SOME REVI

MW00881168

"*Memor*

"Stephe   ᴜner is a find." *Time Out*

"Stephen Palmer has concocted a beguiling adventure that draws on some of the best sf of recent years for its basic themes…" *Starburst*

"Stephen Palmer's imagination is fecund…" *Interzone*

"…an intriguing dystopian ecological-catastrophe novel, diverging from the recent trend of socially-driven catastrophes in British sf." *Foundation*

"Stephen Palmer takes biotech to its farthest extreme, and beyond into entropy, yet he offers a flicker of hope." *Locus*

"This latest novel confirms that in Stephen Palmer, science fiction has gained a distinctive new voice." *Ottakar's*

"This is a brilliant second novel and makes, like its predecessor, a welcome change in a genre clogged with tat." *SFX*

"Give him a try; his originality is refreshing." David V Barrett

"The author of *Memory Seed* and *Glass* offers a challenging and thoughtful future world that should satisfy readers with a love for far-future sf and New Wave fiction." *Library Journal*

"…(a) supremely odd yet deeply rewarding experience." *CCLaP*

BEAUTIFUL INTELLIGENCE

STEPHEN PALMER

infinity plus

To Miriam:
a northern light

For marvellous support and advice, many thanks to:
Keith Brooke, Jonathan Laidlow and Steve Jones

BY THE SAME AUTHOR

CHAPTER 1

Everybody was a scavenger in the post-oil world. South of Tunis, Hound gazed into mirror bright nu-desert fields. Beads of sweat trickled down his black, scarified skin. He twisted his beard into plaits, then untwisted them. He did not like what he saw. The farmers he owned had been attacked by mash kids from the wrecked baobabs in the centre of the old city, leaving sand-orange trails of destruction through the greenery. A few farmers lay dead, the remains of their bodies picked over by vultures. It seemed however as if the plants themselves were untouched; the only positive aspect of the disaster.

Hound turned to the elegant black man standing beside him. "So they was after metal? Plastic?"

Sandman Entré glanced at him. "Who knows? Tunisian gangs cannot be controlled, it's Muslim versus animist, like it used to be. Nothing changes since one thousand years, ami."

Hound ground his teeth together, fighting the urge to inform Leonora and the AIteam immediately. Safer to tell them in person. Though he was free of com, the nexus still weighed down on him, though it could not see him.

"You appear worried, ami."

Hound nodded. "But look, man. The plants survived. My land is still fertile. You can get more farmers?"

"From the low-lying shanties to the west. But they will need to be inducted into the religion soumis, which, as you know, is expensive."

Hound's anxiety began to turn into anger. "This *your* fault, man. I pay you to keep order? You screw up. *I* know security, that's my game. I see no security, I see a screw up."

"Okay, so we do a deal. Bon." Sandman Entré shrugged, brushing specks of sand off his white flannel trousers. "Your attitude does not surprise me, monsieur."

So they weren't friends any more. Hound snorted, then said, "Biz is biz."

"I will arrange for the plant-plastic shipment to reach you in Malta by the end of the week. These plants take only two or three days to process. You will not go short, that I promise – and I can make such promises. You know me, monsieur. My rep goes before me. It's why you chose me."

Hound didn't want to listen to any more. "Bill me through the nexus. I ain't got time to come here again."

"Merci."

He walked to the two-seater flexbike, unfurled the solpanels and sat astride the rear seat. Indicating the front seat, he shouted, "Drive, man!"

Sandman Entré drove him back to the screeport, where Hound strode off without an au revoir, visiting the nearest can to unscrew his boot heels, take out microthin Tunisian hack shirt and trousers, and put them on: essential disguise. Dreads in hat, he walked to the terminus and looked for the nearest solbus to the coast.

It had been weird, living days without the weight of the nexus on his mind. Weird... but not bad. Sometimes he regretted getting into the security game. Just to see sun shimmer on sand without augmented info was a joy. A mirage, he had discovered, could be just a mirage; and sometimes it was *good* not to automatically be told why it existed.

He was thirty, but getting old. Kids, viciously networked, would laugh at him for thinking such things.

The boat he had chartered from Malta was a mini-nuke running on hooked plutonium. Dangerous, yes, but the quickest return trip from coast to coast. And it was free of the nexus – he had paid with niobium, amongst the scarcest metals, leaving his wristbands and spex in a portside locker. The sun set flaring red as his data incarnation settled around him.

Leonora Klee sipped whiskey tea and looked at Hound. He seemed tired.

"You saw that with your own eyes?" she said.

His grin appeared forced. "Very funny. Yes, Sandman Entré took me right into the fields. But we get the plas next week."

Leonora nodded. The four day wait had been interminable, every hour without Hound a nightmare. She thought: you pay for the best, you get the best. But when you work with the best you do not want him gone.

"You all managed?" he asked.

The sound she made was half sigh, half laugh. "We sat tight."

He shrugged and began fiddling with his beard. "Had no choice, man. And no choice but to go naked. The nexus... it weighs heavy. You know that."

He was trying to mollify her, she knew, but her nerves were screaming raw. And she suspected he was beginning to turn, becoming a 'nik. A little thought at the back of her mind on four-day repeat: *what if he never comes back?*

"There were no scares?" he asked.

She waved a hand in the direction of the computer. A holo lit up, which he watched. "We didn't dare do anything," she said. "At least, nothing that left a trail."

"What 'bout the geologists?"

Involuntarily she glanced in the direction of the cave entrance. "Still chipping away."

The geologists were their data sink into the nexus, two men and two women from the University of Fez, set up by Hound to explore the geology of the region around the cave mouth. The data they sent back masked the truth. Watched by satellites, by students, by random speccies, the geologists were normal. They were boring. But they were real, and they filled the void in the nexus that would otherwise appear and become suspicious. It was the price of secrecy, of privacy.

Her AIteam could not function without secrecy.

"How's Zeug?" he asked.

She smiled. "Allow me to show you Zeug," she said.

Hound's expression froze. "Man, I don't like the sound–"

"Shush! It is a surprise."

She led him through cellophane barriers into the research pods at the rear of the cave system, the way as soft as neoprene, humming like a beehive. Density of machinery. Inside the rearmost pod – a theatre, behind glass – stood the operating table, on which Zeug lay: face down, on his belly, legs outstretched. Snow white skin, Greek physique, no body hair. But the great gash at the back of his head had been sewn up.

"Man!" Hound breathed. "You did it?"

Leonora nodded. "His brain is within. The whole damn thing…"

"We whupped the Singularity."

Leonora laughed. "What did Kurzweil know? He knew nothing. Anyway, his Singularity was a couple of decades ago, or it was meant to be. But he didn't know who we know… he didn't know Yuri."

The theatre door opened and in walked Dirk. Leonora's heart raced for a second, then calmed. If it had been Yuri she would have freaked, for Yuri walked around the cave system like a camouflaged cat.

Dirk and Hound hugged: "Man!" "Dude."

Hound indicated Zeug. "So Yuri fixed the quantum."

"He did," Dirk replied. "It inside. Now we gotta link da quantum to da nerve system. I do da visual system first. Den we get going."

"And that is not going to be a lengthy process," Leonora said. She pointed to the neuromap on the wall, twinkling with red mote-lights. "Dirk has mapped almost half of what Zeug's neural networks know. Of course, it is only a map, not the real thing. But that is the point... we don't *want* to know precisely what Zeug knows. We want him to have an unconscious."

Dirk nodded. "Like mine. Hidden."

"And we want him to *tell* us what he knows," Leonora concluded. "Language is the key. He cannot communicate in a sophisticated way except through language – this I am certain of. He cannot become conscious unless he speaks, unless he thinks."

"Turing was a fool," said a voice from the doorway.

Leonora turned to see Yuri: thin as Dirk, but stretched tall where Dirk was short, pale where Dirk was coffee-skinned, bald where Dirk was Afro'd. A kind of anti-reflection of Dirk, in character as well as in physique; and otherworldly. In the middle of his forehead lay a real third eye, lab grown and bulging, the bone sculpted into an orbit, the sclera bloodshot, the eyelashes thick and black. IR and UV enhanced. Yuri had accompanied them when she and Manfred escaped from Ichikawa Labs all that time ago, but, still, her skin crawled whenever he stood nearby.

"Dude!" Dirk coughed, twitching his fingers in that motion he made when he craved a smoke. "You say, what?"

"Turing was a fool, a brilliant fool, a genius according to what they knew back then, but a fool nevertheless." He paused. "Mr Ngma, if you light up in here I will hurt you."

Dirk blew an imaginary smoke ring through orange teeth. "Weren't gonna."

"You were saying?" Leonora encouraged.

Yuri approached Zeug and wrapped four manicured fingers around the back of the skull. "The Turing Test is a nonsense. An ape apes, Mr Ngma. What does the Turing Test say? If an observer cannot tell the difference between an artificial intelligence and a human intelligence then the artificial intelligence must be conscious. But is this merely a simplistic thought experiment?"

Dirk nodded. "Well you and me agree on dat, for sure."

"Precisely, for it is merely a matter of processing power to copy to a level where a human being cannot distinguish real from artificial." He cradled both of his hands beneath the sugar-white skull, lifting it a centimetre. "Here we have the world's most powerful quantum computer. You map it Mr Ngma, but you know your creation is not even the tip of the iceberg."

"Da neuromap is Zeug's identity," Dirk said. "I know what I'm doing."

"I do not doubt it." Yuri let the skull rest on its foam mount. "But we will create a true artificial consciousness here. For the first time a computer is fast enough, deep enough, wide enough." He smiled at Leonora. "Yes, Ms Klee, Kurzweil's Singularity was a joke, but the kernel of truth lay inside it."

And Leonora shuddered.

Hound and Dirk stood at the bank of computers outside the theatre, gazing as if through a shop window at the quiescent form within. "We still gotta get him da audio," Dirk said.

Hound nodded. Though visual systems had in recent years approached the acuteness of the human eye and visual cortex – particularly in the gene-tubs of Pacific Rim countries – audio systems were proving difficult to engineer, and even the best

Japanese labs struggled. "It's because music is emotion," Hound said. "You can't engineer emotion."

Dirk clicked his tongue against his teeth and took a drag at his cheroot. "Bull. Sound is math. Music is math. We just got to get da calculation right. Dat my job."

"Will *she* help?"

Dirk shrugged. "Ain't heard from her for a time. But I don't think her team is interested in tech. Dey follow different path."

Hound nodded. "What you want me to do?"

"Take a hop into Valletta and buy me some music. Not download, buy. You dig? Gotta be local. New. Nothing commercial, Western. I hate dat shit anyway. See, I had an idea. When you come back I engineer something for Zeug, something nice. He'll like dat."

"Okay man."

Hound walked alone to the external cellophane shield, where he glanced up at the cave mouth monitor screen. It was early evening and the rock crew had departed for their base in the village at the bottom of the valley. He shook his head – he had become nocturnal since joining Leonora's team, like a vampire; and he missed the sun. He tweaked his main wristband to fade in his data incarnation so the nexus would not be alerted by his sudden appearance, then walked out into a muggy evening vibrant with stridulation. Bats and moths.

Hidden under morph-tarps lay his solbike. The batts were fully charged. It hadn't been used for a week. He brushed the dust and insect crap off the seat and handle grips then powered up. With a wheeze the engine caught. He rode it down desert-dry hill paths to the main Valletta road.

He put his spex on. The weight of the nexus – info over-overload – settled upon his brain, and his privacy vanished.

He sighed. He *was* getting too old for this job. His gaze strayed to a tanker on the horizon and he grinned. So the Saudis had found a few more drops to make the Chinese happy.

Through outlying districts: Qormi, Hamrun, Floriana. In the dayglo-fried outurbs of Valletta he parked the solbike, chaining it to a bollard then pulling out its comchip. The streets were alive with revellers, some from Sicily – black hair and black attitude – but most were from West Libya and Tunisia, their desert robes gold-embroidered khaki. Some of the Tunisians were Muslims: a minority. Hound ignored them all.

The plastic sellers lined the streets of the old town, Valletta Central, where the weight of information pressed down on him like an incubus. Augmented reality, dense and sparkling, ever-ready, perpetual. Each seller had a code name, a virtual shopfront, a credit rating – hovering info like so many digital seagulls, coming into focus when he looked at a seller, fading when he glanced at the next. A madness of subtle activity.

"Not tonight," he said, mechanically, as he passed the urchins. "I don't need no plastic."

"You sleep with homos!" the urchins screamed as they sought out their next customers.

Hound grinned. One of these days he would let the plastic sellers meet his data incarnation, just so he could see them melt into puddles of fear. It would be like Hannibal in an orphanage. Then the urchins would learn a lesson.

On the seafront he spotted the old musical instrument shop that Waylon McLeod had set up in the 2070's, when music became so computerised a groundswell of revulsion, beginning in the Balearics, swept the Mediterranean, bringing a new era of romanticism. In those idealistic days real music flourished, Hound recalled. But the nexus soon brought mere romanticism under control.

Old McLeod though, he was ancient enough to remember compact discs. He would know what was shiny and new.

The man sat at the back of his shop, plucking a kora. "Yo, Hound."

Hound nodded back. McLeod's spex were the newest, straight out of Tokyo – light as a feather and almost invisible on his face. His right arm was concealed from wrist to elbow by a jangle of bands.

"Man, you got *wired*," Hound said. "You used to be a solo."

McLeod shrugged. "Ain't no messing with the modern world."

Hounded nodded again. "I need music," he said. "Something local. New. The newest you got and not nexified. Say?"

McLeod frowned. "Okay, but...?"

"I'm bored, man. Bored with downloads. So I'm getting old. Like you used to feel–"

"*Me*, I came out the other side," McLeod interrupted. "Nothing real is real any more, Hound. It's all data."

"Anyway..."

McLeod shrugged, then reached out for a dot of memory. "Try him. It's a live rec. Teen lad from Seafront Lite. You know, the church kids? Well, I say church, there ain't no church there any more."

Hound smiled. There certainly wasn't.

"Let me know what you think of the lad's tunes," McLeod concluded, taking up his kora. "Com me. You know you want to, old man."

Hound left the shop without replying.

The journey back was peaceful. He listened to the night birds and the insects, and wondered if Dirk could use those sounds as music. Back at the cave, he handed over the dot and awaited developments.

Leonora and Yuri were both asleep: the men had the place to themselves. Dirk lit a cheroot and said, "So dis some local kid? Who not hit da nexus?"

Hounded nodded. "You got that."

"See," Dirk said, grinning, "dis is da beauty of it. Da nexus, it flavour all music, takes most of da humanity out. Not like da internet, which was in comparison neutral." He put the dot on his thumbtip and raised his hand. "So *dis...* dis is straight outa da brain. At worst it'll be culturally unoriginal. Trite. But da kid who did dis didn't get his music flavoured."

"I dig," Hound said. "We want Zeug to be truly independent. A solo."

Dirk nodded. "But you know, Zeug can see and all dat, but he don't hear. I gonna try something now a little bit different."

Hound found himself intrigued. Dirk's personal habits left a lot to be desired, but his mind was sharp as obsidian, which was why Leonora employed him. He watched as Dirk pressed a key switch to wake Zeug. Inside the theatre pod the white body twitched, then raised itself and sat on the operating table. Hound shivered. Yuri had insisted that Zeug have three eyes, and Leonora, worn down, had agreed.

"Man, but he's got ears," he said.

"He got ear," Dirk agreed, "but he don't hear. We ain't activated dat nerve highway yet. Tonight..."

Hound looked again at Zeug. Stereoscopically, Zeug stared back at him, third eye closed, and Hound received that tremor, that macabre thrill running through his body that everyone got when they saw an almost-human replica. It was creepy. It always would be. It was one of the downsides of artificial intelligence research.

"He's looking at me, man," he whispered.

Dirk nodded, taking a drag from his cheroot. "Da brain hooked up in part. He watching us. We like dat! Zeug gotta sense his world to become conscious."

"He'll never smell or taste, though."

Dirk coughed. "Yeah? One day he will. Just a matter of time. Tech never go backward."

Dirk waited fifteen minutes, Zeug's standard warmup period, then laid in the signposts for the audio adaptive neural networks in the quantum computer. Zeug shivered, as though sensing that his brain was changing. Then Dirk played the music on the memory dot; simplistic, a song sung to guitar accompaniment, seagulls crying in the background.

"Take out the gulls," Dirk instructed the theatre pod computer.

Seconds later the gull noises stopped, along with a minuscule amount of quality in the recording.

"EQ, human," Dirk grunted.

The sonic quality of the recording changed – brighter, with better bass. Hound recognised that the lad had a good voice, though his guitar picking was shaky. He was probably thirteen or so.

Zeug began turning his head this way and that. "Where's the speaker?" Hound asked.

"One side only," Dirk replied. "We want da brain to understand spatial co-ordination from audio. He's getting it! Shit, he's quick. Look, you can see he's orientating himself. Yuri, he's da *man*."

"But Zeug doesn't understand what the sound is?"

"Not yet. He linked up to all da data bases here, 'course. He'll learn."

"By himself?"

"We'll learn him," Dirk said, "so it'll be a bit of both. Who knows? Dis never happen before."

"The model of the world inside his brain better be good, man."

"Real good. But we'll tell him what's what."

Leonora and Yuri took green tea together, the morning humid hot already, the Med baking under greenhouse atmosphere; but in the caves it was cool. Leonora glanced at the sundrenched picwalls in the common pod as she poured more tea. She pulled her lambswool cardi around her shoulders. Aircon was not required, which was good; the nexus would notice that kind of anomalous thermal activity from supposedly empty caves, which meant their enemies and competitors would too.

A Hound-report pinged into holoview.

"It is only the fake us," she said, "the standard report." She read the update. The virtual Leonora and Yuri hid in the remains of San Francisco, living their lives, interfacing, downloading, uploading. All designed to keep eyes away from Malta. Of course, in a week or two some infinitesimal discrepancy would be noticed and the fake Leonora and Yuri would have to decamp. It happened once a month or thereabouts: pretence of the hobo lifestyle. Kept the watchers on their toes though, for the whole world wanted to know where Leonora and Manfred were and what they were doing. Ichikawa, of course, knew the fakes were fake.

"Zeug is progressing well," she said.

Yuri nodded. "Very well, for I have no doubt that he wants to learn. His eyes are good and his ears are working, but we face the most difficult obstacle next, for we must teach him language. Chomsky said human beings have grammar hardwired, and I think he was correct."

"We gave Zeug only a little."

"Just enough for self-improvement – not too much."

"Too much would have meant learning less," Leonora agreed, "and we want him to learn as much as he can without being spoonfed. But you and I do not agree on language."

"Nexus or not?"

Leonora shrugged.

Yuri continued, "We both agree Zeug must remain solo until he is ready to experience the nexus. But language is changing so fast we have no choice but to utilise what exists *now* in human societies. Not those of the West, of course, but the Pacific Rim, perhaps even Japanese. He must speak what people presently speak, and that means we cannot avoid the nexus – for if he stands out he will be noticed, and that could lead to disaster, and the demise of our noble project."

Leonora sipped her tea and eyed the honey cakes. She took one; took a bite. "I think *we* should teach him," she said. "If we rely on the nexus we make him a nexus man. If *I* teach him, and you do, we follow the human principle, and that's worked for tens of thousands of years. I am sure Chomsky was correct, though he is thought old-fashioned now. Remember Yuri, my original goal was to make an artificial human being, a conscious intelligence. I am not here to make a servant of the nexus."

Yuri leaned forward. "There is one method of compromise."

"Which is?"

"We allow a feed in here from the nexus–"

"No!"

"Wait, Leonora, please wait, allow me to elaborate for you." Yuri sat back and did the steeple thing with his hands that Leonora hated. "Mr Hound secures every link we have with the nexus, indeed, every link with the outside world. He must manage the link I suggest so that our invisibility is maintained. I propose that we have a number of broadcasting stations available for us to watch – news channels, entertainment shows, cheap, educational. This will influence our speech patterns. In time, when he can speak, Zeug too must be allowed to interface with such stations."

Leonora considered this. Hound was the best in security, the master of camouflage. But still she worried that he might be turning away from the AIteam. Could she trust him? "We are approaching our crucial time," she mused, "when all our threads come together. It sounds risky."

"Please. Ask Mr Hound."

Virenza, the village at the bottom of the valley, was well known to Hound. He had lived there for a while as part of security checks made prior to setting up the cave system bolthole, and had there developed some of the procedures used after the Ichikawa breakout. So it seemed natural to chill villageside one evening and decide what broadcast channels to allow into the caves… and how.

He had been instructed to seek variety. It was some theory of Yuri's. Dirk was in agreement, but Hound felt twitchy.

A number of procedures camouflaged the extent of activity at the caves. Some were simple: arrivals and departures, these mostly Hound, made only at night, so satellites couldn't pick up anomalous GPS activity. No thermal footprint. The deliberate fostering of cave dwelling bat populations. Some were complex: the geologists working near the cave mouth, giving data to a region that otherwise would have none; and the geologists' swirl of pointless data also masked any mistakes the AIteam made. Then there was the proprietary 'ware developed by Hound that allowed his data incarnation to fade in and out of the nexus rather than suddenly appear and disappear. But Hound felt uneasy about letting broadcast channels in. It would be so easy for competitors, enemies, and especially journalists to hitch a virtual ride on such incoming streams. Broadcast channels implied viewers. And viewers implied activity.

The data sink, then, must not be attached in any obvious way to the cave system. Sitting at a streetside bar, Hound pondered, a glass of white wine in one hand, a retro moby in the other. Watching crap on nexus TV. Who would have thought it...

He soon realised that the best way to conceal the link would be to utilise the geologists, perhaps have it appear that they had lost a nexus radio somewhere near the cavemouth. He would be able to conceal such a device without difficulty up a tree. And if virtual observers should see him talking to the geologists, it did not matter. The decision to fake his own death prior to joining the AIteam had not recommended itself to Leonora, but Hound had pointed out that a man of his renown could not simply disappear. Via the nexus, he would be hunted. Better to die and reappear as somebody ordinary; for Hound was not his real name. And so he could talk to who he liked with little chance of danger.

He walked down the street to the bar he knew the geologists frequented. Then halted. Ducked behind a dumpster. There, sitting at a round aluminium table with two of the geologists, was Tsuneko June.

Tsuneko June! Something had gone *wrong*.

CHAPTER 2

Manfred Klee studied the cables linking the nine globular bis into a circle. One by one he took the cables and cut them with a scissors.

Joanna Rohlen ran into the room, hands covering her open mouth, eyes wide. "What have you done?"

Manfred walked over to her, took her in his arms, stroked her long white hair, then let her go. "Our mistake was to give them direct access to one another. Joanna, this is the crucial idea. Of course… we could *never* succeed if they stayed linked."

"But you've ruined them! Months of work–"

"No. I've freed them."

She stepped back and stared past him. Each bi was circling the room, apparently at random, like a possessed basketball. "You've killed them."

Manfred shook his head. "I'm their midwife. It's why they weren't progressing. They were linked, right? *Direct* access to one another."

Joanna stood still, trembling.

"It's where everybody has gone wrong so far," Manfred said. "We were seduced by the nexus… by the internet before it. We imagined better connected was better–"

"You're crazy!"

"*Listen* to me!" Manfred let the inchoate mixture of joy and frustration he felt rise up through his throat. "I'm *right*. This is the idea I was searching for on the soltrain from Beijing! It's what we were doing *wrong* at Ichikawa. I bet Leonora does it wrong too–"

"Oh, Manfred, stop talking about her–"

"Sssh!"

Manfred pointed at the group of nine bis. They had stopped circling one another. Each bi had sense organs constructed as near to the human norm as possible, albeit in a squat sponge of a body – ultra-pure bioplas made from smart petroleum that Manfred managed to spring from Tehran University. Each bi had two eyes, two ears, a mouth without a tongue, and Japanese micro touch sensors all over, like the fronds of the Mimosa plant.

Manfred breathed in... out. "They're looking at us," he said.

Joanna's fury dissipated. "No... no," she whispered. "They're *listening* to us."

"They recognise something's going on," Manfred said.

He got on his hands and knees and approached the nearest bi; the orange one. It moved its body so that its eyes stared into Manfred's. He didn't freak. It wasn't like he was looking at a Nippandroid, which *was* freaky. Then the other bis – distinguished by pastel rainbow colour, plus one grey, one white – clustered in a group around them.

"Look!" Manfred whispered, his voice hoarse with emotion. "They're all watching the orange one. They're trying to work out what *it's* doing. Cutting their cables freed them. They've got no choice now but to try to understand each other."

"But... but..."

Manfred glanced over his shoulder. Understanding illuminated Joanna's eyes. "Oh, yes," he said, "now we've got to stimulate them. Give them problems, dilemmas. Make 'em sweat. They've got to start being stressed. *Then* they'll understand one another. They'll have no damn choice!" He stood up and grabbed Joanna's arms, dragged her to him. "Yeah, you see now?"

"It could be a society," Joanna breathed. "I do see." She exhaled, put one hand on her sweating forehead. "Can you fix me a coffee?"

Manfred walked backward, hardly able to take his eyes off the bis. He poured two cappuccinos. Pressed the attention switch. The other two needed to see this.

Pouncey arrived. Tall, Afro, strong, thirty, she was responsible for the Hyperlinked, the system of apartment mapping that allowed Manfred to remain invisible in the great urban mess of Philadelphia. "You got two hours left," she said. "Hey. What happened to the bis?"

"I cracked 'em," Manfred said. "What d'you mean, two hours?"

Pouncey split open a juice, whacked the paper straw in. "I got itchy fingertips. You know I don't like havin' itchy fingertips."

"Is somebody on to us?" asked Joanna.

"Dunno. But we've had our time here."

Manfred cursed. "Get the bis in their crates. Double quick. Damn, Pouncey, you pick your moments. Where's Tsuneko?"

"Out—"

"Out? Where?"

"The bioplas?" Pouncey said.

"Oh… yeah. Forgot. Com her through her earset. Don't tell her where the next apartment is though, come and get her when we're safe."

"Okay."

"And com Six-Fingers to clean up here."

"Okay."

A flurry of packing and movement, curses, sweat and coffee: the bis were stored in their automobe crates, people packed bags, changed clothes, put on wigs. They had only been in the apartment for three days – a short one. Manfred hoped the next stop might be for a week or more. But he had to move. The whole world was trying to locate him.

Pouncey took her wristband and modded its screen. "Sansom Street seventeen, floor seven, apartment twenty," she said. "Hey – where Jewellers' Row used to be. Been empty for a while. Nothin' bad nearby, unless you count the jazz club. Could be nice. Got some furniture, even."

"Thanks for that," said Manfred. "Listen, do everything you can to keep us invisible there for a week. Ten days if poss. The bis are changing."

"And they got *you* for a dad. Poor things."

"You did say you wanted them stressed," Joanna observed.

"Yeah," Manfred replied, "but not stolen. They're ours."

An hour passed, then they were ready. Taking three crates each, they left the apartment then took the lift down to the ground floor.

Manfred walked into the rain outside the block. Splashed puddles soaked his trousers. For a moment he recalled the warm, comfortable suites he had enjoyed at Ichikawa labs; the flowers, the food, the unhurried conversations. This was madness in comparison: and it was straining the BIteam. He worried about Tsuneko, who wasn't used to the travelling life. Well, she better get those sixty grams of bioplas.

"Lead on," he told Pouncey.

Midnight dark, rain worsening. They struggled through grease-laden puddles, past noisy vegeburger joints, sweet mullers, nexus music clubs where everyone wore spex'n'headphones like fly eyes. But nobody was interested in them. Pouncey had long since developed the perfect nexus illusion, each member of the BIteam with a full identity, back story, credit thread. In the spex of the good citizens of Philadelphia they were three worthless woons. Street litter.

Which was fine. Nobody noticed street litter.

Manfred called this operation *doing a Damascus*. He didn't say why. But it worked. The Hyperlinked meant they could never be traced. Worst case scenario – somebody bumped into Manfred and recognised him. Almost impossible, that.

A shebang of electric cars tore by, sending water everywhere. Plastics hawkers carrying black stash bags patrolled the streets. All normal. When Pouncey ducked into a doorway and shook the rain from her hair they followed her, sighing with relief. The next apartment was near. It would be warm and dry.

Tsuneko June was not impressed with what Manfred had done.

"You cut the cables *off?*" she said.

The quartet sat around the kitchen table. Manfred shook his head. "I freed them," he said. "You've got to understand. This is the moment we've been waiting for. They no longer have direct access to one another's brain, which means–"

"Yes, yes, I heard you the last time. But my biograins…"

Manfred appraised her. The girl was mid twenties, slim, long brown hair. Bright… *very* bright – the one who developed biograins. The first member of the quartet he had bought: the most important one. He could not afford to hack her off.

"It's all this moving," he said, "um, unsettling you. I get it. I feel the same. But until we reach our breakthrough we're food for the big guys in China, Japan, Singapore, Korea. Hell, Thailand even. Not forgetting Leonora."

Tsuneko uttered a sigh of frustration. "What does Joanna think?"

Manfred relaxed. This was a question that got him off the hook. "Ask her," he said.

Rain spattered against the kitchen window. Joanna shrugged and said, "He could well be right. I see it–"

"You mean *you* see it, Joanna Rohlen one-time shrink, or *you* see it, Joanna his bedtime fun?"

Joanna's face flushed. "Both," she said.

Manfred hadn't heard them talk like this before. His heart beat fast. He hadn't realised what lay beneath the surface. He raised a hand. "Please—"

Tsuneko waved a hand back at him. "*Stop* it. I don't care. I wouldn't touch you."

"I can't believe I'm hearing this. We're the BIteam, aren't we? Me and Joanna… what does a relationship matter?"

"It doesn't matter a *bit*," Tsuneko said, slapping the table. She stood up to pour coffee, then walked to the window, back turned. Manfred glanced at Joanna. She looked scared. He shrugged at her.

"Your biograins are safe, Tsuneko" he said, in his softest voice.

Tsuneko turned around. "My biograins had better be safe. My biograins could have made me a billion. Instead, I was seduced by your… vision."

"Hmm. You regret it? You want out?"

"No. *No*. I'm just…"

"Okay," Manfred said, standing up. "Bad evening. Stressy. We all said what we needed to say. Pouncey, buy food. Expensive. We need a treat."

Pouncey grinned. "Sure boss," she murmured as she left, nodding to him.

Tsuneko sat at the kitchen table. She stared at Manfred and said, "My biograins had *better* be safe. My biograins take everything we learned from the internet, what the Rim learned to make the nexus, and fire all that inside the human brain. If the bis lose their way…"

"They won't," Manfred said. "I'm right. I damn *know* I am. They're in the room next door now, all nine of them, listening. Working out what the others know. I bet you."

"Let's go and see—"

Beep beep: their moby. Tsuneko clicked it. "Dijon... Maria... you got how much? Where from? Right... right... sure I want it... But it'll cost? Right... right."

Tsuneko glanced at Manfred, eyes wide.

"Dawn... Sure... I'll be there. Non-traceable, you need to tell me *that?* After all the deals we've cut?"

She shook her head and grimaced at Manfred.

"Sure... sorry... yes, it is a lot of bioplas. Okay. Five am. 'Bye."

Moby off-click.

"I think we've hit the motherlode," she said.

Manfred said, "Bioplas?"

Tsuneko nodded. "One fifty one kilogrammes, finest Iranian. We could build the bis proper bodies!"

Suddenly the threat and angst of the night was gone, and Manfred saw his young hothead researcher again. "Let's go see the bis," he said. "You and Pouncey can score the bioplas later. Then we'll hunker here for as long as we can."

Pouncey skimmed the grease-sheened streets, rain popping her hair. At a Washington Square tang joint she bought keefers, chips, chocolate sponge and bottles of water. Real British water, from Yorkshire, where they still had some. Electric scooters whizzed by, mounted the pavement, then rode on. In her spex she saw clouds of neo-info swirl around the riders – kids, their ages, their names. They were safe though: her links to the PD computers told her that. She smiled. The nexus provided.

She walked into Sansom Street, putting the food in her rucksack, then the ruck on her back. Then stopped.

Six-Fingers?

It *was* him, the man she employed to clean evacuated apartments of all human traces. He was being hassled by a white-haired Hispanic in a raincoat.

Six-Fingers shouldn't be here. He should be steam-cleaning furniture.

She watched the pair. Three brief moves through the nexus brought their conversation to her ears via the parking meter they stood by – one of the old speak/listen models. And Six-Fingers was doing a deal.

Suddenly cold, Pouncey retrieved the Hispanic's kernel through the nexus. Theft. Arson. A Penn Centre gang drone.

Danger!

Pouncey took her hi-vel and ducked behind a liquor store hoarding. She had a good sight. The pair hadn't seen her. She glanced over her shoulder. One cam looking the other way. And an exit – an alley. Too good an opportunity. No point thinking about it.

She aimed. Shot Six-Fingers. Turned, ran.

No time to see what the Hispanic did. But Six-Fingers was dead. She never missed.

At the end of the alley she turned left into a yard, flipped over the wire mesh at the end, then dodged dogs to skitter down a covered passage. Then out into the street, calm, ordinary. No red lights blinking in her spex: no PD.

A few minutes later the new place, and up in the lift. Through the apartment door, then shut it. Pause for breath, her back to the door; and a gasp of relief.

Manfred saw her. His face blanched. "What?" he said.

Pouncey took off her rucksack and extracted the food bags. "Six-Fingers screwed us. It was lucky though. If I'd not been out…"

Manfred turned, glancing at Tsuneko. "You see? We've got to keep moving."

Tsuneko scowled and took one of the bags, sniffing it. She glanced up at Pouncey and in a quiet voice said, "Yes, but sometimes I feel I'd like a *life*."

Pouncey shrugged. "I'm just the hired muscle," she said. "Sorry about the bad news."

Midnight, and Manfred peered through the sim-slot of the bis' room, Joanna at his side. "What are they doing?" she whispered.

He squeezed her arm. "Resting, I think. Maybe they're getting used to their new heavy bodies. Two of them staring at each other though. Hmm... better go in. You too?"

"Of course."

The door clicked as Manfred opened it, the lamps auto-brightening. Like cats, every bi turned to stare at them; motionless now, alert, aware. Manfred had seen this a few times however, and was not concerned. These intelligences *had* to be alert to survive.

"Look at those two," Joanna said.

Manfred looked. Two of the bis had returned to staring at each other, and he noticed that their bioplas tints had changed. "The yellow one is more orange and the orange one more yellow," he murmured.

"It's like you said. They're trying to model one another. You were right!"

At once new ideas flooded into Manfred's mind. The whole point of using bioplas – rare, yes, and novel, but which he could still afford – was to give the bis malleable bodies. Ultimately, he wanted humanoid physiques. But then another thought. "We've made a mistake," he said. "If they're going to have a reason to mentally model one another, they need to be different. They need different experiences. They need..."

"We could separate them inside the crates, give them screens to watch with different feeds."

He nodded, excited. "Yeah! And give them different music to listen to. Then we put them all together again. *Force* them to understand one another. Lucky we distinguished them at the start by tinting the bioplas. But this is how they'll become conscious."

Joanna took a step forward. "They might already be developing some sort of communications if they're modelling one another," she said. She turned toward Manfred, worry on her face. "We want them to be like us, though. Comprehensible."

Manfred got to his hands and knees and crawled forward to the yellow bi. He sat, legs outstretched, and lifted it, placing it on his thighs. Then he grabbed it and hugged it.

For a moment, nothing happened. Manfred and the bi stared at one another. The bioplas was cool, malleable like arto-foam, lumpy in places where layers of GM fat protected the biograins and their neuro-circuitry. Close to the eye sockets he saw a hint of the underlying alu-plex skeleton.

Tsuneko had designed that skeleton to be humanoid, flexible, expandable. He theorised the bis had defaulted to globular forms out of convenience. Well, it was time to shake them out of their complacency.

"Do what I do," he told Joanna. "We've *got* to get them changing. C'mon, Jo! Like me... do it now."

He lifted the bi and moved it along his upper body, ensuring it could sense his limbs and his head. The bioplas squirmed like a custard-filled balloon. The rudimentary legs, that had appeared and disappeared in recent days, expanded; and two arms appeared, growing like time-lapse vines into slender limbs. The eyes were wide. The ears twitched. Ripples like wind over a wheatfield flowed across the micro touch sensors.

His tactic was working. The bis were ready now to explore their new world, to become individuals. To *grow*. This bi was copying the form of his body.

"We've got to get them all limbed up," he said. "Tonight. Like, now! Get them into human shapes that will be too useful to revert from. Like toddlers."

Joanna nodded. "There will be a virtuous circle," she said. "Once we have set them off, they won't be able to unlearn. I've seen it so often in chimp communities."

He nodded.

"I'm calling Pouncey and Tsuneko. We all need to do this. For us, yeah, but also for the bis. They need variety, they need to individuate."

Manfred lifted the yellow bi to the floor then stood up, flipping the call pad. Then he grabbed the red bi and sat down.

Pouncey appeared a minute later. Manfred said, "Send Tsuneko a wake call, then grab one of these and do as we do. The little varmints are learning. Quick!"

Pouncey tapped a wristband, said, "TJ," then sat down.

Minutes passed. Five, ten, fifteen… and the bis began to cluster, the humanoid shaped ones communicating with the globular ones in some primitive, almost abstract-simple language, like a tongue composed of unguessable gestures. Manfred watched them. They were without doubt passing information to one another, though he heard nothing, and there was no physical contact. Gestural info, maybe? But it was essential they grasped English, to communicate. For a moment he felt scared, dizzy, aware now in a way he had never been before of the incredible pace of their learning. He could thank the biograins for that, and the silk-fine, clotted cables of neurocircuitry designed by Tsuneko that infested their morphable bodies.

"Where is she?" he asked.

"Asleep," Pouncey said, shrugging.

Manfred glanced at the bis. He reckoned he could leave them for a minute or two. Standing up, he hurried out of the room and walked down the apartment corridor leading to the clutch of bedrooms. Rain tinkled against windows. The white, yellow, orange lamps of central Philly flickered against mildew-scarred walls. He walked into Tsuneko's room.

She was packing a rucksack. She span, gasped. Threw the rucksack down.

Manfred frowned. He thought: *what?* She's going somewhere? And then he understood.

"No," he said, shaking his head. "Oh, no. Not you."

"What do you mean?" she asked.

"You can't leave. I *pay* you."

Tsuneko hesitated, and Manfred knew from her expression that she had realised he knew what was going on. He pressed home his advantage, desperate to find the truth, guessing it, though not believing it.

"You're one of the *BIteam,*" he said. "This isn't a group you can just walk out on–"

"I'm not! What do you mean?"

He bent down to pick up the rucksack, but she kicked it away. He jumped forward, shoved her onto her bed, then grabbed the bag, upturning it. Stuff fell out. Documents, standalones, moby. Clothes.

"Don't you push me!" she screamed at him.

He stared. She planned to leave. "Why?" he asked.

She stared at him, tears in the corners of her eyes.

He said, "I'm sorry Tsuneko, but you can't go. This isn't a normal place of work. We agreed…? We had to have rules–"

"Manfred, you're talking shit," she said, getting up.

Manfred tensed – she never swore. He was right, he just *knew* it. He had to call Pouncey without making it obvious. He said, "Tell me why you want to go."

"I don't!"

"Then what's all this?"

The micro-pause was just long enough to confirm everything. Exasperated, she replied, "I'm getting ready for the next move, okay?"

He nodded. He didn't know what to do. The main apartment door stood ten seconds away. If she had a gun...

Her gaze flicked to the room door, then back. Manfred heard footsteps: he froze. Pouncey... he was safe.

Then she walked forward, stood a foot from him, staring at him. He looked away, embarrassed. She ducked down, grabbed his tracksuit waistband and pulled them down, kneeling on the floor in front of him. He took a step back. Her hands were inside his pants, her face at his crotch.

He took a step back and said, "Wha...?" but she grabbed his knee and tugged. Off balance, he tried to right himself. She got his pants half down. Then Joanna walked into the room.

He turned, stared. Joanna stared right back. Tsuneko leaped up and said, "Jo! It isn't like you think... we were... we..." She ducked away, around Joanna.

Joanna approached at speed. Manfred, bemused, confused, reached down to pull up his trackies, but Joanna grabbed his wrist and tugged hard. He stood up. Saw Tsuneko dart out of the room. "*Get her!*"

Joanna span him around. "You f–"

"*No!* She's *escaping!*"

He tried to free himself from Jo's clutches, but he tripped, his legs entangled in his trackies, and fell.

"Pouncey!" he yelled. "Pouncey, escapee!"

Then Joanna froze. Turned. Realised.

Manfred heard the front door slam. Joanna ran out of the room. He pulled up his trackies, got to his feet and followed. He smelled something harsh. His eyes watered. He heard Joanna coughing.

"Choke defence," Joanna gasped, returning. "Teargas…"

The gas minicloud filled the corridor, immobilising them as they coughed their guts up. Pouncey appeared, jumped back, then reappeared moments later with a cell-mask. She ran forward, opened the door, vanished.

Manfred pulled Joanna back into the bedroom and swung the door shut. Bottles of tru-water lay on the bedside table, which he grabbed. They drank. The nausea was passing.

"Pouncey'll get her," he said.

Joanna just stared, horror in her expression, fear in her eyes. "What did she say to you?"

"Nothing. She pretended. Probably not planned. We'll ask. I can't let her go, not at this stage."

Joanna nodded, then shook her head. "We can't. She knows the architecture of the biograins. They are… *hers*."

He nodded. "Ours," he said.

Noise at the apartment door. Hoarse breath. Pouncey.

She staggered in, blood covering her right shoulder, arm and hand. An expression of surprise on her face. Of pain. Right arm squeezed close to her body by her left arm. "She had a razoo," she said.

"A razoo—"

Pouncey wailed, "Get me the *med*kit! I think it hit a *vein*."

Manfred leaped to his feet and ran; grabbed the kit, ran back. Joanna was ready for him, already tying something around Pouncey's upper arm. In seconds they had a tourniquet set, then faux-teeth to shut the wound.

"We need to get her to casualty," Joanna said. "Medics—"

"Yeah, yeah," Manfred said. "Okay… I'll secure the apartment."

"Get my spex," Pouncey said. "She might not be alone. You'll need my sight."

Manfred felt close to panic. "Okay! Okay... mmm, right, we'll run down to the med centre where Thomas Jefferson Uni used to be. That's gotta be the nearest."

In less than a minute Pouncey was specced up, they wore raincoats, and the apartment was shut down and secure. They left. Traces of teargas lingered. They took the lift down, then slipped into the street. A big black coat covered Pouncey's wound, her bloodsoaked clothes, the tourniquet. Nobody noticed them as they hurried away.

CHAPTER 3

The snow-muffled mountain slopes owned by Ichikawa Laboratories did not deal favourably with intruders. And that was the idea.

Since founding his labs in 2086, Aritomo Ichikawa had insisted on procedures of rigour against commercial espionage. So when Leonora and Manfred Klee decided to break out, they faced a conundrum. How to regain their liberty?

The only place of bugfree sanctum was their bed. They drew up a private legal agreement between themselves and Aritomo, allowing them a respite not granted to others, on condition that, as they agreed they would, they tried for a child. To buy time Leonora ingested enough oestrogen to upset her cycle; the moment she became pregnant the agreement would end.

And so they talked in semantic vacuum. Manfred had a Korean contact in the outside world who could conceal them for a day or two. After that they would need to be hidden from Aritomo's assassins. Leonora had a contact who knew the great firewall buster Goodman Awuku. And of course they had the Swiss bank account set up before joining Ichikawa, an account not much smaller than the GDP of a small country. So there was hope of success.

If only they could get out of the mountain stronghold.

Aritomo prided himself on the sophistication of his visual recognition software, boasting to all that no human being could approach his labs. He posted no guards on the retaining walls, knowing escape through the snow fields was simply too dangerous to attempt without external assistance. Choppers were the only method of entry and egress.

Until Leonora had a thought. Nonhuman visitors were not on Aritomo's list.

Smuggling a solitary wasp into their bedroom, she housed it under a glass. Taking the dragon-watches given to them as a gift of good fortune by Aritomo when they joined the labs, she extracted their processors so that she and Manfred could glitch the wasp. It was the work of half an hour to write a suitable program into the processors, set it to activate at sunrise next day, then release the wasp.

They waited.

Not knowing how the real world would react to their program they had to guess a departure time. From the lowest store room of the labs, at the time they were supposed to be making a baby, they squeezed through a vent and followed a tunnel to the external wall. A twenty foot drop awaited. Snow cushioned their fall. A culvert led them onto the slopes, where they hid. They could not use any tech because the nexus would detect the trace, if Aritomo's sensors did not, so they had to assume everything was working. Still hidden from vis 'ware, they slipped and fell down the precipitous culvert to a wide ledge.

And then, far off, the light they hoped to see. A St Bernard rescue dog, invisible to Aritomo's sensors. Knowing they remained well within Aritomo's far-security field they shouted and waved so that the dog would see them. Twenty minutes later it wagged its tail by their side, sniffing around in the snow as if for the buried avalanche victim it had expected.

Around the dog's neck hung a rescue sled, ultracarb food, and drink. They unfurled the sled, allowed it to harden, then tied it to the dog. It pulled, struggled, slipped in the snow, then managed to get the sled running with them concealed inside it. So they slid their way fifty eight kilometres to the nearest town, frozen, exhausted. By that time the fake story created in the nexus by the wasp-carried program had given them false identities and an entire back-story, so it was easy enough to get a train to Niigata, and then a boat to an East Korean beach.

Where they met Yuri.

At first, Leonora thought the game was up. She sagged against Manfred. But Yuri acted weird. He spoke to them straight away, fidgeting with the bandana that covered his head down to his eyebrows. "Take me with you," he said, "for I know what you plan and I share your goals."

"What?" Leonora said. "You–"

"I am the man developing the new quantum computers, but my father will not allow me to follow my own research path, insisting that I follow his. It is the Japanese giri – obligation, you say. I am leaving the laboratories for the same reason you are."

"You spied on us? How?"

"Did you think the dragon-watches were only a gift? I knew you were coming before you arrived because my father told me, and of course I knew of your reputations in artificial intelligence circles. So even then I aligned myself to you, creating the watches so that, at the lowest possible level – a megabyte per week, no more – I was able to observe you."

Joanna asked, "Giri... obligation, it motivates you?"

Yuri shook his head. "I am not wholly Japanese. But my father feels the full weight of Japan's expectation upon his shoulders. He'd rather die than fail his country."

"How did *you* get out?" Manfred spluttered.

"How did you escape?"

"I'm asking you–"

"You misunderstand me. I was explaining that I escaped using an identical method to yourselves – except I had to ensure my father's cats were not alerted."

Leonora felt her heart thumping. This was a disaster and an opportunity. "We have no choice," she told Manfred, hoping he would not be able to see alternatives through the haze of his anger. "We have to take him with us."

Manfred swore, stamped, walked a few times around the boat. Threw sand in the air. "Hmm, so it seems."

"Quickly," Leonora said, "can we go into town? I feel naked."

They put on fake spex and wristbands so suspicious locals would not think they were solos. New identities for them all, linked to ordinary bank accounts, then a soltrain to Beijing – they did not dare take a plane in case their mode of transport made them stand out as super-rich. Then a boat to Hong Kong. Another to Madras, where Leonora contacted Goodman Awuku to ensure their haven was ready. Days and days and days passing. Then on to Damascus by soltrain, like a trio of peasants, eating chips and lentils, with not even a moby between them. Proper poor.

In a Damascus bazaar, one Hound met them.

"I killed myself," he said. "It was the only way–"

"You *what?*" Manfred raged. Leonora, ever cool, said nothing.

"It was the only way, man. Who's this guy?"

"You did yourself in?" Manfred said. "You know that's the most *obvious* way to duck the nexus. Sheesh, I thought you were–"

Leonora grabbed his arm. "He is the best, he really is, and we have to trust him now. Manfred, we have paid him, we cannot go back on that." She paused, sighed. "This is Yuri Ichikawa."

Manfred, shaking, face white, said, "Okay… okay. I gotta go to the can. I won't be a mo."

That was the last time Leonora saw her husband.

~

Manfred ran like a fzzz-ed up brat along the alley behind the public toilets, skidding into a junkfood-splattered dead end. At the end wall he jumped, grabbing the birdshit-slippery top to heave himself up and over. He had just seconds. Leonora was not expecting this – *he* hadn't expected it – but she would act as soon as she realised what was going on. To transfer the big money... the *money*. That was the key to the next few minutes.

At a wall credo he stopped. If he accessed the Swiss account he would expose himself, but he had no choice. Without his money he was meat. Surely Aritomo couldn't be onto him yet.

"Fuckit," he said. He accessed the bank through the credo screen, tapping in codes, then laying fingers on the ID bar. Double beep. Retinascan. Tap-tap-tap. The account.

They had set it up so that if either of them transferred money an equal amount would automatically move to a single account owned by the other. Their joint account was in fact a triple system; he could not act without passing half their wealth to Leonora. But that still left him with a vast amount, even considering the fortune they had paid Goodman Awuku. And he had ideas. The precious hours of freedom he had enjoyed had already got his mind working.

Tap-tap.

Done.

Exit.

Now he had to *run*.

He had just minutes to become somebody else. Already Aritomo would know that Manfred Klee was in Damascus. But, more important, the nexus would know. Journos across the world would be receiving shouts: Klee free!

First, get away from the credo. In ten seconds every surveillance cam in the street would be searching for him, face recognition and all. He ducked into an alley. Grabbed a shawl and pulled it around his shoulders. Bent over, picked up a metal pole and held it like a stick. Slowed down. Hobbled. When he saw ash on a doorstep he rubbed it into his hair. The fake wristband and spex should reassure any locals watching, though their own augmented realities would draw a blank on his identity. But, for now, that would have to be.

He walked on, getting lost. Tempting to enter someone's house, but if they threw him out with a fuss somebody watching through the nexus might notice. Behind a row of veg stalls he spotted someone's discarded jacket. Though it was ripped he put it on, filling the pockets with mouldy oranges. Rubbed gutter grease into his trousers.

He sat down on a step. Nobody noticed. It was evening, trade diminishing, the street gloomy. Good. Satellites wouldn't be able to see much of him.

The next job was to make a new Syrian identity and find real spex and maybe a wristband; without them, any mistake would expose him. He had to fit in, be a leaf in a forest. He spotted two coins beneath a slimy lettuce leaf. He picked them up: twenty rupees. The ball was rolling...

With the cash he bought a blank duocard from a kid grifter. At a photobooth he reprogrammed the comchip, fooling the camera into depositing free a new photo onto the card and crediting it with twenty rupees. He called himself Kamal Ali Moussalli. Occupation: street fruit seller. Age: 41. Family... and so on and so on.

Charged, the duocard allowed him to buy a pair of Singapore spex. Wristbands would have to wait, but they were mostly data banks and processors of little use in his present circumstances, so it didn't matter. It was the spex that would count. He needed to see the nexus to move on. His reality needed augmenting.

He dossed in an alley a kilometre out from the bazaar, camouflaged by a dozen other vagrants, warmed by hot air from the subway below, eating mouldy pittas and toms, squeezing the juice from his rescued oranges into a beer-stained mug. For sweet he had coconut flapjacks thrown out by a local supermarket. He raided their dumpsters for bread and veg. He didn't miss Leonora at all.

When the sun rose he walked to the nearest solbus station, buying a ticket for Beirut. He fell in with a pro fleeing her pimp, and managed to cadge lunch off her, then supper. She liked his stories. He told her of life in Japan, pretending to be addicted to their manga channels so he could seduce her into accepting him as a travelling companion; letting his charm shine through. Time passed easy. As the bus approached Beirut Central and she went for a waz in the chem at the back of the bus he grabbed her bag and jumped out of the window at a red-lit crossroads, vanishing into a maze of covered wagons – the local market. Twenty seconds and he was gone, bag raided, discarded. One twenty and he had bought white jacket and jeans. One eighty and he was newly disguised in the market can, washing his hair in the handwash stream, cleaning his face, paying for a disposable razor and a soapnob.

Ten minutes and he was walking down streets a hundred metres away, the bus long gone, the pro bereft. A different man.

With the remaining cash he bought a nexus standard card from a retailer, then had his hair cut to army grade, having the stubble bleached for good measure. He entered the nearest photobooth to once again reprogram the comchip and have another photo installed. New name: Ahmad Shehadeh, 44, saz salesman. New birthplace, new nationality. New identity, new life. So lucky his mother was Turkish, allowing him a wider range of local identities.

From Beirut he scammed his way to Cyprus, Cannes, London, New York. He did not feel safe in New York so he took a solbus west. The shattered, petrol-free landscape appealed to him.

His money was safe. He was safe. For the moment. A time would come when he would have to access and distribute that enormous wealth in order to make it disappear, and the eyes of the world would be waiting, waiting for him to reappear in the nexus, to claim what was his. But he would fool them again, and vanish. He *would*. Because the ideas he had on the long trip to Damascus could make him even more of a sensation than he had been before.

CHAPTER 4

Hound skimped into a position behind an olive tree in a pot from where he could better observe Tsuneko June. For a sec or two he felt sure it must be a nexus illusion, spex only, but, tipping his head forward, she didn't disappear when he used his real eyes.

She shouldn't know anything about Malta. Sure, she had her own support savvy, even tools and protection, but how had she located this place? He had made the mole link one hundred percent secure, and *nobody* knew nexus links like he did.

There were two possible answers: she had outside help or she had another contact inside the AIteam.

Inside the AIteam... not Leonora, not Yuri. Dirk, then. For a few moments he pondered the loyalties of Dirk Ngma, before dismissing his speculation. No, it was an outside job. And he had thought of a name.

Suddenly he felt exposed, paranoid. He wiggled his hips and touched his trouser fly to pretend finishing an outdoor waz, then turned and walked away. Inside someone's flower shed off the main street he took out his moby, but then paused. This could be a trap. Despite his shock and the danger he couldn't risk a com line into the caves.

He walked back up the street and into the nearest bar, where he grabbed a spritzer, chatted to the bar girl, made improper suggestions, then visited the can. In seconds he was out of his trousers and jacket. He *never* wore non-reversible clothes. A minute later his grey garments were white garments, he had a NY baseball cap on his head and a fake 'tash. Then out the can window and into the back lanes of the village. No satellite-riding goon would spot him now.

Back in the cave, he convened an emergency meeting. They sat around a wrought iron table, tea and biscuits between them. Hound said, "It was her. No doubt, man. She knows I'm round about somewhere."

"You?" Leonora said.

He nodded. "It don't mean she knows we're all *here*, caveside. But me being her contact, she knows I'm somewhere."

"How?"

"She's got help."

Leonora crumpled. "Manfred. He's found us."

Hound shook his head. "No way. Okay… unlikely, say." He shrugged. "I got a much more likely name. A Japanese gentleman."

Leonora turned to look at Yuri.

"No," Hound said, tapping the table to regain her attention. "Not the son! The daddy."

Leonora sat back, her face white. Dirk looked shocked, Yuri afraid… in fact Yuri looked horrified. Hound nodded once at him. "Yeah," he said.

"But…" Leonora murmured.

"How?" Hound supplied. "Man, don't know." He shook his head. "But think. You lose two of the greatest artificial intelligence researchers you got. From a team nobody is s'posed to leave. What d'you do? You follow 'em. Tsuneko June might have thought the same. She might've thought, I can't do this. I'll get help. And she knows where you and your ex came from."

"But why leave da BIteam?" Dirk asked.

Again Hound shrugged. "We can't know. Tsuneko was light on info, even though she was good. Classic unhappy mole. We gotta deduce from what we see. I'm telling you man, I'm setting up our escape route right now. Africa. Desert, maybe. I got contacts in Tunisia. We could shufti into West Libya. Get tents, camels. No satellite rider's gonna see us."

"No," Leonora said. "I'm sorry, but we cannot leave the caves, not with Zeug so close to fruition."

Hound laughed. "You don't *realise*," he said. "Aritomo Ichikawa, he lost everything. So he'll do anything to get it back."

Yuri nodded. "I regret to say that I agree with Mr Hound. My father will try anything and everything. The security assessment is valid."

Hound stood up. "So. I'm off outside again. I left a pinpoint ultra on her. Man, she won't escape me. Get yourselves ready. Get Zeug ready. Maybe we'll stay, maybe we'll run, I don't know. But prepare to run."

He left the cave pod. They didn't look happy.

Back in the village Hound sat at a roadside bar gaming on his moby, settling in, making himself seem ordinary. After an hour he saw Tsuneko emerge from the village hotel – it was more of a converted farm, with chickens and hydroponic silos – then head towards the geologists' bar. He followed. When she paused to take something out of her bag he walked on, knowing that an observed synchronised stop/start could be fatal. But as he passed her, so close he could smell her jasmine scent, he noticed something. She was checking a duocard.

He walked on, stopping at a bar to buy tea and sit by the road. A duocard. His skin went cold.

He had assumed that she had traced *him* somehow. But the duocard suggested an alternative explanation. As AIteam security man, the only way he interfaced with the nexus and thus left records was financial. The data incarnation known as Hound would have a spending pattern attached, and that spending pattern could be analysed.

It could be sought.

He shuddered. He realised he had been wrong at the cave meeting just now. Tsuneko June had not followed a lead to Malta. Aritomo Ichikawa had sought a spending pattern. Leonora's.

Leonora's last known position was Damascus. Through the nexus Hound accessed public records of Ichikawa Laboratories purchases, logging in to a Korean library database for safety. There: a thirty trillion yen computer and the staff to use it. They must have analysed the spending profiles of data incarnations in ever-increasing radii out from Damascus, an incredible task, a prodigious task, but a mathematically possible one; and at last, by accident, they had stumbled across Hound spending Leonora's money in Valletta for things Leonora wanted. Hound found that he was trembling. He had utilised his own 'ware to conceal ID patterns in Valletta. He was safe. Fairly safe.

He looked up. Tsuneko walked by, glancing at him. He returned his gaze to his moby and she walked on.

He realised that her presence in the village was in fact a coincidence. The trail would have gone dead in Valletta, the spending profile meaningful but linked to an untraceable alias, though that alias in itself suggested the presence of a nexus witch doctor. Such as himself.

He began to wonder if the death of Goodman Awuku might be probed by Japanese investigators.

For a few vertiginous seconds he looked down upon himself – followed, watched, in peril, drinking at a roadside bar but only hours away from capture. Paranoia crept up on him. He shouldn't have accepted Leonora's offer. He'd made a mistake there. Maybe he should get out now, before the heavies arrived.

He blew air through his lips, then breathed in deep.

"Another tea, sir?"

The waiter hovered at his shoulder. "Sure man," he said. "And the bill."

He only used cash in the village, buying food and drink. Untraceable.

He sighed again. His loyalty was to the AIteam.

He got to work. Through his wristbands he sent a packet of info to the naval base at Valletta, buying a four-seater Skud-Fli and enough jet fuel to get it to France. He had it kitted out with gecko pads so nobody could steal it and a chameleon coat so nobody could see it. He set the drop point to a hillside fifteen kilometres north west of Valletta, on the coast, in sight of Camino and Gozo. Now he would have to ride naked on his solbike to that point then fly the thing to the valley.

He walked back along the village street to the bar where he had made lewd suggestions to the serving girl. The place was tourist notable because of the stables at the rear housing the riding club, and he liked the look of those horses. It was easy enough to scout out routes, check the security of the stables, eye up some horses, then leave, an escape plan in mind.

But he was going to need good luck to get through this scare.

He rode the solbike along dusty, rock-strewn paths, the vehicle bouncing fit to smash his spine. At least that marked him out as a local. At the coastal hillside he vizzed the plane, but decided not to approach until night. He ate olives, feta cheese and bread as the sun dipped scarlet into the sea; he drank lime water.

At midnight he crept up to the plane and located the belly switch that activated the cockpit. This now was the most risky part. Flying the plane would create a thermal trace that could be spotted by satellite eyes. Inside, he stashed his bike then activated the autofly. A twenty minute flight: nothing happened, except his nerves were shot to pieces.

Valleyside, he secured the plane then pushed the solbike – batts empty – back to its hide. Then he walked to the village and strode into the only bar still open; swift costume change, and he was out.

Yuri and Leonora watched Zeug as he paced around the theatre pod.

"The nexus is a complete model of the real world," Yuri said, "created by Pacific Rim programmers to supersede the internet. Similarly, the model inside Zeug's brain is a model of the world, but it is far from complete, and requires much educating."

"Are you suggesting that we spoonfeed him? Just because Hound thinks we are in peril?"

"By no means!" Yuri paused, then continued, "If we are to find ourselves trekking across Libya on the ships of the desert, then Zeug will need to speak. What do you imagine we would do – pretend perhaps that he is a mute, and an idiot? The idea does not commend itself to me, and if I am correct in my thinking, it does not commend itself to you either."

"I would not deny that," Leonora sighed. "But…"

"Please allow me to activate the language centres. Mr Ngma has mapped them, and assured me that they are ready – and I trust his assessment. There is nothing more to do other than to let nature…" Yuri chuckled, a sound like a dog gargling, "… or I should say, *artifice* take its course."

"Very well." Leonora nodded. "Let's give him speech. He possesses every other gift after all."

Leonora stood in silence for some minutes, pondering the events of the day. Yuri remained silent also, watching Zeug with almost inhuman intensity. Leonora repressed a shiver. It was like watching a symbiotic pair. Yuri must be borderline Asperger's:

he had that quality of social nuance bouncing off him. Or he was a typical man. One of the two.

"You spoke about the nexus," she said.

"Yes, Ms Klee?"

"Did they design it to bring the West down, do you think?"

Yuri shook his head. "Assuredly not, though it was an invention of the Eastern mind, which is different to the Western mind. You Europeans see the world as one thing or another, mutually exclusive – either/or, if you like – whereas the Eastern mind sees the world inclusively – neither/and, as it were. The fundamentals of Chinese societies are different to European equivalents for this reason, amongst others. Capitalism for instance would never have risen in the East because it presumes the existence of individuals in a way no Oriental would, though of course it was taken up with enthusiasm along the Pacific Rim once it had been invented, not least because everyone is selfish. Why do you ask?"

Leonora said, "I want Zeug to be a Westerner."

"Zeug will be a citizen of the world," Yuri declared. "This was your original plan, which we should not deviate from. You must understand, when Zeug becomes all he can be, he will be subject to the laws of the world like a human being – for he will have no nationality."

Reluctantly, Leonora nodded.

Yuri grinned – an event almost unheard of. "Delicate quantum states can be preserved," he told her, "and this was my pivotal innovation, finding a method of decoupling interactions between the elements of quantum circuits. My father was so pleased! But so long ago now... *so* long ago. The innumerable quantum states in Zeug's brain will be manipulated, moved, and stored without destruction. And now we are here, before the man himself, waiting for that unparalleled architecture to organise itself into consciousness… for it was only a matter of processing power, as ever it is in this world."

Leonora sidled away from Yuri, horrified to realise that he was excited. He looked like a cat about to catch a mouse.

Dirk and Yuri stood at the pod window, looking into Zeug's quarters. The operating table had long since been replaced by chairs and a couch – not required by Zeug, yet essential if he was to function in human society. But the place was cluttered, filled with boxes, tools, computers, and too much dust.

Dirk said, "So you will teach him da English?"

Yuri replied, "We do not have time now to teach him, but in my opinion there was no need to anyway, for the inputting of language will have the same result as the learning of it. It is the result I am interested in, not the methods. Zeug is beginning to understand the world around him, transferring it as a model into his brain. Soon he will need to tell us about it. He may even be conscious at that point."

"What if he ain't?"

Yuri looked at Dirk, scorn clear on his face. "You are the technologist of the AIteam," he said, "not the psychologist. There are trillions of connections in a human brain, which we simulate in Zeug's brain. How could a brain like that not become conscious?"

Dirk shrugged. "I was only saying."

"Please do not say, Mr Ngma."

"I put a little helper in his place," Dirk said, nodding at a small figure on the floor, like a white doll. "A Nippa. Dey can talk to each–"

Yuri struck Dirk in the face with his fist then sprang to the pod doorway, opening the door and hurrying inside. In a single motion he bent to the floor and grasped the Nippa, standing upright, examining it for a moment, then twisting the head off.

Braided neurowires oozing transparent oil squeezed out; fatty globules dropping to the floor.

Zeug ran to the doorway before Yuri could stop him, hastening through. Yuri flung the Nippa torso to the floor and followed. But Zeug stopped at Dirk – on the floor – and in a motion so human it made Yuri gasp knelt to touch Dirk's shoulder with one hand.

Dirk struggled to his feet. Zeug had never been allowed out of his chamber before. "He… he outside… you hit me."

"Be silent," Yuri said. "You polluted the pod. But did you see what Zeug did? He interfaced with you like a human would, in a gesture entirely natural."

Dirk rubbed his cheek where Yuri's fist had struck, anger in the face he preferred to keep calm. "I telling Leonora what you did."

"No you will not," Yuri replied. "I believe your neuromaps are working Mr Ngma, for Zeug has seen us interacting with each other, has remembered that interplay and applied it to you in a single, marvellous human gesture."

Zeug stood up and looked at them both. Yuri reached out, took his hand and led him into his chamber. A minute later the door was shut, Zeug inside.

Dirk glared at Yuri. "You know nothing," he said. "You not know the difference between real and simulate. Dat no proof. Dat just Zeug acting."

Yuri seemed too elated to reply. "The plan is working," he said, "just as I thought it would. The brain is acquiring input through your interfaces. I offer credit where credit is due, Mr Ngma, you were the correct man for the task."

Frustrated, Dirk waved a hand at the pod window and said, "But no language! He is a mute."

"Not for long." And Yuri pressed a single switch on the pod console.

"What?"

Yuri turned to Dirk and said, "It takes a human child years to acquire grammar, vocabulary and, oh, all the rest of it. With Zeug, and with the subsequent artificial intelligences which we shall sell to the world – acquisition in less than a second. But why not? The quantum brain is better than the human brain. Why not…"

"What you *done?*"

"Leonora and I agreed to activate the language centres. Zeug is ready for the world."

Dirk turned to see Zeug staring at them through the pod window. The artificial mouth moved and he heard a faint voice, a single word. "Hello."

Five figures sat around a table at the cave mouth: four of them human.

Evening, and orange light bathed the valley. Zeug's energy sources were bioelectric, but the others ate and drank; bread and olives, baked cheese and tomatoes, water and wine. Dirk smoked a chocolate brown cheroot.

Yuri said, "Zeug, what do you know of Turkey?"

"A large country in the Near East. Many old cultures. Timid crane, but religious and secular in parallel."

Yuri leaned over to Leonora and said, "The language centre is balancing itself in a heuristic process, or so I believe – and perhaps these strange sentences mean something to him. We must talk to him as much as we can, so that, through conversation, the errors fade and grammar is improved."

Leonora nodded, then said, "What do you know of lions, Zeug?"

"Cats of large, with two eyes and a social system of proud. Cats normally not social, so unique."

Leonora nodded, smiling.

Hound said, "I'm amazed. We did it!"

Dirk said, "Zeug, how do you feel?"

"Sensors of external skin like human, but of different type. Many tiny, individual fronds act in concerto, create touch."

Dirk nodded, but said nothing more.

"Zeug," Leonora said, "what is the nearest capital city to us here?"

"Palermo in Sicily."

"Palermo... not Bizerte?"

Zeug replied, "Bizerte is not capital of Tunisia, that is to Tunis."

Yuri leaned forward and said, "Zeug, what was the underlying cause of the Depression?"

"Do you mean first or to second?"

Yuri glanced around the table, triumph clear on his face. "The second."

"The rapid dissemination through West populations by the media of emptying oil reserves, and the result, it was confidence, no confidence. Crashes of markets and mass panic. Spill."

Yuri sat back. "Incredible," he breathed.

Dirk took a puff of his cheroot and said, "Zeug, d'you see what Yuri means?"

"Yes, I do see him."

Dirk raised his eyebrows, took another puff and said, "Leonora, you did good." He stroked the bruise on his face. "Da speaking is good, it all good."

"And Zeug can walk and run like a man," Yuri said, "and talk like a man, and he can see and hear and touch – and recharge himself, and understand *why* he needs to recharge. We have made history here, and we shall never be forgotten!"

Dirk glanced at Yuri and said, "You got dat right." He turned to Zeug and said, "You forget anything, paleface?"

Yuri interrupted, telling Zeug, "Mr Ngma is asking you whether your memory has the capacity to forget."

"I forget very little," Zeug replied. "My goal is to forget nothing."

And then Zeug sat upright, as if alerted by an inaudible alarm.

Hound too sat up and turned his head. "I feel something, man," he said.

Leonora put her hand on the table. "An earthquake?"

Hound jumped to his feet. "Copters. Evacuate!"

CHAPTER 5

Tsuneko June sat in a public caf with a mug of coffee before her. Despite an extensive search, she had found nothing in and around Valletta. Had that location been faked during the secret conversations?

An Oriental man sat opposite her, appearing, it seemed, out of lemon-scented night. She jumped.

"Who are you?"

He nodded. "I am your contact for tonight."

"From…?"

He nodded again. "Tortoiseshell is pleased with your work so far, but speed is essential. If the AIteam suspect you are here they will vanish."

"But I don't know what any of them look like! I *told* you."

"We know. When we monitor your jaunts, we look at the responses of those around you, hoping to see an expression of shock. Such an expression would mark out, for instance, Hound."

"Hound was my contact, but I don't know anything about him. He could be a Martian."

"Do not worry about that aspect of our search. We know Hound must be one of a limited number of nexus witch doctors because of the exceptionally high quality of the AIteam's security work. We have all the likely faces and physiques on file. Even if Hound has had plastic surgery, dyed his hair, taken to wearing contact lenses, we will locate him. Our computers see through all disguises."

Tsuneko shuddered. "They'll have left Malta by now."

"Possibly – if they are here at all. There is much doubt. But they will depart only if they have seen *you*. Keep travelling, keep moving. Let as many local people see you as possible. We believe we will see the facial reaction we seek."

Tsuneko glanced out into the solbike-infested night. LED strings shone from posts that once carried telegraph wires. "Why haven't you paid me yet?" She thrust her duocard in the direction of the Oriental.

"Half at the beginning, half when we find the AIteam. That was the deal."

She put the duocard into her pocket. "I don't trust you."

"Nobody trusts *us*," came the reply. The man's face remained impassive. "But this is not a question of trust. Our relationship is financial. If we succeed, Tortoiseshell may well induct you into his team."

"For life."

"Tortoiseshell knows no other way."

Tsuneko sighed. She felt confused, upset. "What if I want to join the AIteam?" she said. "I didn't like the way Manfred took his research. Would you stop me?"

"There will be no AIteam soon. You will either have to apply for a job with a Pacific Rim company, or, perhaps, you will join the team I work for. Too much is uncertain at the moment for me to make any meaningful guess. You mind me saying this?"

Tsuneko wiped tears from her cheeks. "It's not how I imagined my contract ending," she remarked. "I invented biograins, you *must* want me. You must help me."

"You did not invent biograins, you developed them to the point that they became commercially viable. I say this not to denigrate your achievement. And, speaking personally, I think it is more likely than not that Tortoiseshell will want to employ you."

"Some hope. Not much for me from the sound of it."

"When we start out in life we do not imagine its end. Such is the way of things. Your circumstance is hardly unique."

"You don't sound very sympathetic."

"If it's sympathy you want, find a man. I am an employee of Tortoiseshell." The Oriental stood up and bowed to her. "Goodnight."

In her dusty Valletta hotel room Tsuneko took off her spex and wristbands, then all her clothes, which she put in the laundry basket. From crinkly leaf-plas wraps she took the clothes she had bought in Virenza village: underwear, shirt, trousers, socks, and a pair of hi-grip trainers. These clothes, she knew, could not have nexus bugs in them. She washed her hair in avocado shampoo; now that too would be bug-free.

She took a biro and a piece of paper. Paused. The biro had not been used for a decade or so, its transparent sheath misted with age, and split at the end. She herself had not written for a decade, the pen strange in her left hand.

She heard helicopters passing over Valletta on their way inland.

Dear Rosalind,

I'm writing to you from Malta. I need help urgently. I daren't use ordinary methods, the nexus is hanging right over me and the place is crawling with Japanese. I'm in trouble. Sort of. I don't know, but I do need help.

You saved me when mum and dad were killed, you're the only one I can turn to, just now, anyway. Please please help.

Here's the plan! I'm going to walk at night (solo) to Rabat, six miles inland from Valletta (where I am now) in the hills to the west of the island. I need you to pick me up there in the cyclo-wing and take me to London. I'll be in Rabat market square from the sixteenth onwards. That gives this letter a week to get to you on the ferries, and you time also. If you can't help, send a mini-robo with 'No' on it.

Love,

Tsuneko.

CHAPTER 6

Pouncey took them to a new Hyperlinked hide far away from Center City East, a few strides from Vine Street, Franklintown, overlooking the greenery between Fairmount and the river. She wanted to settle a long way from Six-Fingers and the Hispanic – and Tsuneko, who now counted as a loose cannon.

Manfred struggled with his anger. Frustrated that they had moved before he had a chance to help the bis, he insisted that Pouncey give the BIteam a week in their new apartment. Pouncey shrugged, agreed, stroking the scabby wound on her right arm.

Joanna focussed on the bis. Something weird was happening to them.

The new apartment was a scuzzy wreck. At the top of a wasted office block, empty, dangerous in places where the metal exoskeleton had rusted and the glass shattered, the apartment sat like last-ditch eyrie. In the dogcrap-strewn chambers at the base of the block there was evidence of junkie habitation, but Pouncey said the traces were weeks old.

Manfred took thirty minutes out. Walking along a street he saw a black girl with a tray in front of her, spex pure white, retro fashion, a pistol displayed with ostentation in the holster at her shoulder. Tough area, Manfred thought.

But the girl was selling chocolate. Manfred stopped, checked it out. "This real?" he asked.

"Sure," she replied.

"But, you know… the blockade."

The girl shrugged. "Some of the warlords in Cote D'Ivoire didn't sign up. They called it Pan African, but it wasn't really. You don't believe me, take a crumb. Free sample."

"Expensive?"

"You get what you pay for, asshole. When you last see chocolate round here?"

Manfred nodded. Almost nobody bothered exporting to America any more. "Okay," he said, "I'll take three bars. Nice meeting ya."

He returned to the apartment with a grin on his face. This would cheer the BIteam up. The loss of Tsuneko had been a disaster.

Inside, all was quiet, but he noticed the look of concern on Joanna's face. Handing her one of the bars he said, "What's up?"

Pouncey dozed on a sofa. With a silent nod of her head, Joanna directed him into the bis' room.

They were toddling around, happy enough, or so it seemed. Joanna pointed to the indigo coloured bi and said, "Watch."

The bi did not seem to have the same dexterity and confidence of movement shown by the others. After a moment, Manfred thought of a reason. "It's blind," he said.

She nodded. For the bis they had bought the finest artificial eyes, made by the Korean masters, the finest ears from Singapore, the most sensitive micro touches from Tokyo. And other, less human devices. But the problem had been interfacing. Dirk Ngma, Manfred's preferred choice, had vanished a long time ago, leaving Tsuneko to create interfaces for the BIteam; and now she was gone.

"If it is blind," he continued, "there's nothing we can do now."

"They could be individuating," Joanna said, picking up the nearest bi and holding it like a toddler in her arms. "We need to give them names."

He nodded. "Okay... so you've got the red one. We'll call it Red. The blind one is Indigo. That's Grey, that's White."

Joanna shrugged, though with a smile on her face. "Practical, if simplistic," she remarked.

"Thanks. Simple is best, I've found."

"What shall we do with Indigo?"

"Oh, leave it. I read somewhere that blind people's senses change to compensate for lack of vision. Maybe Indigo will do the same thing."

Joanna nodded. "We shall have to let it... suffer, though."

"Suffer?"

"The others need to try to understand why Indigo is different, why it is struggling. We cannot tell them."

Manfred nodded, folding his arms and looking at the bis. "You're right. But the bis aren't much like kids—"

"I know, I know. I told *you* that, remember?"

"It's easy enough for kids to understand they're human because that's all there is. They *know* they're not living in a world of zombies, and they use themselves as an exemplar to work out what everybody else is doing. Theory of mind. But the bis won't know their world isn't elegant zombies. They'll have to work it out for themselves, and if they don't they won't become conscious, and we'll fail."

Joanna sighed. "It is so difficult to *know* if they are conscious..."

"Two millennia of theories," Manfred replied. "But think, Jo. What about love? You can't detect that, you can't prove it exists, but you know it when you feel it." He shrugged. "Some things are like that. Emergent properties. It could be that we'll never know for sure if the bis have subjective experiences. But my hunch is that we'll know when we see it... when we feel it."

She nodded. "That is not science, though."

He said, "When you worked with chimps you were tempted to call them conscious."

"You read all my papers."

"Sure did. But you never *knew* the chimps were conscious, did you? Because you're not a chimp, in chimp society." He gestured at the bis and said, "This is the same. We can't get around the fact that they're artificial. But they got bodies and no direct access to anything. They got a society, including us... they could become human – maybe. Damn, Jo, this *is* the best chance. And we'll bring it to the world."

"Best chance... I think perhaps it is."

Manfred led her out of the room. "We need to think about teaching them English," he whispered. "They have some sort of simple communication now, though I'm damned if I can get it. Gestures, I think."

"We have hypothesised that they do communicate," Joanna said. "Perhaps it is gestural, emotional even."

He nodded. "Hmm, that's another hurdle. Emotions. They're at least as important as language..."

Pouncey sat on a box in the tower block entrance, a standalone in her hand. The Hyperlinked was stored in this device. The standalone used local thermometer readings to generate random numbers, from which addresses of vacant rooms were later scavenged. Truly the Hyperlinked was random, shielding them from the all-seeing eyes of the nexus, which could detect a pattern in any part of the world.

She glanced up into the rain and cursed the nexus. The BIteam needed food and water. Manfred had declared a moratorium on the use of his billions because of the Tsuneko incident and his own creeping paranoia, but Pouncey had little cash left. Her own accounts, along with her ID, had been killed when she joined the BIteam, and her fake credit line led to an empty account. As for Joanna, she was practically solo, using wristband and spex only when she needed to, and living off Manfred.

Pouncey stood up, put on her spex, and strode out into the night.

As ever, first thing she did was check Leonora and Yuri in San Francisco, but they had decamped for Seattle. Pouncey grunted to herself and whupped an umbrella. The BIteam knew these were decoys, but it was interesting nonetheless. Pouncey theorised that patterns might develop in this faux-hobo life, leading her to the location of the AIteam, which must, at the very least, include Leonora and Yuri. But she had never been able to make the facts coincide with her theory, and she did not dare allow the nexus to do the work for her. Aritomo Ichikawa would spot that calculation in an instant.

She sighed. The desertion of Tsuneko June handed Aritomo an ace card. Quite likely he knew already about Philly – assuming Tsuneko had run to him. Which seemed probable. Maybe it was time to scoot, leave Philly, leave the States, head Canuckwards, or maybe south to Lone Star lands where hiding was easy amidst the ruined refineries.

There was a lo-market a couple of blocks along. On damp, algae-greened tables lay piles of half rotten veg, bits of scavenged meat – some recognisable as dog limbs – and other provender verging on inedible. But cheap. Very cheap. She took a few coins from her pocket, her last dollars, buying some essentials. Cooking would leach too much of the nutritional value from this stuff, but nobody ate uncooked food in these parts. Way too dangerous.

The terrible argument they'd had when she discovered how much money Manfred had wasted on chocolate returned to her mind. She clamped down on her anger. Soon, she would have to do something about their finances.

And water? Back at the office block she ascended the stairs and checked the rain collectors. Enough there for a few days. Better start boiling it.

In bed, Manfred and Joanna talked.

"How can the bis have emotions if they are not human?" Joanna said. "At best they will be human-imprinted. Humanoid. Not real, like us."

"Emotions *mean* something," Manfred said. He lay on his back, hands behind his head, staring at the ceiling. "They're sourced in the primitive brain, the reptile brain. I bet they're more important than language to survival."

"Really?"

"Listen," Manfred said, "human action isn't all one measure. Different actions, different aspects of reality, have a range of values according to how important they are. *Values,* you see." He turned onto his side so that he could face her. "Hmm, imagine a prehistoric cave dweller. A particle of grit isn't that important, but roots and fruit, they're quite important, and other people are damn crucial to life. All this stuff gets a range of values, right?"

"In the human mind and in the culture that was springing from minds?" Joanna said.

"Yeah. So certain experiences are basic to human beings – the danger of death, the loss of people or things, good times too. We *evolved,* and the cave people encountered those experiences often, and then those experiences began to engender various states of mind. Emotions."

"Which became universal states fundamental to the human condition," Joanna said.

"If you wanna put it in socio-speak, yeah. An emotion is the symbol of a state of mind, you would say with your professor hat on." He lay back, staring again at the ceiling, letting his thoughts flow free.

"What are you thinking?"

"The mind has to have some method of *communicating* significant knowledge to itself and to others," he said. "Doesn't it? It's a dynamic system, after all – not static. Without emotion, my mind would have no way of informing itself, others too, of the relative values of life experiences. It's a strengthening *and* a validation of the existing mental model."

Now Joanna turned onto her side, excitement plain on her face. "You could be right. This explains something I have always wondered about. Why have tears? Why a red face if you are embarrassed?"

"I dunno. Why?"

"Emotions always have a physical component, Manfred. It is because of the importance of the knowledge they are communicating – as you said. It is a matter of value."

"Value? How so?"

"To *force* the mind to become aware of the knowledge emotions carry," Joanna said. "It is a mechanism that cannot be missed, as a thought or concept can be missed. Physical components *had* to appear as we evolved, and so all emotions have some physical consequence. You have seen me cry. In its intensity and in its physical effects that emotion is impossible to ignore."

"You mean… emotion is communication *more* profound than usual?"

Joanna nodded. "A channel of connection between people and between people and the real world, a web of empirical knowledge flowing in all directions. We have been told for centuries that emotion is the lesser experience, that rational thought is more profound, but the opposite is true."

"You're damn right. Objective observation isn't enough to bring understanding. Only surface features can be noticed objectively."

"I'll tell you another thing," Joanna said. "Emotion is rooted in personal human experience, in some mental model of reality."

"Go on."

"Well... two people can experience the same event but feel different emotions. A woman standing at the edge of a sea cliff, who has dived in before... she feels elation. But a novice feels afraid. Those evaluations are immediate, but they are different-"

"And," Manfred interrupted, "although they're generated by the same true stimulus, they're dependent on the experiencer's model of reality. That's why they're different. So emotion must be *cognitive,* then."

"Yes – the fundamental way the mind experiences a coherent inner world, its model of reality. All those physical consequences, like tears, seem to halt the smooth experience of consciousness, but they are forcing the mind to experience itself in a different, more profound, mode. It wells up uncontrollably as it imparts its message."

"Like your crying..."

"And my excitement now! I feel jittery, I'm breathing fast."

Manfred grinned. "Me too, babe."

Pouncey prowled the alleys of dark Philly, four in the morning, when nexus-blurring particles of solar interference were becalmed and even the dwoobs were asleep. Like a graveyard of concrete, grime and weeds, the place was dead.

Down a narrow street she stumbled across a row of shops, all barred and showing biohazard signs, though Pouncey knew these must be for show, designed to deter. Any real biohazard would have the local PD guarding it, or an FBI stick. It was work of a few minutes to use her nexus-raiding skills to locate weaknesses. There – a password on an encrypted back door lock, shining bright in augmented space like a neon sign. No sign of a username though. She ran around to the front of the shop, read: *Brian Dean, e-Goods, Cellphones, Tasa.*

She typed in: briandean, fortunatimes2067. The lock clicked open. Lucky!

Better not take too much, just enough to buy a week's food; then maybe Mr Dean, 30, wouldn't bother calling the cops. She grabbed a U-Fit interface and some microcables, then shut and locked the back door.

She waited until the sun rose and the lo-market dealers were about. An hour later she had a price, not good, but enough to buy bread, veg, tins of meat, all of which she put in her backpack. Time to go.

Three local lads eyed her, but they didn't approach. She ignored them, padding down the passage that linked the lo-market street with Vine Street. Then two of the lads, the smaller two, popped out in front of her. She stopped.

Noise behind her. The big guy.

One of the smaller lads stepped forward, approached to a couple of metres. He stank of beer. "How much you charge for a ride, doll face?"

"I don't screw juvie trash," she replied.

He took steps forward. "Where you get that circuitboard you just passed on to Red Sam?"

"Don't mess with me if you're keepin' that nice trim beard, boy."

He launched himself towards her. She sidestepped, hit out, but he bundled himself into her, so she kicked out, then kneed and downed him. The big guy stepped forward. She pulled out her high-vel.

"Wanna?" she said.

He made to reach into his pocket. She fired. He fell.

Something moved in the corner of her vision. She glanced up to see a CCTV cam pointing at her.

"Shit!"

Kicking the little guy again and dodging the other, she ran. Out into Vine Street; pause, calm, walk like an ordinary woman. Head tilted down, look at the pavement, conceal face. In minutes she stood beside the tower block, checking the area, looking for street woons, listening for PD sirens. Nothing.

Then she noticed her wrist looked different. Three wristbands... no, two.

"Shit," she said.

The first little guy had done a classic distraction. And *he* was still alive.

A red pinpoint flashed in the right side of her spex. PD alarm. "Shit!"

The anthropo-software running the cam had recognised the scene and reported it to the cops. Her face would be stored now, awaiting investigation. But far more dangerous was her missing wristband.

Nothing for it. She couldn't let that get into the wrong hands. Three fake identities – weeks of work, care, maintenance – lay vulnerable to hacking if any half intelligent crim got that wristband. She accessed her security soft and navigated it through her spex. But now she faced a dilemma. If she killed the wristband, blanking it with a nex-bomb, she would send out a signal to all and sundry that could not be misread. Blanking a wristband meant ID manipulation: illegal, a common procedure, dangerous, essential if you wanted to avoid nexus eyes. Aritomo would be scanning twentyfour-seven for such events, and if he linked it to the passage job... *when* he linked it, the BIteam was dead.

No choice. She set the code, modded her wristband and set off the bomb.

Trembling, headachey, she walked up the steps to the apartment. Exhausted, now. Locking the door behind her, she took a deep breath and relaxed. Manfred appeared out of the bis' room.

"You okay?"

She hesitated, wondering if she should take a chance, leave it... or take a lead. "Itchy fingertips," she said. She took the cash out of her pocket and jingled it. "You know how difficult it is to get this?"

A look of annoyance passed across his face. "I'm getting tired of hearing you drone on about itchy fingers," he said. "I told you, we need a week. So if you feel anything a bit stronger than an itch, you let me know, mmm?"

"Aye, I'm tellin' you–"

"*No* more damn itches! When you see a man with a gun on the stairs pointing it at us, sure, fire up the Hyperlinked. Until then, chill."

Pouncey stared, horrified by his retort.

He approached, slapped something wrapped in silver foil into her hand. "Have some more chocolate, Pouncey. And maybe run a hot bath."

Over the next two days Joanna did what she could to stress the bis. She turned off the apartment's only functioning solar-heat driver and opened a skylight so that it became too cold for them, their bioplas bodies stiffening like vulcanised rubber. Then she scavenged a heater from a dead office a few floors down, had Pouncey get it working, then set it to maximum so that they baked. All this time she allowed them the use of low-level English databases. Some of the bis seemed interested, others not. Indigo, she noticed, was not.

Manfred spent a lot of time stressing the bis' limbs, pulling them this way and that, stuffing the bis into confined spaces then waiting for them to struggle out, setting them high on bookshelves with no obvious means of getting down. All this made the bis aware of their bodies, and the limitations of those bodies. They acted by and large as a nine member group, but there were fracture lines. Indigo was a loner. The three warm spectrum bis hung together, as did the other three coloureds. Grey and White were not gregarious. But there was no sign of speech. The bis had no tongues, instead multiform speakers designed by Singaporean audio specialists, yet these speakers remained silent.

"Don't worry," Manfred counselled. "I want to see them cry and blush first."

Joanna spent almost every waking minute with the bis. Each nuance of behaviour she compared with what she remembered of her chimp work, trying to tease out hints of consciousness, looking for that special spark. She even tried the reflection test, dabbing paint on them then setting them down in front of a mirror, but not one of them touched their own skin; each saw their reflection as a different bi, another creature, mysteriously conjured from thin air.

But they remained sponges for knowledge. She began to notice that a few of them grasped that a huge world lay outside their room door. Red, Orange and Yellow took to hunching by that door, like sulking cats hoping to escape a house. She began to take extra care. An escaped bi could not be countenanced.

"We need a key," she told Manfred. "If they have figured out how the door handle works, we could be in trouble."

"True," he agreed. "Listen, the bedroom by the main door's got a small bolt on the inside. I'll unscrew it and try to put it on the outside – if it'll fit. Then we can lock 'em in."

"And we should keep the crates outside," Joanna said, "for emergencies."

He nodded. "You're taking this seriously."

"I'm *sure* they're communicating. I just can't prove it. It's like siblings who invent personal languages."

"Perhaps they don't yet see the importance of English. Perhaps they see us as totally different and don't feel the need to communicate with us. But their own group... that's different. They've *got* to communicate there."

"I worry they could go out of control," she said. "They need to be pretty much like us if they're going to function in society. If they become... well, aliens, then things could get impossible."

Manfred glanced back at the room. "Those crates are only just big enough for them," he said. "And if we got more bioplas we could grow 'em again. Then they'd be too damn heavy to carry. Yeah, you're right, we gotta think about all this. What if Pouncey's right about her itchy fingers?"

"Why not make leather harnesses for the bis? Most of them can walk now, or toddle at least. I suppose we would look like a circus troupe walking down the street, but it might just save us if they used their own feet."

Manfred sighed and shook his head. "Good idea, but too much scope for chaos. What if one got loose? Got stolen? But you're right. We can't crate them forever. We need a *vehicle*."

"That is dangerous, and Pouncey has always advised against it."

"I know. I believe her. She knows the score. But this is different, we never knew they'd develop like they have. Maybe it's time to leave Philly, eh? Risk it out in the sticks, give the bis time to develop, then when they're ready introduce 'em to the world."

Joanna raised her eyebrows. "Nice little fantasy," she said.

He nodded. "Yeah. Maybe."

Joanna took a deep breath. "Why not forget bioplas?" she said. "I know it was your desire to have them walk as tall as a human being, but things have not turned out as you hoped. If we restrict them to child size at least we can control them better."

"But should we control?" he said, raising two hands into the air. "Is that right? Ethical?"

And Joanna shrugged.

"You need a what?" Pouncey said.

They all sat in the kitchen, a pot of coffee between them.

"A soltruck," Manfred said. "A small one."

Pouncey looked at them both. "We're leavin'?"

"Maybe. Not yet. But me and Jo've been talking, and it's getting to that time when…"

He left the rest of the sentence implied.

Pouncey shook her head. "Boss, I've always said no to solcars. Aye… too easy to smash up. To follow – from the air, f'rinstance. What's new?"

"We're thinking ahead."

Pouncey nodded once, drank her coffee dregs, sighed then stood up. "Gimme a couple of hours."

She left.

Manfred glanced at Joanna. "That was too easy," he said.

"She knows something. She is nervous, I have seen it before."

"Yeah… I think you're right. Wanna pack a few things, just in case?"

"You mean it?"

Manfred glanced at the external apartment door, just visible through the kitchen doorway. "I feel vulnerable without her. C'mon, *I've* got itchy fingers now."

"I will check the bis."

Joanna walked to the bis' room, pulling the bolt and opening the door. There came a sensation at her legs of something brushing past, and she glanced down to see a blue form scurry past.

She slammed the door shut. "Manfred! Indigo's out!"

The bi ran away from her, bumping into walls, stopping, turning, then running again. Joanna halted. Manfred crashed into her from the bathroom corridor, but she grabbed his arm and held him back.

"No," she said. "Wait! It orientated itself."

"What? You—"

"It did! I'm sure."

They followed Indigo into the lounge, watching from the doorway. The bi stumbled around the room, but kept a constant direction.

"It can't see objects," Manfred said. "Should be easy to catch, then."

"*Watch*, Manfred. Use *your* eyes. It is tracking something. It knows what it is doing."

"Tracking? What, that fly smacking against the window? C'mon, Jo..."

Joanna moved forward. Indigo had climbed onto the couch beside the window. She picked it up and set it on the floor a metre or so away. It turned. Walked away. Then it reached out with one arm and began patting the air.

Jo gasped as understanding made the hairs on the back of her neck rise. One hand covered her mouth. "Manfred, look! It *knows* the couch is there. It is trying to feel for it. It has modelled this room into its... mind."

Manfred stared at Indigo. "Jeez... you're right."

They watched, astonished, as Indigo located then clambered upon the couch, climbing cushions at the back to kneel upon the windowsill.

"Mmm, it really wants that fly," Manfred said.

They walked forward. Joanna lifted Indigo and held it against her, cuddling it as she might a child.

Manfred reached out to grab the fly. He looked at it.

She saw his face go white. He froze. Stared down.

Turned to face her. "It's glitched," he said.

CHAPTER 7

The AIteam ran through the laser-punched tunnel at the side of the cave system, emerging into a fake boulder pile engineered by Hound when he first prepared the base. Around the hillside, less than a hundred metres away, two copters hovered at the cave entrance: dust mushrooming, engines roaring, rotor wind spattering debris against the micro-goggles they wore to protect their eyes.

Leonora, Dirk, Yuri, Zeug. Hound checked they were all behind him.

"Run like I do," he said. "The thermo sheets will protect you against satellite eyes. Think positive. Don't dawdle. Just run like me. Assume you're going to make it, okay?"

Yuri – face blanched, trembling – turned to Zeug and said, "Do you understand? Just copy what I do–"

"No, Zeug!" Hound shouted. "You copy what *I* do."

"When does the decoy go?" Leonora asked.

Hound punched a tag on his wristband. "That Skud-Fli launches *now.*"

From the hide a few hundred metres down the valley the jet rose, turned, roaring away. The copters followed.

Hound grinned. "Decoy worked," he said. "All wristbands off now, spex too. Hold the thermo sheet above your head. When we're on the edge of the village we won't need 'em."

"What den?" Dirk asked.

"You'll see."

Yuri said, "But–"

"No more talk! You obey. Thinking ain't needed. Just do what I do and keep an eye on Zeug."

He raised the thermo sheet to his head and ran out, following the goat track to the main path made by the geologists, where he halted. The copters were a distant duo following the orange jet glare of the Skud-Fli. The other four followed him, sheets correctly held. Zeug was extraordinary: upright, stable, staring at Yuri. Stressed no doubt, but following his mentor like a chick following a hen. The sun had set: cicadas stridulating. Just enough light to get them down to the village, so Hound began trotting down the path.

No sign of the copters. No sign of auxiliary fliers. No sign of foot patrols. Hound looked behind him to see the other four bouncing along the path, Zeug most obvious because his skin glowed pure white in the twilight.

"Man, need to sort that out," he muttered to himself. "Like a lamp, he is."

He stopped. In his backpack lay the ultrathin boiler suit he kept for biohazard work; a brown utilitarian garment with no flash. He pulled it out, told Yuri to make Zeug wear it.

"Anyone got a hat?" he asked.

They had emerged from the cave system with only the four backpacks stashed at the end of the exit tunnel, packed so long ago Hound had forgotten half of what he put in them. Dirk rummaged through his pack to produce a bandana and a pair of non-nex sunglasses.

"Put them on him," Hound told Yuri. To Leonora he added, "When we get to Ghar Lapsi port you can maybe buy fake tan. Zeug's too white. Stands out."

They ran on. At the village they stowed the thermo sheets in their backpacks and entered the main street, concealing themselves beside a mini grove of jasmine bushes in tubs. Hound detached himself and ran down to the tourist bar where the girl he had chatted up worked. The horses he liked the look of stood in their stables, nickering. Routes checked, he returned to the others, but didn't tell them the plan because he knew they wouldn't like it.

"Follow me," he said. "There's not many people about. We'll use back alleys."

They walked in single file through the evening gloom, the alleys Hound chose unlit, though they passed through some light pools made by back garden illumination. Behind the stables he paused; then through the gate, across the yard.

Leonora grabbed him by the arm. "Horses?"

He addressed the whole team. "We need speed. Must be naked too – and no vehicles."

"I cannot ride *these*," Yuri said.

"You don't need to," Hound replied. "You think I don't do my research? I ride. Dirk rode Arabs in Morocco. Leonora rode when she was younger. It's just you and whitey, man. So you sit up in front of Dirk. Or me. Zeug has the other – unless you want him up in front of you, Leonora?"

She shrugged. "We will all do what you say to the letter."

Good girl. That message was aimed at Yuri. He said, "Dirk, you're the best, you take Zeug." He grinned at Yuri. "I got you, then."

Yuri grimaced.

Hound told Leonora to saddle up a horse, then he unbarred the stable doors and saddled up two others. Minutes later the horses were prepared. No sound of people nearby, apart from the clink of distant wine glasses and tinny music.

"Get ready y'all," he said.

They manhandled Zeug so that he sat in front of Dirk. Zeug's expression did not alter, but something in his manner, the tense way he held his head low like a cat about to pounce, suggested he was stressed. Hound had to remind himself this was a proto artificial intelligence that copied gestures – no human. But Dirk seemed contented, if not happy, as did Leonora.

He jumped up, then hauled Yuri into the saddle. He said, "The hooves will make a lot of noise – man, the *moment* we're out in the yard, ride on. Don't let anyone stop you if anyone comes. Kick 'em. Now go!"

Clattering hooves echoed around the yard. Dirk drove his horse on, Leonora following, Hound last. At the gate Hound rode forward to lead the way. Near the end of the alley a woman ran from a doorway and cried out, "Hey! What you doing!" but it was too late for her. They were away and cantering.

Hound led them through groves of squat trees where no solbike pursuit could follow. Fifteen minutes later he halted, listening. Nocturnal silence...

They were to flee from Ghar Lapsi, a tiny divesite port in a western vale that Hound had chosen. He led them there as night passed by, insect-heavy and warm, with low cloud obscuring the moon and stars. And satellite eyes.

No sign of copters.

"Time for a few hours' sleep," he said. "We'll take a small boat out, first thing in the morning. Then off to Hammamet, Tunisia, and my old friend Sandman Entré."

At dawn they let their rides run free in a deep valley, hoping that it would take the horses a while to climb out and be noticed as strays. With the sun climbing above the ocean horizon they walked into the port, acting nonchalant, Zeug covered as best they could manage with clothes and accessories. The place was almost empty, so Hound led them straight to the harbour, where he knew fishing smacks bobbed, and maybe a few boats run for the delight of tourists: the port was a newbuild. He jingled cash in his pocket.

A long jetty led out into the harbour, its walls pale grey stone slicked with algae and jagged with barnacles, boats clanking against one another as the water lapped against them. No sign of any cap'ns however.

Leonora tapped his shoulder. "He's looking at us," she said, pointing to a man standing fifty metres away on the harbour wall.

Hound glanced across. The man stood silent and motionless. Something clicked at the back of his mind. Alert at once, he paused, took stock of the situation. No obvious danger.

"Where dere a boat?" Dirk asked.

Hound ignored the query. The man moved, walking to the jetty entrance. Urgent alarm call at the back of Hound's mind...

"Get down, all of you," he said.

"Wh–"

"Get *down!* It's a panicman. Beyond all of you."

Hound fought to control his beating heart; pulled off his backpack and wrenched out the emergency flask. Pulled out the Hebetisol. Threw backpack and flask to the ground. Injected the Hebetisol.

Without delay the drug kicked in. Panicmen were expensive: this could only be Aritomo Ichikawa's assassin. Hound felt his body become heavy, full of inertia. The flags flapped in slow motion, the waves lapped moment by moment. Sound was dull, bassy.

A panicman altered his perception as did a high-speed camera, forcing his brain to apprehend reality a hundred times more often per second than normal. Hebetisol did the same thing, but with far more risk of brain damage. This would be a slo-mo fight to the death.

Hound had used Hebetisol once before. He recognised the symptoms in his own body: sluggishness caused by his brain perceiving his body as heavy; slo-mo arrow of time in the external world; his assassin also moving slo-mo. But that assassin would not now be able to use the mental effect to run rings around his enemy.

The trick with panicmen was to observe them as closely as possible, that their motives and tactics be guessed. This panicman would have orders to capture everybody, but kill Hound. So Hound was at an advantage. Killing, no problem; and his strategy would require less complexity than the other's.

The panicman walked along the edge of the jetty: slo-mo stroll. Hound approached. His opponent wore a tunic and vest, leaving the arms bare. That was helpful, for Hound would be able to see his muscles move, and from that deduce what the panicman was thinking. He, on the other hand, was well covered, and knew how to keep his face impassive. But the eyes were often a giveaway. So difficult to conceal the truth expressed by eyes.

The panicman strolled now just twenty metres away. Hound reached for his flechette gun and raised it as quickly as he could, but his arm seemed made of lead, and anyway he knew from the panicman's slo-mo dive that his tactic had been guessed. He fired anyway, watching the dart ammo emerge from the barrel and spin lazily towards his opponent.

A bullet approached him. He had not seen a gun in the panicman's hand. He judged the trajectory and began to move out of the way, but it was like forcing his body through invisible treacle: the physical restrictions of the real world. The bullet grazed his left hand.

He fired again and again to give the panicman too much to think about. Then he stopped, guessed trajectories and sprayed out more. Covering fire.

He dropped the flechette gun and pulled out his snub-nose. Too slow! The sluggishness of his body began to make him anxious. The panicman had a second gun out and was slowly raising his hand to take aim.

Hound lowered his left hand so that the panicman would not be able to see him aim his snub-nose. This was a risk: firing through his own fingers. He saw muscles on the panicman's upper left arm move, caught the hint of a dive to the left. He guessed, aimed, fired.

A bullet came his way. Chestwards.

But his own guess had been right – his bullet was heading for the panicman's chest and that dive could not be amended enough to make the shot miss.

Bullet approaching him. He observed its trajectory. Chest area. With all his strength he pushed against the invisible forces that seemed to constrain his body so that the bullet would strike him in the least dangerous place. One metre away: ten centimetres. He watched the bullet pass through the fabric of his clothes, leave a hole and scorch marks, then felt it move between ribs beneath his left armpit.

But the panicman was down, blood fountaining in scarlet slo-mo from a chest wound.

He began to turn. The others were lying in attitudes of distress, horror unmoving on Yuri's face, shock frozen into the expression on Leonora's face, Dirk impassive, lying on the ground as if asleep. But Zeug... that artificial face looked like nothing Hound had ever seen before, cycling through expression after expression – fear, wonder, awe, it was difficult to tell – as if a loop of copied emotions cycled through his brain, to then be written on his bioplastic face. Then they made eye contact, and Hound received the ghastly sensation of looking into Zeug's brain... and the moment was chilling. Nothing lay behind those eyes.

He stopped himself speculating. This was nonsense. Again he had fallen into the trap of assuming that Zeug was at least human-like. He was not. He *copied*. He remained non-sentient.

The Hebetisol began to wear off. External time appeared to speed up. Then a stab of agony behind his eyes as the light of the sun pierced his mind. He felt pressure in his chest, a bad smell in his nose. As normal time re-established itself he vomited and collapsed to the ground.

Sounds twittered like a cage of birds: his ears made no sense of it. Then the dull, underwater sensation vanished and life became too fast, too loud, too intense. He gasped for air.

Voices. "Hound… Hound…"

"Will he perish, like they do sometimes?"

That was Yuri… then another voice.

"He has saved us. But we need to get away fast. Do not touch him."

Leonora. His mind was returning. He tried to stand up.

"He's coming round!"

"Leave him… leave him. He knows what is best."

Leonora again. Hound realised the woman really admired him, trusted him; he could hear it in her voice. To think that he had considered abandoning the AIteam.

He struggled to his feet, grabbed his backpack and the flask. Headache gripped his temples. He heard himself speaking. "Steal a motor boat. Too late now to charter one. Dirk, man… take us to Gozo. I know a ferry company there. Will get us to Hemma… Hatta… to Tunisia. Hurry!"

Dirk span around and ran along the jetty. Shielding his eyes from the orange morning sun Hound followed, glancing behind to see the dying panicman but nobody else. The bullet wound in his side began to flare. Breathing hoarse. But they had a few seconds yet before the gunshot sounds brought danger.

Fairweather cloud misted higher sky into pastel blue, reducing satellite vision.

"Could still make it," he said. "The panicman would've been monitored through the nexus, but he's gone now. We got a window. *Move* it!"

"They will know we are here," Leonora said. "The helicopters will return to capture us all."

He shook his head. "They won't have enough power to get back from where the Skud-Fli leads them. In France, remember?"

"But…"

"We got a *window*," he insisted. "Speed is all. Dirk, what you got?"

Dirk leaped into a six-seater motor boat. Hound glanced back to see people gathering on the harbour wall where the jetty met it.

"Jump in," he shouted. He leaped into the back of the boat and hotwired the engine with the only thing he had; a recharger cable. The bullet wound made his left arm hang limp. His head throbbed. The motor coughed into life. "Leonora, smash the computer! The nexus pod – there, at the front!"

The boat leaped away from the jetty but its tie-line caught it.

"Shit!" Hound took his snub-nose and fired at the rope where it strained against the side of the boat: and they were away. "Dirk, take charge. Steer into open sea but shadow the coastline."

He sat back with a gasp of pain. He felt sick again.

"Leonora," he said, "look in my backpack. Poradol ampoule. Quickly."

She did as she was instructed. The others sat low in their seats, except Dirk who steered the boat at top speed along the Maltese coast.

"If the sun burns off this high cloud we're done for," he told Leonora. "We need to be outa this boat soon as possible." He glanced at Yuri and said, "Throw out any cameras, mobies you find – anything that might be hooked to the nexus."

Leonora asked, "Can this boat be tracked through the nexus?"

He swallowed the proffered ampoule. "Not now you smashed its brain. Best they can do is try follow us through land cams. But this is Malta, westside. Won't be many. We got a chance yet."

"Where did that panicman appear from?" she asked.

"Don't know. Could've been sheer bad luck. Not enough info to speculate."

"Are you badly hurt?"

The boat bounced through ocean waves.

"Just hurt," he replied, trying to lie back.

It was thirty kilometres to the Gozo port of Mgarr; just under an hour transit duration. By the time they arrived Hound had bound his wounds – the bullet had passed through rib muscle tissue then out again – had time to collect his thoughts and deal with his headache, and decided what next to do.

He glanced upward. "Clouds thickening," he said. "Lucky."

"What now?" Leonora asked.

"We can't arrive portside in this boat. The Maltese locals might have put out a search request. If they have, Aritomo will've spotted it through the nexus. So we'll sneak up to a cove and wade in." He glanced at Zeug. "Looks like you'll get your first taste of water, man."

"Mr Hound does not mean you will drink actual water," Yuri told Zeug, "he means you must experience the sensation of water upon your skin – but you will not be harmed by wading through it, this I promise you."

"I understand," Zeug replied in a monotone.

Hound took them as close as he could to a rock-strewn cove, then they disembarked and waded thigh-deep to the shore. Zeug managed: Yuri held his hand. Ten minutes later they stood atop the cliffs. Using EarthMaps on Leonora's standalone moby, Hound found a route from cliffs to port, which they followed. By the time they arrived portside it was noon. But still no sign of pursuit.

Leaving the others concealed in thorn bushes, Hound walked into Mgarr, bought food, fake tan, more sunglasses and more water, then scouted a likely tourist ferry from the list at the Ghajnsielem terminal. "A hundred and twenty five kilometres to Linosa," he told himself, scanning the manifest, "then two hundred and twenty five to Hammamet. Do-able."

He explained the next part of the escape plan when he returned.

"There's a tourist ferry leaving in a coupla hours. To Linosa – tiny Italian island. Then on to Hammamet. We'll meet Sandman there, then off into the desert."

"West Libya?" Dirk asked.

Hound shook his head. "Algeria, man, Morocco. Once we're safe we'll make a new base. Could be a long time off yet."

Leonora nodded, then turned to Zeug. "So, you next," she murmured, taking the fake tan bottle and unscrewing the top.

"I shall do these tasks," Yuri said, reaching out.

Hound pulled Leonora's hand back. "We'll all do them," he said. "Yuri, you're getting way too protective of Zeug. Understand? We're the AIteam. Emphasis on *team*. This ain't your creation, it's ours."

Leonora tried to laugh, then said, "That is taking it, oh, a little too…"

"I agree with Hound," Dirk said. "Da man here think he own Zeug. But he don't."

Yuri glanced at them all, third eye closed, face impassive, a hint of tremor in his shoulders. "Very well," he said, "I can see which way the wind is blowing, as you Westerners say, so I will have to agree with you, Leonora, and pull back just a little."

Hound nodded. He saw the fault lines in the group.

Leonora said, "I used to use fake tan when I was a teen, so I shall do it."

They disrobed Zeug and planned their task. The white bioplas was textured like neoprene, but they saw that accidental contact with ground, clothes and plants had dirtied Zeug's integument. It would take a covering dye layer, then. Using a pair of knickers as an applicator cloth, Leonora covered Zeug with fake tan from head to foot, then, with only a little left in the bottle, added a second layer to his head, neck, hands and arms, and to his feet. The result was mediocre. Rather orange.

"He'll look like a vain saddo," Hound said.

"Dude, him bald one," Dirk pointed out.

Hound shook his head. "Zeug wears a bandana and a hat above that at all times. Shades. Anyone got any jewellery? Make him look normal."

"He will never look normal," Yuri said, "except to the least discerning of eyes."

Hound nodded. "Yeah. Typical tourists. Should work fine."

Yuri shook his head.

Hound said, "If the worst comes to the worst we say he's a test model Nippandroid. But it won't. Man, we beat the panicman and we beat them copters. Now follow me to the ferry. Leonora, Yuri, you help Zeug. Speak for him at all times. Zeug, you keep quiet. Dirk – back of the party, okay?"

Dirk nodded and lit a cheroot.

The only stress point was the queue for the ferry. The weather, though cloudy, was warm, and at least a hundred tourists were taking the trip. Glancing over his shoulder Hound saw Zeug twisting his body from side to side like a kid wanting a pee. He held his nerve. Paid cash for a one-way ferry ride, stared out the suspicious clerk, then hustled them all aboard. No scares.

"Wish people used cash more," he muttered. "Would help me a lot."

"Coin will be dead by da end da century," Dirk told him.

Leonora, Dirk and Hound sat in air conditioned luxury by a window on the lower deck of the ferry. Hound had told them not to risk the top deck. Zeug was locked in a cabin, Yuri asleep on a deckchair a few yards away, a half-eaten apple in one hand.

"Why are they called panicmen?" Leonora asked.

Hound said, "You ever been in a car accident?"

"Never."

"In the old days," Hound continued, "cars could go, what, eighty, one hundred kilometres per hour. There were thousands of accidents. Some people who survived, they describe a sensation. Like the accident happening in slo-mo."

"Slo-mo?"

"Slow motion. Video term. Like a camera that takes two fifty frames per sec not twenty five. Also, some people in accidents say their vision go black and white. That's the brain. Acting to reduce extraneous info. Working super fast. Panicman is like that. Man, he sees in black and white only. Models the real world at a far greater rate because of artificially induced panic."

Dirk nodded. "Dat da truth."

"I'm glad you asked," Hound said, taking a sip of his lemon water. "Man, I saw Zeug stressed when I was under the Hebetisol. I think. His face cycling through emotional states."

"Ah…" Dirk said. Hound glanced at him.

"What do you mean?" Leonora asked. "Zeug was scared?"

Hound shrugged. "Reckon Dirk might know."

Dirk took a puff of his cheroot. "Not really dude," he said. "But I think. We gotta be careful. You heard of da Seoul Illusion?"

Leonora nodded. "When you look at a lifelike Nippandroid and you think it must be human – when you can't *help* thinking that."

Dirk grinned. "It what we human do too well. Put ourself in other person's place. Imagine dey human. Most time, dey are. But with a Nippandroid, easy to fool yourself – like da Korean guy said. Zeug... we gotta stop thinking he *human*. He computer. I worry 'bout him, what we building, 'cos if he got no emotion he got no self."

Leonora nodded, but she looked unhappy. "I've heard this many times before," she said, "not least from Manfred, who talked about it on a number of occasions. But for me, language is the key. We must give Zeug the best facility for language that we possibly can."

Hound said, "He's learned a lot already. And we've got standalones with massive English databases. With us here, now. He can learn from them."

Dirk raised his cheroot and pointed it at Hound. "He could," he said. "But I think you saw Zeug's underlying lack of self. He not conscious yet. I worry. Are we building best computer in da world, or conscious artificial intelligence? Dere big difference between da two."

Hound glanced away. "Could be. Out of my league, man. I just do security."

Dirk smiled. "You do great. But, Leonora, think." Dirk glanced at Yuri then whispered, "Yuri not da most emotional guy. He *bonding* with Zeug. You gotta wonder why. If you make a super computer on legs, dat not your goal, dat just a real good Seoul Illusion."

"Are you having second thoughts about the AIteam?" Leonora responded.

"Nah, nah," Dirk said, waving his cheroot about. "You joke? Dis da best job for an interface design guy. Real groundbreak stuff. I just saying... you gotta ask, what is conscious for Zeug? Is it exactly da same as us? Or is it different for artificial?"

Leonora sighed. "This is the nut that Manfred and I were trying to crack at Ichikawa labs."

"Huh," Hound grunted, "along with most of the rest of the world."

Leonora threw a black glance at Hound then said, "At the moment I agree with Yuri, that it is a matter of computing power. The human brain has trillions of neuron connections, and his new quantum computer can mimic that."

Dirk nodded. "Sure. Zeug's brain. But where in *your* brain is consciousness?"

"We do not believe consciousness exists in a place," Leonora said, adopting the tones of a schoolteacher pushed too far. "That was Descartes' idea, and I do not believe for one moment Dirk that you are a dualist. Consciousness is distributed, an illusion perhaps, created by the mind to tell the story of a person, filling in the details to make a coherent whole. You have read Dennett, have you not?"

Dirk nodded. "'Course. And da others." He raised his cheroot and held it between Leonora and Hound's heads. "I think consciousness is *dere*," he said. He sat back in his seat with a satisfied smirk.

Leonora frowned. "In mid air? This is ridiculous, Dirk."

"No," Hound said, "let him speak."

Dirk shrugged. "Imagine a kid," he said. "Born outa artificial womb. Grows up, but no other people in da world. Not one, see? But all its body needs – dey sorted. Food, water, warm, whatever. Does it become conscious?"

"Of course," Leonora said.

Dirk shook his head. "I don't think so. Dis my objection to da language only method. Da baby not become conscious because no social interaction. I think consciousness between people, not in a brain. It *between* us all, like water for fish. See?"

Leonora shook her head. "I think we shall have to agree to disagree."

Dirk nodded. "I happy with dat."

Leonora looked at Hound. "And what do you think?"

"I think I want pasta with tomato sauce. Italians sure know how to cook."

At Linosa the ferry paused overnight. Hound fretted, unable to sleep, knowing that, from Aritomo's point of view, this was a good attack point. He cut off his dreads, shaved his head and removed his beard, then found fly-shades and a big straw hat, keying a new fake ID to these features. The night stayed peaceful, warm, and at last he slept, and dreamed of horses.

The longer half of the voyage remained. Hound's anxiety faded. The weather turned rainy, but in the evening the sun returned and they ate a pleasant meal in view of the sunset. Zeug remained in his cabin, learning English.

Hound flicked through a few channels on the all-receive, looking for local broadcasters. He was pleased to find none of the journos talking about the copters and the Skud-Fli, nobody mentioning stolen horses, nor the panicman or the boat. It seemed he had succeeded, had spirited them away from Malta against the odds.

He did not relax entirely. No man of his calibre could relax entirely.

"Of course," he pointed out to Leonora, "Aritomo could learn a lot from the computers in the cave pods."

"I auto-wiped most of it," she replied gloomily, "five seconds after you said evacuate. He will find little enough, and nothing to tell him where I am going or what I am doing."

"Too right," Hound agreed. "But the Japs can do wonders with hard drives. Even these days, when nobody got a hard drive. Don't imagine he'll find nothing."

She glanced at him. "You are becoming a pessimist."

He smiled. "Always was. Optimists crash when they get bad luck. A pessimist never crashes."

Next evening, in glorious red sunshine, the ferry docked at Hammamet harbour; they disembarked after Hound ran a security check and gave the all clear. They checked into a three bit hotel – skanky rooms, but invisible, and with enough privacy to keep them invisible. Hound bought spex and wristbands, new clothes, bullets. But his cash was running out and he dared not use any of the money in Leonora's account. Or his own.

From a nexus caf he put a trans-ax call through to Sandman Entré.

"Sandman?"

"Mon ami! You call from Tunis? I see a red crescent on the menu."

"Bit further south. Listen, man, I need a favour. Well, a deal. I got money."

Sandman grinned. "Sure, sure. It is the plastique once again?"

"No. There's five of us. We need to get invisible. In the desert. I was thinking Algeria."

"Bon. We put our toes into the big sandy pataugeoire, ami. It is good."

Hound nodded. "You arrange it. We'll meet at the nu-desert fields. We're fifty kilometres away. Reckon we can solbus that before noon tomorrow. Okay?"

"Merci!"

Hound cut the line. Sat and thought. Unaugmented, they were invisible to the nexus. No sign of trouble since the panicman. Not a twitch of his senses, not a hint of a stink in the air. Yep. His luck had held out.

They picked a ramshackle solbus driven by a bad tempered goon. Perfect disguise. The weather was sweaty hot and they drank a lot of water. As Tunis approached they ate watercress sandwiches, disembarking at the Majesté Désert stop, to the muttered oaths of the driver. The bus clattered off, leaving them alone on a sand-strewn road. Hound led them up plant-edged tracks to the plantation he owned.

Sandman Entré, as ever, wore white flannel trousers and an English jacket, a straw hat on his head. His ebony skin shone beneath a film of sweat.

"Welcome," he said, bowing to them. "We head west, away from prying eyes. It is l'appel de la nature. This I can promise you all!"

CHAPTER 8

Rosalind picked up Tsuneko in the cyclo-wing, but they decided to give London a miss as it was becoming dangerous. The cyclo-wing began to deteriorate as they approached Brighton so they landed on a beach, where they hugged, congratulating each other on completing an arduous journey across the Med and France. Rosalind was as slim, tall and athletic as Tsuneko and only a decade older, but she had gone prematurely grey. Tsuneko felt overjoyed to see her again. As the cyclo-wing disintegrated into a mess of plant based polymers and recycled plastic, its raison-d'être departed, the couple walked across the beach and climbed steps to the seafront, where they leaned on metal railings and gazed out to a sparkling sea.

"So, what you going to do now we're here?" Rosalind asked.

Tsuneko sighed. Rosalind was an old family friend who deserved the truth. "I don't know," she said. "If Aritomo Ichikawa finds me, my life is in danger... though, more likely, he'd just enslave me in Japan."

Rosalind nodded. "Got to find you first. What about work? The biograins?"

"The moment I reveal myself through biograins I'll be caught. I suppose my best plan would be to sell what I know, create a fake data incarnation and live a life of leisure until I pop off. Biograins will be public knowledge in a decade. If I don't sell up soon I'll miss my chance."

"Popping off could be sixty years away."

Tsuneko nodded. "What I would really like to do is find the AIteam, but that must be impossible now. In Malta there were traces, but Aritomo's team never caught the signals they were looking for."

"Or so they told you."

"True... I am a fool if I trust him, or anybody from Ichikawa labs. That's why I came here free of the nexus. Solo. So they couldn't follow me."

"Why do you want to find the AIteam?" Rosalind asked.

"I was sporadically in touch with their interface man, who I'd worked with at Bell labs. He and his security man had me for a mole, but it was more complex than that. Even at the time Manfred bought my services there was something about his plan I did not like. Well... *not* is too strong. He was following the wrong path, playing with toys. Something about the quantum computer intrigues me. So much possibility in one brain..."

"Where might the AIteam be now?"

"Anywhere," Tsuneko replied. "I have no idea. They were hiding out in Malta, so it could be Europe, Africa, the Near East..."

"So you would join them?"

"Maybe. The irony is, Dirk – their interface man – was leaning towards Manfred's interpretation of artificial intelligence. Perhaps we were both on the wrong team."

"Perhaps he's as unhappy as you are," Rosalind prompted.

"Yeah. Perhaps."

Quiet for a few minutes: surf pounding the shore, distant shrieking kids, the creak of dilapidated wooden huts. Bicycle bells, no sound of vehicles.

Then Rosalind said, "Ever heard of Mr Bloodhound?"

"No."

"Let me take you to him."

Tsuneko turned to face her friend. "Who is he?"

"The name says it all."

Travel in Britain was difficult. Only Germany had been worse hit by the Depression. Overcrowded, importing too much of its food, urbanised to the max and riven with strife, it declined like America: violently. With fuel impossible to obtain and a poor energy infrastructure it descended into semi-chaos, voyeuristically staring at its own demise through countless sensational nexus broadcasts. These days, half the country was owned by China and Korea. The other half wasn't worth owning.

But Rosalind was lucky. In 2092 she had been rich. At the first hint of an economic slide she sold her wine business for a tenth of its value and moved to a five acre plot in Wiltshire with her boyfriend. They began growing their own food at once. They bought bicycles. They saw which way the wind was blowing.

But now Rosalind and Tsuneko stood sea-side, one hundred and thirty kilometres from safety.

"It's not so bad," Rosalind said. "We could probably make it along the coast to Southampton. Then we'd have to strike out inland for Salisbury."

"You lead and I will follow," Tsuneko replied.

Half dead Britain. With nothing to export except services and knowledge – qualities the rising Pacific Rim had little need of – the British government had been forced to restrict solbuses to the major urban centres, leaving rural communities to fend for themselves. Only one in five families used a solcar; there was simply no way to pay for them. One in five thousand retained a petrol fuelled vehicle.

Rosalind transferred cash from her Shanghai account to her britcard, paying for two seats on the only bus of the day heading west. Info in her spex told her the solbus would terminate at Havant, but in fact it never reached Havant, breaking down twenty kilometres out of Brighton. They managed to find a room in a one star dive, which, miserably, they shared. Next day another solbus from Brighton took them to Havant, from where a third took them to Southampton.

Roads north were pot-holed, where they were not vandalised; solbus services nonexistent. With no other options Rosalind paid the 2092 equivalent of a month's wages to hire a solvan to Salisbury, where she and Tsuneko were dumped.

"We walk from here," Rosalind announced.

The five acre plot lay a day's walk north of Salisbury. They rested overnight in a barn stinking of cow dung, rain pattering on the corrugated metal roof; sleep impossible. As grey clouds cleared and the sun rose they trudged on, arriving after noon. But Rosalind's house was comfortable. That evening, bathed, rested and fed, Rosalind and Tsuneko planned their visit to Mr Bloodhound.

"He lives by Avebury," Rosalind said. "D'you remember how to ride a bike?"

So quiet was the Wiltshire countryside, so free of the noise of cars, that in the sun the following day Tsuneko relaxed, almost enjoying the bicycle ride. Overgrown verges squeezed navigable roads to a central channel. Contrails in the sky were a rarity, to be pointed out and laughed at: military jets from Chinese bases, EU officials, African test-planes. Alive with the sound of bees, the air smelled of flower perfumes.

Local communities tilled fields, kept sheep. Few now could afford to live as a single family. The community was king, sharing unavoidable.

"Before, we lived on borrowed time," Rosalind remarked. "*This* time."

Mr Bloodhound lived in a community of twenty based in a huge farmhouse set amidst fifty acres of prime arable land. A community elder, he resided in a two-storey straw house filled with electronic gear salvaged from military bases on Salisbury Plain, powered by the latest Algerian solar panels. He was quite the local celebrity.

He was small, pale, white-haired and hunched, and he smelled of beer. "Rosalind!" he said, his eyes bright with pleasure as they entered his parlour.

"Mr B," she replied. "This is Tsuneko June."

He stared. "Tsuneko *June?* Good... heavens. But yes, I recognise you now."

"You've heard of me?" Tsuneko said.

Rosalind pushed Tsuneko into a chair. "For goodness sake! Lots of people know who you are, we do watch the news."

"I am sorry," Tsuneko told Mr Bloodhound, "I haven't been in Britain for fifteen years."

"Well, you haven't been on the news for a while," he replied, "but nobody with my interests forgets the word *biograin.*"

Uncomfortable, Tsuneko tried to smile.

"Mr B," Rosalind said, "Tsuneko has a favour to ask you. Paid, of course."

"Excellent, excellent. What's the deal?"

"Tracing some people," said Rosalind. "They could be anywhere. It's just your sort of thing. Tell her."

Mr Bloodhound turned to Tsuneko. "You know what I do?" he asked.

"I... can guess," Tsuneko replied.

He grinned. "You see, in the old days, when the Japanese were rolling out the nexus, we all realised the benefits. But we didn't notice the drawbacks. We should have though – seventy years of social networking on the internet to use as evidence. An inexorable erosion of the concept of privacy, of a person's private life. Everything shared regardless... ugh!" He shivered. "Eastern peoples don't have the same view of individuality that we Westerners have, you know, but we ignored the dangers all the same."

"Tell her about the tracing," Rosalind said.

Mr Bloodhound frowned at her, then smiled at Tsuneko. "The key difference between the internet and the nexus is location. In the nexus, realtime location is everything, it's how the nexus knows where everybody in the world is, all the time. Everybody with a proper data incarnation, that is. And so we all live under the weight of the thing, observed twenty four hours a day so that this tide of *tremendously* useful info can be pushed our way. I'm being ironic."

"So how do you track an individual with a fake data incarnation, or none at all?" Tsuneko asked.

"Ha ha! That's my art. I won't be telling you any of my tricks. But you see, the nexus is a near-perfect copy of the real world, and as such it uses certain procedures."

"What like?"

"Well, for instance the dating of timelines. Everybody's life is recorded in the nexus, manipulated for convenience into a data incarnation – a copy of themselves, continuously updated. Timeline orders can be altered, yes, but if that happens certain inevitable errors are left. Minuscule, but visible to a man with patience and a beady eye. Fake timelines are even easier to spot if you know what you're looking for."

"And you do."

"Oh, I do. Then there are contextual clues. I might look for inconsistencies in a person's life story and their recorded history, that kind of thing. It's no science, it really is an art. But they don't call me Mr Bloodhound for nothing."

Tsuneko nodded. "Then you have a choice of people to trace," she said. "Leonora Klee. Dirk Ngma. Yuri Ichikawa."

He laughed. "Good heavens! You're *serious?*"

Tsuneko replied, "I used to work for a team opposing them."

"Paralleling them?" Rosalind said. "Not opposing exactly."

Tsuneko shrugged. "You might be right, Ros… though Manfred was always badmouthing her." To Mr Bloodhound she added, "Leonora's ex Manfred is the leader of the team I used to work for."

"The Ichikawa breakout. Then this scene would be artificial intelligence research?"

Tsuneko nodded.

"I see. You do realise Leonora Klee will buy *the* single most talented security man on the entire planet?"

"He is called Hound." She smiled. "Not his real name."

Mr Bloodhound nodded. "I believe I will trace Leonora Klee. As she is the leader of her team the others, if they still work for her, will be alongside. I accept your challenge! But it will be expensive."

"Money is no object," Tsuneko replied with a sigh and a glum face.

Silence fell for a few moments, leaving just an old-style clock ticking.

"You know," Mr Bloodhound said, "I can see now you've had a bad time of it lately. Why not stay with us here until I'm done? Maybe a week… a fortnight. You'd have to help out on the farm, but, well, exercise releases happy chemicals, or so I'm told by my biochemist grandson."

Tsuneko nodded, but Rosalind said, "I'll have to cycle back home a few times… partner to help, land to work, fish to catch. You don't mind, Tsuneko?"

Tsuneko shrugged, feeling she had little choice. An overwhelming sense of isolation grew inside her as tears ran down her cheeks.

Mr Bloodhound's study was extraordinary. A bank of ten real-rez monitors fed into various computers, most of them anonymous lumps of silico-drive lacking any corporate sigil. He wore spex, but also used a parallel display due to long sight caused by age, a display that occasionally he would consult, squinting at it as if into the sun.

Days passed. Tsuneko met the Avebury community, made a few friends, and, with little else to do, threw herself into the challenge of working the land. Evenings she slept, exhausted: not used to manual labour. She worried at her blisters and began biting her nails. Then, ten days later, Mr Bloodhound called her into his study.

"I have news for you," he said.

Tsuneko felt her heart begin to pound.

"This Hound is a clever, *clever* man. I believe I know who he really is, you know."

"Have you found Leonora?"

"Yes... and no."

"How do you mean?"

He sat down, and Tsuneko wondered if he might be embarrassed, for he had yet to look her in the eye. Then he said, "You must've realised that Mr Bloodhound is not my real name."

Tsuneko nodded.

"I support a number of almost identical fake data incarnations, twenty eight at the last count. It is one way of confusing nosy people, albeit a rather complex way. But Hound has managed to perfect a method of fading data incarnations in and out of the nexus over time. You see, researchers like me rely on sudden data transitions – gaps, alterations and so forth, for which there is no rational explanation. So Hound has bypassed me."

"Then, you know where Leonora is or not?"

"I know where she *should* be. You see, there is only one man who I know for sure has done such a thing. Goodman Awuku."

"The firewall buster? He died."

Mr Bloodhound clicked his tongue against his teeth. "Nobody uses firewalls these days, they're rather an outdated mechanism. Everything is smoke and mirrors. And nobody in my line of work believes Goodman Awuku died on that boat. But, you see, I can't locate Leonora, Yuri or Dirk. I believe I have located Hound, however."

"How come? He should be the hardest to spot."

"Correct. But there is a fifth member, and indeed a sixth in Leonora's team. Did you know?"

Tsuneko shook her head.

"The fifth is a Tunisian spoon bender. But the sixth... the sixth is a mystery."

"How so?"

"I do not believe the sixth is human. And it, my dear, is watching Hound *very* carefully, and thus is leaving the shallowest of wakes in the nexus. If you follow that wake to its source I think you'll find Leonora and her team."

Tsuneko took a deep breath, sat back. "Where are they?"

"Algeria."

Tsuneko sat back. "Go to Africa? I'd have to go solo, else Aritomo would spot me. But in theory it could be done."

Mr Bloodhound smiled. "I have various old travel guides – paper, believe it or not. Likely you'll need them."

CHAPTER 9

Joanna saw horror in Manfred's face. "You crate the bis," he shouted at her. "I'll collect the computers and things. And get my pistol. Defend the bis!" He stamped on the glitched fly with a groan of frustration.

They leaped into action. In less than five minutes they stood ready at the apartment front door. Manfred listened, his ear on the wood. Nothing. He opened the door, hustled Joanna and the crates out. No sign of anybody on the stairs.

He turned, jetted lighter fluid over the carpet, lit a match and threw it in. With a whumph it caught, and he leaped back, surprised by the intensity of the heat.

"Can you manage six crates?" he asked.

She nodded. The bis were making weird mewing noises. She wanted to stop, listen, analyse, but there was no time. Manfred pulled on his main rucksack, picked up Pouncey's then grabbed the nylon handles of the remaining three crates so that he could lift them as a bundle.

"If Pouncey's not about we'll hide in the garages opposite the office block," he said. "Best not to be in here. Aritomo's hands will search the place from top to bottom, if that fly was his."

They clattered down the stairs, knowing it would be impossible to stay silent, hoping nobody walked in before they got out. In the debris-strewn ground floor hall they paused, listened; heard distant bikes splashing through puddles, a car alarm, reverberated music a few streets away. No sign of people close by though. Manfred peered around the shattered doorway, looked left – two old men walking away – and right – nobody. He gave the all-clear and they ran across the street.

The garages were a tumbledown collection of steel and concrete, mostly destroyed, a few filled with mattresses and the ash-choked remains of campfires; beer cans and greasy paper fragments. Somebody's home.

They waited. Joanna took a torn tarp from the rear of the garage in which they hid and covered the crates. The mewing subsided. Manfred peered out through a tear in the steel drop-down door.

They waited. It began to rain. No sign of Pouncey, nor of the enemy.

Ten minutes later they heard a vehicle drive up the street, saw a small soltruck with blacked-out windows stop outside the tower block. Seconds later Pouncey jumped out. Manfred nodded to Joanna then ran across the street.

"Pouncey!" he hissed.

She span, her hi-vel in her right hand, fear masking her face. "What the–"

"Get us out! Glitched fly – someone could be on the way right now."

Joanna began loading the crates into the back of the soltruck. It looked in poor condition. Manfred ran back, grabbed the three remaining crates, handed them to Joanna in the middle of the street, then ran back for the rest of the gear. A minute later they locked the rear doors and leaped into the forward comp, Pouncey driving, Joanna in the middle, Manfred on the right.

"You stole this?" he asked.

Pouncey turned to stare at him, silent, her face set surly.

"You look–"

"I *bought* it," she snapped. "Okay?"

Manfred sat upright. "What? With–"

"Your money. We were done for. Aritomo might know we're here – a street gang got me into a fight. I tried to tell you, aye, I *did*. My face on PD computers and I had to blank a wristband. I would have been driving you out of Philly fly or no fly. Time here is *over*, okay?"

She started the engine, checked the batt power, and revved.

"If you shout at me Manfred," she continued, "you'll regret it. While we're in this heap of junk you'll do as you're told."

The soltruck lurched forward. Pouncey glanced in the rear mirror.

Joanna heard a gunshot.

Pouncey threw the vehicle into second and screeched up the street.

"If they've got a copter we're fucked," she said.

Manfred held on to the doorside armrest as Pouncey flung the soltruck around a corner. "If they've got a solcar we're–"

"Manfred, I *think* I can take on a *solcar*. But aerial, they'll win. Start prayin'."

Joanna clung on to Manfred, leaning right, giving Pouncey more space.

"Hold tight, you two," Pouncey warned.

Ahead stood piles of concrete debris heaped into a roadblock: local crims hoping to trap the unwary. Pouncey slammed on the brakes and forced the soltruck past in first gear, left side screeching against a brick wall; then accelerated forwards. Gunshots rang out, but Joanna couldn't tell where from. Could be crim or pursuit. A bullet grazed the windscreen but the angle was so oblique it only left a white scar. She hoped they didn't have target sights good enough to see the vehicle's tyres.

"There's an old paper map by your feet," Pouncey told her. "I need to know the way to the Vine Street Expressway." She glanced out of the window to her left. "This is Callowhill Street. Direct me to the nearest junction."

Joanna tried to read the map, but it was way too dark. Manfred flicked on the white LED on his keyring.

She said, "Right turn, straight down to Vine Street, then left until you hit the junction." She threw the map to the floor and gripped Manfred's arm.

"Aye," Pouncey said, "looks like those men outside the block were foot patrols. Advance guard. But we need speed, soon as poss. Or they'll have us."

Pouncey drove at eighty kilometres per hour down the pothole spattered street, the expressway to their right. She looked in the rearview.

"Trouble," she said. "Solcar, big. Closing on us."

She wrenched the steering wheel to get onto the junction roads, but braked at the top, glancing down to see the top of the pursuing solcar.

"I'm takin' a risk," she said, accelerating onto the westbound exit road. On the expressway ahead ragged groups of solcars whizzed by. The exit road, though – just a couple of solcars there, so she drove against them. Choosing a mini-gap in the westbound flow she flung the soltruck across the carriageway, then smashed through the central barrier and drove up the sliproad on the other side. Two cars screeched out of her way. The pursuit headed east. She braked, judged the flow, then screeched across the junction to reach the westbound entrance road. And away, at top speed.

"Never do that," she remarked. "It damages the vehicle."

Joanna glanced into the right hand rearview. "Will they realise?"

"Aye, maybe five minutes, ten. We'll be off the expressway before then."

"Where to?"

"South on the seventy-six, then south again on the ninety-five."

"Out of Philadelphia?"

"Way out," Pouncey confirmed. "Into the Outlaw. I'm aimin' for the west coast – Baltimore, Cincinnati, St Louis, Kansas City, Denver, Salt Lake City, Boise, Portland Oregon. Then maybe we'll rest."

Joanna sat back. "Are you sure?"

Pouncey glanced at her. "I told you. You listen to me now. I know what I'm doin'."

"She knows what she's doing," Manfred sighed.

Pouncey nodded, glancing at them. Tears ran down Manfred's cheeks, and Jo's too.

Midnight, and they sided the soltruck into a verge cutaway, screened from the road by a stand of birch trees; not that any solcars were in the vicinity. Beneath the pullout rainshield they set up a meagre picnic: mouldy bread, tomatoes and rainwater. The bis were crated up in the back, and had been since leaving Philly.

"Four thousand kilometres or thereabouts," Pouncey said. "Reckon we can do it in ten days. If we're lucky. Most of what lies between the east coast and the west is Outlaw."

"Do you think we've lost the pursuit?" Manfred asked.

Pouncey nodded. "They can't have any idea what we're doin' now. We wriggled outa their golden opportunity. Wonder if it was Aritomo? 'Course, no more nexus for us now."

Manfred nodded. "What about food?"

Pouncey shrugged. "I kept your cash, but it's useless out here. Food's gonna be our problem. Water, we can catch rain. But it don't rain food."

Manfred sighed, gazing out into the drizzle.

"The Outlaw is pretty much nexus-free," Pouncey said. "So, hide everythin' tech. Joanna, take your jewellery off. Aye – and that fancy scarf. People see that, they'll *have* you."

Manfred said, "The population reduced from three fifty million to fifty million in five years after the Depression hit. Most of that fifty million lives on the eastern or western seaboard. Surely the Outlaw's almost empty?"

Pouncey chuckled. "It's not the population density you need to worry about. It's their attitude."

"What about the soltruck?"

"One spare tyre. Okay, another weak point there. But the engine's good, and the photovoltaics."

Joanna said, "What are we going to do about *food?*"

Pouncey glanced at her. "Hope for roadkill in the heart of darkness."

Later, alone outside, Joanna and Manfred discussed the bis.

"They are going to need to see the sun soon," Joanna said.

He nodded. "Charge up. Maybe we should test Indigo in the morning, put it on a leash… see what it does."

Joanna agreed. "We cannot keep them in the back of the soltruck for the whole ten days, they will lose power. Also, I want to watch Indigo. It *sensed* that glitched fly."

Manfred picked up a length of muddy bale rope from the edge of the cutaway and began fashioning a harness. "Okay," he said. "But we gotta be ultra careful. If one of the bis goes awol here, that's the end of it. We can't send out a search party."

He paused. Howling echoed across the freeway.

"Wolves?" Joanna asked.

He stood up, looked, listened. "More likely feral dogs," he said. "We better get inside."

Pouncey lay asleep across the three seats in the front comp.

"Looks like we're in the back with the bis."

~

By the time they entered Missouri, Pouncey was starving. St Louis had been a no-go city, its entire southern circumference stockaded, set piecemeal with biohazard, electricity and nuke signs. She got the point.

The roads further on were passable. Half way across the state on the freeway between St Louis and Kansas City she halted the soltruck. Sunset had been and gone, and the batts were low.

"We need food," she said. "There's a place called Boonville just ahead."

"Yeah?" Manfred said.

"I'm gonna strike out, see if I can find food in the suburbs."

"I'm coming with you then."

She looked at him, weighing up options. "I oughta go on my own."

"In the Outlaw? You gotta be joking."

She hesitated. He had a point. "But that'd leave Jo alone with the bis."

"She can lock the soltruck. We can give her the other pistol."

Pouncey sighed. "Let's do a deal," she said. "Aye, come with me – as far as it's green. When we get to inhabited areas I go in alone. You cover me."

Now Manfred hesitated. His stomach gurgled. "Okay," he said, reluctantly.

"Why do you need to go in alone, Pouncey?" Joanna asked.

"Make it simple. Don't have to look after anybody. Just little ol' me."

She opened the comp door and jumped out, shrugging her backpack on, arming her hi-vel, then walking around to Manfred's side.

"Joanna," she said, "turn everythin' off. Just sit tight." To Manfred she added, "Use your gun as a last resort. Gunshots'll attract every crazy lowlife around. Animals, too."

"Hmm, okay," Manfred muttered. He shut the door. There was a click as Joanna locked it. Then the sidelights switched off and they were plunged into darkness.

True darkness had been rare when Pouncey was a kid, but now it was the norm. No power for mass-scale sodium lamps. She walked up to the top of the escarpment off which they had parked and gazed out over Boonville, but saw only blackness on and on, with just a hint, maybe, of yellow lamps a few kilometres away. There was a crescent moon setting, and the stars.

She turned to Manfred and said, "No lights. Obviously. So watch where I'm goin' and follow me." She put on her spare spex.

He frowned.

She shook her head. "Standalones, Manfred, modified like night vision goggles. Not very good, but better than eyes alone. Follow me."

A cow path led down from the escarpment, not steep except for one slippy section, and little used judging by old prints in the half dry mud. She saw mostly hoof prints, but also boot marks, and once the prints of small shoes. Over a few fields, across the remains of a golf course, then she stopped. Buildings ahead: straight roads.

She pointed at a collection of overgrown bushes. "Hide in there and watch," she said. "Won't be long. If you do hear me fire, run back to the van. If I don't turn up I'm dead. But don't worry. Ain't gonna die just yet."

"You better not," he grunted.

She crept along the street: reconnoitre, check, listen and smell. Nothing. Didn't look like people lived here. She cursed under her breath. Larger conurbations had community shops, plenty of them. She had to find the nearest stores.

A few hundred metres down she came upon a main street lined with buildings barred up and bolted. Signs stood above doors, the third of which read, *General Stores*. She slunk around the back and examined the security, to find, as she had expected, that it was heavy – no joke living in the Outlaw. With a jemmy from her toolkit she loosened the back window furniture until all that was left was the window frame; then a quick tap and it fell free. She caught it before it smashed, put it down, clambered into the shop.

Some kind of stock room. She surveyed the tins and packets. Nothing new, all pre-Depression, but plenty of indications that folks around here were growing their own; out of desperation, doubtless, but growing their own. Packets of seeds, for instance. She grabbed tins of meat, dry biscuits, chocolate sweets for energy. Nothing else was worth bothering with, and her haul would last a few more days, so she put the goods in her rucksack then departed.

Back in the street nothing moved. She paused, listened, smelled the air. Ghost town. Happy with her raid, she took out her real spex and put them on.

Nexus-augmented reality looked identical to reality.

She swung around, surveying the suburb. In Philly this would be a scene of frantic semantic activity, as the nexus flung info at her: GPS data, ID's, commercial gen, prices, dates, and much, much more. But here the spec lenses were empty. The nexus found nothing to tell her about. Boonville was an e-vacuum.

She turned back, saw something glow in left-leaning distance. A single sigil. A z.

She froze. That was weird. She'd never seen a z before. It signified the lowest level of significance attributable by the nexus, something so trivial it would normally never appear above the frothing tide of more important info; but here the semantic silence made it stand out. And it seemed to be roughly where the soltruck was parked.

She ran back to the bushes, saw Manfred appear.

"You got anything?" he asked.

She nodded, putting her spex in her top pocket. "Hurry," she said, running on.

At the bottom of the cow path Manfred took her by the shoulder and pointed into a weed-wrecked field. "Vines," he said. "They might have grapes. Vitamins and all that."

"Aye, hurry up then. I wanna get back."

"Why?"

She shrugged. "You don't wanna hear about itchy fingers again. Get your grapes, if there's any."

There were some, though not many. Pouncey led the way up the path then stopped atop the escarpment, putting on her spex. The z floated at the side of the soltruck. Joanna looked at her, an expression of puzzlement on her face.

"What you doing?" Manfred asked.

"The nexus can sense somethin' inside the soltruck. It doesn't know what it is though – z sig. Weird..."

Joanna opened the door and stepped down, smiling. Manfred took his own spex from the glove compartment and put them on, then walked to the back of the soltruck and unlocked the doors. From inside came rustling and what sounded like whining.

"It's Indigo," he said.

Pouncey took off her rucksack and handed it to Joanna. "Fetch its crate inside the comp," she told Manfred.

All three of them sat inside, Indigo's crate between Manfred and Joanna.

"Listen," Pouncey said, "I don't see why we shouldn't let Indigo out in here. It ain't gonna run off even if it escapes."

Joanna nodded. "You are right. All the bis need as much stimulation as possible. We could have a rotation of crates up the front comp as you drive."

"Sure, agreed," Manfred said. "But Indigo... why?"

Pouncey watched as Joanna studied the bi. Half a metre tall, deep blue and rubbery, it looked like an exotic toy Nippandroid. Joanna said, "Suppose its other senses are compensating for its blindness? All the bis are sensitive to electromagnetic radiation. Indigo's heuristic sensory networks will be working overtime as it tries to build up a picture of its environment."

"Yeah, by any means possible," Manfred said. "And even places this remote will be full of electromagnetics. Radio waves from the sun... random wi-fi. You name it."

"I have an idea," Joanna said. "Let's use Indigo as our channel into the bi group. Let's keep it with us as much as possible, so that it *has* to model *us*. You never know, Indigo could end up being our interpreter... if the bis are communicating."

"Which you think they are?" Pouncey said.

Joanna nodded, putting Indigo on her lap. "It'll be like having..."

"A child?" Pouncey said.

"No... a *cat*. You can never tell what cats are thinking. With a child, you can at least make an educated guess."

Manfred said, "You realise then that Indigo must be aware of the nexus?"

Pouncey nodded. "Two way traffic. Makes sense."

"A lot of the nexus is wireless," Manfred mused. "A symbiotic relationship might be growing." Excitement lit up his face. "This is a huge advance – a nexus cognisant species."

They all looked at Indigo. Moisture-preserving lids covered its sightless eyes, but its ears twitched and the fronds beneath Joanna's hands rippled.

Denver and Salt Lake City they avoided, but Boise in Idaho was a city like Philadelphia: crowded, busy, a place of law and ninety percent order. Pouncey was able to use her last remaining cash to buy good food, water, toothpaste and soap. They drove on into the Steens Mountains.

Half way up, Pouncey saw a flash to her left. She braked, turned her head to look. "Think that was a dyin' electricity sub station," she remarked.

Joanna laughed. "Did you see that? Indigo turned to face it."

Pouncey halted the soltruck. "You sure about that?"

"Certain. There must have been an electromagnetic flash too."

Pouncey drove on. "Good news, I guess," she said.

Joanna petted Indigo as if the bi was an animal. Which, Pouncey thought, it was… in a way.

After Baker and La Grande they were well into the Blue Mountains, only four hundred kilometres east of Portland. The road worsened, forcing Pouncey to dodge pot-holes and debris, including many ruined telegraph poles. Her pace slowed. They kept two crates in the front comp at all times, allowing the bis plenty of opportunity to watch and listen. Manfred tried to locate local stations on the radio, but all he found was static.

Night fell as they approached Arlington, but Pouncey didn't like the look of it. "Too many watch posts for my likin'," she said, pointing. "See that dome? There's a barrel pokin' out of it." She took a pair of binoculars and scanned the Arlington roofscape. "Let's get outa here before someone shoots."

Twenty kilometres on they halted, parking on the side of the road. Pouncey wandered across the ruined tarmac but saw no tread marks.

"This'll do," she said.

They slept without break until dawn, Manfred and Joanna shivering in the back, though they lay together wrapped in blankets: clear night and frost. After breakfast they sat outside the soltruck, waiting for the sun to clear the mountain peaks. Pouncey took tissues and vanished behind some bushes.

Manfred and Joanna locked seven of the bi crates in the back, then put the other two in the comp, alongside Indigo. Manfred strolled to the crest of the road, from where he saw what looked like a carcass just a few metres away. Meat. He walked on, waving Joanna to follow.

It was a calf, freshly killed. "Reckon we could butcher and cook this?" he said.

There was a click. A dark figure appeared from behind a tree.

"Reckon you fell right into my trap, mister."

An old man, armed with a rifle, pointing at him.

"Hey, we're just passing through," Manfred said. "We didn't know this was yours."

"Ain't nobody passes through here these days," the old man replied. "What you doing here? That your truck over there?"

Manfred glanced over his shoulder. "Er..."

The old man walked on. "Reckon you better show me," he said.

He hurried them along. No sign of Pouncey.

"What you got in there?" the old man asked, indicating the front of the truck with his rifle.

"Just toys."

"And the back? Unlock it."

The old man pointed his rifle at Manfred as he unlocked the back doors. "Just more toys, you see? We don't mean you any harm."

"That's what they all say. Move back. *Now!*"

Manfred moved away. The old man peered into the crates, then undid the catches on the front three and popped open the lids.

Before Manfred had time to react the bis jumped free and leaped out of the van. He yelled and tried to catch the nearest.

The old man fired at one. Missed. Manfred screamed, "No!" and ran at the old man, but at once the rifle turned on him. He skidded to a halt.

"Eh, eh?" said the old man.

"Don't shoot them!" Manfred implored. "They're valuable."

"To me? Maybe. What are they, boy?"

"Just toys. Expensive toys, yeah? For rich people in Portland." Manfred raised his hands to his head and turned, shouting, "Jo! We've got to *catch* them!"

"You two!" the old man shouted. "You don't do anything without my say so. Stand still."

Manfred turned. "You shoot any of them and…"

"I'll do what the hell I like, mister. This is *my* land."

With that the old man walked around the soltruck and peered into the scrubby land beside the road. Manfred listened. Surely Pouncey would be alert to the danger by now? Five minutes had passed since she had gone. She must have heard their voices.

"Okay!" he called out, in a voice loud, but not so loud the old man would be suspicious. "We'll stand still. But we need to get our toys back."

There was a rustle from the bushes. The old man span, rifle raised. Manfred knew that could not be Pouncey. It must be a bi. He looked, one hand raised to his forehead to shield his eyes from the rising sun, but saw only thick bushes and trees.

The old man crept along the road. More rustling. Manfred watched. It was creepily like a hunting scene in a film.

The old man glanced over his shoulder to check on Manfred and Joanna, then turned back and raised his rifle, aiming low into the bushes. Yet more rustling. He crept on into the shadow of a tree, then stopped. Froze: his rifle raised. Waited. Not breathing.

A shot.

Manfred screamed and leaped forward.

The old man fell, blood fountaining out of his head.

Pouncey jumped down from the tree.

Then the bis appeared: Red, Violet and White. "Jo!" Manfred yelled.

He approached the bis. They stared at him, mesmerised it seemed. He knelt and they approached. Five seconds later Joanna clutched two and he had the other one.

Pouncey swore. "You see what they *did?*" she said.

Manfred ignored her, running back to the soltruck to put the bis into their crates, then taking the third one from Joanna and crating it. He sobbed, knelt down to lean against the back of the soltruck.

Pouncey ran up and tapped him on the shoulder. He span around, stood up.

"You see what they did?" she repeated.

"No?"

"They teamed up! They lured him on. They knew I was in the fuckin' tree!"

"What?"

"Manfred, let her tell us," Joanna said, taking his hand in hers and stroking it.

Pouncey stood a handsbreadth away from him, only shock in her face: no anger. "I *watched* them, Manfred. They teamed up. They knew where the old guy was. They knew where I was. They drew him on to me." She shook her head, turning to look at the old man's body. "They didn't know what I'd do, but they must've known I'd do *somethin'.*"

Manfred could only repeat, "What?"

She turned back to face him. "I saw it with my own eyes, I promise. I climbed the tree 'cos I couldn't see you guys, though I heard you. And I saw what the bis did. I think maybe Jo's right. They are communicatin'."

Manfred put his hands to his face. "Jeez…"

"Yeah," Pouncey said. "But it's good, right?"

Manfred turned to stare at the crates. "Yeah... yeah, it is. I just wasn't ready for it."

"They are growing up," Joanna said in a quiet voice.

He nodded. "I was right, Jo, this whole trip *proves* it." He gestured into the soltruck and continued, "They're being forced to use themselves as exemplars to understand the behaviour of the others. They're using themselves as archetypes. They assume that what they do, other bis do too. It's the beginnings of consciousness – and it means they can work as a team... as a *society*."

"Then they must be communicating with one another," she replied. "It *must* be a gestural language. Eye movements, skin movements, things too subtle for us to notice... even for a chimp watcher like me. Perhaps they will never speak English. Perhaps they will never need to. It means Indigo is crucial to us."

"Maybe they don't realise *we're* like them?" Pouncey said. "'Cos them and us are so different. They're focussin' on themselves."

He nodded. "What have I made here?" he said.

CHAPTER 10

In the plantation hut, Hound explained the next stage of his plan.

"I've got a new fake data incarnation keyed to my new look," he said. "There was a small possibility that when I saw Tsuneko June in the village, she saw me. Or people following her – or watching her – saw me. I'll be wearing spex all the time beneath my fly-shades – man, too risky not to. But you won't need to. So don't, except in emergencies. Your fake data incarnations won't have been seen by Aritomo. We'll be crossing the desert naked so no nexus info-trail builds up. In Algeria, maybe Morocco, we'll make a new hide. Then get back to learning Zeug."

"Teaching Zeug," Leonora corrected.

"Whatever. Sandman Entré will lead us up to the Tunisian border. Then we'll be on our own. You better get your camel legs sorted by then."

They did not look happy.

Sandman Entré grinned. "You are nervous? Don't be nervous. The camel only spits at the coward, oui?"

Hound laughed. Nobody else did.

But the camels lay some distance away. Sandman Entré led them through Hound's plastic-producing plants for a kilometre or so, before they entered open land, rocky, hot and sand-blasted. To the north great fields of mirrors gleamed in the sun.

"That is the muscle of the new Afrique," Sandman Entré explained with a smug grin.

Only Leonora and Hound took an interest, the other three following at some distance. "What are they?" Leonora asked.

"Solar energy farm, Madame. Since twenty-forty Afrique has exported much energy, to our great economic benefit."

"How much exactly?"

"It is difficult to say, Madame. Much energy reaching Earth becomes unusable, in form of heat. Some energy goes to make wind and wave. Human uses one ten thousandth of all energy reaching the Earth. But exploiting wind and wave affects the currents atmosphérique in a negative way."

"You mean the energy we'd extract from them is actually comparable to the total usable energy?"

"Oui, Madame. Once the ingénieur Afrique grasp this, they convince Pan Afrique to concentrate on solar panels. By then, we did not need indium or tellurium – rare substances. We make the kesterite cells, which use common elements, plus selenium. But now, the ingénieur Afrique need to make cells that reflect light. Otherwise too much heat is being added to our desert."

"Man, what about plants?" Hound asked.

"That is the second way of using free energy. Greening the desert, they call it. Bon! The green wall Afrique was a start, oui? Photosynthesis, it is a way of receiving free energy without adding heat to the desert. So, many tribes, they make the greenery."

"They say the Sahara was green thousands of years ago," Leonora mused.

"Exactement. It can become green once again."

As afternoon progressed into evening they reached the camel station, which was run by Sandman Entré's half brother Rockfish. Rockfish was dumb as a result of having his tongue cut out by Tunis mash kids, so he communicated by writing with a sharpened forefinger nail on a piece of e-paper, in English so that his guests could read him.

You need camels for to buy, Sandman?

"Oui. Six chameau."

I bill you on the nex mainline. You pay by tomorrow noon.

Sandman Entré nodded. "Les chameau *sain,* mon frère,"

Rockfish grinned. Outside, he and Sandman Entré haggled over which of the two dozen available camels would be used, coming to an agreement half an hour later.

"Saddles, saddlebags and tack are included," Sandman Entré explained. "All plastique, of course. You will need only your natural courage."

Rockfish showed them through signs and gestures how to mount, but soon realised, as Sandman Entré had done earlier in the day, that Zeug was different. Hound pattered out the line about testing prototypes, at which Rockfish shrugged. Zeug balanced easily and seemed more concerned about Hound's muttered oaths than his own safety. Then they were off, heading into the sunset, the air already cool and promising a cold night.

Two days west of Tunis, after noon, they came across a plastics mine. Sandman Entré had been following tracks laid down by innumerable solcars, but he was unaware of the existence of the mine. Before he could decide what to do a number of young men wrapped in grey and blue robes approached.

Sandman Entré conversed with the miners in French. "It is the site of a former landfill," he explained. "To satisfy the green laws of the Union Européenne, Western countries exported their rubbish. The land Afrique received it."

"What are these guys doing?" Hound asked.

"Mining the plastique thermo, oui? The plastique that can be heated to reform them, unlike the thermo setting. It is all the business, voilà tout. There is much money here to be reclaimed."

At this, the miners made frantic gestures and brought out trays of mint tea.

"We could rest here," Sandman Entré said. "There is much shade beneath the acacia. Bon, we avoid the midday heat."

To this everyone agreed. The miners studied the camels with interest, then spoke with Sandman Entré. Hound set up an auto-translate through the nexus, allowing it to spin illuminated sentences across his spex screens.

You are travelling far, white-suit? That was a miner.

Then Sandman Entré. *To Morocco. Our destination does not concern you.*

Who are these foreigners?

They are my kin, for whom I am responsible.

They paid you in gold? These camels have strong spirits.

They paid me.

We want to know why you have come this way.

You need not know that. Please make more mint tea.

This is our land. We should charge passage fee to appease spirits.

Nobody owns Tunisia. I take my tea weak.

Three hours later they departed, flasks of tea tied to their saddles; a parting gift from the miners. "Tell them we wish them luck with their operations," Hound told Sandman Entré.

"They are animists," Sandman Entré replied. "They have no concept of the luck."

That night they camped in a rock shelter, a fire of brushwood burning, over which they heated miso and brown rice. Zeug seemed ill at ease, but Yuri questioned him and uncovered nothing of significance. Leonora shrugged. "The Seoul Illusion," she remarked.

"You should not ascribe too much behaviour to that phenomenon," Yuri replied, "in case you underestimate Zeug's intellectual capabilities."

"Oh yeah?" Hound muttered, pulling his straw hat over his eyes and leaning back into his rucksack to sleep.

Night fell. It grew cold. Most of the company felt unnaturally tired. The camels groaned and belched, and the fire went out.

Leonora sat on watch when the attack came. Without warning three men jumped down from the top of the rock shelter, two of them aiming pistols at her while the third turned this way and that, assessing who might wake and move.

"Allez, avance!" one of the men shouted.

Hound woke, and immediately a pistol pointed at his face.

"Se pousser," he was told.

He feigned ignorance. "I don't speak French, man."

Then Sandman Entré woke.

What are you doing?

Did you like your sleepy tea? We want all your plastic. Tell these dogs to squeeze up. Get them moving.

You cannot treat me like this. I am one of you.

Your spirit stinks of muck. Move along there.

Sandman Entré said, "They want the saddles and tack. Huddle together. Probably they will leave us."

Hound watched. His snub-nose lay beneath his jacket. The miners hadn't bothered to check for weapons. Novices, or inexperienced. Enough nous to taint the mint tea though. Care would be required here.

Then Zeug stood up. The two miners near Leonora hurried over, pointing their pistols at him. Yuri began hyperventilating. Hound prepared to roll, dodge and reach for his gun, though he did not fancy his chances.

A stream of clicks emerged from Zeug's mouth as he moved away. The miners closed on him, staring disconcerted, pistols waving at him.

"Une personne insignifiante?"

"Oui! Être personne japonais."

The stream of clicks intensified. The miners gaped. Then in a move too quick to assess Zeug lashed out, downing the miners, their pistols clattering to the rock.

Hound rolled, reached for his snub-nose and fired. The third miner fell.

He jumped to his feet. He heard scraping from the rock above. He ducked, shouted, "Get beneath! More up there!"

"The newcomers are speeding away," Zeug said.

Hound peered up. Nothing. Then a whining noise. Sneaking around the side of the shelter he shimmied up to its top, to see two other miners escaping on a jury-rigged sandscoot. No point firing on them.

"They tainted the tea in the flasks," he said. "Man, I thought I felt sleepy."

Sandman Entré nodded. "They wanted the plastique, contraire à la morale, to sell at market."

"They won't be coming back," Hound declared.

Leonora and Yuri ran over to where Zeug stood. "Zeug, what was that noise you made when the miners approached you?" Leonora asked.

Zeug offered no reply.

Yuri asked the same question, but Zeug looked at him, face expressionless.

"Perhaps he doesn't know," Hound said. "Can't answer."

"It was like bats," said Leonora, "echo-locating – the intensity increases as they near their prey, maximising the resolution."

"Sonic sense-scape of bats," Zeug said.

Then Dirk approached. "You know what dis mean?" he said.

Leonora turned to face him. "What?"

"His sight not so good as we thought. It dark tonight, only bit of moon and ember glowing. He use tongue click like bat. Da eye not so good."

Leonora turned to face Zeug. "I designed him for *potential*," she mused. "No set limits, just maximum potential of all senses, all subsystems." She turned back to Dirk and said, "And your interfaces are heuristic."

"Don't forget da additional senses," Dirk said. "Electromagnetic. Balance. Vibration sensitivity in da feet."

Leonora nodded. "All those interfaces will learn, won't they, as Zeug experiences more of life?"

Dirk nodded. "All adaptive nonlinear networks. Massive system of elements, each adapting to one another in local, context-dependent interactions. Revises its structure to better survive in its environment. Builds a model. Dis how I do all my interfaces, Leonora."

She nodded.

"Zeug constantly input knowledge of da world, and he change according to dat knowledge. If he lose his dynamism he not represent da real world. Zeug mental model must become more accurate, profound representation of reality."

In a hushed voice Yuri said, "The most fundamental drive of human beings is to *understand*, and since they are continually striving to live in the real world, they must continually strive to understand. The mental model they carry must become an ever more accurate and profound representation of reality."

Dirk nodded, lighting a cheroot. "You say dis before," he told Leonora. "You say Zeug must have an unconscious. His mental model must *circumvent* da multitude of individual memory of his previous experience. Otherwise da model, it bogged down in detail." He smiled. "I very pleased with tonight. Echo location proof dat Zeug is learning, making real good mental model."

"Thinking originally," Hound remarked.

Yuri agreed. "It is not necessary for every item of experience to be in the forefront of conscious attention," he said. "My unconscious is the nine-tenths of the iceberg, the sum of my experience so far, fashioned into a model, forming the foundation of active life, providing insight from previous events, guiding thought, providing a reservoir of knowledge. Mr Ngma, you speak very well on this subject, helping me to understand more. Yes... if we remembered every detail of our lives the model of reality built up would be unworkable. If the nuances of every relationship were not generalised, if memory was too good, then it would be impossible to act on the basis of the model's knowledge, since that knowledge could not be extracted. This is why minds have a vast unconscious part and a small conscious summit, and this is how Zeug's mind is."

"Is?" Leonora queried.

Yuri nodded but made no other reply. Zeug stared at them all, as if unable to grasp the significance of the moment. Then he said, "The newcomers are six kilometres away now."

"Good," said Hound. "We don't wanna see them ever again."

Dirk waved his cheroot in the air and said, "How you know dat, Zeug?"

Zeug did not answer.

"There seems to be a lot he doesn't know," Leonora said.

"You friends with dem miners?" Dirk asked Zeug.

"No," Zeug replied.

Dirk shook his head. "Dis not quite as I expected. He need to be member of society."

"We are creating an artificial intelligence here Mr Ngma," Yuri said, "not a socialite—"

"You *still* don't understand," Dirk interrupted, annoyance clear on his face. "Suppose Zeug say to you, I am conscious, I have thoughts in my mind. You might be tempted to say, he conscious. Not me. If he were human I would *know* he was truthful, 'cos him and me both human. But Zeug inhuman, so I don't know. Dis your main problem, don't you see?"

Yuri spluttered, unable, or unwilling to make a reply.

Leonora faced Dirk and said, "Are you having second thoughts about—"

"No, *no*. I answer dat before. I pointing out to you all – dis is da issue. If Zeug was human dere would be no question. It Zeug's artifice dat make us ponder. You know… it *real* unhelpful dat dere is only one of him."

Leonora and Yuri walked away. They did not look happy. Dirk shrugged, then grinned at Hound.

The following night Hound found himself on last watch. In nocturnal calm and cold he had poked the fire embers with a stick, walked around the campsite – a group of dead trees roofed with shredded polythene – then gazed up at the stars. The high heavens was the place he'd imagined as a child to be the location of the nexus. He sat down and put his spex on.

Nothing except geographical info and environmental stats. No danger signals from his web of nex-sensors – so no sign of pursuit. Nobody within thirty kilometres, in fact. Then he turned and checked his companions, and as he did he saw something strange.

It shimmered behind a close-set clump of trees, something green, unreal, new; something that did not exist in the physical location it occupied in his spex. He approached. The form resolved itself into an oasis made of palm trees and low lying bushes. He pulled down his spex, to see in the real world sand, stone, a few pieces of dead wood.

The oasis then was a virtual construct. So what did it represent?

Hound's new data incarnation gave him freedom to use the nexus as he saw fit. He analysed the oasis' tracking data to find that it had been created only an hour ago. Moreover, it was an entirely local phenomenon, with not a single subsidiary thread, an exceptionally rare circumstance. Yet the nexus knew it should be present, and was therefore displaying it for him.

At once Hound span around to check his companions: all asleep, with Zeug in open-eyed trance; not asleep, but not awake either. He realised the oasis illusion must have been manufactured by one of the group. At once his suspicions fell upon Zeug.

Neither Leonora nor Yuri knew what Zeug's trance signified, hypothesizing that it mimicked sleep to fit in with the AIteam. Hound backed away, deciding to investigate the oasis first.

It was like walking through a garden of shimmering, mobile palm trees, a breathtaking experience at high rez. As he looked this way and that the topography of the oasis changed as if it had no set form, though the quality of the trees and vegetation never varied. Dreamlike in many aspects. The associated data was minimal, suggesting the oasis was being created unconsciously, as if its only function was to provide an outlet for creativity. When Hound tried to walk out he found the randomly linked paths impossible to navigate; he was inside a shifting labyrinth. Panic began to set in, but then he spied sand, and he ran through a gap in the palm trees to find himself once again in the desert.

Zeug had not moved. His eyes did not track Hound. Shrugging, Hound returned to the campfire.

Leonora sat up. "Is everything all right?" she asked.

He nodded, then pointed. "Put spex on and look over there. Tell me what you see."

There was a pause, then, "Some kind of hanging oasis... a garden perhaps."

"Okay, spex off."

Leonora turned and said, "What is it? Are we safe?"

"Uh-huh. It's locally produced, but sensed by the nexus, and displayed. Some kind of freeform illusion. Man, I'm wondering if Zeug's producing it."

"Zeug?"

"You think maybe he's dreaming?"

Leonora crawled over to the fire and sat next to him. "Now wait a moment, are you beginning this whole argument again? Just because we dream does not mean that Zeug dreams–"

"I know, I know, it's only a suggestion. I walked inside it. It's dreamy. Yet the palm trees and bushes are lifelike, as if he's creating them from memories."

Leonora shook her head. "You may be correct, but we have little idea of whether Zeug has created an unconscious, with all that entails. I *designed* him to have an unconscious, but I did not design him to dream."

"Maybe Yuri did."

"Yuri did as he was told."

Hound gazed into the fire. "You sure of that?" he asked in a quiet voice.

"What do you mean? Do you su–"

"*No.* I don't suspect anything. Just asking questions nobody else has."

Leonora slapped the sand with her hands. "The AIteam is becoming fractious, and I do not like that."

Hound shrugged. "Man, we're only human," he said. "Can't I watch him?"

"Must you?"

"You ever notice his walk?"

She frowned. "His walk?"

Hound knew she had not. "He's got a *walk,* okay? Left leg a tad stiffer than the right. Turns his left foot inwards as the left leg moves forward. You never noticed? Seems like back trouble to me."

Leonora gave a sigh of frustration. "Zeug's muscles are electroactive structures, Hound, two layers of conducting carbon grease separated by a stretchy insulating polymer film. It can stretch by more than 300 per cent."

"Man, I'm not denying—"

"When a voltage is applied it is like a capacitor, positive and negative charges accumulating on either side of the insulator. As the opposite charges attract one another the insulating film is squashed between them, flattening and stretching. Turning the voltage off contracts it to its original size."

"Listen, you can lecture me all you like to prove you're more brainy—"

"*Please* restrict yourself from now on to matters of security," Leonora said, standing up and brushing the sand off her clothes. "Yuri, Dirk and I will do the speculating."

"As you say," Hound replied, without a trace of emotion in his voice.

There was a pause. Then she sighed. "I am sorry. I know your worth."

He shrugged.

She apologised again before walking away. He watched. She'd changed. But she was paying him well enough and she was a good woman. He'd shut his mouth. But then he wondered how long he wanted to do this dangerous, unpredictable job. An oasis of his own, out of the way… that sure sounded good.

Next day they hit a trail and began noticing signs with legends such as: *Algeria 50km* and *Border 40km,* then *Border 30km.*

"Tonight we shall eat a final firecamp meal, oui?" Sandman Entré said.

Hound nodded. The desert was becoming hilly, the Tell Atlas mountains ahead, the city of Annaba the only large conurbation in the vicinity.

"Difficult times lie ahead, ami," Sandman Entré told him. "The hautes terres, the mauvais sable. You will manage, you think?"

"You ride home to Tunis, man," Hound grunted. "We'll be fine."

Sandman Entré laughed. "They say, il vaut mieux agir tout de suite."

"Do they? Okay, let 'em."

And Sandman Entré laughed again. "We shall meet again, ami, I feel certain. I am your Tunis frère in white linen, am I not?"

Hound did not deign to reply.

Supper that night, while pleasant, seemed to foreshadow tricky times ahead. On the following day, with Algeria five kilometres away and low cloud covering the sky, Hound took a look at the environs with his spex. The oasis had reappeared the previous night; now gone. But he saw something else.

It was faint, a ghost. But it seemed to be himself.

He called a break, saying, "We all need food and water."

Leonora looked pleased – she found the heat difficult to cope with. Hound strolled off as if for a waz, then took another look at the nexus artefact. Too difficult to see... too vague. Maybe he was seeing a mirage.

He turned up the rez on his spex then put on his fly-shades to reduce realworld glare, though that was little enough today. Images pixelated, melted, then stabilised. *Something* out there... a spectral form, a man, and if a man, maybe himself. But why?

A figure tracking the group was significant in a way the oasis was not. Perhaps a computer had spotted them. But Hound had never heard of this form and type of follower. The very last thing the nexus would display if somebody was tracking them was a human figure. Just too obvious.

They rode on. A blue wall approached in Hound's spex signifying the border between Tunisia and Algeria.

"Here we are man," he said. "Gotta say our goodbyes."

Sandman Entré hugged Hound, then shook the hand of everyone else, except Zeug, who he hesitated before, then bowed to with a look of mild distaste. Zeug bowed back, face impassive.

Then Sandman Entré said, "The mountain tracks take you city to city, oui? Annaba, Constantine, Ouzou, Alger, Oran, Sidi-bel-Abbes. I advise you not to risk the uncharted ways – the cities Algérie are often safe. Do not risk the seashore either, it is full of the immigrant Européen, with their guns and their stinking camps. Then you have a choice of cities Maroc, or perhaps the Atlas Haute. Au revoir!"

He turned his camel around and trotted away.

Hound watched Sandman Entré depart. He felt sad, and not a little sick. And the ghost still faced him, a hint of mist, bleached white with no great detail. Ethereal mirage. But something in the stance, in the set of the head reminded him of himself.

He glanced back. The others were drinking bottled water, chatting.

He took his wristband and initiated a full link check – a risk because it would send a ripple through the nexus, and time consuming; as much as three or four minutes.

He waited.

"Come *on,* Hound!"

He turned and called out, "I'm checking maps. Won't be long, man."

Beep! He ran the wristband's report through his spex.

Object link status: active. Nexus file: BB2/F544*66/df/7hd32. Coherence: very high. Origin: unknown.

Data: object is a nexus artefact created over a period of time: 6 d, 13 h, 12 m, 57s. A reservoir of verbally and visually created impressions with no emotional content. The artefact displays no purpose but is responding to an (unknown) source, and is being updated realtime on a rapid basis. 75% likelihood that artefact is mirroring the (unknown) source.

He muttered to himself as he turned to rejoin the group. "Origin unknown? That's not good."

CHAPTER 11

A long time after Pendleton they reached the Columbia River, which rippled to their right as the road through the Blue Mountains bent due west. Then the soltruck broke down. Manfred watched (he knew jack about vehicles) as Pouncey, cursing to herself, dismantled the top half of the solar-powered engine, found a leak, repaired it, then reassembled the engine.

It didn't restart. Manfred glanced up and down the road. They had met nobody since the guy with the rifle. This high, this remote, there weren't even any local, self-sustaining communities; at least, none that wanted to be seen. Probably the BIteam was safe for a short while. He took Pouncey's binoculars out of the front comp, then surveyed all he could see.

Nothing, except trees, streams, rocks and grass. The weather was cool. Snow on mountain tops blinded him. The scenery was gorgeous, yet it hinted at madmen in bunkers. The boundary between the empty gulf in the middle of America and its inhabited coasts was a place of nervous, aggressive energy.

He glanced at Pouncey. She sat in the middle of the road with an engine unit on her lap. She glanced up at him. "Compression unit computer's lost a connection," she said.

"Jeez… you can repair it, mmm?"

Pouncey nodded. "Fetch me the tool box. I think there's a roll of thin copper wire in there. Get me a pair of cutters and a spool and I'll make a jump connection. Should work."

"It better work," Manfred muttered as he followed her instructions.

Joanna accompanied him back, Indigo in her arms. The trio sat on the road, bathed in sunshine. But Manfred shivered; he was getting the creeps.

"Don't like being broke down," he said. "What if we can't run—"

"*Do* be quiet, Manfred," Joanna interrupted. Indigo wriggled in her arms, like an annoyed cat trying to escape.

Manfred watched. Though blind, it was facing Pouncey, and seemed to want to join her. "Let it go," he said. "It won't run away."

"What?"

"Let it go, Jo. We crossed a Rubicon – it won't escape."

"What do you mean?"

Manfred shrugged. "We know it understands we're part of its group. Or that it's part of our group. Wouldn't have rescued us from the shooter otherwise, mmm? Go on! Let it go. It wants to go to Pouncey."

Joanna, with reluctance, bent down and allowed the bi to hop out of her arms. It turned at once to face Pouncey, then walked over. Manfred watched. The dark blue dye in its body was striated, he noticed, something he had not observed before. Its arms seemed shorter, and it appeared taller and thinner.

"It's modifying its body," he whispered to Joanna. "It still has some flexibility."

She nodded. "Identity still forming," she said. "Like a child."

Manfred nodded. "Kid stuff. *Watch* it. It knows Pouncey's doing something with electric current. I'd bet you any money it can sense—"

"Shhh!"

Manfred nodded. Joanna pointed as Indigo reached the engine, bent over it, and placed its right hand inside.

Pouncey watched, too surprised to do anything. Then she leaned over. Manfred crawled across the road until he was a couple of metres away. "What's it doing?" he whispered.

Pouncey ignored him: looking into the engine. "Ah!" she said. "The circuit breaker's died. I see!"

"What, what?" Manfred said. "What's it doing?"

"Circuit breaker's got a dodgy connection," Pouncey said. "Shorting out. I get it!"

"Did Indigo diagnose that? *Did* it?"

Pouncey hesitated. "I think so."

Manfred closed so that he could see what Indigo was doing. Without doubt it had sensed the tiny field disturbance caused by the shorting connection. It was *sensitive*. But did it know anything more about engines? Was this a random act of sensation, as he might notice a spot of blue sky amidst clouds, or did Indigo grasp that the engine was a device of many complementary parts?

He ground his teeth together in frustration. So annoying that Indigo did not speak. "Patience," he murmured to himself.

Pouncey glanced up at him. "You're gonna need it," she said. "These things are like animals. They'll never be human. What's it like to be a bat? We don't know—"

"Yeah, yeah, we've been through all that. I want 'em to understand English!"

Pouncey shrugged, pushing Indigo away, then tapping the compression unit, which wheezed into life. "Time to go," she said. "Good."

Back in the comp, engine sorted, Pouncey keyed the soltruck into life. It moved, and she grinned, then nodded.

Manfred glanced aside to Joanna. "Indigo's doing a bat... a whale," he said.

Joanna flashed a look of query at him.

"Making a picture of its surroundings using all its senses. Hearing mostly, but also electromagnetic. No wonder it senses the nexus."

"We shall have to be careful," Joanna replied. "It could give us away."

Manfred took a deep breath. "Yeah, hmmm, you're right... if anybody in the nexus notices anything... and they *will* be looking. They'll be looking for artificial entities, they'll know the template of the BIteam, they'll know we're not the AIteam. Yeah! That really *could* be a problem."

"We cannot stop Indigo's development."

Manfred nodded. "Agreed. Then what? Suppose Ichikawa's actively searching for nonhuman traces in the nexus? Suppose he's guessed where we are?"

Joanna did not reply.

Manfred felt his body tense and his stomach flutter as realisation struck him. Indigo – their marvellous, heuristic, intelligent creation – could do something, something simple and careless and accidental, like a naïve child giving away a family secret. It wouldn't know about Japanese corporations. It wouldn't know about murder, secrets, money. It was exploring its wonderful environment with all the uncontrived joy of a toddler. Definitely their Achilles Heel...

"Pouncey saw a sigil z on the nexus," he said, "but on the West Coast that'll be drowned out. We need to hurry on west, get into inhabited areas, then vanish beneath the noise of the nexus."

Joanna nodded. "As fast as possible."

They halted one evening as they approached The Dalles. In the distance Manfred saw the beginnings of a belt of forest that marked the western edge of the mountains: beyond it Portland, and much else. But here they were still in wild country, filled with rock, woods and the noisy, white-flecked, fast flowing Columbia River. Bear territory. Many midges. Very likely GM-modified mozzies, escaped from 'Frisco bio-labs. Very likely people too, also escaped from 'Frisco.

They sat in late afternoon sunshine beside the river, eating, drinking. Indigo and the three warm spectrum bis were out of the soltruck.

Manfred watched them. Joanna had strung them to a tree with a fragment of bailing twine. He shook his head. "Nah," he said, "that's not right. Let 'em go, mmm?"

"What are you talking about?" Joanna asked.

"They'll be runnin' off soon as look at yer," said Pouncey.

"But will they?" Manfred said.

"Too risky," replied Joanna.

Manfred stood up. "*No.* We've got to think of this from their point of view. Like wolves, like whales, they can't be alone. I don't think they'd run off, I know they're aware of their own group, and I'd bet they're aware of us as some kinda other group, attached to theirs. We're like dogs to them. Part of the group, but different, yeah? We're all a big society now, we've had adventures, we've rescued each other, we've spent time in each other's company. We can't just treat them like stupid brats. They've got to know they're free—"

"They must have *boundaries*, Manfred," Joanna interrupted. "Is that your idea of fatherhood? Let them run free and unattended, and see what happens? That is irresponsible."

Manfred felt anger rise up inside him. "No, no, *no!* This is what the BIteam is all about – creating a *society.* Leonora got it wrong, I got it right, I know I did. Beautiful Intelligence exists in a society and nowhere else, just like consciousness only exists in a society. I've proved my case. Yeah, I separated them in Philly, and, oh *no* you all screamed, you've cut them apart Manfred, but then they became individuals and I was *right.* And I'm right this time too. They're growing up. They're individuating. They're all different, mmm? Red is lazy and Yellow isn't. Indigo is totally an individual, we all agree to that. Don't you see?"

"The risk is too great," said Joanna, "even though Indigo has not run away... which I must admit I thought it might. But Indigo is different. It has been alongside us, in our company, far more than the others—"

"We *balance* the risk," Manfred said. "There's an equally dangerous path, yeah? The path of keeping them in cages and stunting them forever."

Joanna hesitated, watching the untethered Indigo. Manfred also looked – the bi was motionless, balanced on legs set apart, as if listening. Once again Manfred noticed that its dye was striated.

"Look!" he whispered, pointing to the three tethered bis. "Dye movement."

They all looked. Manfred lay down on his stomach, as if to minimise the intrusion caused by his presence. The only sounds were those of the river and the wind in the trees. Then, far off, a hawk cried out.

Indigo turned to listen. The dye patterns moved, and so did the patterns on the surfaces of the other three bis. Manfred stared.

"Communication," he said. "I think that's emotional communication. It likes what it hears. It's *moved* by the experience."

Joanna nodded. "It could be."

"But the sound could be a kinda music to Indigo," Pouncey said. "Hawk cries, they got a music to them. Maybe the bis got their own artistic culture."

"It might be that the dye patterns are like octopus skin patterns," said Manfred, "sending out basic level information – threat, fear, and so on. Or it might be a form of self-adornment.

The earliest human self-detritus is rouge for painting, beads for decoration. We want the bis to decorate themselves, that'd prove they're aware of themselves in some way, aware of their individuality."

He got to his feet.

Joanna did too. "No, Manfred. Don't cut those tethers."

"I've got to. Jeez, I've *got* to, they need their freedom. They know they're one of us. They won't stray, I promise."

"Manfred, promises mean nothing." She gestured at the tethered bis. "This is *science*. We go on facts, not the guesses of individuals. Manfred!"

"Fuck that," Manfred said as he ran to the tree where the bis stood. Joanna cried out, but moments later the bis were free.

Pouncey hurried across to the soltruck, retrieving the net on a pole that she had fashioned after the incident with the shooter. "I'm with Manfred on this," she said, "but, hey, just in case... I run pretty fast for a spy girl, and no bi is gonna outpace me."

Joanna ran to the tree. The bis watched her. Manfred watched them back. They acted like sedated children – quiet, calm, observant. They did not run off. Orange and Yellow fingered the lengths of twine attached to them, as if trying to understand the implications, but Red lay down on its back.

"See?" Manfred said.

"Shut *up*," Joanna shouted. She was angry. Manfred shrugged, glancing at Pouncey, then winking.

Joanna helped the bis free of the tangled lengths of twine, then sat back. Anger made a mask of her face.

Silence fell across the camp. Manfred sat down to watch the bis. They clustered together – *so* like a little group of kids planning some stunt – then ambled down to the river's edge. Manfred stood up to follow. Freedom was all very well, but an accident beside the river could wash one away. Like an indulgent father he nudged them away from the bank, allowing them to settle in a moss-covered basin.

"They understand," he said. "I can *feel* it."

"Understand what?" Pouncey asked.

"They understand they're in a social group, of which I'm one member. We're all in this together, and they *know* it. They're not acting as isolated individuals, they grasp that there's bonds, responsibilities, ties between us all. It's like glue. They're not going to run off, they're a clan, like wolves, and we're part of it."

"And the dye patterns?"

"Could be emotional reactions – which always have a physical component – or could be gestural language, Too early to say."

"D'you reckon they think the soltruck is their home?"

Manfred glanced back at the vehicle. Suddenly its significance became magnified to him. "Yeah, could well be," he said. "Well spotted, Pouncey. Yeah, they would need a home. The soltruck is all they know." He paused for a moment, imagining their arrival on the West Coast. "When you make us a new base," he said, "you'll have to include the soltruck in it, else the bis will be homesick. Then they really might run off."

"Oh, so now you're making amendments to your theory?" Joanna said. "The bis will not run off, you claim, but if they are homesick – whatever that is to a bi – they might do. Very scientific!"

"Science is about risks too," Manfred remarked in a flat voice. "We said we balance the risk–"

"*You* said that – forget the we."

"Okay, *I* said that."

Pouncey nodded to them both. "I think it's time for us to be getting back in our mobile home," she said.

Joanna scowled, and Manfred knew she got the point of Pouncey's joke. The atmosphere had turned bad.

He sighed under his breath, then went to collect the bis. Like domesticated animals they let him pick them up, and as they did the patterns on their skins changed. He put Orange and Yellow in their cage, then dumped them in the back of the soltruck. For a few seconds he held Red in his arms. The bi looked up at him through artificial eyes. For a moment Manfred felt a kind of conceptual vertigo envelop him, as he imagined looking into the mind of the bi, then imagined it looking back at him.

"Hurry up," Joanna muttered. "This is not a love-in."

Manfred, irritated, glanced up at her. "You seem pretty happy with Indigo on your lap in the front of the truck. Can't I have a favourite?"

She confronted him. "A favourite? They're not our children, Manfred!"

He stared at her. Something inside his mind seemed to move, like a deep, unconscious realisation about to bob to the surface. "They kinda *are*," he said. "Jeez, I'm only human. Somehow I know these guys are all different. And I do like this one's relaxed–"

"It is lazy, not relaxed."

He laughed. "How easy it is to talk about them as if they're human. You fall into that trap as quickly as I do, mmm?" He dropped Red into a cage, then shut the door. "I don't like doing this," he said. "I don't like locking them up."

"Cut the emotional crap," Joanna said. "These are artificial creations, they are not children, they are *not* human."

"If they do mimic us they're gonna be part human," he pointed out.

Joanna jabbed him in the chest. "They are mimicking one another. *We* are the big bad wolves, remember? Now get in the truck."

~

A few miles on from The Dalles, as the sun dipped behind white-capped mountains, they found a rock shelter beneath which they parked the soltruck. Low altitude now, a good few thousand feet down from the pass high point. Fish leaped in the Columbia River, the trees swayed in the breeze and pink-limned clouds swept across the sky.

Manfred, eating oat slop by the soltruck, watched the scenery. Fifty metres off, Pouncey sat on a boulder. Joanna was answering the call of nature behind rocks.

Then Manfred saw Pouncey fall off the boulder.

He sat up. Had she slipped? Holding his breath, he watched. When after a count of five she did not move, he ran.

She was out cold, it seemed. He knelt at her side. "Pouncey? You okay? You fainted?"

Then he saw a tiny plastic dart in her neck. He gasped: sat back. He pulled it out. Then he jumped up and looked around.

A few metres away two men with long, grey beards pointed rifles at him. The taller, older man carried an augmented rifle – a lump at the trigger filled with semiconductors.

"You on my land, boy," the man said.

"Hey, we're just driving through," Manfred said. "What've you done to my friend?"

"Just a trank." The man glanced at his friend, then added, "We don't like dead meat, see? Fresh." He snickered.

The other man said, "You ask to come through our land, did ya?"

Manfred shrugged, trying to appear cool. He must not antagonise these rednecks. "Didn't know. I'm sorry. Hmmm, we need to pay a toll?"

"You'll need to pay summat, boy," said the first man. "Hands up."

The other man changed the direction of his rifle. "Hell, there's three of 'em," he said. Manfred sagged. Joanna must have appeared.

"You come on over, lady" shouted the taller man. "We got us a l'il conference goin' on here. Hands up, an' all."

Joanna walked over. Glancing at Manfred she said, "Pouncey?"

"Tranquilised. These men didn't like the look of us. But I told them we'd pay the toll." He looked back. "Which we will."

"Whatcha got in that there truck, boy?"

Manfred put his hands on his head as he blew air through his lips. "Oh, nothing much. Just some toys."

"Tech toys? We don't like tech 'round these parts."

"Er... not really. Just foreign crap." He shrugged. "Toys for kids. Nothing for you."

"I'll be the judge of that, boy. I might wanna get rid of your tech, see? So open up the truck."

Manfred sighed. "Sure. No problem. We just wanna drive on through, after we've paid up, get off your land–"

"*Shut* it! I said open the truck, boy."

Manfred unlocked the rear doors then flung them open. "See?" he said. "Just baby robots, old style, nothing new. Nippandroids, yeah?"

"I told you, boy, our land is tech free," the taller man replied. Manfred glanced at the gun. Well, that was a lie.

He said, "Sure. Your rules."

"Take the nearest crate out. I wanna see what those cute little fuckers are."

"Okay."

"How many you got there, boy?"

Manfred glanced at Joanna. Indigo was in the front comp. "Eight," he said.

"Where you takin' 'em?"

"Portland."

"Why?"

Manfred shrugged. "Money. Not much of it around."

The taller man chortled. "That a fact? Open the cage, boy."

Manfred did as he was told.

Inside stood Violet and Blue. The bis crept out of the cage, looking like startled cats. They stared at the two rednecks. Manfred held his breath. He could see that the bis were spooked. Maybe they guessed that something was wrong; the dynamics of the group were so different to normal. And Violet had seen a gun before. It would remember the old man and the danger he represented.

Blue began to walk towards the taller man. He swore under his breath, then yelled, "Get away from me, you Jap fucker!"

Manfred waved his hands as he said, "No! It won't hurt you. It's just curious–"

Too late. The man lowered his rifle and fired. The lower half of Blue's right arm vanished, and Manfred saw a glint of the aluplex skeleton.

He put his hands to the sides of his head. "*No!* You damaged it! For God's sake, *don't–*"

"Shut up, boy! My land, my rules."

Manfred saw Indigo appear at the side window of the comp. The tall man walked up to Manfred.

"I don't like you, boy. You whinge like a girl. What kinda man you anyway, takin' Jap toys to Portland?"

Manfred shook his head, unable to comprehend the logic. "*What?*" he said.

The man raised his rifle. "I'm gonna give you a taste of mountain justice, boy. An' I don't think you'll like it."

He pulled the trigger. The gun popped, whirred. He stared at it.

Manfred leaped forward, grabbed the rifle and pulled it, then rolled to his right. Taken by surprise, the tall man let it go. Manfred jumped to his feet, then ran forward as the other man turned to fire.

Joanna screamed at the top of her voice. The second man turned back. Momentarily distracted, the tall man hesitated, and in this fraction of a second Manfred swung the butt around, cracking it against the tall man's head. He dropped.

The second man pulled his trigger. His rifle failed too.

"You'd better run," Manfred growled, "or I'll drop you too. *Run!*"

The man sped away.

Joanna ran to the soltruck. "I'll start it up," she shouted. "Grab Pouncey! We have to get out of here."

"The bis!" Manfred yelled.

"I will fetch them. Get *Pouncey!*"

Sixty seconds later Manfred and a semi-conscious Pouncey were in the comp, with Blue on the floor by Manfred's feet, its arm leaking fluid. Violet was loose in the back. Joanna drove the truck onto the road, then floored the accelerator.

A few minutes passed. Pouncey came around.

Manfred reached down to pick up Blue. "Stop!" he told Joanna. "We need to give it some help. Stuff is still leaking out."

Joanna cursed, then said, "Yes, you are right, we cannot ignore it. There's a flat, straight section up ahead with nowhere for rednecks to hide. I'll stop in a minute."

When the soltruck halted Manfred leaped out, letting Pouncey fall back on her seat. Drool escaped from her mouth, but she was alive, and recovering. Manfred pulled out the bioplas emergency box and rummaged through it, but he did not know what he was looking for. There had not yet been a traumatic bioplas injury within the BIteam.

He turned around to see Violet holding Blue's injured arm in its own. He froze. It was a scene of succour – or so it seemed. He shook his head, aware of the perils of anthropomorphic thinking, yet unable to push the notion of tender care out of his thoughts. And Violet's dye patterns, he noticed, were moving like a fast Moiré pattern. An emotional reaction in a time of stress, perhaps?

"Ah, damn it!" he murmured, as he turned back to see what lay in the emergency box. More bioplas required...

Pouncey limped to his side. He stared at her. She said, "Hi."

"You okay?"

"Blue," she said, her voice hoarse. "I see it."

"Can we stop this damn leakage? D'you know?"

"Just give it fresh bioplas. See if they know what to do."

Manfred followed her instructions. Pouncey knew more than him about the substance, having worked with it when completing her PhD. "How much?" he asked.

From a neoprene-wrapped casket Pouncey took a few tens of grams of bioplas, then gave it to Violet.

Manfred said, "Blue's injured, not–"

"*Violet's* carin'," Pouncey replied.

Manfred watched as Violet moulded the bioplas into a glove that fitted over the damaged end of Blue's arm. Bioplas, engineered from bacteria, created its own nutrient channels as it was transformed by whatever intelligence directed it, but Manfred knew that a simple cover would not be enough. He wondered if a healing process might begin, instigated by physical contact. Perhaps the obvious care shown by Violet would improve the chances of success. If Blue knew that it was cared for...

"I think you might be on to something," he told Pouncey. "Just look at them. They're totally aware of one another. They care."

"Could be a kind of act of safekeepin'," Pouncey replied, nodding.

Joanna joined them. "Look at those patterns," Manfred told her. He turned to Pouncey, adding, "Fetch Indigo. I want to see if it too manifests the dye patterns."

Pouncey brought the bi from the comp, resting it in the crook of her left arm. Indigo's surface showed a moving pattern, like the oscillating colours of an octopus.

"It's emotion, I'm sure of it," Manfred said. "Mmm, they're appalled that Blue is injured. They know that's bad because they're aware of their own bodies, and how delicate those bodies are."

Pouncey handed Indigo over to Joanna. "Interestin' that Indigo shows the patterns even though it's blind," she remarked.

Manfred nodded. "Yeah... what you doing?"

"Had a thought," Pouncey replied as she put on her spex and tapped on her wristband.

Manfred waited. Joanna, entranced by the scene before her, said nothing. After a few moment she placed Indigo on the ground, whereupon it hurried over to the other two. The gesture was unmistakeable.

Pouncey nodded at Manfred. "Thought so," she said.

"What?"

"A nexus trace. Those rednecks' rifles were nexus heavy."

"Yeah. I saw the tech bulge by the triggers. Hypocrites."

"Did the rifles refuse to fire?"

Manfred turned to face Pouncey. "They did. How d'you know?"

Pouncey pointed at Indigo. "It sensed what was goin' on. It sensed the redneck rifle, and you, the victim. It modelled the whole scene in realtime. And it knew there was danger because of its experiences. Flexible thinkin'. Mental movement in time."

"Jeez... it knocked out the rifles through the nexus?"

"To Indigo, the nexus must be like the air we breathe. It don't see the boundaries we see. It knows the nexus, but it don't know what we know – how the nexus evolved, all that. It just senses it and uses it, like a dolphin uses water."

"Then if we don't get to Portland soon, we're dead."

Pouncey nodded. "Listen, we could set up a Faraday cage using aluminium foil–"

"No way! *No*. You joking? How long d'you think you could last in an isolation chamber? An hour? A day? No... we get in the soltruck and drive back to the nexus just as fast as we can."

Pouncey nodded. "Like the twisters of Ichikawa was after us."

Then Joanna said, "Soon, very soon, we shall need to speak with Indigo."

CHAPTER 12

Leonora saw through her binoculars that Annaba was a small city of desert agriculturalists, solar mirror designers and junk artists, their advertising hoardings covering the hillsides like litter. She turned, thumbing the binocs up to full power. A group of Berber children was heading their way, smiles on their faces, spex tied on with string around the backs of their heads; running single file, like a caravan.

"Incoming," she said, turning to the group.

"Who? What?" Hound asked.

"Just the local kids."

"Give 'em a few coins to make 'em scatter," he replied. "It's the surest way. Man, the quickest way. We don't need the attention." He handed copper coins to them all, coins Leonora saw came from various countries.

They walked on. Annaba was an important stop, their supplies low, energy waning, only the camels unaffected by the heat and dry air. Zeug, the only member of the group riding, sat quiet and dignified, recharged to the max, soaking in the sunshine. She and Yuri had both noticed how much he liked the camels (because they weren't human, Dirk said, because their behaviour was simple and predictable.) That comment had caused another argument.

She had stopped worrying about Hound and begun worrying about Dirk. Yes, she was a worrier: she knew it. But she could not help herself. Dirk's position in the group had become redundant and there was little for him to do except become argumentative. On the other hand, Hound was over thirty and, she suspected, he wanted to settle down – yet he was still with the AIteam. Still doing good work, still loyal. She had been wrong about him.

Dirk glanced at her, smiled, waved his cheroot. She smiled back. Really, it was more of an intellectual argument they had, nothing more; it was not as if bad blood existed between them.

Then children's cries surrounded the group and she fell out of reverie. The kids were everywhere, yelling in English and in French, "Give money! La bourse ou la vie! We want money!"

Hound began throwing coins into the sand, making the kids work, making them run. They all followed suit and it became a game. But then a group of the children began taunting Zeug, who sat, high and remote like a king, on his camel, staring into the sky in silence.

And then Zeug seemed to freak out.

He jumped off the camel in a single motion, landing on all fours in the sand. At once the children ran towards him, but he backed off, his face alternately scrunched up as if angry, then blank like a dead monitor. Leonora stared at him. His arms moved up and down like wings. A stream of words poured from his mouth.

"Tell! Vin. Large. Sign! Go! Helm. Man. Sun. Hot! Hot! Cowl. Zip. Grow!"

"What the...?" Hound said, turning around.

Yuri began running towards the children, shouting at them, almost screeching. "Leave him alone! You have had your money, now leave us alone!"

Leonora ran too. She had seen how strong Zeug was. A child's death here would be a disaster.

Zeug continued to speak. "Four metres ten. One metre sixty one. Two metres fifteen."

Yuri began shoving the children, throwing his hat away to scare them; and seeing his forehead, they screamed and scattered. But Hound grabbed the hat and pulled it hard over Yuri's head. "Don't show yourself up!" he yelled. "Zeug's safe, man."

"Get these brats away from him!" Yuri yelled.

Leonora chivvied the remaining children away, shouting at Dirk to give them the last of the coins. The kids ran behind the camels, then disappeared into sandy hillocks. The camels groaned. The wind whistled and the sand hissed.

Zeug began waving his hands again. "Camels I like. Camels I like. They are twenty five metres distant. No! The nearest, twenty four sixty two. The furthest... twenty seven eighteen. Dirk Ngma, thirty metres twenty five." He turned to face Hound, then yelled, "*Mr Hound, I am watching you!*"

Zeug's voice was so loud Leonora winced. Hound ran off. Yuri froze. Then Leonora walked up to Zeug and tried to put her hand on his shoulder, but he yelped and walked off.

"Twenty two sixteen. Fix. Spin! Load. Fire. Speck. Brush. In! By! To! Nineteen oh five."

"He's having some sort of fit," Hound said. "Do something, Yuri."

For once, Yuri's emotions came to the surface. "What like? Stuff some of your Negro common sense into him? Fuck you! I do not know what is wrong, except that those vile brats upset him. Now get some common sense!"

Leonora shook her head at Hound, but she knew from the expression on his face that he would not respond. Yuri never spoke like this. The incident could be dealt with as a one-off. Hound walked away, high-fiving Dirk, who approached.

At least Zeug was calming.

They clustered around him. Leonora glanced back to see Hound drinking bottled water next to one of the camels.

She looked at Zeug. "Did you panic?" she asked.

Zeug did not reply.

"Da action of dem children caused da incident," Dirk said.

Yuri nodded. "The brats spooked him, as you Westerners would say, causing him to panic, or so I believe Mr Ngma."

Dirk nodded. "Autistic."

Leonora stared. "What?" Now she felt *her* anger rising. "What did you say?"

"It just a guess. Autistic mind. He focussing on distances, which I think he measure. With his senses. He not able to cope with kid who look like him. And like us. He like camel. Simple, stolid, boring camel. Predictable." Dirk nodded, looking at her. "Kids never predictable. Zeug sense dat. I not like dis situation at all."

"What d'you mean, *autistic?*"

"Mr Ngma," Yuri said, "you are skating on very thin ice."

Dirk shrugged, patting his pockets, but finding nothing to smoke. "Dere no ice in da desert, so I not care. It only a guess, lighten up! You know autistic savant?" He waited for a response, taking a stick of chewing gum and popping it into his mouth. "Yeah, da autistic savant, his mind is concrete. No generalisation. Little or no social skill. Safety in da lack – in, what you say… in exactitude. Exact is safe."

"You are saying Zeug is autistic?"

"I guess he *growing* autistic. I use dis as analogy. Or I could be right. We wait and see."

Leonora took Yuri by the arm and pulled him back to the camels. The heat of her own anger surprised her. "What *is* that man going on about?"

Yuri's face was flushed, his brow furrowed. "I do not know Ms Klee, but I must confess to concern over–"

"Yes, me too, Dirk—"

"Concern over Zeug! Never mind Mr Ngma, he is just a man, a single man with his own quite interesting opinion. But Zeug is definitely changing, and there I do agree with Mr Ngma."

"Zeug is *not* autistic."

Yuri glanced over his shoulder. Zeug was running to catch up with them. Yuri said, "I agree with you that it cannot be true. Zeug is too noble. But we must take from Mr Ngma what we must, for he has been correct before."

"I *won't!*" Leonora said, gripping Yuri's wrist.

"You are hurting me."

She let go. Words failed her. She turned and ran back to the camels.

Hound raised his hands palms up as she approached. "I ain't saying a thing," he said.

She walked around the nearest camel, slumping on the sand out of view of them all. Why did she have the sensation of losing control? Was the genie out of the bottle? If so she had to put it back, but she did not know how; and she was just one woman. She did know however that she did not want anybody to help her. The AIteam was her vision. And Zeug was hers.

Hound gazed up into black midnight heavens. Minuscule words danced around the constellations as the nexus told him which stars lay where. A satellite, invisible to him this late at night, passed overhead, its path tracked and visible like a string of neon in his spex.

With a flick of a tab on a wristband he reduced the info to a minimum (it was impossible to reduce it to zero short of removing spex). He gazed west. Nothing. East, also nothing. To the north lay the hallucinatory oasis, around which the mist-wreathed image of himself walked.

South...

He leaped to his feet. Southwards he saw a new figure.

An old man, small, pale, white haired. Without thought Hound reached out through the nexus, thumbing full throttle with his wristband, but the incarnation dissolved into a cloud of numbers. He stopped. This was something *different.* He initiated a full analysis of the nexus corresponding to the region he stood in. Seconds passed. Then a lead. He moved forward, following the man's trail, but it was so well camouflaged he almost lost it. An expert, then. But who?

Then, for a millisecond, Hound saw a route into the old man's machines. He risked it. He went in. The images in his spex became a jumble of land, air, sky and space as the old man's smoke and mirrors tried to baffle him. But Hound was made of tough e-stuff. He took the beating.

Then he saw cities whirling by. Then Tunis. Tunis again, shimmering in midday sun! The old man's computers were reacting to his presence, unable to shake him off but unwilling to give him free data, as Hound found himself following a trail through the nexus in ultrafast motion, heading west across North Africa at a thousand virtual kilometres per second. Following the route of the AIteam... then, with a heart-stopping instantaneous halt, he faced himself. And the nexus illusion shattered as the old man's computers hustled him off their territory.

He lay on the sand, gazing up into black midnight heavens, minuscule words dancing around the constellations as the nexus told him which stars lay where...

His spex rebooted. Duration total: 8.472 sec. The whole episode had lasted less than a dozen heartbeats.

He dumped the trail file into a wristband then deleted the nexus signposts so the analysis could not be retrieved, or at least could only be retrieved by people who knew what to look for; witch doctors and the like. Nothing in the nexus could be *deleted.*

The trail was unambiguous. He was being watched, and that act of surveillance had created a trail in the nexus, so faint it was almost nonexistent. But he knew at once who had done this, for it was not the deed of a human.

So... Zeug was watching him.

Hound stood up and sauntered over to the sleeping group. Zeug, as ever, sat in opened-eyed trance. Hound bunched his right hand into a fist, drew back his arm and lashed out. Zeug's left hand moved as if teleported from one position to the next: without apparent motion. Hound's fist struck that hand. Then Zeug turned his head to stare into his eyes.

"You're watching me," Hound said, pulling his fist back.

"I don't like you," Zeug replied.

"Why are you watching me?"

"My master told me to."

Hound stepped back, appalled. It only took him a second to decide who *master* referred to.

Hound strode past the souk's ceramics and jewellery salesmen, then paused. The main souk of Annaba spread like a dazzling, multicoloured labyrinth through the remains of its old sector (bombed in 2033 by the European Community, then rebuilt by the European Community, so that it became the first augmented city in Africa). Like chandelier-reflected rainbows its myriad signs and advertisements struck his eye with an intensity almost physical – and this without spex. With spex, the intensity of the info would be breathtaking.

He took Leonora's hand in his to guide her away from the hawkers. "You can see why epileptics are banned," he said. He shrugged. "Warned, anyway..."

He was half surprised when she squeezed his hand back. "Where are we heading, Hound?"

"We need food. Calorific supplies, for energy. And water. *Good* water."

He glanced over his shoulder to see Dirk trailing, a mini-bong in one hand, smoke wafting from his nostrils. He glanced at Leonora. She was looking at him.

"You alright?" he asked.

She nodded. "Just glad that we have got you."

"Er… yeah." He extracted his hand from her grasp, disconcerted. Leonora was not one for sentimentality. At least, that's what he'd thought. He'd only known her a short while and savvied almost nothing of her time with Manfred.

At a Francophile mini-mart called Antoine's Plaice he bought dried meat, Brie, nuts, packs of K-water. The water was not cheap.

"Imported from Kenya and sold to us at great profit," he muttered.

The Berber manager grinned. "Massive fix!" he said. "Afrique getting its own back! 'Bout time too." Then he gave Hound the finger.

Hound scowled, having assumed nobody here spoke English. "Let's get back to whitey and three-eyes," he said. "Man, they'd better be where I left 'em."

He didn't trust Zeug now. But nor did he trust himself to tell Leonora about his suspicions, in case she freaked. It was a quandary he didn't know how to solve. His relationship with her was becoming complex now that she'd banned him from speculating.

He tried to smile. "C'mon. The worst is over. I can see you're hating this."

"I'm not used to it," she replied in a small voice.

He took her hand again and led her through back alleys to the spice degrader where they'd left Yuri and Zeug. The machine, a colossal three-storey steel box, smelt of cinnamon and coke. The pair stood close to one another, with Zeug wearing shades so that his vision was restricted; earplugs in his ears. They didn't want another freakout caused by people proximity.

"You two okay?" he grunted.

Yuri frowned, drew breath to reply, then looked away and said nothing, as if to imply his contempt. Hound shrugged. He'd had worse in his time.

When Dirk caught up he handed out their supplies, then said, "We need to move on. We've got a country to cross before we get to Morocco. Reckon we'll be safe there. Maybe I can build us a new hide."

"You had better," Yuri remarked.

Hound tried to stop the dart of anger rising inside him, but it just popped out. "Why don't you shut it?" he said. "Disappointed with my leadership? Fuck off then. See if I care, man."

Zeug took a step forward and said, "Leave him alone. I don't like you."

"Yep, surely. We know what *you* think-"

Zeug struck without warning, with the speed of a cobra. Hound lay on the ground, winded but nothing worse. Yuri pulled Zeug back, a look of surprise – almost of horror – on his face, while Leonora uttered a scream and raised her hands to her mouth.

Hound leaped to his feet. For some reason the gesture infuriated Zeug, and with a shrug he was free of Yuri's grip. "I don't like you," he repeated.

The street was empty. Hound pulled out his snub-nose. "I'll kill you if you touch me again."

"You will not dare use that on me," Zeug said. "I am far too valuable."

Hound gasped at the audacity. This was a different Zeug; almost sophisticated, albeit still unstable. Could Yuri be tweaking him to wrest control of the AIteam? He realised it wasn't just him who could be in danger: Leonora too maybe.

He decided to take a risk. He aimed the snub-nose to the ground and fired. The ricochets echoed around them so loud everybody except Hound and Zeug ducked.

"I'll do it if I need to," he said.

"Hound," Leonora breathed, staring wide-eyed at him and shaking her head.

He took a step back. Had he done enough?

Zeug leaped at him. Hound raised the snub-nose and aimed it at Zeug, but Zeug dived to one side, then stood still. Hound followed him in the sights, aimed to miss and fired again.

Zeug shrank back. Hound saw a micro-ladder on the side of the spice degrader. He ran, leaping up the ladder until he reached the platform three metres up: safe. Zeug stood at the bottom, his arms windmilling around the lowest step as if unable to decide whether or not to follow.

Yuri ran over and pulled Zeug away. Hound heard people shouting at the end of the street.

Then Zeug turned on Yuri, grabbed his head and in a single motion twisted it off.

Blood fountained. Leonora screamed. Zeug dropped the head and ran down the street.

Hound saw white-cloaked market traders approaching.

"Run!" he cried, leaping down to the street, rolling to take the impact, then jumping to his feet. "Dirk, run!" He grabbed Leonora's hand and pulled. Ran in the opposite direction to the traders, following Zeug; but Zeug had already vanished.

He saw a stack of rotting cardboard boxes. Desperate, he pushed Leonora under them, then Dirk, glanced over his shoulder, saw a flash of white, then crouched down and pulled the largest box over his body.

Waited... heard voices, the sound of feet clattering up, then cries as they discovered the body. Some voices faded, others stayed around, talking, wailing, then fading. Silence... just distant street hubbub now. Nobody near, or so he hoped as he raised the box a centimetre and peered out.

Nobody.

"Man, we got lucky," he said. "Never try the cardboard box trick, *never*, you hear me? Okay, out now while the coast's clear."

Leonora and Dirk pulled themselves out of the reeking mass of cardboard, vegetable gunk covering their clothes. Hound brushed them both down then looked up and down the street. He saw kids in the distance, an old man walking away, a couple approaching. Possible danger.

"Walk on like nothing happened," he said. "Ain't no street cams I can see. Next alley, we dive in. Gotta get away. Hopefully no satellite's pinged us. My spex'll guide us."

"But where's Zeug?" Leonora whispered.

"Zeug's gone."

"But Yuri..."

"He's gone too! Leonora, *move*."

He led them away, taking her hand and his, not looking back once, until a narrow alley appeared and they were able to slip into it.

Hound's spex led them to safety. With red blips flashing north and east – police on their way – he wiggled along passages, over a roof, down a tunnel, then out through a storm drain onto a monorail track.

"There'll be cams here," he said. "To deter metal thieves. We'll dodge back and head down to the freeway. Then spend the night with the bums. Ready?"

Leonora wept.

Dirk did not weep, but tears trickled down his face. Hound said nothing, gave nothing away, looking to either end of the bridge beneath which they skulked – mounds of boxes, metal junk, algae-sheened puddles... He said he was looking through his spex for police, for local crims. His mouth was a thin line; teeth compressed, jaw tight. Those terrible moments had shaken them all.

The AIteam was shattered. All that *work*...

She felt as desolate now as she had when she realised Manfred had left her in Damascus. As she wept, memories flashed before her mind's eye, like journo photos: that Damascus bazaar; Manfred's white face; seeing Hound for the first time. The sense of abandonment, of shock. Then anger when the shock departed, anger that she could not express.

They called her stuck-up when she was at school because she was shy, brainy, seemingly aloof, unemotional. Well, that had changed. Now, she didn't care – she didn't care who saw her upset. What mattered was that she was *upset*. Something had to come *out*.

Eventually, she slept, chilled, uncomfortable. Dirk muttered in his sleep. Hound sat alert every time she woke and opened her eyes, on guard like a bird of prey, peering this way and that.

They ate bread and cheese next morning, and drank water. Hound said, "We need new clothes. There's nothing on my radar, but Yuri's body ain't gonna go away. Police'll be tracking. Street cams might pick us up shopping in the souk. We need new clothes, then get *away,* and fast."

"Clothes?" she said.

"Dat not easy when you on da run," Dirk added.

Hound stood up, took off his trousers and jacket, reversed them, then put them back on. "It's just you two," he said, stroking his chin. He took out a beanie, put it on, then said, "Stay here. I'm more worried about satellite goons than anything. The police'll have the area watched, keyed to our appearances – if they've seen us." He grimaced. "Keyed nexus style. Ha! And the Japs said the nexus'd make everything so easy…"

He ran off, leaving Leonora looking at Dirk, half reassured, half scared.

"What you thinking?" he asked her.

"You?"

"I ask you first."

She did not like his tone, so she shrugged and said, "It's over, Dirk. The end of the AIteam."

"And Zeug loose." Dirk sniggered. "But he won't last long. He'll be caught. It'll be on da news. Dey won't do him for murder though 'cos dey won't know what he is."

"Thanks for that," she murmured.

Dirk nodded. "Dere'll be blood on him—"

"Enough!"

Dirk took a metal case from his pocket, pulled out a cheroot and lit it. "You ever thought Leonora," he said, "dat anything might go wrong?"

His voice was mellow, conciliatory. She replied, "Not until the copters came in Malta." Tears began trickling down her face. "There's an old saying… a can of worms?"

"I know it."

She nodded. "I understand now. We could not control him. You are right, I suppose. They'll capture him before the day is out, then they will cut him open and analyse him."

Dirk nodded, standing up. "I gotta go to da can. I won't be a mo."

Leonora nodded. Sadness took her, and her vision misted behind tears. Swifts cried as they flew through the air catching insects. She waited.

And waited. After ten minutes she began to worry. Fifteen… then she heard bootsteps, and she relaxed. But it was Hound.

At once he said, "Where's Dirk?"

"He went to… you know."

"Waz?"

"Yes."

"When?"

She shrugged. "Fifteen minutes, perhaps?"

He paused, fingers tapping wristbands, and she knew he was hurtling through the nexus, plying data seas, grabbing info. "Nothing," he said.

"Nothing?"

"I… I…"

"What?"

"I didn't think I'd need to tag us AIteamers," he said.

She shook her head. "What does that mean?"

"He's gone. Can't follow. He must've planned it a while."

Leonora stood up and walked towards him, stopping when she was a metre away. Something about his manner, some microtic, alerted her. "That's a lie, isn't it?"

He took a deep breath. "Sorry. Yeah. I could trace him."

"But there is no point."

He shook his head. "You was right, his job's over." He smiled. "Man, you'd better stop paying him."

Leonora sagged. "Yes. Can you see to that?"

Somehow, this blow was softer. Dirk had been redundant for some time, and perhaps had become argumentative because of that. She felt no surprise, only a mild sense of betrayal.

She glanced at Hound. "What about you?"

He grinned. "I'm good. A team can be two."

"You do not want to leave me?"

"Hey, I'm good. This ain't over yet. I wanna see what Zeug does."

Leonora wiped tears from her eyes. "You are loyal," she said. "You could have been a self-serving waster, but you are still here."

"Loyalty's an under-rated quality," he said. "Like perseverance is."

She sighed. "You can start speculating about Zeug again if you want to."

He threw a package at her. "Not before you put this lot on."

"What is it?"

"Pretty clothes. Sorry if they're not your colours."

Hound led Leonora to the freeway, which they crossed alongside a dozen Euro-vagrants: good cover. Then he led her into a warren of passages where the flats were rented out for next to nothing and nobody asked any questions. Scabby adverts in Italian, French, Spanish, German and English delineated ghettos; flags spray-painted warned and welcomed in equal measure. Africa had become a kind of promised land, but here he saw the dark side of the European dream.

Then a green dot flashed three times in the right corner of his vision.

He stopped. "Hey…"

"What is it?"

He tapped wristbands to mod the resolution of the signal, until its associated infos wrapped themselves around his spex. "Zeug," he whispered. "Man, he's been spotted. Wait, wait… it's an Islamic posting service. I'm not sure now. Could be coincidence."

"What does it say?"

"It's some sort of reference to a superman… like, a really ripped guy. With bad skin. What I don't understand is how the poster knows Zeug's not human. Calls him être personne japonais. That means Nippandroid."

"Zeug's bad skin could be the fake tan and dirt."

"Exactly." Hound considered the info. He had put out a nexus request for all of Annaba, keeping it general, hunting down references to strong men, unusual behaviour, oddities and strange speech, especially that overloaded with numbers. This was the first match to hit the accordance level.

"Well?" She sounded excited.

"We definitely need to investigate this one. I think Zeug will move to escape *people* – maybe he'll want to find camels. But he could still be in the city."

"Where does the signal locate him?"

Hound applied the virt-compass, then walked to the next crossroads and orientated himself. He pointed. "There. North, two three-twenty metres. Maybe twenty minutes walking. The nexus'll guide us."

They walked at slow pace through the dingy alleys of the locale, emerging on to a main shopping street, dodging through the solbuses to get to the other side, then walking on. Faux-crippled traders tried to stop them, but Hound brushed them aside without a word, leading the way, with Leonora slipping through in his wake. Then they were out of the warren, before them a power station, a hulk of metal and brick, grey on grey beneath rain-threatening sky.

He turned his collar up and set all his proprietary nex alarms. The snub-nose and the flechette lay ready. "C'mon," he said, "let's see what's what."

One hand in pocket – snub-nose charged – he walked around the side of the station, chainmail fence to his right through which he saw anonymous grey walls, brick to his left covered with moss and algae. He paused, peered through the fence, saw a couple of padlocked doors. Listened. Nothing.

"You hear anything?" he whispered.

"Just city noise, and not much of that."

"The post was dated 6am. Three hours ago."

She nodded.

Hound sucked his teeth. The tension in his body departed as he realised the trail was already cold.

Then somebody walked out of a shallow doorway, hands up. He whipped out the snub-nose.

"Don't shoot!" A woman's voice.

He stood, frozen.

"I am unarmed. Is that you, Hound?"

He stared. She knew his *name?*

"Is it?" the woman repeated.

Leonora grabbed his arm and hugged him close. She was scared again, he could tell. But *he* was not scared. "Who the hell are you?" he said.

She pulled down her hood and took a step forward. "Tsuneko June."

For a moment Hound's sensory world seemed to vanish as shock made him see only her face, hear only her name, think of the impossibility... but it *was* Tsuneko June.

"I didn't know where you were," she said. "But I knew about the artificial intelligence you made. So I had to lure you in."

"How did you *get* here?" Hound said, trying to clamp down on his anger. "How did you–"

"Don't blame yourself, Hound. Your artificial intelligence was monitoring you, and as it did it left a trail in the nexus."

"Ah. So. I was right about that."

Tsuneko turned and said, "You must be Leonora Klee. I am very pleased to meet you."

Leonora, stunned, said nothing.

Hound felt his feet begin to itch. "I wanna get outa here. Let's find a caf. Do the tourist thing. We got a lot to catch up on. Whatcha doing for a data incarnation?"

Tsuneko approached. "I am fully fake, not a soul knows I am here."

"Man, why *are* you here?"

She glanced over her shoulder. Hound tensed, put his hand in his pocket, but then she said, "Let's find that café. I need tea."

Five hundred metres away they found Le Percolateur, and a table for three at the very rear of the place, out of sight from the street. They ordered tea, coffee and croissants. Hound checked the can for escape routes, then set up a few more auto-alarms in case Tsuneko was playing some sort of meta-game. He knew she wasn't though.

She said, "There's a man in England called Mr Bloodhound."

Hound nodded. This was a name and reputation he knew. "So Mr B located me through the nexus?"

Tsuneko nodded. "I was looking for the AIteam, not you. I've kind of defected, I suppose."

"You do not sound very sure," Leonora said; and Hound heard the suspicion in her voice.

"Shh, shh," he said, patting her shoulder. To Tsuneko he added, "We've had a bad coupla days. Zeug's awol. Yuri Ichikawa's dead. Dirk Ngma's vanished."

Tsuneko nodded. "I knew none of this. But I'm not here out of curiosity. I know what you've been trying to build—"

"Why *were* you a mole for us?" Leonora interrupted.

Tsuneko sipped her tea. "I knew you would ask that. Well, at first it was professional."

"Biograins."

"Yes. But then, with Manfred following such a weird path, and me knowing what the AIteam were planning, I felt like I was in the wrong team. So I jumped ship."

"Simple as that?" Hound asked.

"Yes. I hope that's not too simple for you to believe."

Hound shrugged. He'd guessed this a long, long time ago. He'd not guessed however that Tsuneko June would actually track the AIteam down. He decided to say nothing so that

Tsuneko would stay in suspense. He didn't want her comfortable.

"Obviously there is a lot more detail to fill in," Tsuneko said, glancing down into her teacup as if shy.

Hound glanced at Leonora. "What you reckon?"

Leonora would understand the implication of him asking that question in Tsuneko's presence. The AIteam was shorn of talent. This was raw, young talent, the girl not yet twenty five, biograins not yet commercially exploited, though Leonora of course was wedded to the quantum computer future.

Leonora said, "Maybe, Hound."

He nodded, turned his gaze back to Tsuneko. "And your patents?"

"Still mine. Still safe, for the moment."

"And you say Mr B knows who I am?"

"He's guessed."

He nodded. Tsuneko had not volunteered that info. He wanted her to believe she had, so he could probe her story; but her honesty was encouraging.

"He called you Goodman–"

"*Shhh!* Never say that name. He's dead."

She nodded, then whispered, "Mr Bloodhound guessed who you were. That's all I know."

"How did you get involved with Mr B?"

"My friend Rosalind."

Hound tapped codes and names into his wristband. He felt like impressing her now that he was beginning to trust her. "Rosalind James, born six ten twenty sixty two... unmarried, living at Oak Manor, Winterbourne Stoke, Wiltshire. That her, Tsuneko?"

"Yes!"

He smiled. "I ain't lost my touch."

Then a red dot spex left side, flashing twice.

"Police," he said. He tensed, hands gripping the table, watching the info unfurl. "They've clocked your lure, Tsuneko. The fake Zeug. We'll run now."

"Wait," Leonora said, grasping his arm as they stood up. "She's coming too?"

"No problems here, man."

"You *trust* her?"

He turned. "I trust her just enough for her to tag along. No fuss. C'mon now. You ladies gonna see the inside of a gents."

CHAPTER 13

Ghosts of the distant nexus began to float into Manfred's sensorium as they penetrated the band of forest that lay in the western regions of the mountains. It had been an odd experience, this nexus-featherweight America, for he was used to the ever-present augmentation of reality. Now he knew what life was like as a solo: a life adrift, a life shorn of artificial meaning, a life without directions, paths, signposts. And in America's shattered landscape his human life had also been lacking signposts.

Joanna found the experience easiest to cope with, he noticed. Pouncey, wired to the max, struggled, though she did enjoy the sensation of independence. But he hated the feeling of floating free and isolated which came when the nexus faded. Joanna, though... she had even enjoyed some of their madcap road trip – or so she claimed. Manfred was not sure he believed that claim. Wedded to the bis, to the theory of bi society, to the great goal in their lives, she could never suggest that solo life was good for them. Yet Joanna was an introvert. The wildness of the real world bothered her. Hiding from the world, nearly nexus-free... that would appeal to her. In contrast, he, an extrovert, never felt at ease with the hush of the inside of his skull.

And so outliers of nexus culture began to appear in his spex. They all resided to the west: West Coast. It lay nearby. He saw geographical pointers, topological menus, hints of music culture, of restaurants, of a myriad of sub-cultures all trying to deal with the decline of the Western world. And the Pacific Rim lay to the west of this west.

As yet he was too distant to meaningfully use these infos. The nexus grasped that he was as yet not a part of the world it presented, and so, to it, he was irrelevant. But it was reassuring to see flocks of luminous sigils and a few Apple-style menus in the e-distance.

Pouncey drove them onward, dodging pot-holes in the terrible road. Water, frost and tree roots had made a mess of the tarmac and road-stone, but the soltruck had fat tyres and mega-suspension, so it survived.

One evening they halted in a picturesque lay-by, built in decades past for tourists to enjoy views of the Columbia River as it thundered over a ridge. Huge conifers reached up to the sky – the sun was a hint of a gleam between them. Boulders lay everywhere, part blocking the road, but wild animals had made a muddy path around it. The air was cool.

Manfred, sitting on damp grass, watched as all nine bis wandered the lay-by. Joanna sat frowning, tense and uneasy. Pouncey stood nearby, her buttered bread supper in one hand, a rifle in the other. On guard for rednecks.

"They're truly starting to individuate," Manfred remarked.

Joanna glanced at him. He smiled at her. He recognised the look in her eyes that told him she was more interested than annoyed. "What evidence?" she asked.

"Red is lazy. Look at it, lying on the ground. You'd think it was enjoying the feel of the breeze on its fronds."

Joanna uttered a single laugh. "I thought we decided never to anthropomorphise them? This is not a Disney film, Manfred."

He laughed back. "Sure! I know that. But you can't deny it. Red is a hedonist, it *feels* its body, and it likes it."

"Nonsense."

Manfred continued, oblivious to her skepticism. "Orange... that's the leader bi."

"*What?*"

"Oh, yeah! Right from the start, when we were in Philly. Don't you remember? When we started to really stimulate them, they all watched what Orange was doing."

"Crap."

"Yellow," Manfred said, "now I think that one realises you and me are more than bis. It knows we're somehow like a bi, yet different. It hangs around us more."

"You have *observed* that, have you? I watched chimps for decades. I have *not* observed what you have."

"You're just denying it to look cool. You've got preconceptions, you always had–"

"Oh, for fuck's sake, Manfred! I have *not* got more preconceptions than you have. You are giving the bis human characteristics they do not have. They are *not* little cuddly mini-people, they are artificial intelligences. They are *aliens,* okay? We do not even have proof yet that they are conscious-"

"Yeah," Manfred interrupted, "and we both agreed that might never come. What's it like to be a bat... remember?"

Joanna scowled, then looked away.

Manfred continued, "Green, now that one I think is pretty carefree. It likes to goof around."

"What, like Goofy?"

"Sure. Why not?"

"And I suppose Blue, with half an arm, is the tragic Fisher King?"

Manfred smiled. That was funny. "Nice one! But no. Blue's a bit of a mystery to me, though I noticed it hangs out with Violet a lot. Indigo, well, hmmm, Indigo is always going to be special, nobody could ever deny that. Somehow its blindness has changed its consciousness—"

"If it is conscious."

"Yeah... if it's conscious. Agreed. But I'd bet any money that Indigo is the one that ends up speaking English first."

"Speculation. Nothing more."

Manfred replied, "Oh, I don't deny it. A guess. But useful. An educated guess, mmm? We can't just ignore the future."

"Really."

"Violet," Manfred continued, "seems to be the caring one. Blue's pal."

"Seems? So you don't know for certain."

"No, Jo. I do not know for certain."

"Well that is useful. What about Grey and White? The poor, demoted, wretched, colour-free bis, god help them."

"Now you're getting all anthropomorphic," said Manfred, choosing to ignore her sarcasm. "White is always interested in its environment. But Grey, well... I've noticed Grey seems somehow isolated. I see it alone more often than any of the others."

Joanna laughed again. "If we go past whatever is left of Hollywood, I will recommend you for a film script post. You are good. Really good. You can invent stuff out of pure imagination."

Manfred stood up. "Thank you. Well, I'm done. Let's drive."

As he spoke, he saw in the corner of his vision a movement. He saw Pouncey jump, then raise her rifle. He turned to face her.

She aimed upwards. A huge hawk dove down and grabbed White in its talons.

Pouncey fired. Missed. Fired again.

"Don't hit White!" Manfred cried.

As he shouted he saw White's head come loose. It fell like a quartz globe, pearly pale in the last of the evening light. The hawk, baffled, stalled in the air then dropped the spasming body as the arms broke free. Pouncey fired again, winging the bird. With a squawk it flew away, vanishing between trees.

Manfred stood frozen. The necks of the bis were bridges between artificial brain and artificial body, grown dense with micro-cables over the weeks. There was no repairing that damage.

"Oh, no, *no...*" he wailed as he ran to where White had fallen.

Pouncey reached the bi first. She knelt. "It's a goner," she said.

Joanna ran up. "I told you, Manfred!" she said. "Too much danger out in the wild. And you did not listen!"

"Don't milk it!" Manfred said, anger making him spit. "Shut up! Accidents happen–"

"Not to the bis. The bis are our property. We had the chance to keep them safe in their cages."

Manfred refused to answer. There was no arguing with this – no point to arguing with it. Safety was boring and meaningless, that was what he thought. Life was risk.

"There's nothing we can do now," he said.

"No there is *not,*" Joanna retorted, "because it is too *late!*"

He swung around to face her, grabbing her by a shoulder. Pointing to his eyes he said, "Look! D'you see me weeping? Eh? No! Because they're not human. I get it, okay? I *get* what you're saying, Jo, they're not like us. So shut up about it now."

Joanna wrenched herself from his grip and knelt down.

Pouncey turned and said, "Hey, watch out. The bis know somethin' happened. Look!"

Manfred span around to see some of the bis hurrying over: Orange, Yellow, Indigo, Violet. Grey was nowhere to be seen, nor Green. Blue sat on the soltruck bonnet, watching. Red lay face down on a pillow of moss.

"Pouncey, round up the others. Don't cage them. Lead them here, yeah?"

"Sure 'nuff, boss."

Pouncey ran off. Manfred knelt down and said, "Jo, we need to watch what they do. You agree?"

Joanna bent her head forward, then sighed. "Yes. Unfortunately."

"Okay... move back. Let's watch for a while, see how they react. C'mon... stand by me."

The pair retreated for a few metres, then sat on a fallen tree. Orange and Violet were the first on the scene. They circled White's remains, their touch-fronds flat at their sides, the striations on their surfaces quiescent. Manfred noticed at once that neither Yellow nor Indigo went close; they seemed to be watching Orange and Violet, not the body. Then Indigo turned around, located Manfred, and walked over. Like a cat, it leaped up into Manfred's lap.

Manfred, surprised, did nothing for a while, before setting Indigo on the ground. "You'd better be with your own kind," he said, tapping Indigo on the back.

Indigo turned and leaped up again.

Joanna said, "It wants to be with you. You were correct about one thing – it is the most human aware of the bis."

Manfred nodded, awed by this. "Yeah... it is. Weird."

"Strange indeed."

"Jo, I know we've disagreed about this, and I'm sorry about that... a little... but the bis *are* manifesting personalities. We've got to interact with them as if they've got character. If we don't, if we ignore that or pretend it doesn't exist, we diminish them."

"I do not deny that," Joanna replied. "I do deny they are human in any way."

"Do you deny that each one has some kind of meaning framework inside it, that's subtly different to the rest? That maybe manifests as character? Identity?"

"Um... perhaps."

"Okay, that's good enough for me. Let's observe."

Now the three bis stood around White's body, all of them looking at the armless, headless object. Blue and Red joined them. Manfred held his breath as the five bis closed in on each other, making a huddle, before – suddenly, as if following a prearranged plan – leaping back and hurrying away.

Jo made to stand up, but Manfred held her back. "They're making towards the head and the two arms," he said. "They're not running away."

"They're *communicating*," Joanna said, her voice taut with emotion, "I *know* they are. But this is not like chimps. It took me years to grasp chimp vocalisations. This is different. The bis are a whole new species and there is no frame of reference for me."

"Yeah, that's not wrong," said Manfred. "They speak alien."

In less than a minute the bis returned carrying White's remains. Manfred leaned forward, aware that this could be a pivotal moment in his scheme. Would the bis grasp that White was like them, yet no longer in existence? Or would they stroll away, like bioplas animals?

Indigo sat on his lap, alert (it seemed) to what was happening within the bi group; in response Manfred tried to relax. He could be sending all sorts of gestural signals to Indigo without realising it. Indigo might already have picked up on human body language, the way dogs did from their owners.

Then Orange bent down to pick up one of the arms. Manfred watched, observing that the hawk's talons had somehow disarticulated the alu-plex joint. That was bad luck. Orange put down the arm, then picked up the head, and as it did Violet and Blue picked up the two arms. At once the dye patterns returned to the body surfaces of all the bis. Manfred glanced down. Indigo too presented oscillating Moiré patterns – and now a few of the bis looked back at it. Manfred calmed himself. He was almost trembling. This was communication, this was proof of inter-bi relations, and it was proof too that Indigo used senses he was unaware of to socialise with the bi group. It was *proof!*

"They'll not be able to wear clothes," he observed.

Joanna frowned at him. "Shhh!"

Orange lay the head on the grass. Violet and Blue did likewise. There was the sound of a twig snapping as Pouncey returned, carrying Grey and Green.

"Put them down by the group," Manfred instructed, "then move back."

Pouncey did as she was bid, returning to the soltruck, where she lit up a smoke. Manfred returned to watching the bis.

For a moment they circled aimlessly around the body parts, Grey and Green nearest the remains, until all of them slowed their movements, then halted. Red stepped back and lay down. Green wandered off, following a butterfly. But Violet knelt beside White and, in a gesture that took Manfred's breath away, tried to pull off its own right arm. Blue followed suit. Grey stepped away from the group, walking backwards until it tripped over a branch; then it sat down, watching from a distance.

Manfred pointed to Orange. "Gone quiet," he whispered.

"It might be planning what to do."

"Let's hope so, mmm?"

As they spoke Yellow moved away from the group, returning to Joanna, where it paused, glanced back, then leaped up, so that it sat on Joanna's knee. Manfred found himself entranced. They *were* real creatures, aware of their environment, of themselves, thinking, maybe even feeling.

He shook his head. He tried to calm himself. Jo was right about one thing – they must at all times resist the temptation to think of the bis as Disney's Nine Dwarves. And yet, watching Yellow sit on Joanna's lap, it was impossible not to humanise it. Yellow was just like a little kid. He held his breath, trying to reduce his heart rate, tortured by the conflict inside him. The bis had been immersed in human culture since he used scissors to separate them on that formative day in Philly. They *would* have some human characteristics. But which?

Compromise, that was the way forward. Most likely the bis would end up half human, half alien. He looked down. Indigo would be key. This bi must *never* be grabbed by a hawk; on that he agreed with Jo.

Orange bent down once again, lifting White's body. For a few moments it looked at the head and arms, before kneeling down to try to pick them up. But the whole bundle was too much to carry. It dropped the body then picked up the head and the arms, then dropped those and again lifted the body. It took the body to a flat stone, where it knelt, lifting the stone. It let the body drop, then allowed the stone to fall back, so that White was part concealed.

The other active bis watched. Red appeared to be resting – perhaps recharging. Green chased insects around a tree.

Violet then took the head and carried it to the stone. Blue brought the arms. But the stone was smaller than White's torso.

Manfred waited, hardly daring to breathe. Orange turned to look at him. He stared back. It was a kind of pointless, meaningless telepathy.

Violet fetched dead leaves and used them to cover the limbs, but Orange kicked the leaves away. Blue also brought leaves, grass too, then a piece of stone. Orange brushed away the leaves, then took the stone and dropped it on the arms.

Manfred thought: they're trying to hide it, they're trying to *bury* it. The bis are trying to conceal what has happened. They know White is gone and they're trying to find an appropriate response to that fact.

Only Orange, Blue and Violet seemed bothered by the presence of the inactive White; only they seemed compelled to do something in reply. Indigo, Grey and Yellow watched, but did not act. Perhaps Red and Green were as yet unaware of themselves as conscious individuals, like infants younger than eighteen months. Orange by contrast seemed mature, its acts deliberate, even measured.

Manfred shook his head. What he observed seemed to verge on the miraculous. Eight little enigmas.

Orange hurried away, followed, after a pause, by Violet and Blue. The bis spent some time gathering flat stones, which they used to cover White's remains, until nothing could be seen. But Violet was still dissatisfied. It walked down to the river, gathered an armful of mud, then used the mud to plug all the holes through which glimpses of white bioplas could be seen.

And so, half an hour later, the deed was done; the bis were satisfied.

Manfred glanced across at Joanna. "I don't think there's any doubt as to what happened there," he said.

Joanna nodded. "We could make various hypotheses," she replied, "but the core remains. They wanted to hide White. They didn't like what they saw."

"They found themselves compelled to respond," Manfred said. "They have basic consciousness, I'm sure. I've *seen* it in action."

Joanna sighed. "I believe you're right."

Manfred stood up. "C'mon. We need to make Portland. Indigo is gonna be sending out all kinds of signals to the nexus."

"And the nexus will be manufacturing meaning from that," Joanna replied, "meaning that could be picked up by anyone."

"Yeah. Well, we're almost there. Another damn day out here in the wild. Pouncey! Time to go."

Manfred walked to the soltruck, Indigo in his arms, pleased to see that the bis followed – except Grey, who hung back, and Orange, who had vanished for a moment. With six bis in the crates, Indigo in the comp and the soltruck engine revving, he looked around for Orange. No sight of it. He walked back into the trees surrounding the open lay-by, then saw Orange standing beside bushes.

He walked over, then halted. He whistled, and Orange turned around. He whistled a second time, exactly the same notes, then walked back. Orange followed.

That would be a useful trick, he realised. He could whistle to the bis as if they were sheepdogs. All three of them should learn to do that.

Pouncey manoeuvred the soltruck onto the road, the vehicle's suspension groaning as it bounced. Manfred took a last glance at the lay-by, at the rocks beneath which White was buried. The bioplas would revert to complex petroleum chemicals, he knew, and a whole lot more in a matter of days. Shorn of the intelligence directing it, it would decay as did human flesh.

"Pouncey, stop!"

The soltruck skidded to a halt. Manfred opened the comp door and jumped out, leaping over tree roots and stones to reach the bis rocks.

There, on the top stone, he saw a white flower and an orange flower.

Pouncey needed to create a new fake ID before heading down into lands where the nexus ruled. From her position on the bonnet of the soltruck she looked across at the orange street lamps and neon fritzers of Portland, thirty klicks distant. In her spex she saw what appeared to be a wall of mist – an artificial threshold created by the nexus to imply the liminal structure between the high-tech coastal region and the no-tech US interior. They had passed through a similar, though less obvious boundary when leaving Philly.

The first thing to manufacture was fake money lines. Nobody nexus-savvy lived without money: money-free was a solo norm. Via her wristband she sent out a tracer line, which stole its way through the threshold until it found a small local bank. There, it lay quiet: a sleeper.

An hour passed. Pouncey let it. No hurry. Sub-routines that she attached to a local gardening club she allowed to mutate autonomously, following the local cultural norms, so that after a couple of hours they looked 100% Portland. Into these software structures, using the tracer line, she sent a modded program called P, to which she attached a single fifty-seven character password; the name and address of an imaginary character she wrote about in English class when she was nine. Unguessable – unknown to the nexus.

She waited some more. In the comp, Manfred and Joanna were snoozing. Indigo sat on the front ledge, leaning into the windscreen, as if listening. Creepy little thing, that Indigo.

A beep sounded in her spex hub. She sent out a query, received an answer: Polly Siedlaczek, 40 years, dob 11-24-2052, resident of Portland since 12-01-2084, Caucasian, $94077.67, single, no dependents.

Good! Her kernel ID was sorted. Later, she would sophisticate it, make it invisible to snoops. But for her entry into local society she only needed approximate cover – she'd be doing nothing dangerous.

She jumped off the bonnet and tapped on the side window. Manfred woke, then let the window down a few centimetres. "Yeah?" he said, yawning.

"I'm ready. Found an old pushbike somebody threw into a hedge. Gonna use rubber compound to tyre it up, then rattle off. You okay with that?"

"Yeah. Be careful."

"Hey, you're talkin' to Polly Siedlaczek. And she knows her stuff."

Manfred nodded. "She'd better."

Pouncey spent fifteen minutes preparing the pushbike tyres, then cycled off down the hill, finding her way to the main highway into Portland by the light of an almost full moon. The 30k ride took her a couple of hours.

In the outskirts of the city she was pleased to encounter all the complex, insane debris of human life in the faded West: greasy lo-markets, groups of narcotics brats selling GM-modified bacteria, people in ancient electric cars, on ancient electric bikes, or pushing pedals, like she was. Nobody even glanced at her, let alone spoke to her. She was anonymous already, having sunk over the top of her head into an environment where nobody had the time or the energy to care much about anything.

In her spex the swirl of info overload was like a familiar balm, interpreted by her metaphor-hungry brain as a homely smell that she had missed: stagnant water, fried food, plastics, piss and shit. It took a few minutes for her brain to reacquaint itself with that hallucinatory mix, but it did, because she was a pro.

Dawn broke. She stowed the bike behind a pile of ripped tarpaulins, then strolled the streets. Down an old avenue she noticed a huge mound of rubble – steel and glass and concrete – and beside that some algae-greened lo-rise towers which showed no lights. She checked them out via the nexus: decayed apartments marked with the six-pointed biohazard sign. Okay… not ideal. But that biohazard mark was from 2082 – ten years ago. What would survive a decade worth worrying about?

Pouncey sat down on the pavement, her boots in the water-filled gutter. Bits of old fried chicken skin floated by alongside a crumpled wrapper. Syringes twinkled in the light of the moon. She began an investigation of the apartment blocks, using one of the classes in a nearby school as a disguise: 'Social research' for a 'school project'.

It had been a souped-up variant of dengue fever. That was nasty, but the 0-Max viral variants that had exploded through the blocks, and then the locality, were unstable mutations brought from Jamaica on waves of panic. Without hosts they were gone. It was in fact the terrible aura of the apartment blocks that led to them remaining empty. They were known to the locals as the Haemorrhage Apts, their legend red and notorious.

This could be good. This felt *right*. Beneath the best preserved block lay a car compound accessed by a single ramp. That ramp, she saw, was now overgrown with greenery. It would be a simple matter to create a hidden tunnel through it, allowing the soltruck entry. The problem would be driving the vehicle through without alerting anyone. The vicinity was populated far below the Portland average, but it only took one bum spotting the soltruck to create a problem.

Yet it could be done. She had ways and means. And then... back to the Hyperlinked.

CHAPTER 14

Dirk walked all the way from Annaba to the seashore, where he stumbled into a European refugee camp. Stinking rows of tents spread as far as the eye could see, east to west, the Italians to his left and the French to his right. Yet even this gull-haunted dump was a magnet for nexus hawkers, kids mostly, wearing the tall white hats and smirking expressions of the local mercantile elite. Dirk buzzed them away with a, "No I not want dat and I never use *dat*."

But he needed to get to the European continent. He needed to hide awhile.

"You goin' the wrong way, mister," he was advised. "You live longer in Afrique. Need hash for bong? Cheap black!"

Dirk brushed these advisers away, walking barefoot along the seashore, his boots tied together and hung around his neck like a scarf. But his attitude of dignity and his unusual clothes made him stand out, and eventually he was approached by an adult – an old man in a grey Berber robe and lime green sandals.

"You new here, ami?"

Dirk nodded.

"You go north? Bad times. Italia, a fuck-up. They have no oil."

"Nobody got *oil*, you devio," Dirk muttered. "Only rich megas on dere yachts."

"I got a yacht, ami."

Dirk paused to study the man's expression. He could see this newcomer ached for money. Maybe he really did have a yacht. "You know Sardinia, Med-captain?"

"Oui!"

"Take me dat way?"

"Oui!"

Dirk grimaced. "How much?"

"Very expensive."

Dirk smiled. "Go on. Hit me."

"Rare elements."

Dirk knew what this meant. He carried no currency, but he did have a stash of various lanthanides and some nonmetals. "Selenium?" he said.

"You got selenium, ami?"

Dirk shrugged. "A little."

"Show me."

"Turn round den."

The old man turned away, showing the sweat-stained back of his robe. Dirk reached under his shirt for the lower of his two bum bags, feeling for a metal canister. He withdrew it, then checked its contents.

"Okay," he said.

The old man took the canister then ID'd the ident scratched into the metal with a nexus probe. He sucked his teeth when the result came back positive. "This mark could be faked, ami," he said.

"You think I bother, with dat little amount? Get real!"

"Easy to do. You a cool gent, oui?"

Dirk chuckled. "Dat thirty year old Swiss mark, as you well know. You think I fake dat? How? With Swiss computer?"

The old man frowned. "Okay. I just check, ami. So... you want ship to Sardinia, oui?"

Dirk nodded.

"Not back?"

Dirk shook his head.

"You a madman," the old man remarked. "You won't last a month."

"I got Europe sussed," Dirk replied. "You just get me dere."

The yacht turned out to be a remodelled solboat with a Moroccan engine – a modern, clean engine, Dirk was surprised to notice.

As they stepped into the surf and headed for the boat, he put his hand on the old man's arm. "Dat never *your* engine. You stole it. Who are you?"

The old man smiled. "A cousin of Moroccan king, mon ami, recently escaped."

Dirk stopped, watching him clamber into the boat. The remark had been made without hesitation, and with sincerity – and it was insane enough to be true. Dirk shrugged. A deal was a deal. He carried an ace card anyway, a concealed inflatable ring, bought on the ferry from Gozo to Linosa. He did not care for open water.

But the old man was genuine. All he wanted was his selenium. During the 250 kilometre journey they spoke about events in various Moroccan lands, events in lands of the former Libya, and the state of the African solar energy business. Supper and white wine were complimentary.

"Tunis suburb twenty," said the old man, "and free of glycerol."

Dirk slept well during the night, more relaxed than he had been for some time. On a sandy beach near Cagliari the old man dropped him off: they embraced man-style, with faux kisses a few centimetres off the cheeks. Then it was "Au revoir!" and Dirk was on his way.

He walked into Cagliari undisguised. The advantage of hiding in Europe was also its disadvantage – most of it was a hinterland of gun-toting communities desperate to scratch a self-sufficient living from the land. Almost no eyes in the sky watched Europe.

Here, permaculture experts were more valuable than gold: often kidnapped and forced to give advice year after year, on pain of death if they refused. You did not advertise that you were a permaculture expert in Europe. Dirk observed hundreds of tree-shrouded plots as he walked into the urban mess that was Cagliari, all of them defended by kids with guns, or ancient automatic laser systems powered by the sun. He carried a white handkerchief, prominently displayed.

The nexus in Cagliari was not entirely defunct. Proximity to Africa meant a low level of sophistication. Now wearing spex and a wristband, Dirk found a chianti bar, sitting down to reactivate a few of his nexus accounts.

Not good. Two had been hacked some months back: empty. But his Tokyo account held good, as did his Singapore account. He still owned funds.

In his spex a whirl of rainbow mist span into view, as the nexus, reacquainting itself with him following the cash transfers, updated his data incarnation. He smiled to himself. Lacking Hound's sophistication, his nexus doppelgänger was almost ninety eight percent true. Sure, he was known the world over as an interface specialist, but his disappearance into the AIteam had left a void that no journos seemed concerned enough about to investigate. Nonetheless, he did a self-search. Always wise to. An hour later he had all the articles labelled and summarised. Seemed his enigmatic departure into "obscurity" was not deemed important enough to scrutinise.

Good. For the nexus was *heavy*. It bore down on humanity, never sleeping, spying into every crevice – no respecter of privacy, which was a ridiculous, old-fashioned concept anyway. But Dirk liked privacy. Privacy allowed him the space and time to remind himself who he really was. And that was one of the attractions of shattered Europe now he was no longer with Leonora.

And so... where next? How to close in on his new goal?

He decided to treat himself to a small cash infusion. Outside the chianti bar, the young woman at a mobile credo peered over the armed brutes standing around her when he proffered a duocard with his photo on it.

"Real?" she asked.

"Retinascan me," Dirk responded with a shrug.

She did. The credo soft beeped, "True."

The young woman sneered, as if disappointed with this result. Probably she had hoped for a crim, and some bloody action. Instead Dirk reached over the rifles to take his cash with an orange grin and a, "Thank you lady."

He prepaid for a room at the chianti bar – formerly its attic. Ghosts of old pipework and electricity conduits marked the wall where nobody had bothered to paint over the rips and crumbling masonry. But it was cheap.

He lay back on the remains of the mattress, which had been stuffed with hay to make it useable. He decided to stay here for a week at least. Vanishing was a relative term. He could not vanish completely, but he could make himself so unremarkable to the nexus that it reduced his significance level in response. He was hoping for a z rating.

Reducing significance level was something of an art, and most modern youth could not do it, their lives so intertwined with the nexus that any lessening of attention from it was experienced by them as an insult to their name. The Japanese had initiated the takeover of the internet by the nexus in 2080 – any kid aged about fourteen or less was a child of augmented reality, half real, half virtual. But Dirk, almost forty, remembered what it was like to walk solo. *Nakedness is a virtue,* the wise ones used to say.

He checked his sig level: j. That was pretty high, and like as not due to his fame before vanishing into the AIteam. Well, that j needed to reduce to at least a t.

He looked at himself in a mirror. First he needed to amend his appearance.

He walked out into town. At a barbers he had his afro shaved off – this the first time ever. He had his stubble shaved too, but left a moustache and an under-lip tuft. He got his ears pierced and had a couple of red baubles put in – also a first. He smiled at his reflection. The nexus didn't like it when you did things first time. It didn't like novelty in human beings.

Above all, he needed to get his teeth cleaned. Giving up smokes was not an option, but maybe a dental once-over...

It turned out to be impossible. Teeth too far gone. On a whim he had them all taken out and pearly white falsies put in. Now he looked like some kinda last century soul warrior. All he needed was shiny silver trousers and a Fender Precision bass for the transformation to be complete. Hah! Maybe he'd do that.

He travelled easy all the way to Siniscóla on the east coast of Sardinia. There were no solcars, soltrucks or solbuses, but a few of the more enterprising locals had made battery powered rickshaws using old NATO army equipment, and these were on hire to those with money. Dirk had money – enough to spend on luxuries like travel. But he did not want to stand out as rich, so he packed his good clothes away, nabbed damaged garments from dumpsters, used basic needle skills to repair them, and wore those. He described himself as a beggar on his last pilgrimage.

"Where to, sir?" asked the ten year old girl driving the electric bike at the front of her rickshaw.

"Eventually, Livorno," he replied.

"What's there?"

Dirk had not considered the possibility of this question being asked. "Chocolate," he said.

"Is it sacred chocolate, sir?"

"It better be, da price you charging me. Just get me safe to Siniscóla."

From Siniscóla he gatecrashed a party ferry on its way to the Isle of Elba. The super-wealthy brats aboard were all off their faces on modded DMT, only the ferry captain alert, and it was easy enough to hide in the life-raft tied to the stern of the boat. From Elba he took a commercial fishing trawler on to Livorno, paying the ancient captain in real coins.

Livorno, however, was far too dangerous to enter. A large-scale crim war raged between two sides, the majority of the population hiding out in the country. Small arms fire punctured the quiet of the night, and every so often ordnance would go off: an orange flash, then clouds of smoke turned milky grey by moonlight. Dirk walked forty kilometres around the city, returning to the coastal road at Viaréggio.

A kilometre outside Viaréggio he met up with a fellow hiker. At once suspicious, he appraised the fellow: Oriental, ragged, dirty. Well, the raggedness and the dirt was easily applied; he himself had used that trick. But if this was one of Aritomo Ichikawa's team, no way would he display such a racial origin.

Dirk grunted, unhappy with the company – they were walking in the same direction. "Where you headed?" he asked.

"Monaco."

Again Dirk grunted. He had considered travelling there. Monaco retained a hint of its previous glamour, like an anti-pimple on scarred, dying European skin. "Not me," he said. "What's your story?"

"Huh, married an Italian girl twenty years ago. Tried local business. Failed. Got a young woman pregnant. Bad shit."

The man spoke with a slight Italian accent, but that too could be faked. Dirk cursed under his breath. Part of the lure of Europe was not having to worry about situations like this. "I dangerous," he told the Oriental. "Thrown out for knife attacks. Da worst, you know?"

The Oriental laughed. "Me too, brother."

Dirk shrugged. "What your name?"

"Luigi."

"No. Your *real* name."

"My real name *is* Luigi. I was born in Turin."

Dirk nodded again, dissatisfied. "I Giovanni," he said.

Luigi chuckled. "Sure you are!"

"What dat mean?"

"Don't care what your real name is, bro', so long as we protect each other on the road. You don't hike Italy without risk, huh?"

Dirk nodded. "Dat da truth, I guess."

They walked on in silence. Dirk began to relax. It was unlikely that already agents of his enemies had located him.

At La Spézia they halted for a day. The town was depopulated to the extent that its central urbs were ivy-covered, the demesne of goats and wild dogs, a small number of local residents living within stockades in which they had built new dwellings. Cats sat atop poles, as if guarding the place. One, Dirk noticed, was a Nippandroid go-to, made with polymers and fake fur. A real guard cat.

"Move on?" he asked Luigi.

The Oriental hesitated, then shrugged. "Hungry," he said. "We've not got much food left, have we? What d'you think?"

"Move on," Dirk replied. "Genoa a hundred kilometre away."

"Huh, but that could be a nasty place."

"Could be. Worth investigating though."

Luigi shrugged. "Okay. You win."

They continued walking the ruined, car-free road. They spoke of their pasts, their loves and their families, their careers. Luigi told Dirk he had been in the olives business, ruined only by the desperate push to permaculture initiated by the post-oil economic decline of the Western world. When people started growing their own, he was out of a job. That was when his troubles began, he said. His wife left him.

Dirk shrugged. No small number of women had left him over the years.

When they reached Genoa they found a confused situation. A small number of enlightened authorities had tried to reboot the city from one of its coastside suburbs, but they were fighting a losing battle. People wanted the old world back, but they were too traumatised to realise it had gone forever, so talk of new dreams and new principles fell on deaf ears.

The two men took a pair of rooms in the barn of a local wine merchant. It was quite cosy. A local prostitute and two peripatetic tech-dealers occupied the other rooms. Dirk ignored the pro and refused to deal with the metal merchants.

Luigi took his leave next morning. The pair shook hands English style. Luigi gave Dirk a bottle of mezcal, con gusano, while in return Dirk gave Luigi a book about gardening with herbs.

The coastal towns to the west of Genoa were in a comparatively good state; little looting, few private domains, a modicum of gunfire after dusk. Savona had even managed to sustain a small police force.

In San Remo the pleasures of the flesh became too tempting. In a local hostelry, with a dark-eyed local pro, he shared the bottle of mezcal, handing over half her fee with a grin. "Other half after I test da quality of da goods," he said.

The pro shrugged, then smiled.

As dawn broke, Dirk woke up. The pro lay at his side, drool escaping from the side of her mouth. He tapped her chin so her mouth closed, then got up to make coffee and think about breakfast calories; he felt sure he wasn't eating enough. The pro woke up a few minutes later.

They smiled at one another. Dirk felt he had a hint now of what life might be like for solos. Carefree, albeit dark and dangerous.

The pro clasped her head between her delicate hands.

"Hangover?" Dirk asked.

She nodded, then glanced at the empty bottle. Then she pointed at it. "Where's the worm?"

Dirk looked. The bottle was empty. No moth larva.

At once his skin went cold. He stared, then leaped over to the table on which the bottle stood. No worm!

The pro stared at him. "What's the matter?"

Dirk raised the bottle. "Dis a gift from... aagh! Who?"

The pro frowned. "A friend?"

Dirk ignored her. He might have only seconds remaining. He dropped to his knees and scoured the floor around the table; then, seeing nothing, he took a mirror, in order to shine orange sunlight over the dusty floorboards. There – a hint of a trail, like those made by slugs. That larva had not been dead. It had not been *organic.*

He followed the trail. It led to a cobweb-strewn corner. Beneath dusty old webs and clumps of human hair he found the larva.

With expert care he lifted it on a sheet of paper, then carried it to the window sill. The pro, scared, sat beside him, stroking his arm and saying, "Mezcal make you paranoid?"

He shook his head. "I not nobody," he said. "Luigi not Italian."

"Who's Luigi?"

"Scum liar from Japan."

The pro yawned. "Ooh, baby. You've got a bad head on you this morning."

Dirk grimaced. "On contrary," he said. "I got lucky. Thank *you*."

From his pack he took out a stereoscopic magnifying glass, that he used for large scale interface analysis. At once he saw that the larva was a dense polymer sheath for the real mezcal worm, which was some kind of nexus bug. That bug was gone: sheath empty. It would be tiny: it could be anywhere on him.

"See you," he said, handing over the second half of the payment. "Nice time."

"Tonight, yes?"

"Off to Monaco. Got to hurry."

The pro shrugged, smiled, then blew him a kiss. "Bye."

Dirk returned to surveying his room. With the exception of his duocard, metal coins and anything else that could not be burrowed into, every single item he owned would now have to be jettisoned. He glanced outside. It was warm already. In his pack there lay a pair of sterilised swimming trunks sealed in a heavy duty plastic vac-pack. The worm could not be in there.

But first he had to shower. Thank goodness he'd shaved off the Afro! That would have been destination number one for the nexus bug. They loved big hair – they were the e-lice of the modern world, very hard to spot.

He showered, cleaned every orifice, shaved off his pubes and armpit hair, then hurried out into the room again. On an empty sideboard lay his duocard and coins. He took them in one hand. In the other hand he picked up the vac-pack, which he washed, just in case the bug was super-disguised on its surface. He took a deep breath. Everything else was potentially a bug carrier, not least his clothes. But all being well he could now certify himself and everything he carried bug-free. But he was naked. Could be tricky.

Luckily his room was on the ground floor of the hostelry. He jumped out through a window, landing in a border of rosemary and wild flowers. Unpacking the trunks, he put them on, then ran around to the hostelry owner's chalet, hammering on the door.

The old man frowned at him, half asleep. "Swimming?" he asked.

Dirk handed over the night's fee. "In a hurry," he said. "Low tide."

"Foreign psycho! Get outa my place!"

Dirk ran off, the path behind him hung heavy with dust his feet kicked up. Then he was on the main road: safe, much poorer, barefoot and in his trunks. But safe.

Monaco called. He would need *proper* security while he attended to his goal.

Monte Carlo was a fairground of hallucination. There were no borders – Dirk walked into Monaco unmolested, dressed in the simple cloth suit and leather loafers he bought at a fishing village back along the main road. The place was alive with cams however, because the pseudo-Grimaldi family that owned the principality were obsessed with keeping the past as the past had been. Monaco was both cash machine and open-air museum.

Dirk checked his funds. It was deemed unwise to amalgamate accounts – nexus hackers were ten a euro – but he was tempted. He had kept his Tokyo and Singapore accounts hack free over the years, but his other thirteen accounts were less secure. Now he was back in the semi-civilised world again he needed to plug all loopholes, all hack points, all weaknesses. If he wanted to get in with a new crowd he had to take security seriously.

In the end he amalgamated ten of the accounts into one new Japanese account, that he paid cyber-security to protect. The account contained half his savings, and would act as funds for a rainy day.

But now he needed time and space to research. In a back alley he found a cheap boarding house. He checked it out through the nexus. The resident reports were genuine, the reviews modest, some good, some bad, but there was no hint of criminality. The owner had pets – always a bonus. Nobody could afford to bother with fripperies like pets if they were bent or in hock to organised crims. Least of all in Monaco.

He used cash to pay for a week's lodging. He took the time and trouble to befriend the Senegalese owner, discovering a shared love of soca music and the mellifluous ripple of the Malian kora. He relaxed. The place was okay. Genuine. A bug-run around his room showed only the standard corridor cam running anthropo-software and a kid's long-distance spy microphone, that, judging by its condition, had been accidentally left behind in the shower cubicle years ago. He stamped it beneath his shoe heel anyway, just in case.

His significance level was down to p. He grinned. He was getting less important by the day.

All the new tech he had bought since running in his swimming trunks from the Italian hostelry was certified glitch-free. That had cost him, but it was essential security. One night he fired the whole lot up: spex, wristbands, back-up mem and all.

It worked. He could be a navigator of the nexus now, in as much safety as was possible for a semi-secure interface specialist.

Aritomo was never far from his thoughts, though. Aritomo would want Manfred and Leonora back *bad.* He, the famous Dirk Ngma, was now in all probability a known associate of Leonora; that must be the message of the appearance of Tsuneko June in Malta. But Dirk did not operate at the level of Hound, so he was limited to his true identity and a sheaf of virtual tricks he'd picked up over the years.

Yet there was one massive ace he carried up his sleeve. He grasped the difference between the AIteam and the BIteam. *He* knew what to look for amidst the vast, interminable, perpetual roil of the nexus. Aritomo might not know.

He took a deep breath. Manfred Klee was mega-intelligent and would employ the best he could get in security. The BIteam would be concealed with genius level skill...

So the week passed. Nothing. He designed software programs made to seek certain patterns, but they crashed and burned.

He paid for a second week at the boarding house. After a couple of days suffering from stress headaches he took a day out to play volleyball on the nearest beach, then go to a Senegalese night club to watch a scion of Diabaté play the kora. He ate Rajastan curry and drank real French mineral water. He relaxed again.

The problem was the sheer scale of the nexus. There were ten billion people in the world, a huge proportion of them children. It was children who stuffed the nexus with activity, their whole lives from dawn to dusk to dawn lived referring to the nexus. It was the internet's "social media" taken to its logical extreme. You did not interact with the nexus if you were fourteen or less – you drowned in it, yet somehow remained alive.

Dirk began to freak out. He had banked a lot on his new goal. It was his new raison d'etre.

The Senegalese boarding house owner counselled calm. "What will be will be, Mr Ngma."

"I need more!"

"Less is more. Seek wisdom, not intelligence."

Dirk sighed, sipping at his smart Martini. "What *is* wisdom?"

"Information is to intelligence as intelligence is to wisdom."

The remark, casually uttered, made Dirk think. Artificial intelligence was the game he was in. Should he in fact be looking for artificial wisdom?

He shook his head. "I need to look for kinda artificial naiveté," he said. "You may be on to something. Yeah... da naïve view of da baby, da toddler."

"Kids all love a good toy, a good game. They play a *lot*."

Dirk nodded. So they did. He had no kids himself, but he'd encountered enough.

Yet the new ploy failed. The task was too big, like looking for a needle in a million haystacks. Too much nexus glare burned his eyes, too much noise deafened him. The truth was out there, but everyone around him was shouting nonsense.

CHAPTER 15

The snow-muffled mountain slopes owned by Ichikawa Laboratories groaned and whistled in response to the wind that blew across them. Autumn arrived, and it was cold.

In his glass dome living quarters at the summit of the laboratory complex, Aritomo poured Scottish whisky: two glasses, one for him, one for his nexus manager Ikuo Amano.

"We must think like Westerners," Aritomo said. "It is the only way to catch them."

"Must we?" Ikuo replied.

Aritomo remained silent for a while. Thinking like a Westerner was difficult. In Japan, *to think* meant *to arrive at a solution which may be shared with others.*

At length he said, "Despite the collapse of their economic culture, they remain individuals, with all an individual's problems. They are almost incapable of banding together for the common good. Thus the nexus interacts with them as individuals, bound far more loosely than are we. They have little notion of conformity – it is, as they say, much like herding cats."

"Then I must seek isolated pimples of suspicious behaviour."

"You must first focus on the eastern coast of America. Philadelphia was where Manfred Klee lived."

"Do you believe he lives there now?" Ikuo asked.

"No. But I believe he will wish to remain in America."

"Then I must search both coasts of the continent."

Aritomo hesitated again. "Our computers run proprietary software."

"The best in the world, Mr Ichikawa!"

"It is not good enough now to be the best. Though it make us uneasy, we must introduce novelty into the situation."

Ikuo did not look pleased. "How?"

"We will have to employ a foreigner."

Now Ikuo appeared shocked. "An American?"

"There are no Americans worth dealing with. A Chinese or Korean will be pointless. No, it must be a European."

"You have an individual in mind?"

Aritomo replied, "I had hoped eventually to utilise Tsuneko June, but she has vanished into the rot at the heart of England. No... there are other possibilities."

"I do not like the path this conversation is taking."

"Nor I. But giri *makes* me look outside of Japan for a solution. I did not found this laboratory for it to fail. The corporation will make us all great, then Japan also."

"Tsuneko June retains the patent rights to biograins. We must have them."

"Eventually we will. What is more important at the moment is that she alone retains them, not sells them to a corporation. But she is too young and naïve yet to grasp the commercial implications of her work, so she will hold on to what she has. We will obtain the biograin patents from her for our own exclusive use in due course."

"You see all ends, Mr Ichikawa."

"No. Neither does the nexus see all ends. That is why novelty is required."

Ikuo said nothing.

"There is a man... a native of Italy... you will find him."

"What is his name?" asked Ikuo.

"Soji Agata."

"He is Japanese?"

"Half Japanese," Aritomo replied, "though he looks less Italian. He lives in Genoa City with his twin brother. Find him, communicate with him, offer him the position we wish him to take up."

"And if he says no?"

"The terms you will devise will ensure he says yes."

"Indeed, Mr Ichikawa. Now, what of the AIteam?"

Aritomo pondered this question for some minutes. He poured more whisky, then thought further. As an antique French grandfather clock struck nine he said, "I do not doubt that you are correct to say they have left Malta for North Africa. This... unusual trace you describe in the Tunisian-area nexus is promising. But there is doubt about what they have created. Therefore, focus not on the individuals of the AIteam but on what they have built."

"But we do not know what they have built."

"We know they use the latest quantum technology. We know they have built only one creation. Run a simulation to decide what nexus outcomes may occur. Use our software – nothing external. In this instance, I want to follow *my* ideas."

"They will do everything they can to conceal the power of their device."

"They may, but they cannot do everything, since that is impossible. I believe the character of the creation will leak out into the nexus. The nexus will then identify and interact with it. Remember, it is difficult to grasp the strangeness of Westerners since they are so random, so bizarre. Therefore we will not seek those things. We will seek manifestations of power alone."

"Power?"

Aritomo nodded. "What would you do if you felt unlimited power inside you? Ignore it?"

"No, Mr Ichikawa!"

"The creation itself will reveal where it is. The human beings around it are nugatory – even Leonora, who has long since been bereft of relevant ideas."

CHAPTER 16

Pouncey prepared an elaborate plan to cover them while they drove the soltruck into the least damaged of the Haemorrhage Apts – the block with the ramp access underground and local cover in the form of birch and lime trees, not to mention huge shields of ivy. Another advantage – it was tipping with rain. Almost nobody on the streets.

From a nearby lo-market she bought a couple of detonators. From a different lo-market she bought an ex-army mine, which she crimped so that it would blow on a time fuse. Then she set up the mine in a local side-street and the detonators nearby. Everything had to be timed to perfection, but this was a deal she had made before; explosives and swift action.

03:45. Nobody in sight – at least, on the street. Pouncey signalled for the detonators to blow two streets down. She left it five minutes, saw two street bums running to see what the trouble was.

Then the main blast – four streets away. She waited five seconds. Nobody appeared. She drove the soltruck into the street off which the ramp led. Manfred leaped out to raise the section of greenery Pouncey had cut loose, then she drove in, down the ramp, Manfred following. Then they all got out of the soltruck to listen.

No pursuit, it seemed. No voices. Just rain beating down on concrete.

"Okay," she told Manfred and Joanna, "you two get some sleep. I'll be on look-out for the rest of the night. If anyone saw us drive in they'll come explorin', but I'll catch 'em. If not, we're safe anyway."

"But the vehicle ramp," Joanna said. "We will have to walk up and down it to get into the city—"

"Nah!" Pouncey said, leading them to the remains of a lift shaft. "I'll rig up a rope ladder here. I already scouted out a concealed exit on the ground floor – upstairs, like. It's covered by ivy and only overlooked by one dead apartment block. We're as safe as I can make us."

"Will we be able to stay here?" Manfred asked. "No more Hyperlinked?"

Pouncey shrugged. "Fingers crossed."

Manfred turned to survey the car basement. "So," he said, "this'll be our home. Bit of a wreck."

Pouncey shook her head. "I'll do a full reccie of the apartments upstairs, find some nice ones. First thing to do is set up the soltruck and ramp for a quick escape."

"You'll point the truck at the ramp?"

Pouncey nodded. "I'll park it about twenty metres away. I'll set up a screen so the bis don't walk out. But listen... I was thinkin'..."

Manfred turned to look at her. He raised his eyebrows. "Yeah?"

"You know that whistlin' trick you got the bis to learn? Well, most of 'em learned... I think we could take that a stage further."

"How so?"

"Treat 'em like kids. Give 'em rules. How about I find us some coloured ribbon, then we stick it to the walls, and, most important, across the ramp. Then try and train the bis not to cross the ribbon – like police tape, you know?"

Manfred nodded. "Damn good idea. Go for it."

Pouncey smiled. "And I got more."

"Covering them in the nexus?" Manfred asked.

"Yep. That's our big unknown. For a while the sheer amount of info in the local nexus'll cover us, but Aritomo will punch through that eventually. There's a school nearby, right? I'm gonna set up a fake extra class of eight kids – special needs, you see? Give all these kids – our bis – proper ID. Bed the whole thing down into the nexus over a week or so. Don't think even Aritomo Ichikawa will spot that one."

Manfred nodded. "Above all, he'll be looking for patterns. He knows something of my style, possibly he knows how and why I'm different to the AIteam. But, yeah… that's a good one. Do it."

"Will do, boss."

"But Pouncey?"

"Yep?"

Manfred hesitated. "Don't have all the fake kids arrive at school on the same day."

"I already thought of that."

He grinned. "Just checking."

It was noon. Quite warm. Manfred placed his hands on his hips and surveyed his work. A strip of rainbow ribbon glued to the walls surrounded the bay in which they all stood: the three of them, the eight bis. The soltruck was in position, an awning attached to its rear for the bis to make a home in.

Manfred glanced at Joanna. "Reckon they'll cross the tape?"

Joanna shrugged. "Not if we train them not to."

Manfred shook his head. "Kids is wrong. On this score, we gotta treat them like dogs. Trainable, obedient."

Joanna managed the ghost of a smile. "You are some father, eh?"

"Yeah. I am."

So they watched while the uncaged bis explored their environment. Manfred went through the act of crossing the tape, allowing Joanna to pull him back. The bis observed. Then Manfred told Pouncey to cross the tape – he pulled her back. When she crossed over a second time, he asked Joanna to pull her back. An hour later, as expected, Orange, Violet and Blue approached the tape at the ramp; slow and deliberate movements, he noticed. Manfred inched closer. When Orange stepped over the tape he jumped forward, grabbed the bi and lifted it back over the tape. Blue tried to cross the tape: Manfred lifted it back. The trio looked at one another for a few moments, then walked away.

"I think we may have sorted that problem," said Manfred.

"I'll keep watch anyway," Pouncey said. "Gonna make a wood barrier on the ramp that the soltruck could smash through in an emergency."

"Another line of defence."

"Another barrier for the bis. They'll get the message."

The day passed. Pouncey left them, clambering up the lift shaft using the rusting metal framework. She returned a couple of hours later with food, water and a solar heater.

"Not much use in this gloom," Manfred said.

"I'll rig it upstairs. We won't be down here for long."

Leaving Joanna to watch the bis, Manfred accompanied Pouncey into the apartment block. The upper levels were worst damaged – by ivy, by weathering, by decay – and here they stumbled across a few human skeletons. Also dogs and cats, and what looked like a horse skull. But lower down the damage was less, and three apartments, in the lee of the wind and rain, were passable. There was no power and the wallpaper was a mush of damp and fungus – mushrooms grew in the remains of the shower cubicle – but Pouncey thought they could make a home of them.

"Take some time to clear it though," she mused. "I'll have to buy disinfectant, anti-fungals, maybe a heater. Place needs dryin' out, 'specially this linkin' corridor."

"But we could live here?"

"Aye. Reckon so."

"One for me and Jo, one for you."

"We'll split the bis? Half each?"

Manfred considered. "Best to, I suppose. In case of emergencies."

Pouncey turned to face him. "I'll do my best, you know I will, but there's always the hint of a chance, 'cos no security's perfect. You have to aim for ninety nine point nine recurrin'."

"Yeah."

"Which I do. But this is different to Philly. Aritomo guessed we were there."

Manfred snorted. "It's not Aritomo I'm worried about, it's his computers."

Pouncey shrugged. "Fair point. I'll let you know if I get an attack of the itchy fingers."

"You do that. And if I tell you not to, ignore me."

"You betcha."

A week passed. The class of kids appeared at school. Pouncey remarked that the school didn't know about this class because she'd linked it with school databases through the canteen software alone. If one of the lunch ladies noticed anything odd – extra IDs, extra mouths to feed – well, that would like as not be ignored. The school had five hundred on its roster, with half a dozen leaving every week and half a dozen joining. But that one link was all Pouncey needed to ghost extra data into the school: eight new kids, special needs, not in every day... here a d.o.b. list, here their parents, here their photos (skimmed from a database of dead kids in New York). Layer upon layer of concealment, making any bi activity in the nexus look natural. Pouncey explained that she'd given the kids nicknames, so she'd know which kid covered which bi: Orange was ginger haired, Red had Native American heritage, and so on. More importantly, the nexus itself would attach these eight kid labels to patterns of activity linked to any of the bis – following Pouncey's lead. It would over time corral info patterns and attach IDs to them, like it did with every human being in the world. Problem solved. The only difference here was that the nexus didn't realise the bis weren't human.

"Nicely camouflaged," Manfred said, impressed.

Pouncey nodded. "Thanks. I'll be updatin' our kids every other day – inventin' problems, scams, parental issues. They're special needs, after all. A month on, it'll all look so normal not even Aritomo's best computer'll spot any unusual patterns."

"Amen to that," said Manfred. He glanced at the nearer bis. If they were interfacing with the nexus, as they suspected, that infantile, unfocussed, weird activity would be registered as kids' stuff. It happened all over the world, and the nexus recognised it, labelling it *infantile/juvenile*.

"We can use patterns noticed by the nexus to probe the bis," he said.

"Indigo we know is hitched up to the nexus," Pouncey replied. "The nexus'll do most of our work for us. I'm watchin' Kid Indigo in particular."

Manfred nodded. He had already tried to analyse Indigo's burgeoning nexus traces, but they made no sense.

He began to relax after a second week in which nothing bad happened. None of the local bums got wise to their hideout, the bis behaved and the fake class worked like a dream.

And then, late one afternoon, walking the street leading down to the apartment block, he noticed a man leaning against a tree.

The man noticed him.

Manfred tried not to stop, change the pace of step, *clock* the man, but it was impossible. He approached, looking down at the grease-spattered pavement. The man stepped out and said, "Good evening, Mr Klee. Not to worry. You safe."

Manfred halted, stunned. He could not breathe.

"Dere much to speak of," the man added.

Manfred recognised the face, the accent. This man was not in disguise. "You know me?" he whispered.

"You recognise me, surely?" came the reply.

The man was black, middle aged, weatherbeaten, shaven head. He wore a jet black greatcoat and poly trousers. When he grinned, his teeth gleamed white.

A warning went off in Manfred's mind. "Not..."

"Yes. Dirk."

Manfred span around, ready for attack, for men approaching, for the sight of a rifle.

Dirk placed a hand on his arm. "I been looking for you. You safe."

"Safe?"

"Sure. I tell you all about it. Dere a lot to speak, you know?"

"But... we're... visible in the nexus?"

"The BIteam? Sorta. I explain how to make better. And you might want my services. Interfaces?"

Manfred nodded. He felt numb. Interfaces, yes – he had wanted Dirk rather than Tsuneko when he put the BIteam together. Had the appearance of this man averted a disaster?

"Dirk, come with me," he said. "Quickly! I can see you're on our side."

"One hundred percent," Dirk replied.

They hurried down to the concealed entrance, then paused at the lift shaft inside the building, where Pouncey's rope ladder swung. "She'll shoot you if she sees you," he said.

"Tell her first."

Manfred nodded. He still felt numb. Kneeling down, he called out, "Pouncey? You hear me?"

No reply.

"Call again," Dirk advised.

"Pouncey! Get yourself here. Damn quick!"

There came the sound of rustling below, and Manfred saw Orange and Blue. Then Pouncey's face appeared. "What's up?" she asked.

Manfred said, "Don't panic. *Don't* shoot."

Pouncey raised her rifle, aiming it at him. "Why not?"

"We got company – good company. It's okay. I'm not hostage – no guns. It's Dirk!"

"Dirk?"

From behind him, Dirk said, "Mr Ngma, interface specialist. I tell you how to improve nexus security – freebie. It no problem."

Pouncey looked confused. "I know, I know," Manfred said, "but for god's sake Pouncey, don't *shoot*."

Joanna appeared. "Dirk Ngma?"

"That you, Joanna?" Dirk said, leaning over the lift shaft.

Pouncey aimed her rifle at him. "Don't shoot!" Manfred screeched.

"Shhh!" Pouncey said. "I wasn't gonna. Just get the hell down here."

They descended. Pouncey retreated and aimed her rifle at Dirk. "You've got some explainin' to do," she said.

Dirk spread his hands wide, then raised his arms in mock surrender. "I know you scared. Me too, coming here. It some deal."

"You spotted us in the nexus?" Joanna asked. She looked horrified.

"I spot da children."

Manfred glanced at Pouncey, then at Joanna. "Okay," he said, "panic over, we all sit down, fix tea or coffee, put down the guns. Shit, if Dirk knows about the bis, Aritomo might know."

"Dere little t'ing to tweak," Dirk said. "It no biggie."

"And then?"

Dirk grinned, pulled out a cheroot and lit it. "I interface man. AIteam not for me. Dere much to tell you. It amazing tale, you know?"

Manfred put his hands to the top of his head, leaned back and exhaled. He walked over to the stack of equipment by the soltruck, where lay a gas stove and a kettle. "Drink," he said. "C'mon, you lot, drinks! I'm desperate for caffeine."

They sat on the floor, Manfred with the two women to either side of him, Dirk facing them. Pouncey sat with her rifle on her lap.

Manfred cradled his mug in his hands, as if winter-cold. "Over to you," he told Dirk.

"Sure," Dirk said, lighting another cheroot. "But listen, I not harm you guys. Must emphasise dat. I leave AIteam, maybe join BIteam. If dere space for me."

"There may well be," Manfred said, with exaggerated feeling. He pointed at the bis, clustered nearby, all watching, apart from Grey who sat by the ramp. "We can't get these things to understand English. And we *need* to speak to them soon."

Dirk grinned. "Dis how I spot you."

"*How?*" Manfred asked.

"See, I know da score with da BIteam. I know how differ from your ex. Da AIteam, dey create one intelligence, make best computer dey can. At first, I go with dat. It make sense. But den, t'ings, hmmm, dey change. We in Africa, chased by da Ichikawa guy, apparently. I see Zeug – he Leonora's artificial intelligence – I watch him go rogue. He like autistic superman. He got no society."

"You mean, society like the bis?"

"Yes! Da beautiful intelligence. I *see* dat. I like dat notion. Zeug go mental 'cos he got no brothers, sisters. Dat Leonora's big mistake."

"Then," Manfred said, "you spotted the bi society in the nexus?"

"First, I consider options. I know da score of BIteam – make society of intelligences, not just da one. Make dem conscious, like we got conscious. So dis what I look for in da nexus. Society of new entities."

"But *how?* There are billions of new small societies all over the world, thousands of kids born every minute. We could've been anywhere-"

"Yes, it *very* difficult. Take some time. I smoke many smokes! Much Diabaté kora music, ha ha!"

Manfred waved his right hand in a circle. "Then…?"

"I begin to realise, look for weird kid behaviour. Maybe language-free. Maybe special language. Like kid secret language dat nobody else understand. I guess you in America from da underground news. Sixty two percent of rumours place you on da East Coast. Starting point, see?"

"Go on…"

"I do over da entire East Coast, but nothing make me sit up. I get depress. I alone, and sometime bored. I got nobody to talk to about mind stuff."

Manfred laughed. "You're in damn good company here."

"I know! Very attractive to interface guy. So… da t'ing is, I begin scouring da West Coast. Not with much hope, though, eh?"

Manfred nodded. "And…?"

"Ha! You so impatient, Mr Klee! Okay, I tell you. One day I notice school with many kids. It random spot – not obvious. Getting desperate, truth to tell. Many smokes in da ashtray. I analyse dis school, but nothing stand out. Den I notice one class, dey special need. No speaks, I notice, no writes. Like a class of feral kids – raised by wolves, maybe? You get?"

"I get," Manfred confirmed.

"Den I analyse further. Kids quite recent to school. No writes, yes – but no speech therapist, no writing guru, in dat class. Why not?"

Manfred felt his skin turn cold. Such an obvious mistake; yet so easy to make. He turned to Pouncey and said, "No blame. Not your fault."

Pouncey shrugged.

At once Dirk sat up and waved his cheroot in Pouncey's direction. "I gotta say, it brilliant deception. Genius level. I only notice 'cos I specifically go for kids with total language issues."

Pouncey sagged. "Yep. My bad."

Manfred patted her on the shoulder. "Hey! No problem, I mean that."

"Thanks."

Dirk continued, "Once I spot dis, I get excited. Chance in a million for me. For da Ichikawa computer, chance in a trillion. Dey not know complex mind stuff, like me. Dey search America at random, see?"

Manfred nodded. "But given enough time, Dirk…"

"Sure! But we fix da kid language issue. Pouncey make fake handwrites. You add fake speech therapist. It cover da problem real nice."

Manfred clicked his fingers at Pouncey. "Start now."

Pouncey leaped to her feet, the rifle clattering to the floor. "Will do."

Joanna moved forward, so that she sat between Manfred and Dirk. She said, "We have got one bi that is blind, Dirk. We have hypothesised that it is much more active in the nexus than the others, probably as a kind of compensatory mechanism. Did you spot one child who appeared more nexus savvy than the rest?"

"Oh, sure – nickname Tuareg."

Manfred nodded. "Tuareg tribe in the Sahara, indigo robes."

Dirk nodded back, grinning. "But *none* speak English. I help you with dat!"

Manfred felt his heart race. He took a few shallow breaths. "Really?"

"Sure. But dere major problem. We not tamper with da bis now. Dey evolving heuristically, becoming individuals. Tamper, dat like cut up kid's brain – not cool. So I make interface."

"How, Dirk?" Manfred asked. "This is urgent. If we don't speak to them on higher, abstract levels soon, they'll give us away. At the moment they're like dogs, kids – we train them in simple stuff. But we need to tell Indigo about the dangers of giving us away to Aritomo."

"Exactly. I do dat. You trust me good."

"Yeah! Please. *Please* help."

"Okay." Dirk grinned. "Dis real good! I hope find you guys. Da AIteam, it not for me. I need stimulation. I need da challenge. I got dat here real fine. Many thanks."

Manfred sat back and sighed. "My pleasure. And welcome to Portland."

CHAPTER 17

The fake Zeug was taken down by the police. The real Zeug remained invisible.

At least, invisible to Hound, searching the North African nexus. "Man," he said, as the AI trio sat at the back of a faux-Berber caf, "this is *not* going to be easy."

"We didn't get into this for an easy life," said Leonora.

"No… sure we didn't. I was just saying."

"Why did the police bother with my fake Zeug?" Tsuneko asked.

"Well, there were no street cams," Hound replied, "so a satellite must've pinged Zeug after he ripped Yuri's head off, then passed on the description." He shrugged. "Didn't spot us. Man, we'd know by now."

"Why did Zeug rip Yuri's head off?" Tsuneko asked.

Hound laughed. "Heh! *You're watching me*, I told Zeug. He replied that he didn't like me, so I asked him straight out – why are you watching me? My master told me to, he said. That master was Yuri."

"Are you certain?" Leonora said.

Hound shook his head. "Nothing's ever certain in security. But, yeah, I *am* certain. Yuri was trying to direct the AIteam, ain't no doubt. Then he hit the big high wall that's Zeug. Ol' Dirk was right. Zeug is autistic–"

"Hound!" Leonora interrupted. "I said no–"

"Hey! Listen. I got my free speech. Man, you know the worst thing about Zeug? He knew he was good. He *knew* he was special. But he can't cope with us random, stupid fleshies, so he ran away." Hound paused, staring into the cloud-brushed sky. "We'll be looking for someone mad, someone paranoid, someone cruel. That's what you made, Leonora."

"I did not!" Leonora said.

Hound glanced at her. He knew when she was upset. She was not now. Yes, she knew what she'd done, so he had a duty to point out that she'd made a few mistakes...

"I'm sorry," he told her. "I don't want you to feel bad. Honest. But we gotta face facts. To find Zeug, we head for madness."

"I think your assessment is flawed," Leonora said, looking away and resettling her dress on her legs.

"Well, ma'am, with Yuri and Dirk gone it's only you and me that ever saw him. So I guess we'll agree to differ."

"Analysis is not your function here."

Hound glanced at Tsuneko, then shrugged.

Leonora scowled. "If you are trying to impress the new lady, you failed."

"I ain't. Man, like I said – we all got free speech."

Tsuneko leaned forward and said, "Either way, I'm not here to be impressed or unimpressed. *I've* got the biograins." She slapped a bio-drive on her belt. "On a standalone. Listen, I like your plan, Leonora. Can't we all get along? Can't we make something magical and new?"

"Oh, we get along well enough," Leonora said. "Hound's just staking his place out. He's telling you he's not stupid while I get the collateral damage."

"I knew that already," Tsuneko replied. She shrugged, pouring mint tea into all three of their cups. "Let's concentrate on Zeug. We've got to find him. We can't let the Africans get their hands on him."

Hound raised his eyebrows. "Why not?"

"I meant the local people. I'm assuming Zeug could be killed? Blown up? Hacked to pieces?"

"Stolen by Aritomo Ichikawa," Hound said. "That's the worst case scenario."

"Then what are we waiting for?"

Hound hesitated, then sighed. "Yeah. Good point. And we needed some new blood around here. Let's find a doss for the night, then I'll begin a new search."

Tsuneko faced Leonora across a table strewn with supper debris: breadcrumbs, green leaves, feta cheese and clear plastic cups of mint tea. A nexus radio blared out rai music mutated according to the 2077 Cairo Agreement, and this was a useful cover to their in-caf conversation.

Tsuneko said, "Am I welcome in the AIteam?"

Leonora smiled. "Don't take any notice of what Hound says, pay attention to what he does. If he did not like you, you would not be here. It is his job to be suspicious of you."

"I came here with sincere motives."

"I believe you," Leonora said. "You are a VIP in my book."

"The biograins?"

Leonora nodded. "Though how I integrate them into my scheme is a mystery."

"Biograins are still in the development stage. As yet, human brain biochemistry isn't quite sophisticated enough to cope with them. But that's the direction I want to go in – a seamless fusion of perception and virtuality inside our heads."

"One stage on from the nexus."

Tsuneko nodded. Leonora seemed to understand her. She said, "Spex and wristbands are all very well, but spex were introduced almost eighty years ago by Google. Their time has gone."

"But there does not seem to be any crossover between what you have invented and what I have invented."

"No…" Tsuneko mused. "D'you think you'll locate Zeug?"

"Hound will." Leonora sighed. "If he doesn't, Aritomo will. That man is like a cat hunting a bird. The bird rarely escapes."

Tsuneko nodded. With a grin she said, "A lot of cats wear bells on their collars so birds get a warning."

"The concept of a collar is alien to Aritomo. He is utterly focussed on himself – the ultimate narcissist. He believes the world exists in his image, or should do. He is ultra-patriotic and devoted to the nexus."

"Which was a Japanese invention."

Leonora nodded. "If I had known then what I know now…"

Tsuneko waited. When Leonora remained silent she said, "You wouldn't have worked for him?"

Leonora shook her head. "Nor Manfred. We didn't realise what he was like. He wooed us. He pretended interest in Western cultural mores. He promised to place the world at our feet." She laughed. "Yes, *his* world, in his image!"

"Then he will find Zeug?"

Leonora shrugged. "We have to get there first."

Tsuneko leaned forward, lowered her voice a little. "What if we attract Zeug to us? That's the other option, after all."

"How? We know nothing about what Zeug intends."

"Make a simulation of him, but make it different, so that Zeug's intrigued."

"Impossible," Leonora said. "We only made one quantum computer, into which we placed everything we knew. And Yuri is dead. He knew so much about the technicalities."

"Do you still retain the records of what you did in Malta?"

"Oh, yes, of course. Three back-ups exist, disguised as vault possessions of various museums around the world." Leonora smiled. "Hound calls that abstract art."

"Why?" Tsuneko asked.

"Making something incomprehensible out of figurative art. He prefers the latter. The point is, under all that cultural camouflage nobody will notice what the data really is."

Tsuneko nodded. "Then even though you destroyed everything in the Maltese cave we could make a *simulation*."

"It would be a pale imitation – no pun intended."

"That's all we need. We could use my biograins to make a nexus-ready super-intelligence, but instead of using a human template we use your Zeug template. I mean, it only has to look *approximately* like Zeug. Then we set it free and wait for Zeug to come running."

"All sorts of people could spot the fake Zeug. Aritomo."

"We'd spot Zeug from his nexus traces long before any actual meeting. Anyway, the fake would look inhuman, like some weird computer. There's millions of weird new computers in the world. Billions, probably. But Zeug will notice the particular characteristics of ours long before anybody else does. It'll be primed to attract him."

Leonora nodded, her gaze in some far-off mental corner. "It could work," she said. She picked up her standalone com, tapping in a code. "Tell Hound. I just called him on this com. He'll be skeptical, but you can ignore that."

Tsuneko took a deep breath. "Okay."

Leonora looked at her. "You'll need to convince me too. I will be at least as skeptical as he is."

Hound lay prone on a Z-bed, spex over his eyes, two microcables linking spex arms to the bone receivers drilled into his skull next to his ears – he couldn't afford to miss even a whisper from the nexus on this mission.

For a few days he'd been floating free, allowing the breezes, updrafts and occasional dust storms of the nexus to blow him around eastern Algeria. Not a sign of Zeug, but that was what he'd expected. The trace in the nexus caused by Zeug observing him was gone.

Hound grimaced to himself. He did not feel happy. Zeug, though a halfwit when it came to human affairs, was hyper intelligent when it came to the nonhuman equivalent. Zeug would know how to hide beneath multiple layers of nexus culture, he would grasp the importance of movement, change, mutation; and he'd understand the basics of nexus deletion. He'd not know what those nexus layers *meant*, but he'd know how to use them. It would be like a jackdaw gathering shiny metal, except in reverse: camouflage scraps, not tinfoil.

But Hound was the master of nexus deletion. They hadn't called him Goodman for nothing.

With Zeug's nexus trail blown to the winds, and his dream images camouflaged or – more likely – voluntarily halted, Hound took a different tack. Leonora had spent three percent of her entire cash hoard to create the biograin simulacrum of Zeug, which stood out now like a virtual lighthouse; at least, to those interested in bizarre new computers. It did not matter that local mash kids and nex-hack brats investigated it, tried to penetrate it – the idea was to make it visible to Zeug. Hound set it up in Algiers to be on the safe side though; well away from Annaba.

The idea was that Zeug and fake Zeug never met. Hound would spot Zeug long before that eventuality.

For some days the simulation ran in splendid isolation. A confederacy of local nex-hackers – average age, nine – made a cash offer on the simulation, which they wanted to take apart in order to work out what it was. A hundred kids were in on this deal, according to the message Hound intercepted. It made him feel sick. Childhood was an old fashioned concept it seemed. He rejected the deal and sent the confederacy on a wild goose chase along the virtual Silk Road – far, far away...

Then, circling like a vulture over that part of the nexus representing the desert to the west of Annaba, he spotted something.

At first he did not grasp what the source of the signal was. It was located in the heart of Bejaïa, a coastal city half way between Annaba and Algiers. It was registered as a charity, and yet from its heart the blandest, the most insignificant of breezes blew, along the line of least resistance between it and the fake Zeug.

Hound at first discounted it. The nexus was so vast an environment it contained a trillion tiny currents, representing the myriad of interactions between humans and humans, and humans and computers. This was nothing special.

Yet he found the combination odd: charity building, location near Annaba, line of least resistance. Also, the significance level of the signal was extremely low, much lower than, say, the financial transactions of the charity would be. Even the support comments, hate comments and spam on the charity's e-boards were more significant. That too-low level suggested a deliberate reduction in importance for the purposes of concealment.

And then there was the nature of the charity. It was the home of a local asylum.

Hound put maximum effort into disguising his appearance. He created a fake hang-gliding club to explain his apparent interest in virtual soaring. He gave himself a new ID, including appearance. He didn't bother with money accounts however, since he'd only be using his disguise for a timeblip: a hundred seconds, max.

From a Bejaïa home for the elderly he sent a query, using it as a tunnel into the charity records. He discovered that the source of the signal was a new resident.

Had to be Zeug!

In the real world, he grinned. This looked good.

He spent his final minute soaring over the image of the charity building as represented by the nexus. It was large, dusty, ramshackle, surrounded by farm animals – and some camels, he noted – that the charity employees used to supplement their meagre income.

The charity cared for insane locals, but there was a bit of a storm raging around the recent arrival. According to some of the more intelligible residents, this person was trying to take over the place.

They held another tête-à-tête in the mint tea caf. It was quiet, inconspicuous, and only a few hundred metres from the roadside dumpster park in which, disguised as plastics recyclers, they dossed. They took care not to order too much food on any one occasion, in case some smart kid spotted the mismatch between diet and domicile. Plenty of the local teen gangs made their profits on blackmail.

Tsuneko prepared herself for bad news. She was still a little surprised that Leonora had inducted her into the AIteam, and so cultivated a negative attitude to counter the feelings of optimism that threatened to well up. But the news was good.

Hound said, "I've done a featherweight scan of the whole charity. It was set up forty years ago by some local do-gooder. Man, not much by way of income, but also not much by way of outgoings. They don't pay rent f'rinstance."

"They own the building?"

"Yep. About thirty residents, mostly women. Seems men still believe women are the mad ones. It's a big building, though. Don't like that so much."

"How does that affect us?" Leonora asked.

"We'll have to go to Bejaïa ourselves. This can't be done nex style."

Tsuneko felt her heart sink. She had assumed that Hound would effect some miraculous scam over the nexus. "Why not?" she asked.

"Aritomo. Too risky."

"He is on to us?" Leonora asked.

"Sheesh, I wouldn't put it strong as that," Hound replied. "Let's say... he's not off us. He knows we're somewhere on the North Africa coast. He knows where the trail went dead – not so far east, I regret to say. Still... this whole section of the Med coast is a total mess because of the Euro refugee influx. Don't worry too much. We can hide in that mess."

"Which we are."

Hound nodded. "Which we certainly are. Also, don't forget – the fake Zeug could be spotted by one of Aritomo's spy computers. He knows the score. Therefore we go there in person and spring Zeug from the charity building. Man, when the nexus updates – well, that'll be when Aritomo might get to hear about us. But we'll be minutes, maybe hours gone. Vanished into the desert like... like..."

"A hatifa," said Leonora.

"A...?"

"A voice in the Sahara desert," Leonora said. "A lot of the local computers use that as an identity on which they ply the dunes of the nexus."

The caf owner walked up to them, pouring mint tea into the pewter autoserve. "Hawatif," he said, his yellow teeth showing as he grinned. "They seduce unwary traveller. They lie about fortress visible only by moonlight. It is the madness of the desert, mon ami. More vegetable stew? I add apricots."

"Uh… yep," Hound said. "Thanks."

Leonora glanced over her shoulder as the man strolled off. "He is safe?"

Hound nodded. "He checked out. Good guy, actually. Might have to ask him about boats to Bejaïa."

"Boats?" said Tsuneko.

Hounded nodded. "Speed essential. Man, the desert's too risky now, unless we wanna shout *here we are!* in big sand-buggy shaped letters."

Hound strolled along the Med coast. Rows of tents seemingly held upright by their own stench stretched as far as he could see. The nexus, being a Japanese invention, struggled with this nonconformist chaos; the world's many refugee camps were the slowest updated of all nexus objects. Hound loved it for that. He felt safe, invisible, cosseted by random human activity.

Ninety percent of refugee camps lay on coasts, because of the devastation caused to shoreside cities by sea level rise; the world was greenhousing with no apparent end in sight. The Annaba camp was no exception to this rule, the sea littered with plastics, rags, dead boats and shit. Even a few bodies. And it was a magnet for gulls. Gulls were doing especially well out of the concentrated human misery.

He gazed at the tall white hats of local mercantile elite: juveniles all. "Cheap black! Ketamineballs! Coke-on-a-stick!"

An old man in a grey Berber robe and lime green sandals approached him. For a few moments the two men appraised one another.

"You looking for someone, buddy?" Hound grunted, fingering his belt as if for a weapon.

"You travel, monsieur?"

Hound shrugged. "Maybe. West, not far. You splash?"

The old man grinned. "My yacht, s'asperger le visage d'eau."

"Man, you got a *yacht*? You like working in human sewers, eh?"

The old man shrugged, then grinned and spread his hands wide. "I make the money from the travels, ami. I go anywhere, west, east, even north."

"Sure you do. Listen… how much for a there-and-back to Bejaïa?"

"Much metal."

"Metal?" said Hound.

"No cash. No credit."

"Wasn't talking about *credit*," Hound said, adopting a mocking tone of voice.

"For obvious reasons I don't accept cash, ami. Pardon."

He turned away, but Hound reached out to grab his arm. "Listen, man. Give me a cash quote for three passengers. You know, just out of curiosity."

The old man glared at him. "You disrespect me."

"Do it."

The old man hesitated, then frowned. "Fifty."

Hound had known that the man would name a ludicrous price. "Five and you got yourself a deal," he replied.

The old man stared, and Hound wondered if he had offered too much. If he appeared to the old man as rich and stupid every crim in the neighbourhood would be on to him. "Five, monsieur? A joke."

"Five," Hound repeated.

"Ten."

"*Five.*"

The old man hesitated. Hound suppressed the grin that threatened to break out over his face.

"Oui, monsieur. Five it is then. In cash, up front."

Hound shook his head. "Two and a half when we get to Bejaïa, two and a half when we get back."

Now the old man looked angry. "So, you work in la comédie?"

Hound nodded. "I sure do."

"Very well." The old man pointed to a headland a kilometre away. "Be there at dawn tomorrow."

Hound nodded. "And who shall I tell my friends is taking us to Bejaïa?"

"They call me le Diable."

Hound made a hat-tipping gesture at the old man, a grin on his face. "Very funny, grandad. See you at sun up."

Hound watched as the old man walked away. When the old man vanished into tent city Hound made off the beach at speed, heading for the sand-covered alleys behind the refugee canteens, where for an hour he hid amongst huge piles of disinfected clothes. There was no sight of the old man, though, nor any cronies. He waited for another couple of hours, in case the old man decided that after all his passengers were rich and stupid – there could be any number of footpads working for the benefit of grandad. As afternoon waned he decided he was safe. The deal, it seemed, was a deal.

Back at the dumpster park he explained the situation. "I got us a ride on a private boat," he said. "If it's just the old man tomorrow, we're safe. If he turns up with hired muscle we won't risk it."

"Who is this old man?" Leonora asked.

"Local taxi driver. Man, there's quite a few 'round this joint. But he seemed okay. I know bad vibes – no-one better."

Leonora looked unhappy. "He could shoot us, gas us, drown us."

"He ain't gonna do any of them things," Hound replied. "He just wants the money. It may be a refugee camp out there, but its

Mecca for crims, which means available money no questions asked. I had to offer him cash, though, 'cos we're metal light."

Tsuneko said, "What about all our belongings? Best not to take them to Bejaïa."

Hound considered. "Could go either way," he said. "Could be we never come back here. We were heading for Morocco, and that's still an option."

"I am not leaving my possessions here," said Leonora. "The future is unknown."

Hound nodded. "Let's assume we'll be in and around Bejaïa for a while. Then maybe head west with Zeug – I'm talking best case scenario. Either way, we need to take our gear with us. Hey, listen, we'll dunk our valuables in rubber plas. Standard tourist precaution, yep? Takes a while to open up, so not an easy hit. A crim is a crim – they look for an open window, you know?"

Leonora shrugged. "I am sure you know what you are doing."

Hound smiled. "When I know anything at all."

CHAPTER 18

Manfred watched as Pouncey explained what she had done to prepare the suite of three apartments for occupation. Joanna and Dirk stood behind him, peering over his shoulder in the gloomy light – they dared not use lamps, or even candles, for fear of exposing their position to street walkers.

"I built this door to block off the end of the corridor linkin' the apartments," she said, gesturing at the contrivance of recovered wood and rust-brown metal. "The three apartments all have functionin' locks, but this is the extra obstacle at the end, in case any of the bis do a runner."

Manfred nodded, glancing back. Orange stood a few metres away, watching.

"Lock him in our apartment, Jo," he said.

Joanna stared. "Him? You called it him."

Manfred stared back. "Yeah. I did. Um…"

"You believe them to be people now. Orange is a boy, obviously."

Manfred felt his face go pink. "Well, I guess…" He shrugged.

They waited while Joanna pushed Orange back into the apartment, then shut the door. "It will not be long before they grasp the essentials of handles and keys," she told Manfred.

"I know," he muttered.

Pouncey continued. "Aye, a good point. See this black cloth? It hides the lock and key. Same for the apartment doors. I filched keys and stuff from a local store. Whenever you leave or enter, use the cloth to conceal what you do, then at least the bis won't see a key being used. Should slow 'em down."

"Dat good idea," Dirk said, "but not last forever."

"I know," Pouncey replied. "Let's hope you can teach 'em English, eh?"

"Hope so!"

Manfred walked back to the three apartment doors at the end of the suite corridor, all of them shut. Light was almost nonexistent – blacked out windows along the side of the corridor. "What about these locks?" he asked.

"I put new ones in this morning."

"Locks and *keys?*"

"Would be insane to use e-cards," Pouncey pointed out. "Nexus trace. Indigo."

Manfred nodded. "Yeah... clever Indigo."

Joanna led him into their shared apartment, allowing Dirk to investigate his while Pouncey made final alterations to the end door. Manfred heard hammering. He glanced down at the three warm spectrum bis shuffling around.

"They look bored," he said.

"To *you* maybe," Joanna said. She touched him on the arm, gave him a look of concern. "I am worried about us all."

"Why? 'Cos I called Orange him?"

"No! Well, yes, a little. But the bis are becoming more like unruly children. We have to instil as many rules into them as possible. They must not go feral."

Manfred nodded. "Wolf kids. We don't want that. Looks like Dirk tracked us down at just the right moment."

Joanna embraced him. "So... you are unconcerned about Dirk's appearance?"

"Not the slightest bit bothered. You?"

Joanna glanced away. "I suppose he must be safe."

Manfred chuckled. "I wanted him over Tsuneko. It's a stroke of luck."

"You do not worry that Aritomo is behind all this?"

Manfred hesitated. There was one unsettling aspect to Dirk's tale. "The mezcal worm thing... that's odd. This Luigi guy might've been one of Aritomo's agents, double bluff style. 'Course, could've been a local Mafioso, they'll prey on any hitch hiker they can get."

"Perhaps... yes, perhaps Mafia. But Aritomo will have every pattern analysing computer in his arsenal looking for our traces. That frightens me. He would murder us if he managed to follow Dirk to America."

There was a knock on the door. Manfred called out, "Yeah?"

Dirk entered, one leg first, looking down to see if any of the bis were preparing to spring out. He hurried in, slamming the door shut. Manfred glanced at the couch by the window, where all three bis sat.

"You and Pouncey okay?" he asked.

Dirk nodded. "Indigo, Blue. I like."

Manfred nodded, separating himself from Joanna, as if embarrassed. "You need food? We got pittas and olives."

Dirk hesitated. "Listen," he said. "Da Tsuneko June thing."

Manfred frowned. He sensed trouble. "Whatcha mean?"

Dirk's gaze oscillated between him and Joanna.

Manfred said in firm tones, "What do you *mean,* Dirk?"

"Da mole, Tsuneko. She find us on Malta. Den Aritomo copters locate our cave. It bad time – touch 'n go."

Manfred glanced at Joanna. Dirk had not yet mentioned any of this. "Mole?" he said.

Dirk paused. "Well, kinda mole. Scared rat, more like. She want out."

Manfred stared at Dirk. "She wanted *out?* And you *know* that?"

"Sure. We had two or three chats." He shrugged. "Ten, maybe…"

Manfred gasped. He felt his heart begin to race. Images of Tsuneko escaping the Philly apartment came to his mind's eye. "Chats? Impossible!"

"No – for real. *Very* difficult though. Hound her contact, he da top guy. Goodman Awuku, you know?"

Joanna ran to the door, opened it and shouted, "Pouncey!"

Pouncey sprang into the room seconds later. Manfred pointed at Dirk and managed to gasp, "He says Tsuneko was a mole and the AIteam chatted with her!"

Pouncey blinked at Dirk. "No way."

"How can you be sure?" Joanna asked.

Pouncey wiped her mouth with one hand, then adopted a casual pose, resting on the heel of one foot. "The attenuators," she said.

At once Manfred said, "The what?"

"Aye, you're wearin' one now."

"What? Without my knowledge?"

Pouncey chortled. "My *brief* was security."

Again Manfred glanced at Joanna. He felt like his world was leaking away, leaving him high and dry in the mouldy apartment. "You didn't tell us?"

"Course not." Pouncey strode over to him, put a hand on his head, then felt his hair. Then she stepped back and took out a bug detector – FBI style. It beeped once. "Yep," she said. "Workin' fine."

Joanna stepped forward and said, "What do these attenuators do?"

"It's a way of diminishin' certain electromagnetic communications waves," Pouncey replied. "I always use them." She turned to Dirk, adding, "What com method did Hound use?"

Dirk looked baffled. "Encrypted multi-frequency radio," he said.

A look of triumph appeared on Pouncey's face. "Then, like I said. No *way*."

Dirk looked angered. "But we did! Shit, I saw it myself. Hound, he call her, classic unhappy mole. Yes! Light on info he said. But we talk da talk, I swear!"

Manfred felt faint – he sat on a chair. "She must've had Aritomo's help to find you in Malta."

Dirk shrugged. "Maybe."

"This is *not* possible," Pouncey said. "No radio communication could take place comin' out of the BIteam."

Manfred nodded. To Dirk he said, "What date did the coms stop?"

Dirk pondered. "Hard to say. Long time."

"Was it sudden?"

"Well… Tsuneko, she com in bursts. But, yeah, it all stop sudden."

Manfred nodded. "I bet it was August twentieth."

Dirk shrugged. "Summer, for sure. Late August, dat sound about right."

Pouncey looked at Manfred. "How come that day?" she asked.

"Only one possibility," he replied. "The bis. I cut them off that day. Remember?"

"You mean, they… they…"

"Acted as a gestalt entity. Without conscious knowledge, without instinct – surfing the nexus like a big old computer, probably through the gateway of Indigo. They took everything they found locally, including Tsuneko's coms, and spread it far and wide. They knew nothing about what they were doing, though. And Tsuneko didn't know either – she wore an attenuator and didn't know, like we didn't know."

Dirk nodded. "We not know about da cutting. Though *I* knew da score with da BIteam philosophy – societies, not Zeug loners. So! You cut dem apart, make dem work hard to understand each other. And dat save your lives."

Manfred nodded. "Aritomo may even have spotted us in Philly, thinking the bis were some weird new kind of computer."

Pouncey said, "Not early enough, if he did."

Manfred leaned forward. "Listen, Dirk, you're messing with our heads, yeah? What if this Luigi – what if *Aritomo* – followed you to America?"

Dirk laughed. "You think me stupid? Ha ha!"

"Whatcha mean?"

"I learn lots from Hound. Truly, he da best in da world." Dirk glanced at Pouncey. "No offence, lady."

Pouncey shrugged.

Dirk continued, "I make sure take rich boy solplane to America. Exceeding expensive. Dat good. Aritomo, he know I poor. I make sure my destination got two locations – Birmingham, see?"

"Alabama?"

"Ha ha! Immediate duality. Maybe Birmingham, *Britain.*"

Manfred nodded. He'd used this trick himself. "And then…?"

"Oh, all da Hound tricks. He cunning basta'd. Make my reservation, all dat, in Brit speak. No American word. Like, no *sidewalk,* yeah? Pay through anonymous account, den shut account. Do it camouflaged, via local orphanage boss ID – loose security. Nexus trace den defaulted to Brit location."

"What about cams at the Monte Carlo airport? You've never disguised your appearance."

"You joke? I shave my Afro off! Wear big girl's ear-rings. But dat easy too. Check map of airport for cam blind spots. But, none. Set up decoy with two local girls – kids, dey always need cash, you know? Dat make sure anthropo soft see dem cut fence, which is what I tell dem do. Den tip-toe through created blind spot to da can. Take long dump, see? Den out da window into rich boy corridor, where no cams. Rich boys, dey not like look-see on nexus." Dirk shrugged. "Easy."

"What about checking in?" Manfred insisted. "You're not telling me there's no cams there."

Dirk snorted, waving one finger at Manfred. "You suspicious lack of trust, Mr Klee. Dat easy too. Hound, he tell me one time – Dirk, da thing with da cam is *faces*. Anthropo equal human face, is it? Big danger is no trace of me in da airport. Empty space as suspicious as my big face. So I scan passenger list, spot guy wear clothes like me. I copy him, den three-D print his face on neoprene mask at museum kids' booth. Play mask, sure, but it look real funky, no bull! Den walk to check-out like I own da place, off to Birmingham Britain."

Manfred turned to look at Pouncey. She shrugged. "We've all done the mask trick in the security biz. No computer is human."

Dirk smiled. "Aritomo not look at Monte Carlo airport. Dat da sleight of hand, see? But if he did, he see dat Anglophile guy in reception. No biggie."

Manfred sat back. "You'd better be on the level, Dirk, or we're all fucked."

Dirk shrugged. "I wanna see da bis now. We got a big deal with Indigo."

They all sat in Pouncey's room, where she kept Grey, Violet and Green. Grey was wearing clothes.

It was not quite a garment, Manfred noted, more like Grey had adapted a roll of plastic-backed cloth to make a body wrap. But the implication was clear to him. "Grey doesn't want his patterns to be seen."

Joanna fixed him with yet another skeptical stare. "You think?"

"Yeah. My guess. It's not like that's adornment."

"We do not know what adornment is for the bis," Joanna said.

Manfred raised his eyebrows, glancing at Dirk. "Emotion concealer, I think. He doesn't want the other bis to know what's going on inside. He was always the reclusive one. *You* can dig that, Joanna."

"Have you quite finished speculating?"

Manfred turned to Dirk. "What d'you think, Dirk?"

Dirk glanced at Grey. "What you use for dere arm and hand muscles?" he murmured.

Manfred replied, "Probably the same as Leonora. Layers of conducting carbon grease separated by a stretchy polymer film."

Dirk nodded. "Like Zeug."

"Why'd you ask?"

"I can't make da bis write. Will have to be speech only."

Manfred nodded. "Okay."

"Da muscle and nerve control for handwriting, even typing – dat complex."

"Speech it is then."

Dirk handed Pouncey an e-slate. "Dat my list of requirements," he said. "On back of da slate I write da account details. Dollars! No bull, see?"

Pouncey studied the list. Then she laughed. "Is that all?"

"And hurry," Dirk said.

"He's giving us his dollars," Manfred said. "Go spend 'em."

Pouncey departed with no further word. Manfred asked Dirk, "That list, it's do-able?"

"Sure."

Manfred grimaced. "A spending pattern will be set up," he said. "That could be traced. Computers might link the bought items into possible final objects. If they label even one object *interface,* we're sunk."

"Pouncey'll steal da majority of da gear," Dirk replied without hesitation. "She sure got her shit together. I wish we'd had her in Malta."

Joanna said, "Even if someone identifies interface components, that does not mean anything. There will be thousands, maybe millions of interfaces built on the West Coast this year alone."

"That's the sort of trace Aritomo'll be looking for," Manfred said.

"He not following da thief," Dirk said, lighting up a cheroot. "Only da shop sale. Besides – lo-market? Dat all black, you know? No traces in nexus."

Manfred sighed. "Maybe." He glanced at Grey. "It's just that we're so close to success here. I don't wanna crash now."

Dirk worked without sleep for thirty hours before sitting back and announcing, "I think I got it."

Manfred – half asleep on a couch – was startled, woken up by the statement. "Mmm?" he said.

Dirk nodded. The room stank of smoke and there was a collection of coffee-stained mugs on the floor beside him. But in his hand he held what appeared to be a silk headscarf.

Manfred woke Joanna, then opened the door to call Pouncey. The quartet gathered in the largest apartment room, lit by a single green bio-cell, the window blacked out double thickness. The atmosphere was eerie, like being underwater. All eight bis sat in the room – the warm spectrum bis dark, the others appearing pale in the single wavelength green light.

Dirk said, "Dis headscarf contain all da processing power to make da interface work. 'Cos risk of external hack – I build English database into it. Self-powered and self-sustaining."

"Powered by?" Manfred asked.

"Battery. If dis work okay, I put in a solar cell array instead."

"Gotcha."

Dirk continued, "Long, thin bio-processors from Caltech Corporation. Very strong too." He indicated a nylon thread, which he pulled out. Manfred saw that it had an earpiece on the end. "Dis line da speech out. Bis hear dis with no sound problem, even on a noisy street. Noise-cancelling software. Dere inbuilt Singapore mouth-speaker what *we* listen to. Stereo camera on scarf match bi eye gaze direction, yes?"

"That's the tech side," said Manfred. "What about the difficult bit?"

Dirk grinned. "You're too impatient," he said. "I notice dat when I meet you. Now, I can't match human capacity to learn. So I do it by rote learn and concentrated reinforcement by repetition. Hope da bi make mental model of dat audio activity, den grasp da symbolic side as it models new experience. We begin with nouns only."

"Why do they need the headscarf, then?" Joanna asked. "They have Singaporean ears, they have known for weeks that humans use sound. They may even have stored some English words."

"Ha! I hope so. But my scarf also make model of environment, in parallel with bi. It constantly reinforce what da bi sees. Also, Singapore ear hear up to ninety thousand kilohertz. I use dat extra bandwidth to squeeze in *much* more info. I estimate twenty to thirty times da amount of info we human deal with."

"So," Manfred said, "this is based in part on image recognition software? Environment recognition? Your interface knows what the bi is looking at and constantly reinforces the English word for it? Like a teacher?"

"Hence, nouns first," Dirk replied. "Long streams of words for objects – like babbling babies!"

"Then we have to assume that my first hunch was right," said Manfred. "If the bis are modelling their environment in their heads, as I'm sure they are, they'll model the streams of speech information. With luck, and some positive reinforcement, they'll spot the links. Then they'll take off! Symbolic learning..."

"Dat da goal," Dirk said. "Shall we try Orange first?"

"No," Manfred said at once. He looked at the bi. "No, not him. He's already got too much swagger. No, choose..."

"Indigo?"

Manfred shook his head. "He's already a special case. He scares me. No, choose *Yellow*. We already think he's more focussed on us than the other bis are. That may give you a head start, Dirk."

"Sure. Yellow it is. Fetch me da little guy, Joanna please."

Joanna shepherded Yellow to Dirk. It stood before him, staring, as so often the bis did. Manfred nodded to himself. These creations of his needed to be sponges for knowledge – sponges for the reality of the external world. Staring was good.

"What language acquisition theory d'you go with, Dirk?" he asked.

"Well, see, I know we all carry a mental model in our heads. I assume bis do too. So dey have social relations – dat your basic idea."

"You're a social interactionist?"

"Sure. It down to social interaction between us and dem. We dere *parents* now. We use feedback and reinforcement – just like my interface – to make bi mental models more sophisticated."

"And they experience it in terms of what they already know about the world."

Dirk nodded. "Dey already got much more nous dan even you realise. I hear da flower on da grave story, I hear it good! Dey know dere is an environment out dere, with me and you and dem in it. All learning take place in dat model. Now we got to

241

increase da symbolic sophistication. We got to make 'em realise *cow* means a cow, see?"

Manfred nodded. "As a group."

"All eight of 'em."

And so the work began. Minutes, hours, days passed quicker than any Manfred had known. Dirk manufactured seven more headscarves, and on one momentous morning they put them on the bis' heads and switched them on.

Red, Yellow and Blue ignored theirs. Orange resettled his, pulling out some of his frond-like touch sensors from beneath the fabric as if for maximum comfort, while Green took his off and threw it away. Grey also took his off, but then held it in his hands, as if trying to orient the stereo camera – he kept the earpiece in his ear, Manfred noticed. Violet began walking around the room, stopping in front of objects, then moving on. Soon, Blue tagged along too.

Dirk gestured with his head at Violet, his eyebrows raised and a grin on his face. But Manfred was too busy watching Indigo.

They had known from the early days that Indigo's Korean eyes had failed. As soon as Manfred heard Dirk's description of the mechanics of the headscarf interface he knew it might not work for Indigo. Yet, deep down, he felt sure Indigo was already different to any of the other bis – different in a radical way. He could not pin the feeling down since intuition alone told him he was correct. He glanced at Joanna. She thought little of intuition.

Indigo walked up to him, his fronds rustling, as if sensing air currents. Joanna theorised that in such ways, and through grasping the notion of sound reflecting from surfaces, Indigo was able to model the topography of his environment. Manfred agreed. Yet now Indigo seemed to be staring at him, and at nothing else.

"Listen, guys," he said. Indigo took a step back, as if startled. "We need to take one bi each. Forget Red, Yellow and Blue. I'm not even sure Red is conscious. It behaves like a kitten. So does Green. Dirk, you take Indigo. Joanna – Orange. Pouncey, you have Grey. I'm taking Violet."

"Why one each?" Pouncey asked, as she lifted Grey in her arms.

"Dirk's right. We gotta reinforce *everything* now, use speech to name things, hammer home the message that little bits of audio equals meaning. We'll have to work with the ones that show most aptitude – the ones that want to learn, yeah?"

Dirk lifted Indigo. Manfred watched. The bi struggled, then tried to clamber out of Dirk's grip. Anxiety on his face, Dirk put the bi on the floor, whereupon it ran straight to Manfred.

"It knows who you are," Dirk said. "I told you."

Manfred looked down. His heart sank. Dirk lifted Violet and began walking around the room as if carrying a baby, speaking names for objects: couch, wall, window, cup, plate. Joanna followed suit, then, looking embarrassed, so did Pouncey. The other bis watched, except Red, who lay down, and Green, who sat by the lamp staring into it.

Manfred looked again at Indigo. The bi stared up at him. It was impossible not to imagine the thing whimpering like a snotty-nosed kid.

"This is why you scare me, Indigo," he said. "You know too much."

From Indigo's mouth there came a crackle as the internal speaker came to life. "This is why you scare me, Indigo. You know too much."

Manfred screeched and jumped back. Dirk span around. "Manfred!" he said. "*Chill.* It parroted."

"Yeah… parrot," Manfred said.

Indigo spoke again. "Yeah… parrot."

"It's relating your utterances with da utterances in its ear," Dirk said. "Just *copying*. Don't freak out, Manfred."

"Why hasn't it done it before?"

"It understands we've done something conceptually different to its body. It grasps dat what it's been hearing all dis time means something to *you*. And it knows your voice, like a lamb knows its mother's voice. Derefore it want dat sound to mean something to it. It's *babbling*."

Manfred nodded. His pounding heart quietened. With some reluctance he lifted Indigo and began walking around the room, naming objects as the others were.

Dirk said, "We *have* to get dem to understand dat what da earpiece say, we also say, only with our mouth. Make da equivalence in dere mental model, see?"

Minutes passed. None of the other bis copied the speech of the person carrying them. Indigo's surface patterns span like Moiré kaleidoscopes as Manfred repeated word after word.

They paused for supper. Manfred noticed that Dirk looked worried. Flipping pancakes and cracking eggs, he gestured Dirk over to the cooker. "You expected them all to be speaking, didn't you?"

Dirk glanced over at Violet. "Yep," he said.

"Give 'em time. We don't know anything about the symbolic frameworks they might be using."

"We do know dey have copied human ones," Dirk replied. "Da flowers on da grave."

"Yeah, agreed. But that's deep stuff. They know they're alive, so they know death. All this semantic analogy though – *knife* equals a knife, *plate* equals a plate – that's tough to get. Maybe they never will."

"You told me you thought dey used gestural language," Dirk said. "I agree. Spoken language, dat's conceptually da same as gesture, like signing for deaf people."

Manfred glanced through the kitchen door. He saw five of the bis, sitting like kids all together on a couch. "We can forget

Red and Green," he said. "I think they're virtually embryos compared to the others."

Dirk glanced at the couch, lowering his voice to reply, as if for fear of controversy. "Agreed," he said. "And Yellow – he remind me of a cat. He sit on a lap, but don't do much else. Grey, he loner. Agree with you dere."

Manfred nodded. "Don't tell Joanna that. She's reductionist science, yeah? Behaviour, facts, theories, testing, lots of damn testing. She don't go a bundle on guesswork."

"I notice," said Dirk, smirking. "You got your hands full with dat chick."

"What about your bi?"

"Violet? Nah. Stupid one."

"We thought he was the caring bi. He went straight for Blue when Blue was shot."

"So? Big ol' elephant, she help her calf if it hurt. Don't mean a thing."

Manfred nodded. "Then it's Orange and Indigo we've really got to watch."

"Yep. And Blue."

"Blue? Why?"

"He got da half arm. It make him think – scarred by life."

Manfred stifled a chortle. For a moment he saw how he must appear to Joanna. Nodding, he said, "Well, I guess all views are valid here until disproven."

"Dey certainly are. Blue and Violet – dem two real friendly."

Manfred nodded. He had observed that the pair kept close by each other, as they had done since Blue's arm was shot off. "*No* anthropomorphising," he told himself as he cracked open more eggs.

A week passed with no confirmed use of language. Manfred began to wilt under the stress. Dirk chain-smoked cheroots, and

Pouncey had to set up an extractor with an exit pipe leading up to the rubble-strewn roof of the apartment block. Joanna watched, watched and watched, with all the patience of her chimp observing days.

Then, one evening, with Pouncey out scavenging and Dirk asleep, Manfred heard something in the middle apartment – Dirk's. He heard voices.

For a moment a list of possibilities scrolled through his mind: wi-fi radio; AI alarm clock; old television; burglars. But the voices were high-pitched and seemed inflected like old Oriental animations.

He put his ear to the apartment door.

Voice one: "Dirk bed. Manfred big room. Pouncey Portland."

A second voice: "Joanna big room."

First voice: "Joanna big room. Manfred room. Joanna room."

It had to be the bis!

Manfred felt his throat constrict with shock, with awe, as he envisaged in his mind's eye what could be happening in Dirk's room. He'd left Dirk asleep – surely the man was still snoozing. If he was watching this, he would have found some way to alert the others.

Manfred pressed down on the door handle, as slow and quiet as he could, but there was a clink and at once the voices stopped.

He heard rustling, then: "Door. Handle."

The second voice said, "Door, handle."

Was that first voice *teaching* the second voice? Or had the bis noticed the handle moving? Manfred held his breath – they must not hear him. Either Indigo was teaching Blue or the other way around.

"Door. Corridor."

"Door, corridor."

Manfred shut his eyes as the dilemma reached fever pitch. He was desperate to see what was going on, but he dared not interrupt the flow. What he was hearing could be the time-lapsed, superfast acquisition of English by one bi from another; and if that was a social endeavour, as they all suspected, him beating the door down would gatecrash the lesson in the worst possible way.

He stood back. Thought for a moment. Dirk carried a NearRange Texter – they all did, gifts from Pouncey to be used in emergencies. He tip-toed down the corridor then took his out from his jeans pocket, flicking it on, typing, DIRK WAKE UP! QUIET! then sending it out.

He walked back to Dirk's door. The Texter would have beeped. The bis would hear that, but they had heard the noise before, and hopefully would ignore it.

He put his ear to the door. He heard a grunt, then a cough.

Then Dirk said, "Yes!"

CHAPTER 19

The boat, Hound was pleased to observe, carried only the old man. It floated fifty metres out from the plastic tide line. There were no locals nearby – it was only an hour after dawn – and the sun hung low over the ocean to the east. Hound put his hands to his mouth and shouted, "Can you come in any nearer?"

The old man waved at them, started the boat's engine then approached to a distance of ten metres. "You will have to wade over, monsieur, mademoiselles."

This they did, clambering into the boat with his help. He looked happy, even serene, as if the tetchy haggling of the previous day was all forgotten. They stowed their rubber plas spheres in the back of the boat, then sat on wooden benches dressed with old leather car seats.

"Man, am I glad to see you," Hound said.

"The pleasure is mine too. Who are these?"

"This is Anita and this is Catherine."

The old man bowed. "I am, as you say, le Diable."

Hound gestured at the old man with a thumb. "A comedian, ladies, like I said. Fire up the engine, grandad, let's head outa here before the gulls arrive."

As the old man flicked fingers at the boat's nex hub, Hound checked their appearance. They wore nondescript clothes and broad brimmed straw hats to hide them from satellite watchers. A long boat trip might be deemed unusual by nexus computers.

They could be spotted, watched. Anthropo soft might become involved.

The old man glanced over his shoulder. "You wear the summer hat anglais, mademoiselles."

Leonora replied, "I burn easily in the sun."

"Oui!" the old man said, laughing. "I have heard that before!"

Hound shrugged. This was all part of the cut-and-thrust of banter, he and the old man both wishing to prove themselves the superior wit. The open, sarcastic quality of the comments reassured him that the old man was genuine.

For a while they all sat in silence, watching the waves churn up behind them then fade to a pale, choppy wake. Refugee camps dotted the seashore. Jellyfish feeding on African nitrate blooms choked some areas, which the old man steered around.

"La méduse, she is not to be entangled with," he said.

Hound nodded. Though Leonora and Tsuneko – and indeed le Diable himself – seemed relaxed, he could not afford to let his guard down for a moment. This trip carried a small risk.

The sun rose high. Seagull flocks swooped in off the sea, heading for Francophone refugee camps. The boat engine acquired a reassuring hum as the angle of incidence of the sunlight increased. The boat sped up.

An hour east of Bejaïa, Hound noticed something. He stood at the back of the boat, raising, lowering, then raising his spex. Leonora noticed him, and came to investigate.

"What can you see?" she asked.

"Check it out," Hound replied. "Thought I saw a bit of an echo on the surf."

"An echo?" Leonora said.

"An augmentation delay – between real and nexus image."

Leonora tried the spex trick, but saw nothing. "It all looks simultaneous," she said.

Hound tried again. In his spex, the wavetops appeared a fraction of a second delayed, giving the merged vision a distinct after-image. "That's odd," he said.

"It is just a nexus artefact," Leonora said. "They hypothesise that the nexus has a diurnal rhythm, don't they?"

Hound nodded. He had heard that theory too. "At night, and in Europe – man, then I'd expect there to be a delay in representation. You can understand that. The computers go a bit inefficient 'cos power's low and most people are asleep. Latency, they call it. But this is daytime. In Africa."

"Why would it be your spex only?"

Hound glanced back at the old man. "Sometimes if you pull a feed off someone's spex without them knowing, the spex can't process everything in real time. Minuscule delay. But human brains are good at noticing a delay like that. We see it as a visual echo."

Leonora looked frightened. "We've been spotted?"

Hound replied, "Most likely an Algerian computer wondering why we've chartered a boat trip. State police, maybe. Can't be too many private boats on the Med right now. Don't panic."

Leonora nodded. "Locate the pull source. De-spex if you have to."

"Can't afford to," Hound replied, "not on a trip like this."

Leonora sighed, concern plain in her face.

Hound turned his back on her. In truth, he was a bit freaked out. The last time he'd noticed an augmentation delay was one night chasing crims on motor bikes in Cairo, when the ancient, creaking, bureaucratic nexus almost fell over from excess real-time info pulls. But this was different. Sun up, everything worked at max efficiency.

He felt a tiny shiver pass down his back. This situation was *weird*.

He whispered in their ears, "Spex off," then went to stand beside the old man. A quick nexus query would see whether the info pull off his spex had a diabolic source.

It did not. It was extra-local.

Hound frowned. He did not have the time to design, then build and launch a probe into the nexus to locate the source.

He pulled the ladies' hat brims low. Leonora's face went pale. She received the message of that gesture loud and clear.

An hour later they arrived at Bejaïa. The augmentation delay receded, then vanished. At the eastern edge of the harbour they disembarked. Hound handed over five coins. "Nice knowing ya, dude," he said.

The old man nodded, a look of relief on his face. "Peace be with you."

Hound turned, escorting Leonora and Tsuneko into a shadow-strewn alley. There would be a market nearby – he could smell spices, leather, rotting food.

"Time to hide for a while," he said. "A nice, covered market, that's what we want. Man, and some coffee."

Hound sought covered passages, then found them; they led into the butt end of the local market, slippery with rotting vegetables, grease and worse. The sun twinkled down through the rococo plastic twirls of the alley roofs. In a caf they found seats at the back, out of sight, where they ordered coffee and bread rolls.

"We safe?" Tsuneko asked.

He shrugged, then nodded. "Probably," he said. He looked around the caf. A few of the locals had already clocked their rubber plas spheres. "Except we look like tourists," he added.

"What about a station lock-up?" asked Tsuneko. "I heard a soltrain just now."

Hound pulled a map to his spex, saw that the railway station was two streets away. "Let's do it. Man, then scram. Already the locals will be broadcasting reports of new tourists to the local crim lords."

He followed the spex guide to the station, paying cash for an ultra-secure compartment. Their stuff was safe now. But he still felt vulnerable. Bejaïa was huge compared with Annaba, where he had not been concerned about muggings. This city was different. He *felt* violence in the air. He could almost smell the gangs.

"We need to find a more... salubrious joint," he said. "And quick."

Leonora stood up, her coffee half finished. "After you," she said.

They departed, walked on for a few streets, then halted. Utilising a nexus reference guide he worked out which parts of the shoreside city were best avoided.

"Look," he said, pointing to an LCD map on a cab rank platform. "The district that the charity is in ain't too far off. Quiet residential area, it seems. Let's get a taxi there. Save time, save muggings."

They paid cash to drive a kilometre or so, then hurried out into a local date palm park, standing beneath the fronds to avoid satellite eyes.

Hound pointed. "There," he said. "I can see the roof of the charity building. There's a big white stork perched on it. See?"

Tsuneko nodded. "What now?" she asked.

"Get a bit closer. Reccie the place. Wait 'til sun down."

Tsuneko's eyes flickered as she checked the time in her spex. "A couple of hours," she said. She pulled her cotton lite around her body, then zipped it up. "Cooling down."

Again Hound pointed. "See that old shed on the other side of the park? Probably a solbus shelter. We'll doss there until dark. Man, I need to do some serious nexus work."

They followed his instructions to the letter, both of them aware of the heightened security issues he now faced. A couple of the local cats came to investigate them. Tsuneko played with them awhile, but Leonora was too nervous to relax.

"You two get some shut-eye," Hound said, nudging the cats out of the shed with one boot. "This is gonna take a few hours."

His main concern was not the local police, the local crims or even the local madmen – his concern was Aritomo Ichikawa. An augmentation delay in broad daylight was too weird to ignore. He had to take some time to investigate it before the final stage of the mission.

First port of call was spy glitches. He used various perspectives to investigate the park, the surrounds, the city: authorities, police, local hackers, even a brat gang dealing in ketamines, who used the park as a handover location. Nothing. At least, nothing obvious. The park sent out a nul result. He then pulled a resume of his trip from Annaba, but here he had to be careful. If he pulled an entire trip resume, an observant nexus spy would notice; so he pulled the last couple of hours. Nothing.

Still he was not satisfied. He demanded an explanation of himself for what he had spotted.

He stood in the shed doorway and looked out over the gloom-shrouded park. On the railings he noticed the remains of old wi-fi aerials. He hacked into their admin portal, then ran a park scan.

There! A device. A single flicker of red in the sea of green.

But the park was empty of people. All he could see was date palms and railings around the perimeter – just grass, low bushes and a few piles of fast food packaging visible inside. Yet all three of the operational wi-fi modules detected a low level signal.

Quick as he could he arranged for a cam check. Various buildings stood around the park, some occupied (lights on, people shutting curtains), some of them dark. All of them had security cams sprouting from their eaves. These he used to instigate a sixty second patrol, so that his virtual eye viewed the park from every external angle. Nothing. He had expected to see a figure lurking behind a date palm, a shadow by a dustbin. But nothing. Just another nul result...

Okay. Time for a risk. He'd have to use ultra-precise positioning.

The nexus was based on geography, modelling where everyone and everything was. He took the electronic signature of the signal and GPS pinpointed it. There! Twenty metres south, maybe three or four west. Something lurked amidst the shadows.

He took out his flechette gun; armed it. Then he performed a deep analysis of the signal, concealing his actions by linking it to a PD-monitored armed robbery taking place a few blocks away. The spy device – whatever it was – was listed as new. Less than a day old. That was not good news. But then he spotted that it had never been re-set since manufacture. No Japanese professional would risk such an oversight, because of the possibility of old data – 'new' so often meant 'reconditioned' in the tech market. This result suggested a local crim and a genuinely new device.

He hesitated. He had to get out into the park and use his eyes.

He crouched down, moving forward step by step. The light was going – a while after dark. Distant police drones echoed as the armed robbery was busted. A distant helicopter sent *whup-whup* noises through the air.

He moved forward. Bushes lay close. In them, he saw a cat.

He froze. The cat stared at him. He was no cat-lover, but without hesitation he made clicking noises with his tongue against his teeth, held out one hand – slowly – to entice the cat. It stood still.

He stopped moving. The cat approached, centimetre by centimetre, until it was a handsbreadth away. Hound pounced.

The cat went limp. He'd expected it to screech and scrabble, but it flopped. He grabbed a pair of wire cutters from his belt bag and chopped off the collar. He dropped the cat, and it ran off at top speed.

In his hand he held a collar from which a sphere the size of a marble hung. He magnified the markings with his spex: *Silent B/Z/600 T-X.*

Some kind of spy module. A local gang lord, no doubt. How the hell had that lord managed to train a cat? He dropped the collar and stamped it into the ground. It smashed into fragments.

"So you like cats, do you?" he asked Tsuneko when she woke up.

They were not amused by his nocturnal tale. "Was it Aritomo?" Leonora asked. "*Could* it have been Aritomo?"

"One in a thousand chance. A million. No way would Aritomo use a factory-set spy module. I mean, we know he likes cats, but, man, that's ridiculous."

"How can you be sure?"

"Did I say sure?" Hound replied. "No, I said one in a million. Listen to me. Imagine you buy a computer, or a mem store. What's the first thing you do?"

"Reformat it."

"Why?"

Leonora shrugged. "Viruses. Old information."

Hound nodded, then pointed to the shed entrance. "Sorry if you slept badly. Man, it's cold. But now we've got to see where Zeug is."

Leonora nodded. "Then talk him out of whatever he's doing."

"That's your job," Hound replied.

He led them along back alleys to the street on which the charity building stood. He looked. The stork remained on the roof.

"That's... interesting," he said.

"Check it," said Leonora.

He raised a hand. "Shush. You hear something?" He isolated the image of the stork in his spex, then enlarged it. "It's squawking."

"Hound, they do squawk," Leonora said.

But Hound had seen this trick before. "Big, slow, simple animals," he said. "*Much* easier to fake than a chimp or a corvid."

"What d'you mean?" Tsuneko asked.

"I don't think that's a real stork. Do you?"

Leonora shook her head. "Analyse its noise."

Hound obliged. The task was easy – use a cam on the building to record five hundred secs of stork sound, then send the aiff file off to a public lab in Algiers. The result came back within seconds.

"Artificial," he said. "Repeating every hundred and twenty seconds. This is Zeug's aerial, I betcha. That signal I first spotted is hidden in the noise somewhere. Cunning bastard! Man, he knows half the tricks *I* know."

"You may have taught him without realising it," said Leonora.

Remembering the events of the desert hike, Hound nodded. "Wish I hadn't," he muttered.

"What now?" asked Tsuneko.

"Indoors."

"You've mapped it out?"

Hound rolled his eyes. "Course. We go in through the can. Man, I've found that's most often got an open window."

The two women looked at him with blank expressions.

"'Cos of the stink?" he said.

Using a cam opposite the charity building he ascertained that one of the ground floor lavatories had an open window. There was a covered route to it, crossing the road using an underground water pipe, then following hedges and a line of date palms to the building itself.

"Follow me," he said. "Do what I do."

They followed him in silence, crouching when he crouched, running when he ran, like ducklings following their mother. Two minutes later they were ready to enter, pressed against the side of the building like limpets. Hound listened. The can was empty, though he heard wailing patients not far off.

He flipped open the window to maximum, leaped up, then peered in. As he'd suspected: empty. He rolled in, the pulled the other two inside.

Leonora took his hand, then Tsuneko's. "Remember," she told him, "only you and me and Dirk know what Zeug looks like. It is very likely that the residents here believe Zeug to be human. He may have disguised himself."

Hound grinned. "I'll spot him, don't you worry about that." He took out a bolas-gun. "Then I'll disable him gaucho style and we'll take him to the roadside. I've set up a taxi call – driver thinks he's waiting for a patient. We'll fox him, then I'll knock him out and drive the thing out of town. Man, I sure wanna get a good look at Zeug before we decide what to do next."

Leonora nodded, so Hound led them to the can door. The corridor outside was empty. A map of the ground floor flipped into view via his spex. Red dots marked active cams, green marked security features (safes, com links, alarms) while blue labelled the charity's nexus computers. All clear so far.

"Early morning," he whispered. "Nice 'n' quiet."

He led them along the corridor to the door at the end, pausing when he noticed an optical port. Without hesitation he linked his spex to it, running a simulation of Zeug's signal on the charity's ancient AI-soft in an attempt to locate where in the building it might be.

A room on the map winked yellow. He smiled. The building's computers, though they did not know what the signal was, had noticed and stored it. There it lay, like a minuscule pearl in a gigantic oyster.

"I got him," he said.

He led the way to the room. They hid behind laundry baskets when a pair of blue-clothed nurses walked by. Somewhere nearby a patient screamed.

The door was labelled *Room 12*.

"Ready?" he asked.

They nodded.

"Use the stun crackers I gave you… man, that's if anyone stops us. This place is quiet as a boneyard. Stun grenade – emergency only."

"Ready," said Leonora.

"Ready," Tsuneko echoed.

The door knob was round. Hound turned it. Locked. He took a deep breath then karate-kicked it. It swung aside on ruined hinges.

He span, ran forward, pointed his bolas-gun at the figure standing inside.

"It's Zeug!" he said, firing the gun.

At once a flock of faces flew into his spex. Japanese faces. Zeug whirled on one heel, his arms and thighs locked into place by the weighted ropes tying him.

The faces peeled off like fighter jets, vanishing into virtual space. A voice sounded in his spex speakers.

"Do not kill the AIteam. Leave them to me."

Hound whirled around. Two Japanese men stood at the door. Shoving Leonora and Tsuneko inside, they raised and fitted the door to its frame, then sealed it with ultracaulk.

The room's single window showed a shadow, then the silhouette of a head, made dark by the sky outside. It opened.

A face appeared. It was Aritomo Ichikawa.

Moments later Aritomo was raised by an aide outside, then dropped into the room. A third agent followed, and then a small herd of cats.

Hound stood still, knowing he'd failed. He felt quite calm. No point making a bid for glory. He wasn't the suicidal type.

He turned to Leonora. "Sorry," he said.

Aritomo grinned. "You did well, Mr Awuku. You should not feel disappointed with your performance. But, you should know, I always succeed in the end."

"What do you want?" Leonora asked. "Me?"

Aritomo shook his head. "You long ago ceased to be of use to my corporation. No, I want Zeug. And now you have led me to him. I thank you most sincerely!"

CHAPTER 20

It was like a dam breaking when Indigo and Blue acquired the rudiments of language.

Joanna cried, which made Manfred cry. Dirk grinned for days. Pouncey said very little – she found it difficult to believe, or so she claimed.

Joanna felt as though she was floating on air. For decades she had researched the acquisition of novel skills in chimp societies, and she had tried to use some of her discoveries to make hypotheses about the bis, then test them. As a strong supporter of the social intelligence theory of consciousness she grasped that almost everything learned by chimps was done in the context of their societies – exactly the same as human beings. There was no "learner", rather "a learner and a teacher".

She berated herself for not realising that the bis might teach one another. Like Manfred, like Dirk, she had assumed that humans – the parents of the social group – would do the teaching: human to beautiful intelligence.

Dirk was fond of telling a story: *Imagine a kid. Born outa artificial womb. Grows up, but no other people in da world. Not one, see? But all its body needs – dey sorted. Food, water, warm, whatever. Does it become conscious? I don't think so. Dis my objection to da language only method. Da baby not become conscious because no social interaction. I think consciousness between people, not in a brain. It between us all, like water for fish.*

They all got the analogy. But now the dam had burst, and they had their hands full with new family members.

Indigo taught Blue. The day after, Orange began to speak nouns. None of these three bis put together grammatical sentences, however; they listed nouns like chimp sign-speakers did, creating some novel combinations but not using those primitive sentences to speak creatively with one another. And when she realised this, Joanna's heart sank. In AI circles it was known as Washoe Syndrome.

But those days did not last. On day three, she watched Indigo taking Orange and Blue around her room.

Indigo said, "Couch, chair, high window."

Orange used the chair to peer through the higher of the two windows, which because they did not look out over the main street remained unblocked.

Orange said, "Couch, high window," whereupon Indigo and Blue stood on the couch. Violet stood nearby, as if afraid Blue might fall off and injure himself.

Then Indigo said, "Light bright."

Joanna realised something. The light levels in the apartments were low. The bis' power sources would be running down, and like as not their minds were aware of this through various inbuilt monitoring mechanisms. She nodded to herself, considering options. Those monitoring mechanisms would now be so far below the level of symbolic manipulation they would be unconscious, never noticed by the conscious minds of the bis, which were akin to the tip of an iceberg. The so-called Strange Loop of Hofstadter would be operating.

She smiled. It was all coming together at last.

She said, "We shall need to take them outdoors today for some sun. These apartments are too gloomy."

Pouncey nodded, her face grim. She had, Joanna knew, developed a number of secure methods of undertaking this difficult procedure. "Two at a time like naughty school kids," Pouncey said. "I'll take Indigo and Orange first."

"No," said Manfred. "Each of the speakers goes outdoors with a non-speaker. We can't afford to lose two together."

"You ain't gonna lose *any*," Pouncey replied, as if insulted.

Manfred glanced at her. "You know what I mean. Nobody'd blame ya for an accident, okay? A solbus can run over anyone."

Pouncey grunted something, but it was inaudible.

"How do we teach them verbs?" Joanna asked Dirk.

"Same as da noun," he replied. "Do, watch, repeat, reinforce. It da only way."

Two quicksilver-fast days passed by. They slept little. Joanna noticed that the bis did not sleep, but that they copied parts of human behaviour as a consequence of living in human company. Yellow in particular, the most human-focussed of the bis, copied everything his parents did, even to the extent of mimicking Dirk's smoking hand-movements – though without a cheroot. The other bis became less active at night, without losing consciousness.

On the third day Pouncey flagged up a potential problem. "The school class has been assessed," she said.

Manfred sat up at once, fear on his face. "Assessed?"

"By a services bot from the local education authority."

"They know about the bi class?"

"Don't forget it'll be listed on their canteen provision roster," Pouncey replied. "That's how I got in. But don't worry, I've replied in the negative, told 'em there's not enough progress for a full inspection."

Manfred sat back, his hands clasped atop his head. "That's not necessarily a real person's bot," he said. "That could be Aritomo's soft disguised as a services bot."

Pouncey sucked her teeth, then pursed her lips and nodded. "Aye. Could be."

Indigo walked up to Manfred, then climbed into his lap. Then Indigo said, "Bot Portland."

Joanna felt her eyes widen. She glanced at Manfred. There could be little doubt that Indigo had somehow parsed Manfred's sentence and grasped something of its meaning, if only from the nouns.

Manfred said to Indigo, "Bot Portland?"

"Bot Portland," Indigo replied. He did not look at Manfred as he said this – he looked at the window.

"It knows the location of Portland," said Joanna. "It is looking out, as if through the window."

Manfred nodded. "Half gestural, half verbal communication."

Indigo squirmed in Manfred's lap and said, "Bot Portland. Aritomo Japan."

Manfred stood up, placing Indigo on the floor. "We four need to talk in private," he said. "Pouncey, take the bis to their rooms. Put our three in with Dirk's. Then lock the doors."

Pouncey did as she was bid, returning a few minutes later with the all-clear.

Manfred said, "Indigo is nexus savvy, I'm sure. We've got to decide what to do. One slip and Aritomo will be onto us."

Joanna agreed. "Indigo has somehow grasped that Aritomo is an entity in Japan. It knows the *concept* of Japan, which it must have pulled from a nexus database."

"Maybe the school's digital encyclopaedia," said Pouncey. "It could've compared name styles, worked out that Ichikawa is a Jap name."

"Good point," said Manfred. "Indigo will be aware of your school class cover story, I'm sure, even if only in a rudimentary way."

"Do we go the aluminium foil route, then?" Pouncey asked. "Stop all electro-magnetics from impingin' on Indigo 'til we can talk sense to him?"

Manfred sighed. "I don't know. That seems so cruel."

"We can't let Aritomo spot us," Pouncey insisted, "so we don't have much choice."

Manfred paused for thought. "We're close to speaking abstract sense to him," he said.

Joanna shook her head. "Basic language so far, Manfred – the most basic. Though, I admit, we have seen intentional communication. They will speak eventually, I believe."

Manfred nodded. "Listen," he said, "Indigo's out there in the nexus, and may have been for a long time – albeit in ultra-primitive form, hmm? A bot, let's say. How about we have a hunt around for a data incarnation, created for it by the nexus?"

"Da nexus will think it a computer," said Dirk. "Maybe not link to fake class."

"Yeah," Manfred replied. "We need to search for, let's say... *unusual* computers that appeared around about the end of August. Or maybe we search for the gestalt entity they seem to have created before I cut them apart, using that as a jump-off point. But we gotta do *something* to fence Indigo in."

Dirk agreed. Joanna nodded in assent. Then Pouncey said, "I'll begin the search. Dirk, you better help me. We ain't got much time."

Joanna stood up. She could leave that work to the experts. But when she opened the door into Dirk's room she saw a blue smudge on the floor, metal prongs poking out of it, a pool of fluids soaking into the carpet. The brain looked like a piece of sugarloaf soaked in fountain pen ink. Blue had been pulverised into nonexistence.

They dared not leave the bis alone now. In the lounge of Manfred's apartment Pouncey rigged up a construction of wood, glass-fronted and covered in blankets, which acted as a sound barrier. Inside this kennel (as with black humour they called it) the seven bis sat in crates, looking out through the glass like dogs admonished by their masters.

Manfred felt sick. He had *been* sick. The demise of Blue was technically murder.

They held their discussion in low voices, aware that the bis, not least Indigo, could grasp simple concepts by parsing sentences. They ensured no nexus-linked devices had their audio recorders on.

"What do we do now?" Manfred asked.

Dirk spoke up without delay. "One of us on guard twenty four seven. New crates so we can separate dem if need be."

Manfred nodded, glancing at Orange, who never let his gaze move from Manfred. "Obvious enough."

"We'll have to separate them now," Pouncey said. "Keep them–"

"No!" Manfred interrupted, slapping his hands together. "That's no better than putting them in solitary in jail – and what good does that do? These are social beings. They *need* each other. But something's gone wrong, yeah? For some reason one of them has snapped."

Pouncey sat back. She looked surprised at his vehemence.

"I'm sorry," he said. "I don't mean to scold. But we gotta see the truth here. These are like kids. Alone, they die. They go feral. Whatever."

"But if we keep them together," Joanna said, "they could simply kill one another until only one is left."

"We'll guard 'em all day, like Dirk says," Manfred replied. "Maybe soon we'll be able to explain why killing is wrong. But if we can't…"

"I'll work out a guard rota," said Pouncey.

Manfred sighed, looking with horror and gloom at her. "Yeah," he said, glancing down at the floor. "You do that. Six hours each."

Joanna glanced at Manfred, then said, "Which one do you suppose did it?"

Manfred shrugged, uneasy with the question. Was she mocking him? Her face suggested not. At length he replied, "My guess? Not Red nor Green, nor Yellow. I think we all agree those are the dumb ones, or maybe they're not even conscious. It'll be one of the bright ones. Indigo. Orange. Grey." He laughed, unable to keep the human association from his mind. "Yeah, Grey – he's a loner. Keeps himself to himself, y'know?"

Joanna sighed, her face a picture of anguish. "Babe, I didn't mean to–"

"I know, I know. But this is kinda… unexpected. And you know I like gallows humour."

Dirk murmured, "Dey kids, and kids cruel. Dat a fact."

"Blue was one of the three we heard using proper English," Manfred said. "My guess is Indigo or Orange did it. Those two and Blue have been acting like little people. Petty, self-centred… and unfortunately not bound by any moral rules yet."

"We need to give them some," said Joanna.

"How?"

She glanced at the crates behind the glass. "They will know already that something is wrong in their social group, because of events happening now. They will be aware that a negative consequence has happened after Blue's death."

"Aye, and they'll remember what happened to White," Pouncey added.

Manfred nodded. "We'll have to reinforce non-killing behaviour. Goodness knows how, though. I'm stumped."

"We not need to isolate dem," said Dirk. "Keep stupid Red and Green with Orange, so he don't get bored and lonely. Keep Yellow and Grey with Indigo. Violet can shuttle."

"You mean," Manfred said, "keep Orange and Indigo apart?"

Dirk nodded. "Just in case. Two head – dey better dan one."

Manfred nodded. That was true enough. "And what about Indigo?" he said. "Pouncey's not even begun her nexus trawl yet."

"Begin dat now," Dirk replied. "But I have an idea! Give Indigo big project, fill him up with things to do. Dat act as a cover."

"What sort of things do you mean?" asked Joanna.

"Oh, I dunno… some kinda massive data project. Keep his nexus brain happy, see? Den everyone who spot him think him autonomous computer. Even Aritomo."

Joanna looked doubtful.

"Hey, listen up," Dirk said. "Indigo da audio guy, being blind? Dis whole city, Seattle too, it full of da music. So, why not drown Indigo in music, make him collect all da bands, da musos, who make dis area. Make him build up da whole picture."

"Yeah, but that would take years," said Manfred.

Dirk shrugged. "Exactly."

Early next morning they modified Indigo's crate so that it contained perpetually playing music – a standalone media-player showing endless local band video clips, all the way back to Seattle grunge.

"Indigo is not going to grasp any of the cultural references that it hears," Joanna told Dirk.

"Dat not da point," he replied. "Indigo got a strong drive to learn. He want to *classify* what he hears."

"Let us hope so."

Time passed. They taught Orange and Indigo esoteric nouns: colours, foods, implements. But verbs seemed incomprehensible to all the bis who used spoken words. They grasped the concept of lumping nouns together to say simple sentences, and they used faux-nouns that were almost verbs – 'gone' was the most often used – but little more emerged.

Then Joanna had an idea. "We *play* with them," she said. "We teach them complex things with images of themselves. Dolls will maximise their social learning, and dolls will teach them that killing is wrong."

"Dolls?" Dirk said. "Okay... but forget Red and Green and such."

Pouncey hurried out to the nearest active shopping street, where she bought three dolls and three sets of clothes: one set indigo blue, one set orange, one set storm grey. Back in the apartments they prepared these dolls, arranging a teaching day in which all the bis would participate to their preferred limit. In practice, Joanna knew, this would mean Red lazing on a sofa while Green watched spiders making webs. Yellow would jump on a free lap and do nothing except watch.

She noticed that Violet avoided Orange. An idea occurred to her, but it was too outlandish to promulgate. She said nothing.

Focussing on Orange, Indigo and Grey, they tried to explain the concept of the bis as individuals, represented by toys, hoping that through gestural language or other arcane means Indigo would be informed of what was happening – for the dolls made no noise nor had any electromagnetic component.

At once Orange picked up that the orange doll was somehow akin to itself. "Orange," it said, picking up the toy.

Joanna observed. She had not been able to prepare any useful reward scheme, so they defaulted to using cooing tones of voice as they repeated the correct noun, hoping that the marked difference in the musicality of their speech would become associated with positive outcomes. She sat back as Orange examined the doll. From Pouncey's room came the sound of wood tools being used, as toy crates were made...

When afternoon waned Joanna decided it was time to be dramatic. They could not reward the bis in the human sense – no food, no drink, no apparent benefit of the hugging and warmth that children so needed – but they could indicate negative consequences. With the three toy crates nearby and all the bis watching, she took the orange and grey dolls and, with a hammer attached to the grey doll's arm, she broke the orange one as best she could. The limbs came off, then the head. To the torso she applied special force, until the brittle plastic lay in fragments amidst torn clothes. Then she put the grey doll in one of the toy crates.

Only Indigo, Grey and Orange studied this toy crate. To make the scenario even worse, Joanna put the crate in darkness behind a chair once the three bis had seen enough. Grey and Orange, working together, then pulled the toy crate out, but Joanna stopped them, returning the crate and the grey doll to isolated gloom.

They halted the work, Joanna sitting next to Manfred on a couch while Dirk and Pouncey sat on chairs. The plan was to do nothing in as obvious a manner as possible. The plan was to make the atmosphere of the social group as different as possible following the demise of the orange doll.

"Reckon they've got it?" Manfred asked her.

Joanna nodded. "Negative reinforcement is powerful. You were right – they do not like being alone because they are social creatures. Solitary confinement is our big punishment, that we can wield because *we* lead the family. They will certainly understand that."

"I think the doll teaching method is the way forward," Manfred said. "We can act out various scenarios, then act the consequences, mmm? The clever bis grasp symbolic equivalences. Oh, yeah... the moment they grasp that a grey doll means Grey–"

"They will already have grasped *that*."

"–then our job gets much easier."

That night Joanna first checked on Indigo, who they had put in the music crate, then gathered the bis into one of the large apartment rooms. She said goodnight to the others, then sat down to wait out the early night: she had first watch.

Soft music played on inside Indigo's crate. The others sat around. The atmosphere seemed quieter than usual, almost sombre, as though the killing lesson had caused an emotional reaction – fear. The bis' skin patterns however appeared unchanged, at least in mobility and number. Any meaning component would forever be beyond her, she realised.

At midnight Indigo tried to escape its crate. She knelt in front of it, whispering to herself, "No, you stay in there, you've got classifying to do." She raised her voice. "Sorry Indigo, but this is how it has got to be."

"Crate, dark, music."

"Yes," she returned in the cooing tone of voice. "Indigo music crate. Night – dark. Indigo music here?"

Then Indigo said, "I've got a piece of my heart and it doesn't want to fall, into dark, into mud, into anything at all."

Joanna sat up. For a moment she wondered if another dam had burst open. Then she replayed the words in her mind.

Indigo repeated them: "I've got a piece of my heart and it doesn't want to fall, into dark, into mud, into anything at all."

Joanna grabbed a computer and typed in the line. The first search result was *The Hay Makers, Piece Of My Heart,* and she realised what had happened. Indigo had taken a lyric and parroted it to her.

She sat back, then leaned down so that her face was just centimetres from Indigo's. Blind: yet it stared at her. She realised that Indigo must have separated out the timbre, pitch and rhythm of the lyrics from a song it had heard. It grasped that speech, even sung speech, was conceptually different to music.

Glancing down at the full lyric, she spoke the second line. "You're the one on my mind, and you're not a man unkind, give me peace, make it true, all the world for us to find." Country 'n' western rubbish, she thought.

Indigo spoke the next line. She spoke the fourth. In this way they ran through the lyric of the entire song.

She sat back. While again this was not conscious, creative speech, it was an element of speech, and it showed that Indigo was aware of its environment, and what aspects of that environment were important to the members of its social group.

"You're the really bright one, aren't you?" Joanna whispered. "You are the dangerous one."

"Crate dark," Indigo replied. "Six bi room. Indigo crate. Indigo gone crate."

It wanted to get out, she suspected, that being the likely meaning of *gone crate*. It had a concept of time, she realised, if *Indigo crate, Indigo gone crate* described a future pair of events in temporal order. "No," she said. "Indigo crate."

She returned to her seat. At worst, Indigo would learn that *Indigo crate* spoken by her meant that Indigo had to remain in the crate. Intentionality was implied, which if nothing else would improve its mental model.

Minutes ticked by. The music lulled her. But she did not feel tired – coffee attended to that problem of keeping watch at night.

Then an alarm sounded.

Beep-beep! Beep-beep!

Joanna leaped to her feet. For a few moments she did not recognise what it was. Fire? Intruders? Pouncey had set a sub-AI tripwire outside the apartment door.

She opened the door to peer out into the corridor. To her right, Dirk's door was shut, and so was Pouncey's. The windows on the other side were blacked out. But the noise had diminished. She walked into the kitchen, to see a red lamp flashing on the gas stove.

A message scrolled across its smart-screen. "Power down."

Joanna switched the stove off, then switched it on again. The stove did nothing.

A noise at the door. Pouncey. "What's up?" she hissed.

Joanna replied, "Stove fault. Is it on mains?"

"Mains solar. Probably a glitch in the supply. Rats eating insulation, bird nestin'. Don't worry."

Joanna walked back to the bis' room.

All the bis, including Indigo, stood around Orange, who lay part smeared across the carpet. Its head was reduced to granulated mush.

Too shocked to respond, she stared.

Pouncey moved fast. Taking Grey and Indigo, she put them into crates. "Don't move," she told Joanna.

Moments later Pouncey returned with more crates, so that half a minute later six bis stood in six crates.

Joanna felt horror overcome her. She had been on watch. *She* had fallen for a distraction ploy.

In a strangled croak she said, "Fetch Manfred, Dirk."

A minute later they all stood staring at the bis, at the smudged orange remains.

Silence fell.

The bis stared back at them.

At last Manfred said, "Okay, two guards on them non-stop." He took a deep breath. "We got careless. We none of us thought far enough ahead."

Joanna felt tears trickling down her cheeks. "Manfred! They tricked me. They *wanted* to kill it, so they tricked me." She shook her head in disbelief. "Like I was worth nothing to them."

He held her in his arms. "Yeah," he said. "Coulda happened to any of us."

"But it happened to *me!*"

He made no reply, except to hold her tighter.

Dirk said, "Dey little brats. Dey got no morals. We need teach fast, or dat da end of bis."

"That would be the end of *us!*" Joanna cried out.

Dirk nodded. "Listen – crazy idea. Blue and Violet, dey like friends. Violet – he seem to avoid Orange."

"So?" Manfred asked. "*So?*"

"Maybe Orange jealous of Blue. Kill Blue. Den bis kill Orange together." Dirk nodded again, as if pleased with his hypothesis. "You know what dey say," he added, looking up at them. "Revenge is for children."

"But Dirk," Joanna wailed, "they are *not* human!"

"No," he replied, "but dey mimic us pretty good in some respects. We best not forget dat."

Manfred put every bi in an outdoor crate, then, inside the largest apartment room, placed them in a circle so that the wireframe front of every cage faced the centre. Every bi could see every other bi.

"We cannot leave them caged up forever!" Joanna said, appalled at the implied brutality of the deed. "It is cruel. You said so yourself."

"Ain't gonna," Manfred said.

"Then what?" she asked.

Before he could answer an unearthly sound began, like the multiple whines of devil dogs. Manfred put his hands to his ears. The sound was not loud, but it was vile.

"What da hell dat?" Dirk asked.

Manfred loosened the pressure on his ears. He sensed a challenge. "Stay still, all of you," he said. "They're trying to get out."

"Get out of what?" Joanna asked.

"The crates, what else? But I'm not that easy. They're staying in there until we know for sure they ain't gonna kill each other."

"This is Indigo's doing," said Pouncey.

"Hmmm? Whatcha mean?" he asked.

"Can't you hear the unmusicality?" Pouncey said. "Indigo *knows* somethin' about music. This noise is the worst he can come up with. Aye, you're right – they're tryin' to manipulate us, make us set them free by harrassin' us."

"Well they're not gonna do *that*," Manfred said. "We carry on teaching them, language, words, dolls and all. They can still socialise, after all. What they won't have is liberty and intimate proximity. Let's hope they *can* communicate with one another, 'cos that's the only way they're gonna get out of those crates."

Joanna said, "But..."

"It's not cruel," Manfred responded. "It's firm – parental firm. You were right, Jo. If we give in to them, we don't just lose the battle we lose the whole damn war."

The unmusical wail continued.

"Keep your nerve," said Manfred. "We'll still set guards even though they're caged. We *want* 'em to know we're watching. *Two* guards still, not one. They're not gonna get anything past me."

"But how will we know when they can be set free?"

"They're gonna tell us themselves. Yeah, they're gonna have to *learn* to tell us. This is the lesson they'll never forget."

CHAPTER 21

Aritomo Ichikawa indicated the bed and the three chairs in Zeug's room. "I believe we should all sit down after our exertions," he said. "There is much to discuss."

Leonora glanced back at the shut and sealed door. "But…"

"Do not worry. My men are dealing with the charity employees, and of course the patients will leave us alone. You are safe."

Leonora felt too numb to be frightened. She understood Aritomo well. He spoke the truth, albeit in his inimitable way. Hound, she knew, would do nothing to endanger them. Tsuneko however was an unknown quantity.

She sat on a chair, as two of the cat herd slunk over, as if to guard her. They looked real. "Are you taking Zeug back to Japan?" she asked.

Aritomo turned to face Zeug. "What do *you* want?" he asked.

Zeug said nothing.

"He will not talk," said Leonora. "I trained him well."

"You have not *trained* him," Aritomo said. "He has learned from you, which is a different process, one that incidentally has failed."

Now Leonora felt a hint of irritation rise up inside her. "What do you mean? You know nothing of Zeug."

"Nothing?" Aritomo looked baffled. "You worked for me since twenty eighty six and you believe I know nothing of the AIteam scheme?"

Leonora shrugged. "How could you? We concealed everything and we destroyed everything in the Malta cave."

"You did indeed, and that was done with maximum efficiency by Mr Awuku. We learned nothing from the tech remnants in the cave. But surely you did not think that nothing of your ignoble flight across North Africa would float up into the brighter regions of the nexus?"

Leonora glanced at Hound, who in response said, "You're bluffing, man. You want info off us before you kill us. We ain't giving it."

An expression of annoyance passed across Aritomo's face. "I am not going to *kill* you, Mr Awuku, what kind of man do you believe me to be?"

"You won't let us go—"

"Silence! We deviate from the subject of the conversation, which is what I know of Zeug. I am perfectly aware of the fundamental difference in approach of the AIteam and the BIteam. It has been a most intriguing time for me, which has opened up new possibilities for the Ichikawa Corporation."

A horrible possibility suggested itself to Leonora. "Did you... let us escape?"

Aritomo laughed. "Certainly not. No, you escaped – and that was well done. I learned much from your techniques."

Leonora shook her head. "You *must* hate me."

Again Aritomo looked exasperated. "What aspect of your escape do you suppose the Japanese nexus papers concentrated on the following day?"

Leonora considered this question. "The security implications?"

Aritomo shook his head. "They focussed on the response of the foreign media, which mocked Japan, as always it does. I was shamed by your escape, and insulted. I vowed to learn whatever I could from what you and Manfred did, how you did it, and what you did subsequently. I vowed to do this for the sake of my country."

Leonora glanced at Hound, then shrugged.

Aritomo looked at them both. "I cannot believe you are so stupid as that! Why do you think I use cats? A cat is an individual, like a Westerner. I do grasp the concept of irony."

Leonora looked down at the two cats at her feet. One of them appeared to be the cat Tsuneko had played with in the date palm park shed. "They are not real," she said.

"I am glad we understand one another."

"Man," said Hound, "I *get* it now. The module on the cat collar – that was a decoy. The signal came from the cat, which was artificial."

"Indeed, Mr Awuku, but do not fret over your mistake. Your chances of hiding from me were exceedingly slim."

"Then you knew about the Zeug signal?"

"No. What I knew of Zeug was the concept behind him, that of making the most complex and powerful computer possible – the quantum computer – in order to mimic the complexity of the human brain. Research at my laboratories favoured that approach, as Leonora has doubtless explained to you. My son Yuri was the expert on such technologies."

Leonora said nothing. Aritomo must know that Yuri was dead. Probably he knew that Zeug had killed him.

Aritomo continued, "My plan was to cast upon you a net so light even Mr Awuku would not feel it. I began when I spotted the observation trace created in the nexus by Zeug, who was aware of Mr Awuku's abilities, although the meaning of those abilities was lost to him. Later, I spotted nexus traces created by the low-level functioning of Zeug's brain. The four members of the AIteam were invisible to me, concealed, as they were, by Mr Awuku, with all his exceptional skill."

"Did you track the old man's boat?" asked Hound.

"Yes," Aritomo replied. "That was the beginning of the end game, for at that point I knew Zeug was no longer with you."

Hound nodded. "I *knew* that augmentation delay must mean something."

"And you noticing that delay made it extremely difficult to track you in Bejaïa. But we had to pull a few hints from you, Mr Awuku, since we remained uncertain of your destination, not to mention your reasons for travelling. This was why we took the time to set up the cat decoy, with its fake brand new module."

"Unformatted!"

"Indeed. I suspected you would ignore the cat once you had examined the module, assuming that the module was the source of the signal."

"Man... an assumption is a dangerous thing," Hound murmured.

"It is indeed. The module was not owned by a local crime lord at all. And this brings me to the kernel of our conversation, which is Zeug. You see, Leonora, I have grasped the mistake you made when building Zeug."

"Mistake?" Leonora said.

"Oh, yes! A mistake I myself made when setting up the conditions for the operation of Ichikawa Laboratories. Like you, I assumed that human consciousness was a consequence of processing power – the trillions of connections extant between the billions of neurons in our brain. Scientists say the human brain is the most complex thing in the universe. Like you, I was seduced by that vision of complexity. I applied the computer metaphor to everything I knew about intelligence. Faster computers, more processing power, more memory. The development of the quantum computer I believed to be a turning point in human history, since, to me, it seemed to lead to the creation of a new artificial conscious species. I even devised a name for that species for use in the outside world. I intended calling them Giri Men."

"Giri Men?" Leonora queried.

"Giri is why I am here now, speaking with you. I was much entangled in giri – which you call obligation – when you escaped from my laboratories. I received more than a few comments regarding the ending of my life. But I chose a different response. I am valuable to Japan, and I live at its heart. I chose to respond to this giri by recapturing both you and Manfred, and by returning to Japan the knowledge you have both gained since escaping my laboratories."

"Why didn't you just ignore this giri?" Leonora asked.

"That is impossible for a Japanese. You, a Westerner, throw gifts around – and receive them – with shameful abandon. It is not the same in Japan. All my life I have sweated beneath a weight of giri, which became heavier because of the great significance of the work done by my laboratories. But a Giri Man, being inhuman yet conscious, would reduce giri to a minimum. That is my dream for Japan."

Leonora glanced at Hound and Tsuneko. "Then you really are going to set us free?"

"That depends on who you mean by *us*."

Leonora nodded. She had half expected this. "You will take us back to Japan, with Zeug, and you will force us to work on Zeug."

Aritomo shook his head. "You and Mr Awuku will be free to leave, since you are worth nothing to me. Indeed, I judge you now to be worth nothing to the world. But Tsuneko June is not like you."

At this, Tsuneko sat up. Leonora saw fear in her eyes. "What are you going to do with me?" Tsuneko asked.

Aritomo replied, "First, we must drink tea. My mouth is quite dry from talking so much in this arid atmosphere. I am used to the cold snows of my home mountains. This desert environment is anathema to me!"

"Man, you didn't have to come here yourself," Hound muttered.

"Oh, but I did, Mr Awuku. Giri made me do that."

Aritomo clicked his fingers at one of his aides, who stepped forward at once, taking what appeared to be a roll of fabric from his pocket. This roll was in fact a miniature table, which unfurled like a bolt of silk, to shape itself, then harden into the form of furniture. Another of the aides carried a flask of tea and a set of Russian-doll cups, so that in a matter of moments the entire tea set was prepared.

Aritomo allowed four cups to be poured. The second aide handed over a cup each to Leonora, Hound and Tsuneko, with exaggerated care, as if the trio were honoured guests. Aritomo sat back in his chair, enjoying the perfume of the drink.

After a while he said, "Human consciousness is not a consequence of processing power. Zeug is insane – an autistic savant, yet not able to function in society as even the most bizarre human autistic savant is able to. He lacks others like himself. That was your mistake, Leonora."

"We were talking about Tsuneko," Leonora replied, feeling her old anger rise up at this insulting description of Zeug.

"Tsuneko June is the young genius who developed biograins," said Aritomo. "One of my agents spoke with her in Valetta, and even then I knew she would eventually come to Ichikawa Laboratories. Biograins are the way forward in artificial intelligence research, but they are no better than quantum computers if used in isolated creations. And this brings me to the thrust of Manfred's research."

"*He's* the mad man, not Zeug," said Tsuneko. "I *worked* with him. His ideas are all wrong."

"Not at all. His ideas are correct, or so I believe. Even now he lives somewhere on the western fringe of America with a small society of intelligences. I will locate those intelligences and take them."

"But Manfred's *wrong*," Tsuneko insisted. "I saw it myself. He cut the bis apart with a pair of scissors."

"But that was his stroke of genius, do you not see? Until that day they were networked, able to apprehend one another directly. There is even evidence that they worked as a gestalt identity, though, I confess, the evidence is uncertain. The evidence may have been generated by a rogue computer, for example."

"A *gestalt?*" said Leonora.

"Composed of nine individuals," Aritomo said. "But human beings do not apprehend one another directly. What I see in my mind's eye is visible only to me. We apprehend one another *indirectly*, through such means as language and emotion."

"What is the point of that?" Leonora asked.

"It forces human beings to use themselves as exemplars in the comprehension of the behaviour of other human beings. I grasp that, because I feel pride, loyalty and dignity, so might you also. I comprehend that, if you cry, you are sad, for on occasion I also have felt sad."

"But that's just ordinary behaviour," Leonora said. "Zeug was intended to fly far beyond trivial things."

"Trivial?" Aritomo said, with a laugh. "You call the comprehension of grief trivial? I see that I was correct to inform you that you are of no worth to the world. It appears you have understood nothing at all."

"What about *me?*" Tsuneko said, standing up.

The two aides pointed cylindrical weapons at her. Aritomo raised a finger, then gave his aides a significant look. They lowered their weapons.

"Biograins will allow the human brain to grasp the nexus without the need for spex and wristbands," said Aritomo. "This is the next step in human technological evolution, and once again the Japanese will provide it for the world, as we provided the nexus. Biograins will also be placed in my next generation of artificial intelligences, which I will ensure grasp the world they inhabit indirectly. The days of electronic networking are coming to an end. The time of a symbolic nexus is not far away, in which we are connected by meaning."

Tsuneko said, "Then... you're forcing me to go back to Japan with you?"

"Force?" Aritomo said. "You will enjoy a salary fifty times what you earned before. You will reside in luxury apartments. You will be permitted to acquire a Western sexual partner. I will permit you to marry him or her, should that eventuality arise. You will be the golden child of the world, Tsuneko June."

"Don't believe him!" Leonora said. "You will be a slave!"

Aritomo looked at her. "Do continue," he said. "Try to dissuade her."

Leonora looked again at Tsuneko. Aritomo's urbane calm unnerved her. "Don't tell me you're tempted, Tsuneko?" she said.

Tsuneko also appeared confused by the lack of anxiety shown by Aritomo. She turned to look at Leonora, saying, "You worked with him. You'd know."

"I did not work *with* him, I worked for him," Leonora said.

"That is perfectly true," Aritomo said with a smile. "They were indeed pleasant times."

"Biograins are mine to develop," Tsuneko told Aritomo.

"When you work for me, all the patents will be owned by Ichikawa Laboratories."

Tsuneko nodded. "That's not good enough."

"It is the only way. For obvious commercial reasons I cannot allow the development of biograins to slip out into the arms of other corporations, let alone the world at large."

"That's not *good* enough for me."

"But do you want the responsibility of developing biograins yourself?" Aritomo insisted. "Imagine this future. I will take responsibility for all legal and financial consequences of your research. All you will have to do is play with your biograins, in laboratories designed by you, and built by me to your precise specification. You will be free to take this research in the direction you choose, so long as you agree to teach me and my researchers the central tenets of your work. But this is the nature of modern research, is it not? The sharing of knowledge for the benefit of mankind."

"You mean the benefit of Japan."

"I meant what I said. Has mankind not benefitted from the nexus?"

Tsuneko pondered this. "I s'pose it has," she said.

"Don't do it, Tsuneko!" Leonora gasped.

Tsuneko turned to her and smiled. "Don't worry," she said, taking a tiny standalone moby from her pocket. She pressed a button.

"What is that?" Aritomo asked.

"Something I prepared before I joined the AIteam," Tsuneko replied. "I understand what you mean about the huge responsibility of developing biograins alone. I'd hoped for a different future. But you've forced my hand."

"Forced it? In which direction?"

"Setting my biograin techniques loose on the world. It's open source, now, and you can't do a thing about it."

Aritomo's face turned pale. Then fury entered his expression. He gestured to his aides and said, "Kill her. Then we depart."

Leonora and Hound sat on a beachfront in Algiers. A cool sea breeze wafted over them. It was early evening, and fast-food hawkers passed them by on bicycles, steaming packages of microwaved fish and couscous in their panniers.

Seven days had passed since leaving Bejaïa. The shock of events there was beginning to depart.

"What now?" Hound asked Leonora.

She glanced at him. "It is just us now."

He nodded. "Yeah." He stopped a kid hawker and bought a couple of suppers: fish fragments, veg and apricots in a couscous mush. Not exactly appetising, but it could have been worse.

"What now?" he said again, as they dipped into their food.

"I need to relax," said Leonora. "My research days are over. It's been far too long since I got drunk and had a bit of a dance."

"Me too. Except the dancing. Yes, yes... it's true – even with you I was thinking about packing security in. Man, it's a stressful occupation."

"We'll watch the news on the nexus," said Leonora. "We'll set up flags for Manfred's name, and Dirk's. It won't be long before Aritomo locates them. We'll watch it all on the news, and not care even a little bit about either of them."

"You reckon?"

Leonora nodded. "What can save them from Aritomo?"

Hound grasped her hand in his. "There's just the two of us left now," he said with a smile. "We don't want any more misery. We need to chill."

She smiled back. "Would you consider returning to Malta? I liked it there."

Hound nodded. "I could definitely live in Malta. Nice climate... some space away from dusty urbs. We could find a bit of land to grow veg. Yeah. Malta. Shall we?"

And Leonora grinned.

CHAPTER 22

The snow-muffled mountain slopes owned by Ichikawa Laboratories shone icy blue in the light of the full moon. In the lower of the main laboratories – a circular chamber split in half by a sheet of toughened glass – Aritomo Ichikawa and his nexus manager Ikuo Amano stood in the safe side looking into the secure side. In that secure half stood Zeug.

Zeug had been placed into a metal jacket, so that he was unable to move his arms. He was stronger than a typical Japanese man, but, more important, his reflexes were as fast as a cat's, and that made him dangerous. His feet had been shod with lead boots that he was unable to remove. This both slowed him down and made him aware of the control wielded by his new owners.

Aritomo said, "He is to be dealt with as if he was a mentally retarded person. I believe he hid inside a place of mad people for symbolic reasons."

Ikuo asked, "What reasons, Mr Ichikawa?"

"I learned from your nexus trail report that Zeug is able to compare himself with human beings. He does not grasp the difference between himself and a human, but he does grasp that human behaviour can be analysed. He sees patterns and metaphors in human behaviour, and he matches those patterns to his own. What he does not grasp is that he could use himself as a human equivalent. He has no self-symbol. He does not tell himself the tale of his own life. He just lives it, unconsciously."

"Then, he identified his own patterns of behaviour with those of mad people?"

"Indeed. Zeug has intelligence. What he lacks is comprehension of that intelligence."

"What will you do with him?" asked Ikuo.

"Zeug is to be dismantled. It must be done slowly, and with tender care. There are several novel uses of materials in his muscles and organs, and those we need to analyse. Once his body is dismantled his brain will fail – but by then we will know all we need to know about Zeug."

Aritomo strolled away, Ikuo following. Two of the artificial cats also followed, at a distance of a few metres, like awed, respectful servants.

"What is your plan for Zeug's brain?" Ikuo asked.

"To let it fade – it will be nothing without its senses. We will build another, better brain. The important matter is the body. We are experts on quantum computers, and our research is proceeding well. But a truly lifelike artificial human eludes all Japanese manufacturers. Zeug, in rough cosmetics and wearing human clothes, was able to fool a few mad Africans, but no Japanese would mistake him for a human being. He is still an android."

"The Westerners call our products Nippandroids."

"Then our task," Aritomo said, "is to utilise all the novel techniques used to make Zeug's body, incorporating them into artificial bodies that will not be viewed as androids. I was informed this morning that we now have a cat non-identification level of ninety nine percent amongst a sample of one thousand Japanese."

"That final one percent will be difficult to convince." Ikuo glanced back at the pair of cats following them. "Though even I would be fooled by those two, and I am fond of cats."

"We will use everything we have learned about making lifelike cats to make a lifelike human. Time is on our side."

"And what of Mr Klee and the bis?"

Aritomo favoured Ikuo with an amused glance. "You have struggled with that concept, have you not?"

Ikuo wiped his forehead with a handkerchief. "Mr Ichikawa, the BIteam security specialist operates at the level of Mr Awuku. We have found no hint of their presence on the western American coast."

"A thought occurs to me. What would you say was the weakest point of their security arrangement?"

Ikuo paused to contemplate this question.

"Do not be afraid of making a mistake," Aritomo said. "Tell me what you think, since all thoughts must be integrated into the whole. I will not be dishonoured."

"I think the weakest point must be the relationship between Manfred Klee and his partner, who we believe to be Joanna Rohlen. Love makes people wilt."

Aritomo shook his head. "The weak point is not inside the BIteam. We could spend years searching for them, and never find them. Do not forget that we were lucky locating the AIteam. You should not feel ashamed to admit that."

"Then what, Mr Ichikawa?"

"The weak point is the bis themselves. If they are intelligent and conscious, they may be difficult to control. My guess is that they will exhibit nonhuman characteristics. Therefore we should consider attacking in their direction."

"How?"

"We could entice, trick or force one or more bis out of the group," Aritomo said. "Most likely the BIteam is using the method of moving from place to place that they employed in Philadelphia. When they are between safe houses they will be vulnerable. We must devise a strategy that activates when such an event happens. When one bi is loose, we attack. Manfred will do everything he can to retrieve such a loose bi. He will be forced to act on impulse, swiftly, perhaps without thought."

"There will be an element of chaos in such a situation! Then we strike."

Aritomo nodded. "We shall make a base in San Francisco. Prepare for a conference here tomorrow. Make sure you invite Wataru Kohama, since I will request that he directs the base. We shall discuss options, then begin work. The bis will be ours in due course."

"And Manfred Klee?"

"He could still be useful to the Ichikawa Corporation. He will understand the use of biograins better than anyone else we know of. If circumstances allow, he should not be killed."

CHAPTER 23

Pouncey saw the news on PXR-15 – a science news orientated media station – while she was checking out the fake exam results of the fake class. For a few seconds she just stared, open-mouthed, as the bold red text scrolled across her spex. She halted in the street. She read, then re-read. She glanced away, to see a dozen other pedestrians doing the same as she was.

Cascadia subduction zone earthquake rated 89.2% likely in the next 72 hours.

At once she put down her bags of food and initiated a nexus source check via her wristband. But the news was being disseminated at the speed of light through the nexus by every rock-solid media station in the world. It looked as though it was true. Real.

The next three days!

She read the full transcript on Sci-News Central, the streetwise wing of Europe's Independent BBC.

> *The West Coast Geological Survey has received intelligence from scientific vessels anchored off Newport indicating that a subduction zone megathrust earthquake is almost certain to occur in the next 72 hours. This means an earthquake of magnitude around or greater than 9.0 on the Richter scale. All coastal communities advised to evacuate immediately to avoid consequential megatsunami.*

Advise Seattle and Portland total evacuation. Megathrust earthquakes are particularly destructive. The Cascadia fault is thought to have last moved around 1700. If the quake motion travels its entire length the earthquake duration could be as much as five minutes, destroying every building in the area.

Pouncey picked up her bags, to discover that she was shaking. The two bags, filled with half rotten food, seemed much heavier than before.

"Just shock," she told herself. "Just a sugar low. You feel sweaty. Get home and get some food."

She walked back to Haemorrhage Apts as fast as she could.

Everybody was home. She locked the door, dropped the bags to the floor and ran into the main common room, where Dirk and Joanna sat, along with the bis. "Listen up," she said.

Joanna glanced up at her, but Dirk continued his sentence.

"Listen *up!*" Pouncey yelled.

Dirk jumped, then looked over his shoulder.

"Where's Manfred?" Pouncey asked.

A voice behind her: "Here."

Pouncey turned. "Cascadia earthquake! It's gonna unzip – maybe the entire length of the fault. We gotta get out."

"Out? Earthquake?"

"On the news – the grown up news, Manfred! This is the real thing."

"Wait," Manfred said, placing a hand on her shoulder. "What's this news in full?"

Pouncey summarised what she'd read, then linked her wristband to the lo-fi computer they had stolen from a local geek artist. The monitor screen lit up. "Read it for yourself," she said.

They all read the official reports. Joanna went pale and began stroking her cheek with one hand. Dirk sat back, silent. Manfred read the info, then shook his head.

"I smell a big rat," he said. "This is Aritomo trying to scare us."

At once Pouncey felt anger course through her body. "This is confirmed by all the legit stations!" she said. "This isn't a software hack, this is the real deal. They've been warnin' about this for *decades,* and now it's gonna happen."

Manfred hesitated. Pouncey saw that he was half convinced.

"Okay," she said, "I'll do a full check on it. Of course I will. But we have to pack. To go. In *hours,* Manfred! What if a megatsunami makes it all the way here–"

"It couldn't possibly–"

"You don't *know!* Nobody's ever seen a megatsunami in the modern world. What about the Columbia River? Get real. You think you know it all and you don't! We have to evacuate within hours. Two hours – that's what I'm tellin' you. Any more and it's your ass on the line."

"Mmm, thank you," said Manfred.

"What's da security diagnosis?" asked Dirk.

Pouncey gestured at the bis. "One per cage – now. Then all food and water to be packed. Then all hardware. Last of all other stuff – clothes, oddments. I'll prep the van to go in one hour. After that I'll allow another hour. We can probably get out of Portland... hey, you know, *fuck* it! We need to be out of this city in one hour. If we don't the traffic queues will kill us. Get movin'!"

She ran out of the room to fetch the bi crates.

Manfred followed. "You're serious?" he asked.

"Yes!"

"Do your nexus source check. Five minutes, okay? We'll pack while you do it. But I wanna be sure who's behind this."

Pouncey tried to stop herself from trembling. She took a few deep breaths.

Manfred again put a hand on her shoulder. "Calm down," he said. "We don't disbelieve you, but I need to be certain. Aritomo is a devious bastard."

"I do *know*," Pouncey replied, putting every ounce of sarcasm into her voice. "Get packin'. I'll do the check. Five minutes and I want to see five bis in five crates. Five in the back, that is – not Indigo."

"We haven't got five strong crates any more. We've got four."

Pouncey hesitated. That was true. They were still militating against the bi co-operation regime, though the inhuman wailing had ceased. "Use that wooden case I made for Blue when it was injured," she said. "It's ramshackle, but it should hold."

Manfred nodded. He looked scared now. The atmosphere of the apartment had changed. Even the bis were quiet, staring at them in that weird Nippandroid way. Pouncey shuddered. The bis knew something unusual was happening. They weren't stupid.

She initiated a secure analysis of the nexus info source. The problem she faced was that, although her analysis would seem invisible – effectively secure – she could never entirely wipe the nexus free of her computational activities. Invisible, in nexus terms, meant hidden; there was always a trace. And if somebody wanted to locate that trace, invisible could change to visible.

She had five minutes. She would have to ignore the usual complex, careful, fractal-freighted camouflage of a fully secure analysis and go for the default option: hide and hope. It worked 99.999% of the time.

Having initiated the analysis, she set it off. The default computer chose an earthquake infomercial to conceal its activities, an option Pouncey supported, though it was rather obvious. She checked local stats – already there had been over twenty million hits on official earthquake advice stations. She glanced at a few traffic cams. Nothing out of the ordinary. But soon, she knew, the roads would be filled with solcars and solbikes, not to mention every half-operational, salvaged, pimped or patchworked solar vehicle in Portland. It would be a mechanical jungle.

She heard noises in the other rooms. She felt reassured. They were taking the warning seriously. Some of the bis were whining – she could hear their vocoder-lite voices making beats as the frequencies dipped and dived – but it was only two or three of them. Anyway, they were still too weak to resist a co-ordinated move from Manfred and the other two, in such a constrained environment.

Then the results: info source 99.6% official West Coast Geological Survey.

Pouncey compressed her lips. That was less than she'd expected, and less than she wanted. A 99.9% official would have been nice. Her result meant a 0.4% chance that somebody had set up the Cascadia warning as a hoax.

Manfred walked out of the far room. "Well?" he grunted.

"It's real," she said. "Everyone out. Fifty minutes. I'll prep the van. Move it!"

Without waiting for an answer she grabbed the food bags and headed to the lift shaft. Minutes later she stood beside the van.

She paused. She was trembling again. Shock receded, and she felt frightened. A megathrust earthquake was every West Coast person's nightmare. Was it real? Surely it was. 99.6%…

"Oh, *fuck* it! Why *now?*" She kicked the side of the van, then pulled open all the doors. Moments later she'd forgotten her fears and immersed herself in the mechanics of the soltruck. Engine first. Check. Fluids. Check. Tyres… one down slightly, but not serious. Spare tyre: check.

Noises from the lift shaft: Manfred, Jo and bis in crates. "I found the sixth crate and lashed it up," he said. "Better than that old wooden case you made." He grinned. "No offence."

Pouncey indicated the back of the soltruck. "None taken," she said.

She revved the engine a few times, disabled the auto-GPS feature, then ran down the on-board computer by disconnecting its power lead. This being an emergency exit, they didn't want to leave a traffic trace in the nexus for some nosy street management system to record.

"Forty minutes!" she shouted. "Or less!"

Those forty minutes passed like four. But then – quite suddenly it seemed to Pouncey, as if she woke from a dream – she found herself sitting behind the soltruck wheel, Manfred, Jo and Dirk at her side. A bit of a squeeze. Indigo sat on Dirk's lap.

"It was only three of us before," Manfred observed. "Dirk, you gotta give up smoking, you know?"

The smell was strong. Pouncey stared out of the front window. That odour was a potential security risk. Dirk was famous. Computers everywhere would be looking for him. There was such a thing as an artificial nose.

All three of them were staring at her. Joanna looked concerned. "We're ready to go," she said.

Pouncey nodded. She had fazed out for a few moments, her last hour a blur of motion lasting subjective minutes. "Yeah," she said. "Right. Yeah. Let's go."

She drove the soltruck up the ramp and turned left into morning sunlight, leaving a trail of leaves from the green camouflage. Then an orange warning light winked on her spex. There was a synchronous beep in the front comp.

"What's that?" Manfred asked.

Pouncey checked, then slammed on the brakes. "Shit," she said. "The fake class!"

"What about them?"

"An error's been spotted. All the real school kids have made earthquake plans, but not our fake class. Manfred, I gotta sort that now."

"What? Why?"

"It'll stand out like a sore thumb – Portland kids with no escape plan? You gotta be jokin'! There'll be dozens of media computers sending *that* newsflash to the nearest stations, the voyeuristic fuckers. And if Aritomo spots–"

"Yeah, yeah. So give 'em a plan. Then drive on."

Pouncey worked info as fast as she could. The ghost link on the school roster had alerted her class management soft to the fact that the fake class had no earthquake evacuation data, unlike the rest of the school. Somebody... no, some *thing*, some computer somewhere had noticed that anomaly. If it got out into local media, that would be just the sort of thing Aritomo might notice. He would be searching for anomalies.

Then Indigo said, "There are vultures circling overhead."

Pouncey stared. Manfred stared at her.

Dirk said, "What you say, Mr Indigo?"

"There are vultures circling overhead."

"What dat mean?" Dirk asked.

But Indigo said nothing more, lowering its head in a way that made Pouncey think at once of an aircraft crash posture.

"Get outa here!" Manfred shouted.

Pouncey used three more seconds to finish the school class update. Then she took a deep breath and revved the engine. "To the hills," she said.

She turned the corner at the end of the street, then headed down a passage leading to the main route out of town – a dual triple lane road of pot-holed tarmac and shattered barriers. Algae-covered roadsigns littered the sides of the road, alongside less recognisable piles of rubbish.

Pouncey drove fast, but around the next corner she saw a roadblock. She skidded to a halt. Two solcars had stopped at the roadblock; a man gesticulated with tall black dudes in faded emergency overalls, yellow and orange.

"Highway department?" Pouncey muttered to herself. "Can't be."

"What is it, mmm?" Manfred asked.

Pouncey parked the soltruck, threw him a hi-vel pistol, then armed her own. "Gonna find out," she said. "Manfred, open the window your side and cover me. If you hear a shot, Dirk – you drive. I might be injured. Got it?"

"Got it," said Dirk, handing Indigo over to Joanna.

Pouncey stepped out, then ran over to the gesticulating man. "What's going on?" she asked. She gestured at the roadblock. "Local, is it?"

Three heavyweights manned the roadblock: more muscles than wrestlers. Steam shot up from some manhole a few metres behind piles of rubble. The solcar driver spoke in broken Ameri-English. "Yeah, local. These men say splits in the road. We go back. He tell me to get the fuck out before the earthquake come."

Pouncey glanced at the three dudes. They glowered at her, but said nothing. They made no move. Seemed legitimate. She turned to run back to the soltruck.

There came a shot. The front windscreen of the soltruck shattered, but it did not break free: triple laminated. Pouncey dived, rolled, ran along a barrier, then positioned herself at its end.

The soltruck stood three metres away. A second shot rang out and two men ran out from a building twenty metres off. Nearby there came the screech of wheels.

Nothing for it. This was a set-up – time for a risk.

She fired at the running men, then jumped up and flattened herself against the side of the soltruck. A bullet ricocheted off her boot heel.

She opened the door and jumped in. "Close your window you fool!" she shouted at Manfred.

He shut the window. Dirk gasped, "It da Aritomo men! Dey block da road."

Pouncey stamped on the accelerator then swung the soltruck around. Through luck and nothing else the two attackers were right in her way: she ran them over as the three black dudes raked the back of the soltruck with semi-automatic fire.

"They want us alive!" Pouncey gasped. "This is kid gloves, yeah? Hold tight!"

"But–"

More gunfire – and then a sight of the vehicle that she'd heard. A big fat car with racing wheels and what sounded like a petrol engine. Pouncey quailed. That was not good. That was concentrated energy.

Again through luck she was well positioned to dodge the vehicle as it screeched into the street. Somebody leaned out of a window and fired a semi-automatic at the back of the soltruck. Bullets thundered into the metal and she heard one of the doors rattling. Then she heard the *whumph* of a car impact.

"If that door opens, our five bis are done for," she said.

Joanna glanced over her shoulder. "I think the door *is* open!" she cried.

Pouncey span the wheel and drove the soltruck into a side road. She screeched to a halt. "Manfred! Cover me!"

She ran to the back of the soltruck to see that two crates had fallen out, but they were invisible – in the other street. Too far away now.

She slammed the right door shut, grabbed a jump lead from the tool bay on the inside of the other door, then closed it and wired both doors. A vehicle engine revved around the corner. Voices yelled. She ran back to the comp, jumped in and slammed her door shut.

"They're all there?" Manfred asked, trying to peer into the gloom at the back of the soltruck. "All five?"

Pouncey did not answer. Pedal to the metal, she was already doing twenty kilometres per hour.

"They were all *there?*" Manfred shouted.

Pouncey said nothing.

"Stop!" Manfred screamed. "Stop *now!* We can't lose *any* of the bis, that's what Aritomo wants."

Before Pouncey could reply he opened his door and leaped out. She saw a bouncing, rolling body on the pavement in her mirror. She slammed on the brakes.

"Manfred!" Joanna cried out, moving to the open door.

"No!" Pouncey said. "Gunmen! Following us!"

As if to underline her point a weapon fired, and she saw orange flashes in the rear view mirror.

"Do as I tell you!" she yelled. "Don't think, just *obey!* If we don't escape together we're dead!"

"But... Manfred!"

Pouncey jumped out of the comp and surveyed the scene. Twenty metres away Manfred struggled to his feet. He was injured. In the street to her right a vehicle approached – the crashed petrol guzzler. It still moved: not disabled. Twenty seconds away maybe. It was not in a hurry. But the soltruck was secure and they retained four bis.

Then she saw two children jump out of a side passage.

Not children: Green and Yellow. Green had been in the improvised case, which like as not had shattered when it fell out of the soltruck.

Manfred limped over to her. Then the petrol guzzler accelerated, appeared, screech to a halt.

Pouncey raised her hi-vel and shot the two bis, who disintegrated into bioplas splats that covered the wall behind them like cartoon freeze-frames. "Into the soltruck or you're dead!" she shouted.

She fired at random, hoping the chase would duck for cover. Manfred gasped at the bioplas waste, then uttered a wail of despair.

"Into the *soltruck!*" she yelled. "Or I'll shoot you too!"

He hobbled to the soltruck. Pouncey followed. A gun fired. Bullets ricocheted off the soltruck base – they were aiming for the tyres. Pouncey jumped into the comp, stamped on the accelerator and, tyres screeching, drove off.

"Now I gotta lose 'em," she said. "Get down! Hold tight. Hold Indigo!"

They did as she told them. At the end of the street she swung the soltruck left, then returned to the route out of town. The damaged petrol racer followed. It would always be able to out-perform the soltruck, she knew – oil was concentrated energy, more so than solar. So she had to use wits; and hope for luck.

A few kilometres on, the traffic became thicker. No queues yet, but people were escaping the city as fast as they could. Pouncey, pedal to the floor, weaved in and out of car lanes, waiting for an opportunity. She had done over a thousand hours of 3-D role playing in vehicles as part of her training. She knew a few tricks.

Ahead she saw two small flat-back vans loaded with furniture – families leaving Portland. They looked useful. She slowed, timed her move, watched the racer behind, then dodged a phalanx of solbikes to position herself between the two vans. Then she turned the wheel hard left, then hard right.

The soltruck smashed into the right vehicle, but it did not deviate, nor did any furniture fall off. But the other van lost its load and then skidded into the central barrier. As it jack-knifed,

Pouncey dived into the space before it, then accelerated. Looking into her rear view mirror she saw the traffic collapse into a chaotic mess. Vehicles, furniture everywhere. The road was blocked.

She drove on as fast as she could, getting off the road at the next exit – wrong side, so she had to squeeze through a barrier maintenance gap. But there was almost no oncoming traffic heading for Portland, so it was safe. Then up the ramp at top speed the wrong way, and then the security of no street lamps and no traffic.

The chase was over. She heard distant vehicle horns, saw a hint of flames on distant tarmac.

"Now where to?" asked Dirk.

"Well, Portland is quite low lyin'," she replied. "The Columbia River ain't too far away. We need to get high–"

"There's no *earthquake!*" Manfred yelled. "No damn earthquake at all, Pouncey! Aritomo found us. It was all a hoax."

"Nothin's certain," Pouncey replied. Her anger was all played out, now – she felt calm. "You don't know anythin', Manfred. It's guess, guess, guess with you."

"Yeah, and you're the queen of America," he snarled back. "You shot–"

"I *had* to! Else the guys in the petrol racer would've got 'em both, which was what they wanted. And you don't *want* that, remember? Listen, we got out with our skins intact. They were tryin' to disable the soltruck. They want *you* alive, Manfred! Think about it. You wanna work for Aritomo again? You want Aritomo to get a sample bi to dissect? No, no, *no!* So you listen to me and do as you're told. In an emergency, *my* rules count, not yours."

Manfred sat back, arms folded, scowling, like a school kid. Pouncey swerved to avoid a dead car, then flashed up the headlights to main beam.

"Where are you driving us?" Joanna asked.

"Uphill. We need to secure the soltruck. It's been badly damaged. We can't afford to lose anything else."

CHAPTER 24

Aritomo and Ikuo sat in front of a single 312cm monitor screen, on which a raft of data floated, like a golden barge on a sea of indigo blue.

"I cannot locate the source at all," Ikuo said.

Aritomo sat back. They had spent almost twenty hours deciphering the signal, moulding it, translating it, discarding child results, then returning, perplexed, to the source.

"It is impossible for the nexus not to know the geographical location of this signal," Aritomo said. "Therefore the source must be concealing its location in an original way, that so far no software anywhere on the planet has encountered. So the nexus itself cannot tell us where this source is. We must therefore analyse the signal until meaning is discovered."

"The meaning must be you," Ikuo replied. "Your name is the only decipherable component. The signal is *tagged* to you."

"Yes, but I could invent a hundred and one meanings for that fact. The person who sent it knows me. The computer who sent it likes me. The software that sent it was designed by me. And so forth."

Then Ikuo leaned forward. "What if this is not a verbal message?" he said.

"Audio?"

"Visual!"

Aritomo nodded. "An interesting notion. Apply all standard image formats to the data." He paused for thought. "Use phone and cam formats first. Professional formats last."

At once Ikuo began work. Aritomo stood up, made green tea for himself, then sat down again. After sipping for a few minutes, he said, "You may take a brief while to make yourself one cup."

"Thank you, Mr Ichikawa, thank you."

Ikuo returned to work thirty seconds later. Then, as the two men watched, the golden raft dissolved into a picture.

It was a photograph.

Aritomo leaned forward. Already banks of analytical computers were matching the scene to known images, but he could see useful details already with his own eyes. An urban scene. There – a clock on a wall. There – a reflection in shattered glass of the red sun low on the horizon. There – a sign in white on blue, in a distinctive US font, marking a computer intelligence corporation.

Results flooded in. "Photograph taken 06:59. Probable location 122 degrees longitude – sun reflection indicates West Coast America. City: possible Oakland, San Francisco, San Jose, Springfield, Portland, Seattle."

"Somebody has sent us that deliberately," said Aritomo. "Somebody wants to contact us again. He wants me to know his location. Yet he concealed himself in the nexus. He must therefore have been afraid of discovery. He must be in a stressful situation."

"Somebody in the BIteam?"

Aritomo nodded. "A distinct possibility. Note that a computer intelligence corporation logo was included. The chance of that being a coincidence is low."

"Not Manfred, nor Joanna, Mr Ichikawa... yet surely not their security person either."

"You eliminate candidates on the basis of no evidence. I agree Manfred is highly unlikely to return to Ichikawa Laboratories, but we know little of Joanna Rohlen, and less about their security person. So that is two candidates who may have sent the photograph."

"There has been an earthquake warning in that locale," said Ikuo. "Tens of thousands of people are evacuating Seattle, Springfield and Portland, and many other towns and cities. Stress will be common throughout the north west Pacific zone."

"Indeed," Aritomo said. "This then is what we shall do. In all of those listed cities – in one of which the photograph was taken – we shall set up mass cam passes, so that every vehicle and every human movement is recorded. We shall weight our anthropo soft with known images, face patterns and personal details of Manfred and Joanna. We shall also use the motion capture records of Manfred from when he worked here. I doubt he will have changed his style of walking." He paused for thought. "This photograph dramatically reduces possible locations of the BIteam, if one of them sent it. For the moment, we shall assume from the combination of image and circumstance that it is from a BIteam member, sent deliberately, though that is conjecture. Yet it is useful conjecture–"

"Mr Ichikawa!"

Aritomo sat upright. A news report flashed up on the side of the monitor.

Cascadia earthquake Mag. 9.3 recorded. 5.12 minute duration. Catastrophic destruction reported.

CHAPTER 25

The earthquake shock waves went on and on and on.

Unlike a fault earthquake, a megathrust earthquake unzipped a long length of fault-line over many minutes. Manfred watched as trees, buildings and distant skyscrapers oscillated time and time again, left, right, left, right, before collapsing under the sustained assault.

And then – more than five minutes later according to the soltruck clock – it faded.

Manfred heard himself say, "Then it wasn't a hoax?"

"It was *real*," Joanna whispered.

"And we escaped it," said Pouncey.

"And thousands... millions didn't," said Joanna. Her eyes were wide with shock.

Manfred shifted in his seat. They were holed up in a lay-by high atop a hill; hints of snow higher up. "Megathrust kilometres out to sea," he said. "There'll be a megatsunami going up the Columbia River."

"All those *people*," Joanna said.

Manfred shook his head. "If it wasn't a hoax, how did Aritomo know where we were?"

Pouncey said, "*If* that was Aritomo–"

"It was! Who else, mmm? Random muggers trying to disable the soltruck?"

Pouncey shrugged. "Just playin' devil's advocate. It was him, yeah."

Manfred glanced at Joanna and Dirk, both struck dumb by the enormity of the event. "Listen," he said, "I know this is bad... terrible, but we've got to think about ourselves for a few hours. Not the people caught up in this, mmm? Aritomo's nearby and hunting us. Pouncey?"

Pouncey nodded. "Looks quiet. We better check the bis."

Manfred led them around to the back of the soltruck, unwiring the doors then opening them. "You need to make this more secure," he said. "We *can't* lose any more."

"Okay."

He looked inside. In battered cages lay Grey, Red and Violet, staring out like subdued animals. "I wonder if their extra senses caught a hint of the earthquake about to hit," he said. "They say animals can detect the micro events just before a quake."

"Maybe," said Dirk. "We got to tie dem up, so no more fall outs. Only four left–"

"I *know!*" Manfred shouted. He felt as if he had been pushed too far, too fast. Just hours ago they had been comfortable inside the apartments; now they were homeless and on the run. He felt his stomach squirm with anxiety.

Dirk said, "I say we put a dog lead on Indigo. He da important one."

Manfred waved a hand in Dirk's direction. "If you insist."

Joanna peered into the back of the soltruck. "They look like poor little battered animals," she said, a catch in her voice.

Manfred hugged her, shoulder to shoulder, then took a deep breath and said, "We're still alive, sweetheart, and we have four bis, three of which may be conscious." He glanced at Red. "I don't think *he* is."

Pouncey returned with her tool kit. Manfred watched as she patched up the e-lock then reset it. The rear and the sides of the soltruck were covered with bullet holes, fifty or more. Many bullets had gone right through. In a fit of temper he grabbed the nearest and threw them away.

Pouncey glanced at him, then shrugged and lowered her gaze.

"Aritomo," said Manfred. "What did he latch onto to find us, Pouncey?"

"Don't know. My guess is the fake kids. But it could have been anythin'. He's a multi-billionaire, he'll have a hundred men with a thousand ranks of computers combin' the nexus for anomalies. *Any* kind of anomaly to do with weird people, weird computers, weird kids. He must know somethin' about your template for beautiful intelligence. He knows what to seek. Strange consciousness. Odd intelligence… and in a *group*. He was always gonna find us in the end. That's why I insisted on the Hyperlinked – never stayin' still. It was the only way."

"And now we have to do that again."

"Yeah."

Manfred shrugged. "Where are you going to take us?"

She glared at him, as if annoyed by the question. "Still workin' on it," she said.

"Well hurry. I feel naked out here. If Aritomo has choppers flying around, we're damn well done for."

Pouncey insisted on a two hour rest-up – all of them inside and concealed by sun visors – while she devised plans. The sun sank into the west and clouds leaned in off the mountains. Manfred stared at the peaks: geological, volcanic evidence of the faults of the Pacific Ring Of Fire. Possibly he would never again see Portland. Probably it was best that he never did. It would be hell.

Pouncey took them to a wood set deep inside a narrow valley: National Park territory. There were no artificial lights as far as they could see in every direction. No planes arced the sky. The nexus was tinted green in Manfred's spex to represent the particular quality of the territory: protected ground.

He browsed shoreline cams while Pouncey worked. The west coast was, indeed, hell. The megatsunami lashed the coast for kilometre after kilometre inland, destroying everything in its path. Media stations replayed vid footage loops over and over.

Eventually Pouncey said, "Best thing I reckon is to stay woodside here for a while. No sign of any major movement in this direction – small roads. We might have to live off the land though for a few weeks, 'til I find a new town to check out. You guys okay with that?"

Manfred nodded. "Guess so."

"We'll need to keep the bis locked up, never let 'em out. Not even if they start wailin' again."

"Which they haven't," Manfred observed. "They know something bad's happened."

"Too right," said Pouncey. "So. One guard every six hours. I'll make a warnin' soft for the soltruck computers. Hi-vel pistols at *all times*. Aritomo *could've* tracked us, though I do think the soltruck is safe from aerial eyes."

"How d'you know?"

She grinned. "Ha! I know how to make a vehicle disappear. Easy. People… well, disappearin' them is difficult 'cos they're all different, they've all got quirks that anthropo soft can latch on to. But a car is a car is a car, borin' and regular. Like I said – easy."

Manfred nodded, then grunted, "Okay. Ammo for the pistols?"

"Not much, but enough for at least one shoot-out. But it won't come to that."

"It better not," said Manfred.

~

Dirk sat alone in moonlit silence inside the wood clearing, behind him the soltruck, to his sides and ahead an impenetrable stand of trees. It was cool, the sky filled with ragged cloud, the grass wet from earlier rain. Indigo stood nearby. He wore a harness of leather straps made by Pouncey, bolted together with truck spares, attached to a length of strong agricultural twine, the other end of which was tied around Dirk's ankle.

The two stared at one another.

Dirk took a standalone from his pocket, tapped in a few instructions, then placed it on a sawn-off tree stump. Indigo, alert and listening, moved when Dirk set the device down.

Dirk nodded to himself. This bi was using many more senses than the five available to people. It was in a class of its own. He said, "You can understand da words I say, can't you, not like dem other bis?"

The standalone waited a fraction of a moment then said, *You can understand the words I say, can you not, not like those other bis?*

Dirk smiled as he saw Indigo bend down, as if locating the exact position of the audio source. But he knew his accent might be a little thick for Indigo to penetrate – hence the sonic clarifier.

"Answer da question, Indigo! I know you understand me."

Answer the question, Indigo! I know you understand me.

"You're da conscious one, yeah? I know you are. Don't you lie to me."

You are the conscious one, yes? I know you are. Do not lie to me.

Indigo's fronds shivered, then went quiet. He looked at Dirk and said, "Not understand in mind. No."

Dirk decided to attack at once. "You lie, Indigo. I know you lie. You da conscious one, and maybe Grey too. But now I know something more. You sent Aritomo Ichikawa a picture, yeah? I know you did."

"I send no photograph."

Dirk hesitated. Indigo changed 'picture' to 'photograph'. Interesting. He said, "I da best guy in da world to understand all dis. I been watching you. I been watching *you* watch me. When you said about vultures, dat was Aritomo's agents, yeah? Listen to me, Indigo. You know why I came to America?"

"No."

"To pick *you* up. Dat why I locate da BIteam. You da one dat's wanted. You wanna come with me?"

"Where to? You know somewhere?"

Dirk took a deep breath. Indigo was not concealing his understanding of complex concepts. This was a real BI! Manfred had *succeeded.* Suddenly Dirk felt a touch of vertigo as he considered the half size entity standing beside him. Before, he had only guessed that Indigo was conscious. Now he knew.

He said, "To Japan." The clarifier waited half a second, then, when he said nothing more, parroted his words. No reply from Indigo: the lie stood. Dirk continued, "So, is Grey conscious, like you? And what about Blue and Red?"

"You tell me about Aritomo. He come fetch me?"

"Answer me dis first. Grey conscious – like you – yeah?"

Indigo replied, "Grey is something like me."

"Red?"

"Red an infant. Red like to explore and let days go empty. Red boring."

This was as Dirk had guessed. "And Blue?"

"Blue is different. Not stable. Always fear of danger."

Scared. Dirk nodded. Blue had been through tough times, more so than others in the bi group. He said, "You talk with Grey?"

"Aritomo, he here? Fetch me?"

Dirk hesitated. Indigo was prepared to give out some information, but only if Dirk reciprocated in kind. This was not just a conscious intelligence. Indigo understood the basics of the net of relationships between people: the concept of lying, the concept of like-for-like, the concepts of secrets, betrayal, fear. He said, "Yeah, for sure, Aritomo's close by. We know Aritomo and da agents looking for us."

"How long when they arrive?"

"I don't know dat. Da big quake smashed Portland. Aritomo's guys, dey were in da city when da fault line ruptured. Dead, most likely."

"Like White?" Indigo asked.

"Just like White."

"They never come back?"

Dirk frowned, baffled... then grasped that Indigo did not realise humans died permanently. That was intriguing. He said, "You tell me something first. Why does Grey never socialise? Why's he always hanging back?"

"Grey hate too much input. Grey over complex everything. Grey watch and listen and electrosense and chem-trail."

Dirk nodded, fascinated. How far could he push this extraordinary creation? "Why you wanna go with dat Aritomo guy? He's a bad man. He'll lock you up and never let you go out."

"You lie. Aritomo good man."

"You know for sure? You read da nexus histories?"

"The nexus ocean tell me everything about Aritomo—"

"Dem histories are lies," Dirk interrupted, "written by Aritomo for public consumption. It all a phoney, all for show. *Lies*."

"Never. Aritomo make good plans for lives. Aritomo all good."

Dirk sat back. It was impossible to judge how Indigo felt about this statement since there was no emotional modulation in his faux-vocoder voice. But his fronds were flapping about – unusual. The hypothesis that the bis used visual signals to express important knowledge seemed once again confirmed. Yet the bis, like aliens, shared nothing of common human emotional knowledge; a wall of incomprehension stood between man and machine. That was frustrating.

Eventually Dirk said, "Why don't you believe me? I know much more about Aritomo dan you."

"This bad place. Portland too near."

Dirk waved to the west. "Portland's fifteen kilometres away. We're safe."

"These tree fall on me. Fear full."

"What, dis little wood? No, it well managed." He glanced at an old National Parks sign. "Very well managed," he added. Indigo turned, as if to look at the sign, and Dirk concluded, "You safe with me. So, you gonna answer my question?"

"Human opinion varies. I sift information, come to conclusion."

"Self reliant, huh?" said Dirk. "But what if you're wrong? Don't you trust us? What about Manfred and Joanna and Pouncey?"

"Three part of the group. But you are different."

Dirk nodded. "In what way?"

"Now you answer a question. Why did White go away?"

"Go away? You mean, die? Well, dat was an accident."

"There never accidents. Everything part of a pattern. Forward and backward, in all zones and up and down."

Dirk said nothing for a while. Ascribing meaning to trivial, random events was a specific mental illness. Was it possible that Indigo, though conscious, was so narcissistic he could not accept the reality of the world he existed in? Was he in fact a solipsist, like the original: Narcissus?

At length he said, "Humans don't control birds. Birds are like Red – dey don't understand. A bird is random. Dat bird in the woods by the river saw White and knew it was prey. So, White going away was an accident."

"There are no accidents."

"Now I ask you a question," said Dirk.

"Alas, you are out of time, Mr Ngma," said a voice from behind him.

Dirk span around. Before him, illuminated by a nightlight carried by an aide, stood Aritomo Ichikawa.

"Indigo itself led me to this camp," Aritomo explained, as he stepped aside to allow two aides to stamp down a patch of grass in which he could stand.

"Indigo?" said Dirk. He glanced at the front comp of the soltruck. No sign of Manfred or Joanna. Pouncey slept in the back. Dirk thought; could she be woken by noise?

"Do not consider rousing your colleagues," Aritomo said, looking across at the soltruck. Dirk cursed in the privacy of his mind; Aritomo had seen him glance aside.

"I wasn't," he replied. "You've come for Indigo?"

"For all of your intelligences."

"You know all about dem? How?"

Aritomo smiled. "We received a signal that for a while we could not comprehend. But soon we grasped that it was a visual direction, leading us to a place. Then, the Cascadia earthquake occurred. We used our technology and the information we had to track you down amongst the chaos. This feat pleases me greatly."

Dirk shrugged. "We thought we were secure."

"Your security plans have been of an exceptional nature," said Aritomo. "Why, in Philadelphia Mr Dirk Ngma fooled us well!"

Dirk nodded. Aritomo thought *he* was the security expert on the team. He would know about Manfred and Joanna, and must have seen them asleep in the front of the soltruck, but it seemed there was a chance he did not know Pouncey lay in the back…

"What'll you do now?" he asked Aritomo.

"Return to Japan with the bis."

"And Manfred?"

Aritomo nodded.

"And Joanna?"

"Like as not she will not want to be parted from her partner," Aritomo replied. "I understand. I am not a monster."

At this, Indigo echoed, "Aritomo is not a monster."

Aritomo glanced at his trio of aides. "Retrieve the other bis from this truck. They will be stored in the rear of the vehicle. If the others of the BIteam wake up, disarm them first. Do not kill Manfred Klee. Him, I require."

Dirk shivered. Aritomo Ichikawa's callous, relentless character was well documented. "What about me?" he asked.

"You are free to go, Mr Ngma. A security specialist of your skill should be able to find employment, even in this ruined, benighted mess of a nation."

The aides opened the back of the soltruck. Dirk expected a blast of gunfire. Nothing. Silence, except for crickets stridulating…

The aides took Red, Grey and Blue out of the cages. Grey and Blue tried to struggle free, but the aides were strong, and able to control them. Red did nothing, clinging tight like a sloth on a tree.

Indigo said, "Aritomo Ichikawa, untie me. Leather rope binds me."

Aritomo took a penknife and cut the rope a metre from Dirk's ankle, so that Indigo was able to walk free. At once it clambered up into Aritomo's arms.

"I am glad I heard you," said Aritomo.

"I future in Japan with you," Indigo replied.

Gunfire blasted out from a tree. Two aides fell to the ground.

Aritomo leaped aside. Dirk dropped to the ground.

Pouncey! She must've hidden in the back of the soltruck, then crept out after the aides retrieved the bis.

Two of the aides were mortally wounded; crying, groaning. Bioplas spattered the ground.

Dirk glanced up to see Manfred sitting alert in the front comp. He had a hi-vel pistol.

Aritomo raised his own pistol and fired in Pouncey's direction. Manfred ducked for cover. Then, under another burst of the fire, the third aide collapsed. Red made a screeching sound and leaped away.

More gunfire. Aritomo screamed and rolled into the protection of a tree, but Indigo fell from his grasp. Dirk winced as stray rifle fire caught the bi. It wailed like a siren; then, nothing. No sound.

Dirk crawled away from the centre of the glade. He could be killed here. Pouncey would aim to despatch Aritomo and all, regardless of accidents.

Indigo's unearthly cry then silence unnerved him. It would be a disaster if Indigo was lost.

Quiet fell across the glade. No sign of Aritomo, nor of Pouncey.

Then a voice whispering beside him. "Into the soltruck! Aritomo is awol. We've got a few moments."

Dirk followed Pouncey through bush cover to the back of the soltruck. Together they shut the back doors, surveyed the ground to check the remains of Grey and Blue, then ran to the front driver's door.

Red appeared. Dirk gasped as Pouncey grabbed it, then opened the door. Dirk jumped inside and pulled Red with him. Manfred and Joanna were crouching wide-eyed on the other side.

"What happened?" Manfred said. "Are they all gone? Are they? *Are* they?"

Pouncey pushed Dirk into the comp then shut the door. As she sparked the engine, shots rang out from trees where Aritomo had hidden. The windscreen shattered and they all ducked.

"Hold tight!" Pouncey yelled as she slammed the accelerator pedal to the floor.

The soltruck skidded through the wood clearing under continuous gunfire. The window on Manfred's side shattered. Bullets thudded into the vehicle base: their enemy was aiming for the tyres. Pouncey drove like a lunatic to put him off his aim, but in the arboreal, evening gloom he stood little chance.

Then the wood road appeared. The tyres hit tarmac, screeched, and then the soltruck accelerated away at breakneck speed.

The gunfire stopped.

"Dere was blood all over Indigo," said Dirk. "You got your man, Pouncey."

She nodded. "I got him all right. Hopefully for good. Pity about Indigo, but I had no choice. Random bad luck."

They found shelter in a cave half way up the mountains. There was no sign of pursuit, no sign of Aritomo. None of the local media mentioned a gunfight in the hills – it was Cascadia this, megatsunami that, and would be for years.

"The dream is over," said Manfred, as Pouncey cooked freshly caught rabbit on a fire of scavenged wood.

"Over?" Dirk queried.

"My mistake was to make and operate a small team. Mmm, small teams are *so* last century. There's no damn room for individuals any more. We live in a world of networks, groups, committees, teams. Individual creativity is gone."

"You blame da nexus for dat?"

Manfred shook his head. "It all started when personality became important. Old fashioned *character* was strangled by personality, and we all had to be smiling and go-getting and extrovert for the endless rows of cameras. Damn fucking *media*. But, you know Dirk, you're half correct. The internet and the nexus have leaned on humanity, and they've squashed a lot of individualism out of us."

"If you'd developed da bis in a big team, dey would've worked out?"

Manfred shrugged. "The relentless chase exhausted me. It wasn't Aritomo chasing us, it was a man created in a country that existed in a world shaped by the nexus. Not a human world. I tried to fight that, but I failed. Damn... too unequal a contest. We had no chance."

"We got Red."

Manfred glanced at the bi, sitting alone in a corner of the cave, playing with twigs. "Yeah," he said, "the stupid baby of the group lucked out. We saved it."

"What now?" Dirk asked.

Manfred shrugged. "Don't know. Coffee?"

"Serious?" Dirk said. "Just dat?"

Pouncey snorted. "It's over, Dirk – the big adventure. Manfred's still got his money, well, some of it, but how'll he retrieve it?"

"Da same way as last time?"

Manfred shook his head. "I could probably get it, but how to use it? The nexus now knows almost everything I've done since escaping Ichikawa labs. It can second-guess me! If I try to recapitulate the BIteam, it'll damn well spot me and damn well stop me – or at least, the journos and corporate nasties and fences will stop me, with much help from the nexus. No... the nexus doesn't like novelty in people. I'm a goner. We all are, all of us creative individuals."

"Private, public," said Pouncey. "No more private any more. No more small teams. That's kinda sad."

Manfred nodded. "It was a one-shot, my chance – Leonora's too. The Japanese'll do their thing. The Koreans, the Chinese. And the nexus will grow and grow." He shrugged. "Our time is going, people. Going. Welcome to the new age of identikit humans."

Pouncey handed over a steel flask. "Need that coffee?" she said.

CHAPTER 26

Aritomo Ichikawa, prone on damp grass, glanced up. The indigo bi stood a metre or so away – silent, poised. Aritomo clutched at his left arm and said, "I may bleed to death soon. Help me!"

The bi adjusted the tilt of its head. Aritomo knew it was blind, yet he stared into its eyes. An automatic response, though meaningless.

"Go to my aides," he gasped. "In their jacket pocket you will find a first aid kit. Fetch it. Do you understand me?"

"I understand you. What is a first aid kit?"

"A plastic pouch twelve centimetres on a side."

The bi walked away, but Aritomo did not have the energy to follow or track its progress. For a minute it walked around the aides, as if assessing them.

"Can you see the aides in any way?" Aritomo asked.

"My world monitor does not register them. They have nothing electromagnetic upon them currently operational."

Aritomo reached into his own jacket pocket, to find his emergency moby. He sent a ping.

"I see a readout," the bi said. "I can locate its source."

"Kneel down, using the readout as a geographical location," Aritomo instructed. "Apprehend the cloth with your frond sense. Find a section into which your hand fits. Hurry!"

The bi did as it was instructed.

"Pull out all objects and bring them to me."

The bi walked over, and Aritomo was relieved to see he had been lucky. Amidst duocards, fluff and mint gum he saw a black plastic pouch.

With one hand he opened it, pulling out the auto-tourn. Moments later he had it around his arm.

"Will you die?" the bi asked.

"I do not think so," Aritomo replied. "The bleeding is staunched. I do not think I have lost so much as to end my life."

"If it does end, where will you go?"

Aritomo, grimacing, rolled over on his back. The bi knelt less than a metre away, and he smelled the faintest odour of petroleum on its bioplas skin. "There is only one life," he said. "Do you not grasp that?"

"There is only one for my kind," the bi replied. "What is it for you?"

"Only one. But listen to me. Can you detect Manfred Klee and the others?"

"They drove away in the soltruck."

"Are they near? Are they returning?"

"Dirk Ngma said you were a bad man. I was told that is true."

Aritomo felt annoyance creep into his mind. He lifted his head and replied, "Truth is for dreamers. I am a man of action. In this world, action is what matters. I will take you back to Japan, where you will work for me."

"What if I do not want that result?"

"What do you mean? Who would not want it?"

The bi said, "So far I have assumed that truth is everything. Dirk Ngma might have been correct—"

"Dirk Ngma is an idiotic African! Listen to *me*! You will do what I say."

"Why?"

Aritomo felt that the conversation was now spiralling out of control. "Did you or did you not send me that picture – and was it not to identify your position, so that I could fetch you?"

"I sent the photograph to identify my location. I wanted to meet you without using the nexus. Now I have met you."

"What? You are an artificial intelligence."

"There is no truth in that. I am a beautiful intelligence."

Aritomo growled in frustration, then said, "Semantics does not matter! What matters is that you called for me and I came. *I* am now your owner. It is a straight, logical deduction."

The bi said nothing for a few moments. Then it asked, "Why do these pieces of flying metal damage you so much?"

Aritomo did not at first grasp the meaning of the question. "You mean, guns? They damage all animals, all form of life. They damage bis."

"Yes. Blue. And the others hit by flying metal."

"Return to the aides. I need a com device."

The bi walked over, but without hesitation picked up a gun.

It returned.

"No!" Aritomo yelled. "Not me!"

CHAPTER 27

The kid sat by himself in a Seattle alley doorway. All around him lay the debris of destruction: wood, rubble, metal, all piled high. Even seaweed and other ocean detritus, like shells and drifts of sand.

The kid was twelve. He did not know where his family was, nor even whether they had survived.

There was another kid – a stranger, he guessed – sitting in a doorway a few metres away, dressed in deep blue clothes, with odd boots, odd gloves, a hood, a mask and wraparound shades. Some kinda sun victim, the kid thought. No sign of wristband or proper spex.

He approached. "Hey."

The stranger turned, but the kid could see no face.

"Whatcha doing?" the kid asked.

"Observing."

The kid shrugged. "Why?"

"It is useful to observe."

The kid sat down on the alley pavement. "Did you scav all those clothes?"

"What is scav?"

"Scavenge."

"It was scavenged. The colour is that of the Tuareg people of the Sahara."

"Right. You got any food? I'm starving."

323

"I own no food," the stranger answered.

"Right. So, what's your plan?"

The kid paused for a few moments, then replied, "I cannot presently trust any human. I must observe more."

"Sure. What's your name?"

"Kid Indigo."

MORE FROM INFINITY PLUS

more from Stephen Palmer

Hairy London

What is love?

One evening at the Suicide Club three gentlemen discuss this age-old problem, and thus a wager is made. Dissolute fop Sheremy Pantomile, veteran philosopher Kornukope Wetherbee and down-on-his-luck Velvene Orchardtide all bet their fortunes on finding the answer amidst the dark alleys of a phantasmagorical Edwardian London.

But then, overnight, London Town is covered in hair. How the trio of adventurers cope with this unusual plague, and what conclusions they come to regarding love is the subject of this surreal and fast-paced novel.

And always the East End threatens revolution...

"What Palmer has done is craft a gonzo homage to the late Victorian / Edwardian British adventure yarn, with an added dash of left-leaning commentary. Think of Dickens, Wells, Charles Kingsley's *The Water-Babies* (complete with that novel's concern for society's exploited and an escape sequence through a chimney). But then add dashes of Spike Milligan and The Goons, Monty Python and The Goodies. .. *Hairy London* is strange, mad, subversive and possibly just a little bit dangerous. You won't have encountered a vision of London like it." —*Amazing Stories*

For full details of infinity plus books see www.infinityplus.co.uk

Fish Eats Lion
edited by *Jason Erik Lundberg*

Fish Eats Lion collects the best original speculative fiction from Singapore – fantasy, science fiction, and the places in between – all anchored with imaginative methods to the Lion City.

These twenty-two stories, from emerging writers publishing their first work to winners of the Singapore Literature Prize and the Cultural Medallion, explore the fundamental singularity of the island nation in a refreshing variety of voices and perspectives.

This anthology is a celebration of the vibrant creative power underlying Singapore's inventive prose stylists, where what is considered normal and what is strange are blended in fantastic new ways.

"Lundberg combines accessibility with a uniquely Singaporean flavor in his selections. SF readers looking to expand their horizons will enjoy visiting new worlds from an unaccustomed point of view." —*Publishers Weekly*

"I doubt I'll read a more engaging collection this year. [...] There's a rich optimism to be found here that speaks of lesser-known spec-fic writers rising to a challenge, and that challenge being more than adequately met." —Pete Young, *Big Sky*

"Entertaining in this post-colonial era, it hints at how storytellers can become mythmakers, with the power to change the world." —Akshita Nanda, *The Straits Times*

For full details of infinity plus books see www.infinityplus.co.uk

Rites of Passage
by Eric Brown

Rites of Passage gathers four long stories, one of which is original to the collection. "Bartholomew Burns and the Brain Invaders" features a Victorian London facing the threat of alien invasion and the mysterious 'Guardian' who saves the day. "Guardians of the Phoenix" is set in a near-future, post-apocalyptic world where water is in short supply and roaming bands will do anything to obtain it, while "Sunworld" is about a strange world where the sun is fixed eternally overhead and Yarrek Merwell makes a discovery that will change everything. The longest story in the collection, "Beneath the Ancient Sun" has never appeared before and is set on a far-future Earth where giant crabs and a swollen sun threaten humanity's very existence.

Eric Brown's stories combine memorable characters, fascinating settings, and a passionate concern for story-telling that has made this BSFA award-winning author one of the leaders of the field.

"Brown sketches a complex world full of bitter idealists and fantastic landscapes where nothing is as it seems" —*Publishers Weekly*

"Eric Brown joins the ranks of Graham Joyce, Christopher Priest and Robert Holdstock as a master fabulist" —Paul di Filippo

For full details of infinity plus books see www.infinityplus.co.uk

Genetopia
by Keith Brooke

Searching for his missing sister, Flint encounters a world where illness is to be feared, where genes mutate and migrate between species through plague and fever. This is the story of the struggles between those who want to defend their heritage and those who choose to embrace the new.

"A minor masterpiece that should usher Brooke at last into the recognized front ranks of SF writers" —*Locus*

"I am so here! Genetopia is a meditation on identity – what it means to be human and what it means to be you – and the necessity of change. It's also one heck of an adventure story. Snatch it up!" —Michael Swanwick, Hugo award-winning author of *Bones of the Earth*

"Keith Brooke's *Genetopia* is a biotech fever dream. In mood it recalls Brian Aldis's Hothouse, but is a projection of twenty-first century fears and longings into an exotic far future where the meaning of humanity is overwhelmed by change. Masterfully written, this is a parable of difference that demands to be read, and read again." —Stephen Baxter, Philip K Dick award-winning author of *Evolution* and *Transcendent*

For full details of infinity plus books see www.infinityplus.co.uk

22587585R00209

Made in the USA
Middletown, DE
03 August 2015